BOUGHT BY THE BILLIONAIRE

The Complete Series

LILI VALENTE

Self Taught Ninja

BOUGHT BY THE BILLIONAIRE

The Complete Series

By Lili Valente

Dark Domination
Deep Domination
Desperate Domination
Divine Domination

DARK DOMINATION

Bought by the Billionaire
Book One

By Lili Valente

CHAPTER ONE

Hannah

"Keep the door locked, Hannah, and don't go outside." Her sister, Harley, dug her fingers into the soft flesh of Hannah's upper arms, the arms she could never keep as toned as her twin's, no matter how often she hit the gym. "No one can know you're here. Do you understand me? No one."

"I get it," Hannah said for the third time.

"Even if the hall is full of starving orphans," Harley insisted, her blue eyes hard and focused. "Even if there's a nun out there with her pants on fire, you keep the door closed and your mouth shut. Get me?"

"But nuns don't wear pants." Hannah winked, trying to ease the tension that had festered in the air since she'd surprised Harley at work this afternoon.

But her sister's perfectly sculpted brows only drew closer together. "I'm serious, Moo. You know I love you, but if you screw this up for me, I'm going to lose it."

"Screw what up?" Hannah asked, dread whispering through her chest.

Harley's schemes were never good news. Her twin's flair for the dramatic had taken a dark, twisted turn that summer ten years ago when their family had fractured down the middle. Afterward, their mother had been the one most obviously damaged, but something in Harley had been broken, too.

Since then, her sister never seemed to know when she'd gone too far, or care if people were caught in the crossfire.

"What's going on?" Hannah pressed. "Is this why you've been pushing me away all summer?"

"I haven't been pushing you away," Harley lied, not even bothering to do it convincingly. When Harley was in top form, she could make you believe that the sky was green and the grass was blue.

But she didn't bother turning on the charm for family. She saved that for the art dealers who purchased her sculptures, the wealthy lovers she played against each other like pieces in increasingly heartbreaking games of chess, and the unlucky victims slated to pay for wronging her.

It didn't matter if the sin was real or imagined or if Harley realized halfway through crafting her blueprint for revenge that the punishment she'd conceived for her target didn't fit the crime. She never shifted direction or altered course. Hannah was the second guesser, the person who could always see both sides of a story. Harley was simply…inexorable.

Sometimes, it made Hannah wonder if she had absorbed her twin's share of empathy in the womb.

Sometimes it simply scared the hell out of her.

"Don't go." Hannah mirrored her sister's stance, gripping Harley's arms, but her touch remained gentle. It was her blessing and her curse, her inability to be as tough and pitiless as her father wanted his daughters to be. "Stay with me. Let's make popcorn and watch *Pretty Woman* and pretend it's the end of another perfect summer. Like when we were kids."

"It is the end of a perfect summer." Harley's smile was sharp to the touch. "The most perfect summer ever."

She leaned in, pressing an impulsive kiss to Hannah's cheek. "I love you, Moo. And I'm never going to let anyone get away with hurting you or Mom again. Okay? Just stay inside, quiet as a mouse, and everything will be fine."

Hannah's stomach clenched. "Harley, please, I've got a bad feeling."

"You've always got a bad feeling, worry wart." She pulled away with a laugh, reaching for the black handbag on the polished table by the apartment's front door.

The apartment Harley had chosen for her summer on the Virginia shore was uncharacteristically modest, but her purse still cost a few thousand dollars. When Hannah had left for college at Duke, she had adjusted her wardrobe to fit in with the other undergraduate students in her psychology program, gratefully abandoning thousand dollar dresses for blue jeans and tee shirts. But Harley's taste had only grown more extravagant.

Her twin was making a killing in the art world, had sweet-talked their father into granting her access to her trust fund two years early, and was always getting gifts from her endlessly shifting assortment of suitors. She was never short on money, which was another reason the modest apartment, the summer job serving drinks at a restaurant by the beach, and the beat up VW Bug Hannah had seen parked in her sister's space in the parking lot below made no sense.

Add in the tip envelope with "Harley Garrett" printed on the outside that Harley had tucked into her purse before hustling Hannah out of the bar this afternoon, and there was no doubt that Harley was up to something. Why else would she be using a fake last name?

But Hannah knew from experience her twin wouldn't share a word about her latest scheme until it was a fait accompli. Her sister was as superstitious as she was fearless. She wouldn't risk jinxing a plan by whispering a word about her hoped for outcome until the deed was done and the bodies were buried.

"There's leftover rice and Thai curry in the fridge," Harley said, checking her makeup in the mirror by the door, brushing away an invisible lipstick smear at the corner of her full mouth. "Feel free to have that or any of the stuff in the freezer, but don't order anything to be delivered. Once I leave, this door doesn't open until I get home tomorrow morning, not even for the pizza guy."

"I get it," Hannah said, irritation creeping in to singe the edges of her dread. "But we're going to talk when you get back. A real talk."

She'd driven six hours to spend the weekend with her sister and she wasn't going to spend her last few days of freedom before graduate school locked up in Harley's apartment, hiding from the world.

"And we're going to the beach," she added, glancing down at her pale, spent-the-summer-in-the-library arms. "I need some sun."

Harley's gaze shifted, meeting Hannah's in the glass before flicking back to her own reflection. The eye contact only lasted a moment, but it was long enough for Hannah to be certain the next words out of Harley's mouth were going to be a lie.

"Okay. We'll go to the beach and talk. I promise." She turned, pulling Hannah in for a quick hug. "Never ever, Moo."

"Never ever," Hannah mumbled into her sister's silky brown hair before Harley slipped out the door. She couldn't help repeating the familiar phrase, no matter how frustrated she was with her twin.

Never ever was what they had said to each other since they were little girls. It meant more than I love you. It meant I never ever want to be apart, I never ever want to wake up to a day without you in it, I never ever want to be as close to anyone in the world as I am to you, my sister, my best friend, my other half.

But they hadn't been that close in years and lately, when Hannah thought of her sister, it was with an ache in her chest and a hollow feeling in her gut. She knew from her psychology classes that twins often had a slower, more difficult individuation process than normal siblings. It was just harder for "we" to become "me and you" when you've spent your entire life as one half of a matched set. But what was happening between her and Harley was about more than growing up. They were growing apart, becoming such different people that she could look down the road and see incredible pain in their future.

There would come a day when she wouldn't be able to forgive Harley for something she'd done. A day when her sister would go too far and become someone she couldn't trust, maybe even someone she was ashamed of. Hannah had a big heart and a forgiving spirit, but even she had hard limits, lines in the sand that, once crossed, could never be uncrossed.

Later, after a supper of leftovers and a few mindless hours passed in front of the television, Hannah lay in her sister's bed, staring at the ceiling in the dark, thinking about those lines.

She didn't want to believe Harley would hurt innocent people, but as the years passed, her twin reminded her more of their any-means-to-an-end father than their sweet Aunt Sybil—the woman they'd both sworn they wanted to take after when they were girls.

They'd been eleven years old the first time they'd gone to stay with Sybil for the summer, desperate for a woman to look up to, a woman who wasn't broken and sad like their mother or cold and efficient like Nanny Hammond or the night nurses who had sat watch outside their bedroom since they were infants. Sybil struggled with severe arthritis and other health problems, but she was always upbeat, excited to greet the day, and eager to spread light around her corner of the world. She exuded a quiet strength and was unfailingly kind.

If there was one thing Hannah never wanted to fail at, it was kindness.

But when did kindness become weakness? More importantly, when did her love for and support of her sister make her an accomplice, culpable for the suffering of the people caught in Harley's warpath?

She didn't know, but she knew she and Harley were going to have a real talk tomorrow morning. It was time for Hannah to make it clear that while her love was unconditional, her friendship and support were not. If Harley couldn't assure her that she was keeping her hands clean, then the next time her sister called in the middle of the night, needing someone to talk her down from her latest anxiety attack or assure her that everything was going to be okay, Hannah wouldn't pick up the phone.

Sometimes, anxiety isn't meant to be banished by a gentle voice in the darkness. Sometimes, anxiety is the soul's way of telling the body that there are dangerous choices being made, choices that could lead to pain, suffering, and destruction of the most beautiful things in your life.

Hannah drifted off to sleep battling her own anxious thoughts and didn't expect to sleep well. Even after four years of living in single dorms and tiny rooms in apartments she shared with friends, she still had trouble drifting off without her sister's body close to hers. They'd slept in the same bed from the time they were born until the autumn Hannah left for college and Harley headed to New York City to set the art world on fire.

Hannah's high school boyfriend had thought the single queen bed in their shared room was strange and Harley's boys of the moment had usually thought it was sexy—no doubt imagining what it would be like to be sandwiched in between the Mason twins while they did something more than sleep—but Harley and Hannah hadn't cared what anyone else had thought. They simply rested more peacefully when they were close enough to feel each other's body heat, to hear the soothing sound of another heartbeat, another indrawn breath, another exhalation through softly parted lips.

Maybe it was the familiar smell of her sister's almond

lotion lingering in the air that soothed Hannah into a deep sleep, or maybe it was the gentle patter of the rain on the roof that began to fall around nine thirty.

Whatever it was, Hannah was far past the REM phase, drifting in the slow, sticky waves of delta rest when she was suddenly wrenched awake by the feeling of a heavy body settling on top of her in the darkness and a huge hand covering her mouth.

CHAPTER TWO

Hannah

*H*annah's eyes flew open and her lips parted in a scream, but the enormous man straddling her pressed his hand tighter to her lips, muffling the sound.

She jerked her arms downward, ready to fight him off, only to discover that her wrists were tied to the headboard. Terror rushed through her and her pulse sped, setting her heart to slamming against her ribs as she tugged harder on her bonds. But the rope biting into her wrists assured her she wouldn't be able to fight her way free.

She was bound tight, powerless to protect herself from whatever this man intended to do to her.

"Relax, princess. It's just me." The man leaned down, the water dripping from the end of his nose, landing on Hannah's cheek, making her flinch. "I came in through the window. I thought I'd make that fantasy you were telling me about a reality."

Hannah swallowed, her thundering heartbeat slowing a bit as she understood what was happening.

She wasn't being attacked by an intruder. This man must be Harley's guy of the moment, and he *clearly* thought he was straddling her sister. Once she cleared up the misunderstanding, he'd untie her and she could show him to the door. They'd both be embarrassed, no doubt, but she wasn't about to be raped or murdered.

The realization made her whip-tight muscles sag with relief, an action she realized too late that the man took as an invitation to continue living out Harley's bondage fantasy.

"I've been dying to touch you all day," he said, his dry palm moving from her mouth to her breast, teasing her nipple through her thin tee shirt, drawing a gasp from her throat.

She expected his touch to feel foreign and unwelcome, but his fingers were gentle, teasing her with a sweetness that made her arch into his warm hand. Electricity shot from her breast to coil between her legs, the sensation intensified by the feel of the rope digging into her wrists as her biceps tightened reflexively in response to the stranger's confident touch.

"God, the sounds you make drive me crazy," the man said, pinching her nipple tight enough to make her gasp again.

"No, please, I'm not—" Hannah's words ended in a moan as he pushed her shirt up and bent lower, tugging her nipple into the warm, wet heat of his mouth. His tongue flicked and teased, flooding her body with pleasure and longing so intense she was panting by the time he transferred his mouth to her other breast, sucking and nibbling at the aroused skin as his big hand slipped down the front of her panties, finding where she was already wet.

Wet, from her *sister's boyfriend's* mouth on her breasts. And now his fingers were sliding into where she ached, making her shudder.

If she didn't stop this soon, it would be too late. There would be no avoiding tragedy, there would be only shame and the nightmare of confessing to her sister and this innocent man that she'd done something unforgivable.

"Stop, I'm not Harley." She tensed her thighs only to relax them a second later when she realized her locked muscles were trapping his fingers inside her embarrassingly slick sex.

"No, you're not," he said, driving his fingers in and out of her as he trapped her nipple between his teeth and bit down, making her cry out in pain before he soothed away the hurt with his tongue.

"You're my little slut," he continued in his deep, sexy rumble of a voice, his fingers still busy between her legs, making the tension coiling low in her body fist even tighter. "And I'm going to fuck you until you scream."

"No, please," Hannah said, excitement and fear dumping into her bloodstream simultaneously, making her feel like she was being deliciously, torturously torn in two. "I'm not Harley, I'm—"

This time, he silenced her with a kiss, his tongue pushing between her lips, demanding entrance to her mouth. He tasted of something smoky, hard cider, and the ocean on a day when it isn't safe to go into the water. His kiss was dangerous, wild, and unlike anything Hannah had experienced before. He didn't tease or test her; he fucked her mouth with his tongue, the thick muscle mimicking the movements of his fingers between her legs, bringing her to the edge faster than she'd imagined possible.

She'd had trouble tumbling over in the past. But her former boyfriends had always been sweet men and often too-tender lovers.

This man might be sweet—she had no way of knowing what he was like outside the bedroom—but he wasn't tender. He was demanding, controlling, the type of man who didn't hesitate, didn't change course, didn't stop until the job was done. There would be no easy escape from this bed, she knew it even before he hooked his fingers inside of her, coaxing her into an orgasm that had her bowing off the bed, screaming into the hot, hungry mouth still devouring her own.

Her body clenched down, liquid heat gushing out to dampen her thighs as pleasure rocketed through her core and his tongue continued to fuck her mouth, building her need again even as her pussy still throbbed and clutched at his thick fingers.

By the time he grabbed her behind the knees, forcing her legs up and out—until her knees were in her armpits and she was bared to him, from her ass to her dripping sex—she was beyond words, beyond identity, beyond awareness of anything but the blunt head of his engorged cock hot at her entrance.

Fear flashed through her for a moment—she was on the pill, but she'd never had sex without a condom before—but then he was gliding into her, shoving through her swollen flesh, stretching her so wide she wasn't sure she'd ever be the same again.

She moaned, pain and pleasure warring within her as he claimed her in one long, slow stroke. He was enormous and so thick her body fought to eject him, to banish the burning sensation he caused between her legs. But he kept coming. And coming and coming, until she swore she could feel him in her belly, in her lungs. He was everywhere, his hot thickness filling her up until there was no room for anything but him.

She tried to breathe deeper, to center herself, to hold on to that sacred, hidden kernel of her soul no man had ever touched, but she couldn't find it.

There was only him, his heat, his rain and campfire smell, and his need, spearing her in two, insisting she take everything he had to give.

"Look at me," he said, holding still inside her, his voice demanding she obey. "Look at me."

She lifted her eyes to his, a ragged sob escaping from her strained throat. At this angle, the light from the bathroom hit his face and she was granted her first good look at him, this stranger who was buried inside her, and it all but stopped her heart. He was beautiful—strong, rugged features softened by full lips and dark eyes that burned with passion and intelligence. He was as stunning as all of Harley's men, but there was more to him than a handsome face or a gorgeous body.

There was something in his eyes, something that made her want to know him, to please him.

"I know what you want," he said. "But I can't go there until you tell me that you're mine." He paused, looking so deep into her she couldn't believe he didn't see that she was an imposter.

But in the long, breathless moment that their eyes held and all of Hannah's secrets and fears seeped into the air between them, his gaze only gentled.

"Because you are mine," he said softly, his voice as tender as his cock was merciless. "Your pleasure belongs to me, your pain belongs to me. I want it all, Harley. All of you. Don't fight me anymore. Give it to me. Give it all to me."

Hannah's breath rushed out through her parted lips, but she didn't know what to say, how to tell him she was a liar when this moment felt so real, so right.

"You can trust me." He flexed his buttocks, forcing his cock impossibly deeper, making her groan in pleasure. In pain.

Pleasure-pain. They were one and the same with this man and she wanted nothing more than to give him what he wanted, whatever he wanted so long as he would never stop hurting her, healing her, possessing her in a way she'd never realized she wanted to be possessed until this stranger had claimed her for his own.

But she wasn't his and he wasn't hers.

He belonged to her sister and this was so wrong that "wrong" wasn't a big enough word to describe it—this betrayal, this sacrilege, this terrible, terrible thing she'd allowed to happen. She should have fought harder, screamed the truth until he understood she wasn't playing games.

Now it was too late, and she hated herself for it.

"Please," she said, tears filling her eyes. "Forgive me."

"For what, princess?" His warm palm cupped her cheek with a sweetness that threatened to break her heart all over again.

"I can't…" She swallowed, searching for the strength to tell him the truth, but she couldn't, not when she was exposed, so vulnerable, and so intimately connected to this man that she couldn't tell where he ended and she began. "I can't tell you. Not now."

"Now is the time to tell me anything," he said, leaning down, his lips hovering above hers as he shifted his hips, pulling out until she was acutely aware of all the places that ached in his absence before pushing back into her again, summoning another hungry sound from her throat. "Everything. I'm ready for your secrets."

"No, you're not," she whispered, shuddering as he began to roll his hips, nudging her clit with his pubic bone again and again, building the need swelling inside of her.

"I'm not a fool." He captured her nipple between his fingers, tugging it in time to the undulating rhythm of his hips. "I know you've been hiding things from me. It doesn't matter. What matters is right now. Tell me you're mine and we'll figure the rest out together."

"Stop, please," she said, teeth digging into her bottom lip as she strained against her bonds, but the rough rope against her skin only made her hotter, wetter. "I can't think. I can't—"

"Don't think," he said, his grip tightening on her nipple as he rode her harder, until she was quivering beneath him, so close to the edge she knew she could go at any moment. "Feel. Feel how real this is and tell me you're mine. Tell me and I'll do all those things you've been dreaming about."

He shifted his head, whispering into her ear, his breath hot on her skin as he fucked her with long, languid strokes that completely unraveled her mind. "I'll spank you and mark you and fuck you so hard you won't be able to sit down for days without thinking about how I used you." He pressed a kiss to her throat, where her pulse raced. "Isn't that what you want?"

Hannah nodded breathlessly. She had never even imagined things like that, but suddenly, lying beneath this man, she wanted all the wicked things he'd promised and more. She wanted to be turned over his knee and punished for the lies she'd told. She wanted him to hurt her for letting him believe she was someone she wasn't, and then she wanted him to take the pain away with his beautiful mouth.

That exquisite mouth that made her shudder now as his teeth dragged lightly over the skin at her throat.

"Then say it," he said. "Give yourself to me. Tell me you're mine."

"I'm yours," Hannah said, the words out of her mouth before she could stop them. "I'm yours. Forever. Yours."

"Fuck yes, princess," he moaned, thrusting faster, deeper, demanding her pleasure. "Come for me. Come on my cock. Let me feel you."

Hannah's head fell back as she came with a sound that wasn't cute or ladylike. It was wild and base, a cry of animal satisfaction that ripped from her throat as her pussy clutched at her stranger's pistoning cock, demanding his orgasm with the same assurance that he'd ordered her own.

He came crying out her sister's name, his thickness jerking hard inside of her, the feel of his scalding heat soaking her insides sending her soaring a third time. Lights danced behind her tightly closed eyes, and somewhere deep inside of her, things she needed to live lost purchase and floated away from their moorings. She was adrift, helpless to defend herself, totally at the mercy of this man who gently untied her arms and kissed the red welts on her wrists.

And she didn't even know his name.

Hours later, after he'd had her again—this time with his hand fisted in her hair while he took her from behind, his rough use making her feel safer than every considerate kiss from every ex-boyfriend she'd ever had—that's all she could think about. She didn't know the name of the man who kissed her like she was his world before climbing back out the window he'd crept through hours before.

And she wasn't going to find out until tomorrow, when she would be forced to come clean to her sister and confess the nightmarish thing she'd done.

Harley might actually forgive her—she didn't tend to get too attached to her lovers, especially the summer boys she used to entertain her between epic trips abroad—but the stranger would hate her. He was in love with her sister. He thought he'd been making love to Harley, not a complete stranger.

As Hannah lay in the dark, in sheets that still smelled of sex and sweat, she was forced to admit that she was a terrible person. She wasn't the good twin, after all. She was weak and selfish and obviously unfit to become a psychiatrist and counsel troubled kids, not when she was so messed up in the head that she'd slept with her sister's boyfriend.

The first time, he hadn't given her time to protest, but she could have stopped things before they came together again, before he held her on his chest and promised she would always be under his protection, or before she whispered "I love you, too" as he eased out onto the tree limb beneath the second story window.

Liar. She was such a miserable liar.

She didn't know if Harley loved the man, but Hannah barely knew him. It was impossible to love a man you had just met and barely spoken to aside from some scalding hot pillow talk.

She knew that, but as she got up to put the sheets on to wash and start a pot of coffee—sleep was going to be impossible, might as well help the insomnia along—she couldn't help wishing that she didn't have to tell her stranger the truth. A selfish, wicked part of her secretly hoped that Harley would never come back to her summer apartment, that she would hop the next flight to Paris and disappear the way she sometimes did, usually right when Hannah needed her the most.

And then Hannah could meet the man again, learn his

name, and start figuring out what it would take to make him hers.

In the years to come, she would think of that selfish, wicked wish again and again, wondering if wishes like that had a power others didn't. Wondering if her greedy longing was the reason her sister had been murdered and Hannah would never see her best friend's face again.

Even when her Aunt Sybil spirited her away from Harley's very private, very secret wake, insisting it was past time she learned about the darkness that haunted their family, Hannah couldn't bring herself to blame fate or her father's enemies for her sister's death.

She would never forget that one wonderful, terrible night, or that she had wished that Harley would disappear and that hours later she had.

Forever.

CHAPTER THREE

Hannah

Six years later

*F*reedom doesn't come for free. Neither does forgiveness.

Every step Hannah had taken from the moment she'd learned Harley was dead, to the morning she awoke to find Aunt Sybil crying on the back steps of their storm-battered bed and breakfast, had been taken with one goal in mind: Absolution.

She wanted more than survival. She wanted release. She wanted to shed her skin and leave the sins of her former life far behind her. But the past has long arms and sharp claws that dig in deep and hold on tight. The past was a monkey on her back. A monkey with an ugly sense of humor she swore she could hear cackling at her attempts to escape the Mason family curse.

In the past six years, The Mahana Guesthouse had been damaged by gale force winds, lost three cottages in an electrical fire, suffered through two Dengue fever outbreaks that scared the tourists away for months, and nearly been reclaimed by the sea when Hurricane Isra swept through last week.

The morning after the storm, the Laurents, their only neighbors close enough to reach the guesthouse on foot, had come to check on Sybil and Hannah. The sweet older couple had wept with relief when they found the women huddled in the cottage farthest from the beach—the only structure not falling in on itself—soaked to the skin but safe. The Laurents had taken them to their home, fed them fresh French bread and guava fruit salad, and spent the rest of the day telling them how lucky they were to be alive.

But life was fragile, especially when you were a Mason.

Their savings had finally run out after the last Dengue fever outbreak. Now, if Sybil and Hannah couldn't find the money to repair the main house and guest cottages, their income would disappear, and their lives not long after. They could never return to the States or reach out to their family for help.

They were dead to the world they'd known before. This was their safe place, their one chance to carve out an existence far from the people determined to destroy them. But if Hannah didn't figure something out soon, their safe haven would be a thing of the past. She had to pull it together, get creative, and whip up a miracle with nothing but her hands, a dash of hope, and an abundance of determination.

But first, she had to make sure her aunt didn't hurl herself into the sea in despair.

"I come bearing gifts." She held the steaming cup of coffee beneath Sybil's nose, grateful when her aunt reached up to take the mug instead of staring zombie-like at the horizon the way she had for most of the week since the storm.

"I'm going to figure out a way to get the money today," Hannah added, curling her hands around her own warm mug. "I promise."

She had promised the same thing yesterday, but so far

she'd come up with nothing. Their tiny Tahitian island was a paradise, true, but it was also a place where jobs were few and hard to come by. And even if Hannah could manage to land a job as a maid or bartender at the luxury resort on the south shore, she wouldn't be able to cover basic expenses, let alone the cost of repairs, and the burden of raising the money sat firmly on her shoulders. Sybil could sell her homemade banana bread and other baked goods, but she couldn't hold down a job. Her aunt's arthritis made for days where she could barely get out of bed, let alone work ten hours stripping beds and cleaning toilets.

"I had a dream last night." Aunt Sybil swept the tears from her tanned cheeks with a trembling hand.

"Not a good dream, I'm guessing." Hannah sat down beside her on the steps leading down to the beach.

"No, it was," Sybil said, her gaze trained on the waves lapping at the sugar-white shore. "Aaron, Ezra, and Matthew were alive. We were at the old house eating dinner on the lawn the way we used to in the summers when we were young. But in the dream, we were all grown up and there were children and grandchildren everywhere." She smiled. "Dozens of dirty bare feet and popsicle sticky hands. It was lovely."

Hannah sighed, knowing the sound would be masked by the wind rustling the palm leaves.

They hadn't lost all the trees. Or the pool. That, at least, was lucky.

She was determined to stay positive. She couldn't think about all the things that had been lost. She couldn't think about the dead uncles she'd never met or that Harley might still be alive if Sybil had embraced her conspiracy theorist side sooner. Before Harley's car crash and the series of "accidents" that had picked off their first cousins one by one, Hannah wouldn't have believed that there was a contract killer out there somewhere determined to kill off their entire family. She would have thought her aunt was paranoid at best, delusional at worst. She never would have dropped out of grad school and fled the country without saying a word to anyone—even her mother and father—before the day she was forced to pick out her twin sister's coffin.

No, there was nothing to be gained from the "what could have been" game and dreams like her aunt's only made the waking world seem like more of a nightmare.

"I'm going to head into town to talk to Hiro this morning," Hannah said. "He said he might have some good news for me from his friends on Moorea. Do you need anything from the store while I'm there? Flour? Sugar?"

Sybil frowned but didn't turn her gaze away from the shore. "What kind of good news? You told him we weren't selling, right?"

"I did." Hanna ran her fingers idly back and forth across the wood beneath her. The planks still smelled of fresh stain and were one of the few parts of the guesthouse she'd been able to rebuild herself.

She was handy, but she wasn't a trained carpenter or a roofer or a plumber or any of the other endless skilled laborers they'd need to hire to make sure their tiny resort was ready to receive guests.

Still, she understood why her aunt didn't want to sell. After the hurricane, property values were in the gutter. They'd never get what the resort was worth and it was dangerous for them to conduct any business with a paper trail. Both she and Sybil had fake passports with assumed names, but anything that made people pay attention was a bad idea. That's why they had kept to the tradition Hannah's father had started long ago and never posted pictures of themselves on the Internet. They didn't have host photos on their website, refused to be photographed with their guests, and conducted all of their transactions in cash.

Cash that was growing perilously low.

"I'm not sure what he had in mind, but he seemed hopeful," Hannah said, forcing an upbeat note into her voice. "And if anyone can be trusted to help us wiggle out of this, it's Hiro. You know how much he wants you to stay on the island."

Sybil grunted, but Hannah could tell her aunt was fighting a smile. "You'd think after a year of trying he'd get the message that nothing's going to happen between us. He's half my age, for goodness' sake."

"He's only ten years younger," Hannah corrected, nudging her aunt's knee gently with her own. "And he might get the idea if you'd stop flirting with him like a shameless hussy."

Her aunt's answering laughter was one of the sweetest sounds Hannah had heard in days.

"Oh my goodness," Sybil said, still giggling. "I didn't think anyone had noticed."

"Kind of hard to miss," Hannah said, grinning. "I think it's adorable and I bet you and Hiro would have a lot of fun together. And how many people can say they've dated a pearl farmer?"

Sybil's smile faded as she tucked her gray-streaked blond curls behind her ears. She really did look so much younger than fifty-five, with only lightly wrinkled skin and bright blue eyes that danced when she was happy. She swore that her commitment to looking on the bright side had kept her young, which only made it harder to see her succumbing to despair and losing faith that everything would work out okay in the end.

"Maybe I'll think about it," her aunt finally said in a soft voice. "If we're still here come the new year."

"But it's only November. You know you don't have to wait until New Year's Eve to try something new, right?" Hannah pressed. "Why don't you let me invite Hiro to come have dinner on the beach with us tonight? It's supposed to be a beautiful evening, and I'll be there to chaperone."

"Oh no," Sybil said shaking her head. "I don't even have a

proper kitchen to cook in. I can't feed a guest anything I've whipped up on the hot plate."

"Give him a few beers first and I doubt he'll notice he's eating grilled cheese," Hannah said, finishing her last sip of coffee. "Besides, it's the company he's after, not the gourmet experience."

Sybil's head shaking grew more agitated. "No, Hannah. I'm not ready. Maybe someday, but not now. Not until we know you're safe."

Hannah's spirits fell and she suddenly wished she hadn't pushed. She knew her aunt wasn't comfortable with change and even less comfortable with men. Besides, Hannah wasn't in any position to preach about embracing opportunities for romance. She had only dated two men since the move and both relationships had lasted only a few months before fizzling away.

She told herself it was the need for anonymity and secrecy that made it hard to forge a connection. She refused to admit how often she thought about the night she'd promised herself to a stranger. Or how often she woke up from erotic dreams featuring *his* hands on her body and his lips on her skin.

Her mystery lover, the one who had ruined her for other men.

But she wasn't going to think about him either. Positive thoughts were the order of the day.

She managed to keep her head up and her optimistic attitude firmly in place until her meeting with an anxious, embarrassed Hiro, who told her what he'd learned from his connections on Moorea.

There was a way for Hannah and Sybil to save the resort: a billionaire who was willing to give them the money they would need to rebuild. But what he wanted in exchange was something Hannah had never imagined putting up for sale.

"I don't know if I can do that," she said, glancing over her shoulder, hoping no one else at the open air café had heard

Hiro's proposal or her response. She wouldn't even be considering what the pearl farmer had suggested if she weren't backed so far into a corner she was starting to fear she'd never get out.

When she was certain none of the other patrons of the café were listening, she turned back to Hiro and whispered, "What kind of man is he? Do you know him? Would I be safe?"

"Yes, he's a good man. A very good man. And very rich." Hiro's dark eyes tightened with concern. "But it is too much, yeah? You are a good girl." He ran a tanned hand through his lightly graying hair. "Your aunt would be so angry with me if she knew I'd even mentioned this kind of arrangement."

Hannah shook her head as she picked nervously at an empty sugar packet. "Sybil could never know. If I do this, if I become…" She swallowed hard, unable to speak the words "erotic companion" aloud. "I'd have to make up another excuse for leaving the island. I couldn't let her find out. It would kill her."

And it might kill you. You trust Hiro, but do you trust his assessment of a stranger's character enough to risk your life on it?

She wasn't sure, but after they had finished their tea and she'd walked down the crowded village street to the grocery store and checked her and Sybil's bank balance at the ATM, she knew she had no choice but to accept the terrifying offer. They were almost broke. There was no other way to pay for Sybil's medicines, let alone get their business up and running again.

And it would only be for a month. She could do anything for a month.

Pushing away throat-tightening images of a greasy man with a hairy back ordering her to spread her legs, Hannah pulled out her cell and dialed Hiro's number.

"I'll do it," she said when the farmer answered. "I'll pick up the directions on my way out of town."

CHAPTER FOUR

Jackson

*I*t was time, the moment Jackson Hawke had been working toward for six long years. He was finally going to have his revenge on the woman who had taken everything that mattered away from him and set his life on fire.

The woman whose death he'd mourned even as the wounds she'd left on his heart teemed with hatred, unlike anything he'd ever known.

During his ten years in the Marines, Jackson had been deployed to some of the most violent war zones in the world and seen men commit acts so heinous they deserved no mercy, no trial, no second chance. He'd come face to face with human monsters, but Harley Garrett was the worst of them all.

She was pure poison, venom wrapped in an irresistibly beautiful shell. She was a nightmare come to life, but he'd cried when he'd learned she'd been killed in the car wreck that had claimed the life of his best friend. Still, he'd ached to hold her, even after learning she and Clay had been on their way to Niagara Falls to get married when their car was forced off a dangerous mountain road.

It wasn't until Jackson was locked in a cage, disowned by his family and reviled by his friends, that he'd stopped grieving and started hating with a purity that had transformed hatred into a religion. Hate became his center, his mantra, and the reason he'd been able to rise from the ashes of his former life to become something stronger and better than he'd been before.

He no longer had an honor code, morals, or ethics standing in the way of taking what he wanted. Now, he had hate and the single-minded focus it lent all its devotees.

Without that focus, he wouldn't have kept digging into the details of Harley's death until he discovered that Harley Garrett had been born out of the ether that summer six years ago. He wouldn't have learned that there wasn't a single photograph of the woman on the web or a record of her body being buried anywhere in the United States. He wouldn't have made contact with the kind of men who made a living finding people who didn't want to be found or kept paying them to search for Harley for years after a less vitriol-filled man would have given up hope of finding the monster who had gotten away.

And without hate, he never would have learned that Harley was living the sweet life on a tiny island in Tahiti or had the patience to wait until she was vulnerable and powerless to fight him to take his revenge.

Initially, he'd planned to buy her property for a song and drag out closing negotiations until she and her aging aunt were so desperate to survive that Harley would have no choice but to agree to his demands.

But this…

This was so much better.

His cock thickened at the thought of all the things he was going to do to Harley's tight little body once she belonged to him. He hated her, but he still wanted to fuck her, to get his cock in her lying mouth, into her slick cunt, into the pretty pink asshole she'd denied him access to years ago, back when he'd cared what she wanted. He was going to have her every filthy way he'd imagined and make all the lies she'd told come true, until she regretted ever hearing the name Jackson Hawke, let alone ruining his life.

Once upon a time, his dark desires would have troubled him. But now he didn't care if it was twisted to want his enemy on her knees in front of him choking on his cock.

He didn't care about anything except seeing that bitch get what she deserved.

"She's on her way up, sir." His pilot and right-hand man, Adam, stepped into the artificially cool hotel room, his tanned face shiny from the late afternoon heat. "Is there anything else you need before I head down to the field?"

Jackson shook his head. "No. Just be ready for takeoff when we show up. If all goes well, we'll be there before sunset."

Adam nodded and stepped out of the room without another word. It was one of the things that made the man invaluable to him. Whether they were smuggling guns to drug lords in South America, selling secrets to rebels in war-torn countries, or arranging to buy a woman for a million dollars and change, Adam didn't put his oar in. He did as he was told, got the job done, and kept his mouth shut.

It made for boring company, but Jackson wasn't worried about it being just the three of them and a small number of carefully selected support staff on a private island for a month.

He expected Harley would keep him more than entertained.

Jackson turned to the computer monitor on the desk in front of him, waiting for his prey to appear, wondering if she'd follow the directions she'd been given like a good girl. The Harley he'd known had chosen defiance over obedience at every opportunity, but the woman he'd known had been a cipher, a lie from beginning to end.

Soon he would get to know the real Harley and maybe even learn why she'd made it her mission on earth to destroy him.

Not that he cared anymore.

He couldn't care less if his name was cleared—he'd done his share to tarnish his formerly pristine reputation in the past few years—but he would still make her return to Virginia with him to meet his father. He needed to see the look on Ian Hawke's face when he learned that a lying whore had tricked him into disowning his son. That alone would be worth more than a million dollars.

As if summoned by his thoughts of lying whores, the door opened in the room on his screen and a woman in a simple, sleeveless black sundress stepped inside.

The moment her tensed, frightened features turned to face the camera set up beside the bed, he knew it was Harley. Still, something in his gut pinged, insisting this wasn't the woman he'd been hunting for. But for once, Jackson ignored the gut instinct that had kept him alive and out of prison during the years he'd enthusiastically embraced a life of crime.

It was no wonder his gut was confused. Harley had changed significantly in the past six years. Her once dark brown hair had turned auburn in the island sun and freckles covered her tanned face, making her eyes look even more strikingly blue than they had before. But it was her body that had changed the most. Gone were the relatively boyish figure and stick legs she'd complained about when they used to go walking on the beach. In their place were curves for miles and miles.

She'd been beautiful before, but now she was…a goddess.

She was exactly the kind of woman he'd always preferred, with abundant breasts that would overflow even his large hands, generous hips, and a curvy ass he couldn't wait to get turned over his knee.

As soon as they reached his island, he was going to give her that spanking she'd begged for back when they were lovers. But this time he wouldn't stop before pleasure-pain turned to suffering. He would keep reddening her ass until her flesh glowed and she squirmed on his lap, begging him to release her. But he wouldn't, not until he'd bruised her sensitive skin, making sure that every time she sat down for the next week she'd be reminded that she was his property, to do with as he saw fit.

The thought was dizzying. And so arousing that by the time Harley reached for the top of her dress with trembling hands, his cock was testing the integrity of his zipper.

Slowly, slowly, doing exactly as she'd been told, she pulled her dress down to reveal her breasts, then her tanned stomach, and finally her full hips before pushing the fabric past her thighs. It fell down to puddle around her ankles, taking Jackson's breath away. She had obeyed the order not wear anything under the dress, as well, so the moment the black fabric dropped to the floor, she was bare to his gaze.

From her stunning breasts with the dark pink nipples to the gentle curve of her belly to the small thatch of dark hair that covered her mound, she was perfect.

Jackson's throat tightened and a wave of lust swept through him, making his skin feverishly hot. He wanted her. Now. He wanted to abandon this chair, hurry down the hallway to the sunlit room where Harley stood trembling in front of that camera, and show her how much more scared she should be.

He wanted to see her face when she realized who had come to claim her and then he wanted to bend her over that mosquito-netted bed in the corner and fuck her, hard and deep, until he lost himself inside of her, marking his new pet with his cum.

Instead, he forced himself to relax, to exert control.

Revenge wasn't something to be taken fast and hot. As the saying went, revenge was a dish best served cold.

When Harley laid eyes on him for the first time in six years, he would be cold, glacial. He would give her no power, no hope of using his emotions to manipulate him. She would never know how deeply she'd hurt him or how much he still wanted her. When he did eventually fuck her, it would be calm, efficient, a means to an end, a step on the path to breaking her.

He would not give her his need or his hate. He would give her nothing but what she had given him—suffering and pain.

And so he sat completely still as he watched Harley bring her hands to her breasts, ignoring the fact that the sight of her small hands cupping her full mounds made his balls ache. He remained frozen as she rolled her nipples between her fingers until her breath came faster and the anxiety on her face was replaced with arousal. But when she dropped one hand between her legs and began to rub her clit in circles, clearly intending to reach orgasm the way her instructions had commanded, his control snapped.

As Harley plucked at her nipple and fingered herself, he stood, wrenching open his fly. His swollen cock bobbed free, so hard and hot the skin felt like it would burn his palm as he took himself in hand and began to stroke his engorged length in time to the rhythm Harley had set. He jerked harder, faster, his cock swelling in his own hand as he imagined what it would be like to be in the same room as his prey.

Would he be able to smell her wet cunt, salty and sticky-sweet in the air? Would he be able to hear the sound of her fingers gliding through her slick, swollen flesh? See the flush that spread across her chest right before she came?

Would he have rushed in to catch her as her legs buckled and she dropped to the floor, crying out in ecstasy and fear as her orgasm brought her to her knees? Or would he have simply stepped in and finished with his cock level with her face, shooting his release across her pink cheeks and between her parted lips?

He groaned as he came—hard, exploding in his own hand, his cum splashing across the computer screen, covering Harley's face before leaking down to coat her breasts.

It wasn't as good as the real thing, but it was still pretty fucking amazing. She'd followed his orders and now she would be his. And in a few days—or a few hours, however long he was able to last—he would have her on her knees in front of him, ready to take whatever he would give her.

Jackson fetched a towel from the bathroom and cleaned up his mess, watching Harley get dressed with stiff, jerky motions that made him think she was embarrassed by what she'd just done.

Good.

Embarrassment wasn't shame, but it was moving in the right direction.

Her downcast gaze and flushed cheeks made him smile as he placed the final call to set his revenge in motion. "Hello, this is Mr. Hawke. Release the hundred thousand to the Mahana Guesthouse account."

"Right away, sir," the banker promised in heavily accented English. Jackson could have spoken to the man in his native French—he had become fluent in both French and German during the years he studied at West Point—but he wasn't interested in making other people's lives any easier.

Jackson thanked him and hung up before texting Hiro. It was time for his spy to make one final phone call. The man had obviously begun to regret the part he'd played in the sale of Harley Garrett—or Hannah North as she was calling herself these days—but another deposit in the pearl farmer's account had convinced him to ignore his protective instincts and get the job done.

Moments after the text went through, the phone in Harley's room rang.

She crossed to the bedside table, bringing her closer to the camera as she answered the phone, close enough for him to see the faint tan line creeping around her neck. When she was his, she wouldn't have tan lines. He didn't plan on allowing her the luxury of being clothed. At least, not at first. Whether she was inside the house they would share or out on the beach scanning the deserted horizon for signs of a rescue that would never come, she would do it in the nude.

"Oh, okay," she said, nodding though the man on the other end of the line obviously couldn't see her. "I'll meet the car downstairs in a few minutes. Thank you, Hiro. For everything."

The other man said something Jackson couldn't hear but that seemed to make Harley more nervous. Her voice was shaking when she spoke again. "Okay. I will. Look out for Aunt Sybil for me. I'll see you both soon."

She hung up, hesitating only a moment before picking up the phone and dialing another number. In light, lilting French she asked for the banker who had helped set up the funds transfer from Hawke's Swiss bank account to the bed and breakfast's local Tahitian one.

Clearly she didn't trust the mysterious billionaire who had offered to purchase her escort services for the month.

Hawke smiled again. She shouldn't trust him. Everything he'd told Hiro about wanting a beautiful American girl for a month of fun, sun, and no-strings-attached consensual vanilla sex on the beach was a lie. But when it came to the money he had kept his promise to pay one tenth of the fee up front. He knew Harley well enough to realize she would never get in his car or on his plane unless she knew she'd been paid something for her trouble.

She was a liar, but she was no fool.

She spoke again and was apparently assured that all the money ducks were in a row, because she thanked the banker, hung up the phone, and turned to go. She hesitated for a moment, but then her hands balled into fists, her chin lifted, and she started for the door with a steady stride, obviously determined to meet the man who had bought her with her head held high.

Too bad Hawke would be taking a separate car to the

airport and that Harley would be blindfolded and gagged before he arrived at the airstrip. He wasn't taking any chances that she would see his face and try to call for help while they were still surrounded by friendly islanders who might come to the rescue of a woman in need.

She wouldn't have the use of her voice until they landed on Le Sauvage, an isolated island at the far edge of the archipelago, where no one would be able to hear her scream.

CHAPTER FIVE

Hannah

*H*annah climbed into the back of the stretch limo waiting in the shade beside the Pension La Plage on rubbery legs. By the time the silent driver wound his way through the colorful streets of Fare, down jungle roads tunneled in green, and out to the private jet waiting at the edge of the airfield, she was trembling all over and fighting the urge to dash across the airstrip and make a run for the safety of the tiny airport waiting room.

What the hell had she done?

What you had to do. You're just lucky there was a man willing to pay that kind of price for a twenty-eight-year-old woman with no experience as an escort.

An escort. It was just a kinder word for a whore. Tonight—or maybe this afternoon, depending on whether or not the man who'd bought her joined her on the private jet—she would have sex with a man for money. It was a lot of money—once he paid the remainder of her fee she would have enough to save the guesthouse and make sure she and Sybil were safe from the ravages of their own bad luck for years—but still…

Still, she felt filthy, ashamed, and dangerously foolish.

She'd been bought and paid for. She had sold herself to a

complete stranger. A man who had already seen her naked and watched while she pleasured herself in front of the camera he'd set up in his hotel room. In the grand scheme of things it wasn't that kinky, she supposed, but it was kinkier than anything she'd done before, and it had made her vulnerable to this man in a way she'd never been to anyone.

He'd seen her naked, completely exposed as she'd come on her own hand, and she had never seen his face. Didn't even know his name.

You didn't know your stranger's name, either, and it didn't matter. It was still the hottest sex you've ever had.

As she climbed the steps into the private jet, Hannah swallowed hard, but the bitter taste on her tongue remained. She wasn't naïve enough to believe the billionaire who'd bought her would be a handsome young man with magic hands and a tender light in his eyes. He was almost certainly at least a decade older and probably not much to look at or he would have been able to convince a woman to come to his private island for free.

He might be hideously ugly, obese, or so ancient he'd have trouble getting aroused and she'd be forced to ignore the old-man scent of him as he labored above her, sweating and grunting.

Or maybe he was simply a twisted monster looking for a woman he could use, torture, and throw away, a woman no one would go looking for when she went missing.

Hannah half fell into the sumptuous leather seat on the far side of the plane, her trembling becoming a full-blown quake. By the time the tanned man with the close-cropped blond hair stepped out of the cockpit, she was shaking so hard her teeth were chattering.

Her eyes flew wide as her gaze connected with the man's paler, bluer one, but before she could think of what to say—or fully experience her relief at discovering that her client was a perfectly attractive middle-aged man—he crossed to stand in front of her seat.

"My employer asked that I help you tie this over your eyes." He held out a thick strip of heavy black cloth. "I've got another for your mouth."

Hannah's breath sped. "Why do I need to be blindfolded?" she asked, not wanting to think about the gagging part. The thought of not being able to speak, or even swallow her own saliva, was ridiculously terrifying, almost as scary as taking her clothes off in front of a camera, knowing a stranger was watching.

God, what had she done? What the hell had she done?

"I don't ask questions," the man said, his voice humorless and his blue eyes remaining flat. "My employer doesn't enjoy questions. He prefers efficiency."

"All...all right." Hannah's heart raced as she reached for the blindfold, figuring it was better if she was the one to tie it on. She wrapped the soft fabric across her eyes and tied it behind her head, tight enough to be sure it wouldn't accidentally fall off, but not so tight that it pressed against her closed lids.

When she was finished, she held out her hand, willing her voice not to shake as she said, "I can tie the gag, too. If that's okay."

"Just make sure it stays put," the man said.

Hannah couldn't help flinching as the man dropped the cloth into her outstretched hand. Not being able to see was already heightening her other senses, making the sensation of soft fabric brushing against her skin ricochet through her nervous system in a way it normally wouldn't.

She tied the gag as loosely as she dared, but when she was finished her tongue still felt cramped, forced to coil at the back of her throat like a snake denied the right to strike. The combination of the stressful day, having half her face covered, her eyesight stolen away, and her mouth filled with fabric combined to trigger the worst case of claustrophobia she'd experienced since she was eight years old and Harley had accidentally locked her in the crawl space next to their room.

She'd sat in the cramped portion of the attic, where she and her sister had hidden their secret treasures from their nanny, for hours, sweating and crying in the summer heat until she'd almost passed out. But she hadn't dared call out for someone to rescue her. She'd known Harley would kill her if she let any of the staff find out about their secret hideout. Harley didn't tolerate broken promises, no matter how many she broke herself.

Hannah struggled to swallow, fighting to slow her racing, panicked heartbeat. But it was an exercise in futility. Her heart was beyond her control, like the rest of her life, and the best she could hope for was that she would pass out before her owner joined her on the plane.

The thought made her throat feel even tighter and sweat bead around her hairline and above her parted lips. By the time she heard the door to the plane open a few minutes later, she was sweating profusely, panting through her flared nostrils, and so dizzy she didn't know how much longer she would remain conscious.

She whimpered and pointed frantically to the gag, praying the blond man would understand that she was having trouble breathing and grant her permission to remove it.

But instead of the first man's firm monotone, she was answered by a low grumble, "The gag stays in. You need to relax. You're breathing too fast."

Hannah tried to relax, she really did, but this man's voice wasn't one that inspired relaxation. He sounded hard, cold, and enormous. Until this moment, she hadn't realized that a voice could project size, but this man sounded ten feet tall and bulletproof. He sounded like someone capable of strangling the life out of her with one hand and mean enough to enjoy it.

As the thought passed through her head, her traitorous breath sped even faster and her chest began to shake.

"You're going to hyperventilate if you keep that up," the man grumbled again, his voice so deep she could feel it vibrating through her bones, touching her in places a voice shouldn't be able to touch. "Hannah stop. Right now."

A whimper escaped her cramped throat and her breath came so fast it felt like she was being spun in circles by one of those terrible carnival rides she'd hated when she was a child.

"Stop it," the man repeated, his voice closer and dropped to a soothing whisper. "I'm not going to hurt you on this plane, Hannah. I give you my word."

On this plane. He hadn't said he wouldn't hurt her at all, just not on the plane, and she sensed that she wasn't reading more into the remark than he'd intended. This was a man who knew what he wanted and was willing to pay a million dollars to have a woman at his mercy. He had deliberately left the door open for pain.

Hannah clutched the arms of her chair until her fingers ached, fighting to keep from ripping the gag and blindfold off and making a break for freedom. A deal was a deal. This man had paid for the pleasure of terrifying her. And if she backed out of their agreement, she had no doubt he would take the rest of his money and leave her and Sybil to starve.

She'd made her bed and now she had to lie in it.

To sleep with this man in it, even if the thought terrified her.

"We're ready for takeoff." The first man's voice sounded too far away to still be in the plane, but maybe that was because Hannah was so focused on the new voice, her owner's voice whispering in her ear again.

"Sit back. I'll put your seatbelt on."

She leaned back in the plush seat. A moment later, she felt fingers brushing her hips as the man found both halves of the seatbelt and brought them together across her waist. His touch was calm, impersonal. He touched her only as much as he needed to in order to get the seatbelt snug across her lap, but for some reason she still shivered.

There was something about this man, something in the spicy, salty smell of him that drifted to her nose as he settled into the seat across from hers that made her skin prickle and the hair at the back of her neck stand on end. She felt more than watched; she felt hunted and suddenly didn't know what she feared more—the nameless, faceless people who had killed half her family, or the nameless, faceless man whose foot brushed every so lightly against her own as the plane rumbled down the airstrip.

It wasn't until they were lifting off that Hannah realized the two might be one and the same.

She might have just sold herself to the man who had killed her family and the past six years of hiding, deferring all her dreams, and abandoning the aunt who needed her, might have been for nothing.

CHAPTER SIX

Jackson

*T*he plane was still gaining altitude when Harley started trembling again, shaking so hard he would have thought she was having a seizure if he didn't know better. But according to everything Hiro had told him, "Hannah" was in perfect health. It was her aunt who was frail.

So either she was truly scared out of her mind or she was faking it to elicit sympathy from the man who'd bought her. That would be like her. She was a master manipulator.

Until he'd met Harley, Jackson had been certain he could spot a con around a blind corner. His mother had majored in emotional manipulation at Brown and his sociopath father had taught him early on the importance of realizing when you were being worked like a puppet on a string. By age ten, Jackson was a master at spotting reverse psychology; by twelve, he'd perfected his poker face; and by his fourteenth birthday, he had a plan in place to escape his father's influence: a con of his own Ian hadn't seen coming until Jackson's acceptance letter to an exclusive military boarding school showed up in the afternoon mail.

But despite all his experience with the care and feeding of

sociopaths, Harley had still worked him like a player piano, arranging things so perfectly he'd practically conned himself.

Like that last night, when she'd promised to belong to him forever, fucked his heart from his chest and down to the floor to lie helpless at her feet, only to run away with his best friend a few minutes after Jackson had climbed out of her bedroom window. She had literally gone from coming on his cock to waltzing out the door with Clay moments later. He'd done that math. She had to have left her apartment no later than midnight in order to be driving down that particular stretch of highway at three in the morning.

But even after years of turning over various possible scenarios, he still had no idea exactly how she'd faked her death. That alone was enough reason not to underestimate her capacity for treachery. He couldn't let down his guard or allow compassion to creep into his heart. He had to be on his toes and ready to beat Harley at her own game.

And he had a good idea how to start.

He leaned in, placing a gentle hand on her knee. She tensed and made a startled sound behind her gag, but after a moment, she settled beneath his touch. Her muscles remained tight, but she stopped shaking and held very still, clearly waiting for him to make the next move.

With a hard smile, he reached behind her, into her thick, soft hair, and untied her gag. He set it on the seat beside her before returning his hand to her knee, allowing his fingers to curl around the shapely muscle of her calf. "Is that better?"

She swallowed and swiped the back of one hand across her mouth before nodding a little too fast. "Y-yes. Thank you."

She sounded so scared, so young and vulnerable. Like a woman who had never walked a dark street at midnight, let alone become one of the evil things lurking in the shadows. No wonder the military police had believed every word she'd said. Even without the evidence she'd doctored, her witness statement alone was fucking compelling. She'd been so beautiful in the tapes he'd been forced to watch. So beautiful and broken that he'd understood why the people in charge of the investigation couldn't help wanting to sweep in and do whatever it took to deliver justice.

But her suffering was a lie, like everything else about Harley. She was a monster hiding behind a pretty face and he knew better than to let her play him so easily.

"You're welcome," he said, gentling his voice, letting her think she was getting through to him while still keeping his pitch lower than usual.

He expected her to recognize his voice eventually, but he wasn't going to make it easy for her, and he didn't want recognition to come too soon. That would spoil the fun and he intended to enjoy every stage of Harley's undoing.

"I don't want you to be scared." He traced a path back and forth across the soft skin above her knee with his thumb. "Is there anything I can do to put your mind at ease?"

Her tongue slipped out. The sight of her pink tongue caressing her full lips was sexy as hell, a fact he was certain she was aware of, no matter how unpracticed the movement seemed. "I d-don't know." She took a deep breath, her full breasts rising and falling.

He glanced down at the tempting cleavage visible above the tight bodice of her dress and tried not to think about how much he wanted her gorgeous tits heavy in his hands.

"I um…" She swallowed. "I've n-never done anything like this before."

"I know." He allowed his thumb to slide higher on her bare thigh. Her legs remained close together, not tightening to bar his passage, but not parting to invite him in, the perfect balance of coy and seductive, proving Harley was still at the top of her game. "But you did very well in the hotel room."

"I was scared to death," she whispered.

"I couldn't tell," he lied. "I thought you were beautiful and very, very sexy."

She took a breath, holding it for a moment before she said in a husky voice, "It would help if I could see your face."

"Not yet," he said. "Soon, but first I want you to help me live out a fantasy I've had for a long time."

She tensed again but nodded, slowly. "A-all right."

"I've always wanted to be the stranger on the train," he said, stroking a little higher on her thigh as his other hand reached up to release her seatbelt. "I've always wanted to make a woman come before we've even kissed. Before she's so much as seen my face."

"That's the reason for the blindfold," she said, her shoulders relaxing slightly, seemingly comforted by the confession.

"That's the reason for the blindfold," he lied again. "And why I'm going to ask you to spread your legs for me."

"Now?" Her throat worked.

"Now," he said. "There aren't any midnight trains on the Tahitian islands, so we're going to have to settle for a private plane. Now spread your legs, Hannah, show me that beautiful pussy."

Harley's fingers tightened on the arms of her chair and her jaw locked. Even with her eyes covered, he could tell her expression was that of someone who'd taken a bite of something rotten and was too mannerly to spit it out. He expected her to deny him, to force him to ask again—maybe even threaten to take the money back if she didn't obey—but after a moment she slowly spread her legs, parting her thighs for him, granting him his first glimpse of her pussy.

But a glimpse wasn't enough.

"Wider," he whispered, exerting the slightest pressure on the knee he cupped in his hand. "And move to the edge of the seat."

With a shaky breath, she obeyed, shifting her hips and spreading her legs wide enough for her skirt to bunch up around her waist, revealing her pink outer lips and the entrance to the pussy that had haunted his dreams.

She was fucking beautiful, delicate and deadly, like a flower infused with poison. Hers was a pussy men would kill for, one he might have died for if she'd decided to frame him for murder instead of rape.

Her lips were fuller than he remembered and her sex was quiet and shuttered against him, but soon he'd have her swollen and wet. Soon he'd have her panting and begging for him to bring her over. And then he would, again and again, until his hand was sticky with her desire.

He wanted her thighs dripping and her body hungry for more when he removed the blindfold. He wanted her to know she'd already lost the first battle the moment he declared war.

"Lovely," he murmured as he worked his hands up the insides of her thighs, kneading her muscled flesh as he drew closer to her apex, his cock thickening from a potent combination of lust and this first heady taste of revenge. "You have a beautiful body."

"Thank you," she whispered in a strained voice, her fingers curling tighter around her armrests. She looked like she was bracing herself for a beating.

"Relax, beautiful, I know what I'm doing. This is going to feel good."

She nodded slightly. "O-okay…"

"But?" He hesitated, urging her legs still wider, but not moving his fingers to her delicate flesh.

"I wish I could see you," she said softly. "Just your eyes, just for a second."

"And why's that?" He traced a fingertip down the seam of her thigh, inches from where her leg became something more intimate.

She tensed but didn't try to close her thighs. "You can read so much about someone from their eyes, don't you think?"

"Not as much as you can read from a touch," he said, bringing his thumb to her clit and circling gently, making her gulp for her next breath. "Don't worry about my eyes. Concentrate on my touch. Let me bring you pleasure."

She didn't respond, but she didn't need to, her body assured him she was obeying his command. Slowly, but surely, she blossomed beneath his touch. Her clit hardened against his thumb, her sex flushed a deeper pink, and within minutes telltale slickness glistened at the entrance to her cunt. Jackson wanted to bend down and lick her wetness away, to burrow his tongue into her pussy so deep he would be able to feel her muscles contract when she came, but oral sex was too intimate.

Oral sex was an offering, a humbling of yourself in the name of pleasuring your lover. Harley would take his cock down her throat when he was ready, but he wouldn't put his mouth on her while they were together. She would get his hands or his cock. He didn't intend to kiss her on the lips, let alone anywhere else. Kisses were for people you trusted and cared for. Harley was neither and any pleasure he gave her would be in the name of breaking her down.

Her desire would be his weapon and her orgasms instruments of her own destruction.

"I love seeing you wet. But I want you even wetter." He brought his free hand to her entrance, teasing the edges of her slick cleft before sliding one finger into her heat, all the way up to the knuckle.

She gasped and her head fell back as he fucked her with his hand, all while maintaining his patient torture of her clit, applying enough pressure to drive her higher, but not enough to take her over the edge. He added a second finger, looked up to see her breasts rising and falling faster, and suddenly couldn't tolerate that part of her being hidden from his gaze.

He grasped the top of her dress and pulled it down with a sharp tug. Her heavy breasts fell free, bobbing gently as she cried out. She moved instinctively to cover herself, but he captured her wrist in a firm grip.

"Hands at your sides," he ordered, his voice thick and his pulse speeding as she obeyed him.

Yes, this is what he needed. He needed her tits in his hands, her wetness coating his fingers, but most of all he needed her submission. He needed her stripped bare and vulnerable by the time they landed and the flight wasn't a long one.

"These are mine and I'll touch them when I choose." He shifted his angle of penetration, bringing his left thumb to her clit as his left fingers continued to drive in and out of her pussy, leaving his right hand free to play.

He cupped her breast in his hand, capturing her already puckered nipple between his fingertips. He pinched her flesh hard enough to make her gasp, then pinched it even harder before rolling the bud in a fierce circle between his finger and thumb.

He was rewarded with a moan wrenched from the back of Harley's throat and a rush of heat between her legs.

"Your tits are mine and your cunt is mine," he said, slipping a third finger into her pussy until he could feel her desire-plumped flesh stretching to accommodate the thickness between her legs. "For the next month, you will belong to me. Your body will be my playground and your pleasure my property. You will not touch yourself while you're with me and you will come only when you're allowed to come. Do you understand me, Hannah?"

"Yes," she said, her hips lifting into his thrusts.

"Yes, sir," he corrected, transferring his attention to her other breast, plucking at her erect nipple. "You will show me respect, especially in the bedroom."

"Yes, sir," she said, lips parting as her breath came faster. "Yes, sir, please, sir."

"Please what?" he asked, his cock so hard it throbbed painfully, aching to be buried in the pussy gushing slick honey onto his hand.

"Please, I-I can't stop," she panted. "I'm going to come."

"No, you're not. Wait until I give you permission," he commanded even as he picked up his pace, fucking her hard and deep with his fingers. "Wait or you'll be punished."

"Yes, sir," she said, features twisting as she spread her legs even wider, welcoming his rough use. "Oh God, sir. Please. Oh my God!"

Jackson's lips twisted. He *was* her God, and soon she'd be prostrate on the ground before him, begging him for mercy. The irony was so perfect he decided to let her off easy.

There would be time to delay her pleasure and drag out her suffering later. Now, he wanted to watch her come and know he was only minutes away from the revelations that would leave her trembling with terror and ashamed of how easily she'd become his whore.

CHAPTER SEVEN

Hannah

"Come, Hannah," her owner ordered in that insanely sexy voice of his, the one that was familiar and foreign, arousing and terrifying, all at the same time. "Come hard for me."

She obeyed with a rough cry, her pussy locking down around his fingers, coating him in her juices. She was so wet it would be embarrassing if she had any room left in her mind for worry or shame. But there was only pleasure, white hot and electric, and bliss overloading her nervous system until she felt she might die from it.

She squirmed and moaned beneath his fingers as he continued to drive in and out of her heated flesh. She spun through a dizzy world of pleasure for what felt like hours—her womb pulsing and her nipples burning beneath his wicked, teasing fingers. But she still hadn't made it all the way back to earth when he moved his hand from her breast to her clit, pinching the erect nub between his fingers, dragging her back into the overwhelming spin of bliss.

This time, she reached for him as her pleasure claimed her. Her fingers found his upper arms and dug into the muscles there, not surprised to find he was as huge as she'd guessed.

His biceps were rock hard, without a pinch of fat to soften his flesh.

Based on the feel of those arms alone, he was easily twice her size. Twice her size and terrifyingly strong, but she couldn't bring herself to be afraid.

Logically she knew she should be wary that he had claimed her body and pleasure as his property and demanded her compliance without any assurances to keep her safe while she was in his keeping. But something inside her insisted that any man who could bring her such exquisite pleasure wasn't someone she should fear.

And something else inside her—that veiled part only one man had ever tapped into on that stolen night long ago—reveled in being controlled. In her deepest, most private fantasies, she didn't dream of candlelit dinners and gentle kisses. She dreamed of strong hands, a commanding voice, and a lover who would demand her submission and reward her obedience.

Maybe that's why it hadn't been as hard to put herself up for sale as it should have been. She was a self-respecting woman. She didn't want to be a man's whore, but in her secret heart, she did yearn to be owned.

And now she was, by a man who gently set her hands back on her armrests before pulling her clothes back into place— top of her dress tugged up and her skirt eased down over her still trembling thighs just as the air pressure in the cabin began to shift.

"We're nearly there," he said as he buckled her seatbelt across her waist once more. "Are you ready for a surprise?"

"What kind of surprise, sir?" she asked softly, suddenly shy. It was so strange, to have been pleasured by a man who she knew only by touch and sound.

It made her feel exposed and off-center, but at the same time strangely powerful.

She could tell that she'd pleased him. She'd heard it in his grunt of approval when she'd so eagerly called him "sir," and in the rich timbre of his voice when he'd ordered her to come. It gave her hope that maybe this month wouldn't pass as miserably as she'd expected. Maybe she and this man would find their sexual appetites compatible. Maybe they would even become…friends.

Odd, unexpected friends, but friends nevertheless.

The hope made her heart lighter, but it also made her vulnerable. She was unprepared for the sudden shift in her mystery man's tone, her thoughts too muddled by pleasure to make sense of his words when he said—

"An unpleasant surprise. At least for you."

She frowned beneath her blindfold, her pulse picking up again. "Why? Didn't I please you, sir?"

"You pleased me very much. Today." He spoke louder to be heard over the dull roar of the landing gear descending from beneath the plane, sounding less gruff than he had before.

"But this isn't about today, beautiful," he continued. "It's about penance for the sins of the past."

A sour taste filled her mouth as she cursed herself for being so ridiculously naïve. She was here to play her part in fantasies this man had been willing to pay a *million* dollars for her to help him fulfill. She'd been a fool to think this was about anything so relatively tame as Dominance and submission.

But still, she had to hold onto hope that she could find a way to please him, to mollify him, to do whatever it took to ensure she returned to her safe place in the world with her mind and body intact.

"What do you mean, sir?" she asked, clutching her armrests tighter as the plane dipped toward the ground. "What sins?"

"Do you really need me to tell you?" he asked, his voice closer than it had been before, making her think he was leaning across the small space that separated their seats.

"Can't you think of a thing or two you should atone for, sweetheart? Haven't you done something in your twenty-eight years of life on this earth that you regret?"

She swallowed. "I've done lots of things I regret. But I've never intentionally hurt someone and I've apologized for my mistakes whenever I could. In my mind, a person can't do much more than that when it comes to atonement, sir."

He chuckled softly, but she couldn't tell if he was amused or angry. For the hundredth time, she wished she could see his face. Just for a moment. But she knew better than to reach for her blindfold before he'd given her the order. Her owner had proven he could give her great pleasure, but she sensed he wouldn't hesitate to deliver punishment, as well.

"You really have no shame, do you?" he asked, but before she could answer the wheels connected with the ground and the roar of the plane's brakes fighting their forward momentum made speech impossible.

Eventually, the plane slowed and the pilot's voice came over the intercom. "The car is already waiting, sir. Would you like me to have Jean Pierre meet us at the end of the runway, or do you have business you need to conclude?"

"If you're asking if we're fucking, the answer is no, Adam," her owner said, his irritation clear. "Have JP bring the car around. I'm ready to get Miss North settled in her new home."

Hannah brought her hands to her lap, unbuckling her belt then fighting the urge to fidget with the straps. She sensed she should keep her mouth shut, but she couldn't help asking, "Is it okay for me to take the blindfold off now, sir?"

"Not yet," he said briskly. "But soon. The house is only a fifteen-minute drive from the airstrip. I want us to be alone when you see my face. I don't want to share that moment with anyone, beautiful. That's just for you and me."

Hannah nodded and tried to smile, but her lips refused to cooperate. His words were kind enough, but there was something in his tone that brought all her misgivings rising to the surface again.

What if he was hideously disfigured and intended to punish her for all the women who had refused to look beneath his superficial ugliness? What if he had a grudge against the female sex in general and planned to take his grievances out on the whore he'd bought for the month?

Then you'll show him that you're different. You'll prove to him that you're grateful for his kindness and the pleasure he gives you. You'll make him see you as a person with integrity who doesn't deserve to pay penance for the people who have hurt him.

She heard the door to the plane open and a moment later smelled sea air, damp earth, and lush vegetation. But aside from the soft voices of two men conferring outside the door and the distant screeches and warbles of birds, there wasn't another sound to be heard.

The fact that she was on a private island hit home in a new way, making her shiver despite the steamy humidity creeping in to muddy the plane's conditioned air.

She was going to be completely alone here with this man, surrounded by people paid to do his bidding. Adam had made it clear he honored his employer's wishes without question and she had no doubt the other people in his employ would be the same. Mr. X didn't seem like the type of man who brooked opposition from anyone, let alone the people who worked for him.

She would find no allies among the residents of this island, no one to aid her if she reached out a hand, no one who would care if she cried out for help. Her fate was truly in the hands of the man who gently, but firmly, took her elbow, helping her rise from her chair before leading her toward the door.

"Bend your head a bit," he said. "Now take the first step down with your left foot. There are four steps down to the ground."

She minded quickly, without question, which was a good

thing considering Mr. X didn't slow his pace or make any other concessions for her lack of sight aside from the hand on her arm. Thanks to her swift obedience she made it safely out of the plane, across the pavement, and into the expensive smelling car waiting for them not far away without tripping or falling flat on her face.

As her owner settled beside her and the car pulled away down a gravel road, she prayed that her obedience would be enough to keep her safe as she started this month-long odyssey with a man who owned her—body and soul.

CHAPTER EIGHT

Jackson

*H*e had planned to remove the blindfold on the plane, but that was before Harley made the mistake of pretending to be a decent human being. Before she professed in that sweet and sexy voice of hers that she'd never intentionally hurt another person and always apologized for her mistakes.

As if an apology would have been enough to right the wrongs she'd perpetrated against him, even if she'd offered it.

Which she hadn't.

She had ruined his life, potentially killed his best friend—he didn't know if the wreck had been part of the plan or if Clay was just another casualty in Harley's quest for Jackson's destruction—and walked away without a backward glance. And now she was going to pay for it. Her game was over. It was time for his game to begin and he was going to be sure she realized that in a very visceral way.

As soon as they pulled up at the house, he practically dragged her out of the car and up the wide wooden steps leading to the spacious front lanai, where succulent tropical plants in massive planters lent stateliness to the entryway. He pushed through the heavy wooden front door and hurried

toward the master bedroom without taking time to appreciate
that the home was even more stunning in person than it had
been in pictures.

He didn't pause to admire the beautiful central room with
the atrium that let in natural light, the gently whirring
bamboo fans, or the peaceful indoor pool at the center of the
space. He didn't stop to greet the small, aging housekeeper
with the steel streaked bun who stood silently in one corner of
the expansive kitchen as he charged through, tugging a blindfolded woman behind him.

The housekeeper had known what she was getting into
when she took this job. All of the staff had. They'd worked for
a South American drug lord, before Jackson, and a contract
killer who specialized in discreet murders for the very wealthy
before that. They knew the rules.

They would perform their duties, avert their eyes, and stay
out of his business, and in exchange they would be paid hand-
somely and live to service another monster for double the
salary of their straight-shooting counterparts. He could kill
Harley and bury her body in the jungle behind the mansion
and the men and women he'd brought with him to the private
island wouldn't lift a hand to stop him.

The thought made his hand tighten around Harley's as he
strode down a wide hallway with dark wooden walls to the
master suite at the end. She deserved to die for what she'd
done, but that wasn't in his game plan.

Death was too good for her. Too peaceful. He was going to
break her down, force her to acknowledge the darkness
inside of her, and then feed her soul, piece by piece, through
the shredder, until she was too shattered to face her reflection in the mirror. He wanted every waking moment of her
life to be a punishment to be endured, not a gift to be
enjoyed.

He would make her suffer, make her sorry, make her wish
she'd never been born. But most importantly, he would make

her repent for what she'd done to him or drive them both out of their minds trying.

As soon as he reached the bedroom, he stepped through the door and closed it firmly behind him before recapturing Harley's hand and leading her deeper into the space. When they reached the center of the generous suite, near two small couches and a glass coffee table arranged in front of floor to ceiling windows that showcased a breathtaking view of the lush back lawn, he released Harley's hand.

With his fingers digging firmly into her shoulders, he turned her to face him, his breath coming faster and his heart thudding heavily in his chest.

"Is everything okay, sir?" she asked, in that soft, submissive voice of hers, the one that was innocence and sex mixed into a potent cocktail that had kept his dick hard for most of the past hour.

Even with her eyes covered, she had read him like an open book and adapted to meet his unique needs in less time than it took most people to eat a meal. She clearly had a gift for giving men what they wanted, but it was all an act. Her perfection was only skin deep. In truth, she was a chimera, a mirage, a beautiful illusion that would linger just out of reach until the day she drew her weapon and plunged it into your heart.

"Sir?" she asked again, her arms beginning to tremble at her sides.

"Quiet," he said, his voice hoarse and his breath still labored. He bench pressed well over two-hundred pounds and ran ten miles every day, rarely breaking a sweat until mile three, but his training hadn't prepared him for Harley.

This was more than a battle of bodies. It was a battle of wills, of souls, and it was time she realized that hers belonged to him. She wouldn't set the tone of their relationship. She wouldn't be the puppeteer pulling the strings. She was his property and she would show him her true colors or he'd beat them out of her.

"Stop pretending," he said. "Stop trying to manipulate me. That isn't going to happen this time, sweetheart."

Her breath sped, her chest rising and falling faster, but her trembling ceased. "I don't understand, sir."

"That's because you're a dumb cunt," he said, enjoying her flinch in response to his hard words. "Now drop the act and show me the vindictive, psychotic bitch I bought. She's the one I want right now."

She shook her head ever so slightly and a sob escaped her parted lips. "I don't understand."

"You said that already," he snapped. "Stop playing dumb and don't you dare cry or I'll give you something to cry about."

Her bottom lip quivered as she shook her head again. "I'm not playing, I swear! I just want to please you. I want to make you happy so you won't hurt me. Please." She paused, lips pressing together and her throat working as she fought to keep her tears at bay. "Please, sir. Please, believe me."

"Believe you." He laughed softly, an ugly laugh ripe with his barely suppressed rage. He reached out, driving his fingers into her hair and fisting his hand at the nape of her neck, drawing a mewl of surprise from her full lips.

"I will never believe you," he said, pressing his cheek tightly to hers and whispering his words into her ear. "You will never have power over me and the sooner you realize that, the better. Now, you will show me the woman I want to see, show me the monster beneath your pretty face, or you will suffer the consequences."

She whimpered. "Who do you want to see? Who do you want me to be?"

"Yourself!" he shouted, triggering a full-body cringe from the treacherous woman in his arms. "Be yourself! Stop denying who you are!"

"I am myself!" she shouted back, heat creeping into her tone. "I can't be something I'm not. I'm not the woman who hurt you. I'm Hannah. I'm a good person. I swear I—"

With a growl of rage, Jackson tightened his grip in her hair and jerked down, forcing her to her knees in front of him. She landed with a cry he barely heard over the blood rushing in his ears.

"You are not a good person," he seethed. "I know who you are and I will hear your true name from your own lips. Right now."

She went very still and he could practically hear the wheels turning in her clever head. "Who are you? Why have you brought me here?"

"Right now I want to hear you say your name," he said, ignoring her first question, knowing the truth would be revealed soon enough. "You will not think beyond what I demand of you in any given moment. Your will is mine. Now give me what I want or you will be punished."

With a deep breath, she lifted her chin, somehow managing to project defiance even while on her knees. "Then punish me. I'm not going to play this insane game. I'm not going to pretend to be anyone but who I am. I am Hannah North, and I don't deserve to be treated this way."

"Punishment it is then," he said, reaching for his belt buckle. "Take your dress off. Now," he added when she hesitated a beat too long. "You chose punishment, Hannah, and I'll have you naked to take it. Unless you're ready to give me what I want."

Her lips tight and her stubborn jaw set, she reached for the top of her dress and tugged it down her curves until it fell around her knees then reached down to guide it back down her calves. Jackson watched her bare her heart-stopping curves as he opened his fly and shoved his pants and boxers around his hips, freeing his aching length.

His cock bobbed free, the swollen flesh pulsing and eager. His dick didn't care that he hated this woman. It was desperate to be buried between her legs, shoving into her hot mouth, sliding between her oil-slicked tits, whatever would get him off the fastest. But this wasn't about pleasure— though he fully intended to come—and he had to maintain control, to prove to both Harley and himself that he was in charge.

"Touch your nipples," he said, bringing one hand to his cock and beginning to stroke his own engorged length. "Pinch them, make them tight for me."

Harley slowly brought her hands to her breasts but when her fingers captured her nipples it was clear her heart wasn't in it. She only lightly stroked the pink flesh and her skin remained flat and unresponsive.

"Harder," he said. "I want your pussy wet the way it was on the plane. I want you dripping down your thighs and your cunt hungry for something to fill it."

"I don't want to have sex with you," she said, voice trembling. "Not like this."

"We're not going to have sex," he said, kneeling in front of her. "When I finally fuck you, you will have been begging for it for days. You will be so desperate for my cock, you'll lick the bathroom floor clean if that's what it takes to get me to put it in you."

Her lips puckered, but she didn't speak a word. She didn't have to.

"You think I'm lying," he said, stroking his cock a little faster, aroused by the thought of her begging. "But I'm not. I will not take you by force. I won't have to. Now pinch your nipples for me. That's right. Like that. Now harder."

She obeyed and slowly a telltale flush spread across her chest and her breath came faster. He waited until she was biting her bottom lip and her thighs were clenching and releasing, causing her hips to shift slightly, before issuing his next order.

"Lie back and spread your legs." She hesitated, but he pushed on before she could protest. "Right now, Hannah, or I may rethink my promise not to fuck you on the floor."

Her flush spreading up her neck, she lay back on the floor and spread her legs barely two hand widths apart, playing the prude though it was clear she was turned on.

"Wider, Hannah," he said. "Grab the back of your knees and pull toward your shoulders. I want to see every inch of my pussy."

She moved slowly, efficiently, clearly doing her best not to put on a show for him, but seeing her spread wide, revealing her most intimate places made his cock leap in his hand.

Fuck, she was even hotter than she used to be, so curvy and plush and obedient. He took a deep breath, forcing himself to slow his rhythm, to ease his grip on his swollen shaft. He was going to have his release, but first, he needed her to beg him for it.

And he knew exactly how to make her beg. Harley had played him for the worst sort of fool, but the passion between them had always been real. She hated him, but that hadn't cooled her lust any more than it cooled his own.

And now he was going to use his intimate knowledge of how his kinky little bitch liked it to begin bringing her under his thumb.

CHAPTER NINE

Hannah

Don't respond. Stay cold, calm, above it all. Don't let him get to you.

Hannah squeezed her eyes closed and clenched her jaw, struggling to stay motionless and unaffected as the insane person who'd bought her explored her sex with his long, thick fingers, playing through her folds, dipping into her slickness before circling her clit with a not-quite-firm-enough pressure.

She fought to shut down her nerve endings, but it was no use. This man was out of his damned mind, cruel, and probably dangerous, but he also knew how to play her like an instrument. He was a maestro and she was helpless to resist the erotic song he coaxed from her body.

Soon, her pussy was dripping and her sex plump and swollen beneath his touch. She stayed still as long as she could, but eventually she lost the battle against her own desire and lifted her hips, fighting to get closer to the fingers that stroked her clit hard enough to make her crazy, but not firmly enough to grant her relief.

"You want more?" he asked. "More here?" He tapped her clit, making her breath catch. "Tell me, Hannah. Tell me what you want or you won't get it."

"Yes, more," she said, the words transforming to a yelp of pleasure-pain as he smacked her between the legs.

Pain flashed through her sensitive clit to spread through her belly, but it was followed by a rush of even more intense pleasure as his fingers returned to her clit and what felt like his thumb plunged into her pussy.

"Yes, sir," he corrected as he worked her harder, building the need swelling inside her. "Or I'll slap you again. Do you understand, Hannah?"

Hannah bit her lip, fighting the desire washing through her like a hot, sticky flood, a wild thing that didn't care if this man was crazy or dangerous. That part of her didn't give a shit that this was degrading, it just wanted him to slap her again.

"Or do you want more punishment?" he asked, proving she was hopelessly easy to read, even with a blindfold covering half her face. "You want more of this?"

He slapped her again, twice in rapid succession and she cried out, but it wasn't a cry of pain. There was no mistaking the lust in the sound. She sounded like she was about to come and it suddenly wasn't that much of a stretch to imagine herself at his feet begging him to fuck her.

If he teased her like this for too long, she would be so desperate for relief she had no idea what she would do.

"You like me to hurt you a little don't you?" he asked, his breath coming faster, making her think he was turned on, too. As messed up as he was, he seemed to get off on her pleasure, not her fear, which she could only hope meant he didn't intend to rape her.

It wouldn't be rape. If he pushed his cock inside you right now, you wouldn't fight. You'd beg him not to stop.

The thought made tears rise in her eyes and her face feel lava hot.

What the hell was wrong with her? How could she be falling so easily under this man's twisted spell?

"Answer me, when I speak to you," he demanded, swatting

her two, three, four times between the legs, until her clit burned and the delicate skin around her pussy grew hot from the repeated contact.

"Yes, sir," she panted, squirming her hips though she wasn't sure if she was trying to get closer or farther away. The sensations he aroused in her were dizzying, making her feel outside herself and more in touch with her own desire all at the same time. "Yes, I like it when you slap me."

"What about when I slap you here?"

Hannah cried out again as his big hand slapped first her right breast and then her left, rippling her flesh and making her nipples pull so tight they ached.

Ached for more. Ached for that heady sting and then his mouth hot on her puckered skin, taking the pain away.

"Yes, sir. Please, sir," she said, her hunger peaking as his fingers set a faster pace between her legs, fucking her hard, but not hard enough.

Shamelessly, she spread her legs wider, silently begging for what she wanted, but she should have known her tormentor wouldn't be satisfied with silence.

"Please, what?" he asked. "You want to come?"

"Yes, please. Please, sir!"

"You've already come twice in the plane," he said, his voice husky with the same desire that was driving her crazy. "I think it's my turn, first, don't you?"

"Yes," she said, reaching for him. "Tell me what you want me to do."

"I want you to put your hands back on your nipples," he said. "Then I want you to beg me to come on your tits."

She moved her hands, but when she opened her mouth the words wouldn't come. She'd never said the word "tits" before in her entire life and she'd never been overly verbal in bed. Sighs, moans, and the occasional, "yes, there, more please," were the extent of her dirty talk.

She was still trying to get her mouth to form the uncomfortable phrase when her tormentor suddenly pulled his hand away from her pussy, leaving her feeling bereft and abandoned.

And so damned unsatisfied, she couldn't stifle the groan of protest that escaped her lips.

"If you want to come, you need to beg," he said, his voice underscored by the faint sound of flesh sliding against flesh, making her think he was touching himself somewhere nearby.

The thought was unexpectedly, intensely arousing. She wondered what he looked like, kneeling over her prone body, his cock in his hand, stroking himself while he watched her roll her nipples between her fingertips. Imagining it made her even hotter and her wild, primitive side ached to drop her hands between her legs and bring herself over at the same moment he did.

But that wasn't what he wanted. He wanted her to beg and suddenly she wanted it too. She wanted whatever it was he needed to get off, to lose some of that fierce control and come because she had *made* him come.

"Come on my tits, sir," she said, her voice breathy and strained as she rolled her nipples in firmer circles. "Please come on my tits. Please. I want to feel you."

The sounds of flesh against flesh grew more urgent and when he spoke his sexy voice was an even sexier growl. "More. Beg me, Hannah. Make me feel how much you want me to cover you with my cum."

"Please, sir," she begged, her thighs clenching and releasing as the tension building inside of her became almost unbearable. "Please come on my tits. Cover me, mark me. I want you hot on my skin, I want to feel your—"

He cut her off with a groan and a second later she felt his hot stickiness splash across her chest, covering her hands and her breasts in his release, making her gasp and her clit throb. He smelled like fresh cut grass and lemons and something fiercely, unrepentantly male and his labored breath was music to her ears.

If you'd asked her beforehand, she would have assumed having a stranger come on her chest would be distasteful at best and revolting at worst, but right now all she felt was turned on. She could come from a single finger pressed against her clit, but only *his* finger.

She needed him to touch her, to bring her over until she was panting on the floor beside him. Her nerve endings buzzed and hummed with longing and her sex was so swollen and heavy her longing was quickly approaching suffering. It felt like there was a burning stone weighing down her pelvis and he was the only one who could take the pain away and replace it with pleasure.

"Can I come now, sir?" she asked, teeth digging into her bottom lip as her thighs clenched together, seeking relief. "Please, sir?"

"In a moment," he said. "But first, I want you to see my face. Are you ready, Hannah?"

"Yes." Her tongue slipped out to dampen her lips and her pulse fluttered in her neck. She was nervous, but she was also excited, ready to see the face of this man who both enraged and seduced her so easily.

And scared her, she shouldn't forget about that, but with the magic he'd set loose in her body making her high with desire, it was hard to remember to be afraid. How could she fear a man who, thus far, had given her the greatest pleasure she'd ever experienced?

Bar one night, one man, and she knew by now that no one would ever live up to him, to that intense sexual encounter so long ago that never should have happened in the first place.

She was thinking of him as her owner untied her blindfold. She was thinking of his incomparable body and sharply angled face. Of those eyes that were both hungry and devoted, predatory and so full of love she would have sold her soul to exchange places with her sister, to be the Mason twin that beautiful stranger loved with such devotion and intensity.

She was so lost in the memory that for a moment, when her blurred vision cleared and she looked up into the face of her captor, she was certain she was hallucinating.

It couldn't be...

There was no possible way...

Her eyes widened and her heart raced, slamming against her ribs, excitement and confusion making her feel like she was being pulled in two. It couldn't be him, but still...there he was, standing over her, zipping up his gray suit pants and pulling his belt back into place. His eyes were harder, his face covered in dark stubble, and his body even thicker and more powerful than she remembered beneath his button down shirt, but he was her stranger, there was no doubt about it.

He had come for her, bought her, taken her away, and now he wanted to punish her for her sins.

He must know that it hadn't been Harley he was with that last night. He must know it and be sufficiently enraged by it that he had tracked her down and done whatever it took to get her isolated on this island and at his mercy.

Hiro must have been complicit in the scheme, which meant Aunt Sybil might not be safe. Hannah knew she should be worried about Sybil, concerned for her own safety, and terrified of this man who was clearly as obsessive and mad as he was gorgeous. But she had been waiting years to see his face again, to feel his hands on her, his body moving inside of her, his rough voice calling her name instead of her sister's.

And the part of her that had meant her promise to belong to him forever didn't feel afraid. She felt like she was coming home, finding something precious she'd thought was lost forever.

So when she met his gaze and saw the hard, challenging expression in his eyes, her stomach flipped with excitement, not terror.

She would be his for an entire month and she would finally learn his name. It wasn't much, but for a woman who had dreamed only of *his* hands since the night he crawled out that window into the rain, it was a gift.

A dark gift, but a gift nevertheless. And when a person receives a gift, there's nothing to do but smile.

CHAPTER TEN

Jackson

*J*ackson waited, watching Harley's eyes widening in recognition, not wanting to miss the moment she realized she had been caught in an inescapable snare.

Her hair was wild around her face and her eyes glittered in the sunset light streaming through the windows, making her look like a goddess come down to earth. Even sprawled on the floor, covered in cum, and with lines on her forehead where the blindfold was tied too tightly she was beautiful.

Those signs of his use made her even more beautiful, and if she were one of the submissive lovers he'd enjoyed himself with during his travels, he would be proud of her for her obedience and the way she'd relished the feel of him marking her with his release.

But she wasn't his lover, she was his enemy and any moment her nimble mind would work its way around to the truth and she would shatter before him. She would quake and beg and know with a bone-deep certainty that all her worst nightmares had come true.

He expected her cheeks to pale and her lips to tremble. At

the very least, he expected denial and pointless explanations. He didn't expect her to smile.

But she did.

She smiled.

She smiled like the sun coming out from behind a rain cloud, a relieved, helpless-to-stop-its-spread, hopeful smile that left him feeling like he'd been punched in the gut.

The bitch actually looked happy to see him. Legitimately happy.

Not vindictively happy, not wickedly happy, just pleased.

Grateful even.

What the fuck.

What. The unholy. Fuck.

Jackson and Hannah's story continues in
DEEP DOMINATION

DEEP DOMINATION

Bought by the Billionaire
Book Two

By Lili Valente

CHAPTER ELEVEN

Jackson

Six Years Ago

*T*hey had only been in the stuffy room at the end of the hall for half an hour, but Jackson was already sweating beneath his clothes and dangerously close to losing his shit.

The interrogation was a joke. It was clear, that in the minds of the two military police officers charged with getting his side of the story, he had already been tried and convicted. He didn't know either of them, but they weren't hard to read. The older, red-headed man with the crooked nose wanted to pound Jackson unconscious and his partner—a young, fuzzy-haired brunette who barely looked old enough to have graduated from the academy—alternated between flushing red with anger and paling with disgust.

And fear. She was afraid of him, too.

He could see it in her eyes when her guard faltered. She was horrified by what she was certain he'd done. She was also scared of what might have happened to her if she'd encountered him on one of the more far-flung Quantico trails, deep in the forest where no one could have heard her scream as he'd forced himself on her.

As he'd *raped* her.

The thought made his stomach roil and bile rush up the back of his throat. He would *never* do that to a woman, *any* woman, let alone the woman he loved. Being questioned in connection with something like this was deeply disturbing, but the fact that he was accused of violating Harley was just...too much.

He felt dizzy, sick, and panicked, but also strangely above it all, like a ghost hovering in the air watching a man with dark circles under his eyes protest that he was innocent.

It was all so fucking bizarre.

He'd spent the past two days grieving Harley with an intensity that had left his insides black and blue, crying himself to sleep and wishing he never had to wake up again. All he wanted was for her to be alive, even if it meant she was married to Clay and he would never get to hold her again, never taste her skin or hear the breathy sound she made at the back of her throat as he pushed inside her.

He still loved her, and ached for her so deeply he worried the pain might kill him. He would never have hurt her—*never*.

He'd said as much to the MPs at least half a dozen times, but it bore repeating until these people got the message.

"It doesn't matter if anyone can confirm whether or not I was at home asleep four nights ago," he said, cutting off the red-haired officer in the middle of his latest monologue.

The man and his partner both had nametags on their uniforms, but Jackson couldn't seem to focus long enough to make sense of the letters stitched in black on gray. The entire morning had been too surreal, from the time the officers knocked on his front door to the moment he learned he was being questioned in connection with the rape of Harley Garrett.

"I didn't rape Harley. I love her." The reality that she was no longer alive to love hit him all over again, making it hard to swallow past the fist of emotion shoving up his throat.

"I loved her," he continued, his voice hoarse. "So much. I would never have hurt her. And if she were here right now she'd tell you that. She'd tell you everything we did was consensual."

"So you believe Miss Garrett was a truthful woman?" the female officer asked. She was pale now, not flushed, but Jackson was too frustrated to wonder if that was a good sign or a bad one.

"Yes," he said, shaking his head as he realized that wasn't the truth, no matter how much he wanted it to be. "I thought so, anyway. She always seemed to be when we were together. But two days ago I learned that she was engaged to my best friend. They'd been dating behind my back for months so…"

He ran a clawed hand through his hair with a harsh sigh, trying not to think about the fact that Clay was gone, too. Clay, who had been his best friend since basic training and saved his life more than once. Clay, who would have been the first and only person he would have turned to at a time like this, the only person in his life he'd trusted with all of his secrets.

"So maybe she wasn't always truthful," he continued. "But she would have told you the truth about this."

"Why's that?" The woman—Pearson according to her name tag, though he would probably forget that the second he glanced away—lifted her unplucked brows. "Was she afraid to contradict you?"

Jackson balled his hands into fists on top of the table, fighting to keep the anger from his voice. "Because she was the one who wanted to experiment with being submissive. She's the one who wanted things rough." He lifted his chin and relaxed his fists, ignoring the doubt he could feel seething toward him from the other side of the table. "She wanted to take things even further, for me to gag her and use a whip that would leave marks on her skin, but I told her no."

"Why?" Pearson pressed.

"I wasn't ready to go that far until we had a serious commitment."

"You only hurt the ones you love?" the male officer asked with a barely controlled sneer.

"Because power exchange can be dangerous," Jackson said, not bothering to keep the condescension from his tone. "I've been involved in these kind of relationships before, but Harley was new to the lifestyle. I needed to know that she trusted me to take care of her and help her learn her limits. Like I said, I didn't want to hurt her."

He sat still, forcing himself to hold the gaze of first Pearson and then her older, meaner counterpart without flinching, resisting the urge to fill the silence. He'd offered enough explanation. If there was something they didn't understand, they could ask.

There was nothing perverted or wrong about what Harley had wanted—or in his need to make sure he was entering into a relationship in the way he felt was safest for a new-to-the-scene submissive. Giving your will over to another person for the first time can be overwhelming. Both the Dom and sub need to have similar expectations and be committed to working through the process together from the start.

He'd had doubts Harley was ready to submit to another person's control—she was so stubborn and didn't always seem to enjoy it when he started giving orders in the bedroom. But after the way she'd responded to him the night he'd climbed through her window, his doubts had faded away.

She had been so perfect, so vulnerable and honest and sexy as hell.

For the first time, he'd seen all the way to the heart of her, and known it was safe to tell her that he loved her. Because she loved him, too. She was scared and she had secrets and pain she tried so hard to hide, but deep down she was ready to take the first steps toward abandoning control. To him and only him. She was ready to hand over her power and let him help her find a way to be free of the things that haunted her.

As he'd kissed her goodbye he'd been certain they were on their way to something special.

Instead, it was the last time he would ever see her alive.

"I loved her," he said again, the words out of his mouth before he could stop them. "And now she's gone and I just…" He sucked in a shallow breath, willing himself not to break down. "I don't understand why this is happening."

"Maybe this will shed some light on that for you." Red turned to press play on the DVD player behind him.

The television sat on a dull gray portable stand and had already been in the room when Jackson was led in. He'd assumed it was part of the standard furnishings of the drab interrogation room, along with the chipped table, squeaky chairs, and the plastic water cooler in the corner.

But he'd been wrong. The television was there for him; he knew it the moment Harley's face flickered onto the screen.

His first reaction to seeing her tear-streaked face was joy—to see her again, to see her talking, animated, *alive*—followed closely by grief and then rage.

Someone had hurt her. Badly. Her face was swollen from crying and her big blue eyes darted back and forth, unable to look directly at the person questioning her on the other side of the table. She was trembling so badly he could hear the legs of her chair rattling on the floor, a soft, percussive accompaniment to her words.

To the nightmarish words spilling out of her pretty mouth.

Comprehension hit like a bolt of lightning, sudden and shocking. Jackson's lips parted, but no sound came. His throat closed and all the blood in his body seemed to rush away, leaving him drained and freezing in the room that, only a moment ago, had felt too warm.

But that was before he'd heard Harley describing a date on the beach they'd never had, before he'd watched her lifting her shirt to reveal bruises he hadn't given her. Before she'd sworn that he'd raped her again and again, until she could barely stand and had been forced to call an ex-boyfriend to drive her to the police station after Jackson allegedly left her bleeding in the sand.

He watched the tape in stupefied silence and remained mute for several long minutes after Pearson turned off the television and stopped the DVD.

How...

How could she? How could she have done this?

How could she have told such horrible lies about him when all he'd ever wanted to do was love and protect her?

There had to be some mistake, some explanation.

She was confused. That was it. It had been dark on the beach that night. Maybe she hadn't seen her attacker's face, maybe he'd grabbed her from behind or—

Stop it!

She knew your body, your touch. She would have known it wasn't you, even if she were blindfolded.

She's lying on purpose.

She's lying *on* purpose.

Finally, as his mind continued to echo the terrible truth over and over—like a scratched record stuck on repeat—and his heart continued to break he found his voice. "I didn't do it. She's lying. I don't know why, but it's all a lie."

Red leaned in, his brown eyes flat and cold. "You might want to rethink that line of defense. The DNA results from the rape kit came in last night. We pulled yours from the Marine database. They're an exact match."

Jackson shook his head, anger and confusion warring inside of him. "But we always used a condom. Every single time except..."

His eyes widened as the flaw in Harley's story suddenly

became abundantly clear. "Those bruises were fake! Make-up or something. I saw her two nights ago, right before the crash. We slept together and she was fine. Every inch of her was clear and bruise-free. I swear there wasn't a mark on her."

"Do you have any evidence to support that?" Pearson asked, writing something in the tiny notebook she'd brought into the room, not even bothering to offer eye contact.

"No," he said, voice tight. "Why would I? I was with my girlfriend, who I thought was in love with me. I didn't think I'd have any reason to need to prove I hadn't beaten her to within an inch of her life."

He paused, watching Pearson show the note on her pad to Red, who nodded smugly.

"What is going on here?" Jackson asked, volume rising. "I'm being framed for a felony and you're buying a woman's lie without even giving me the benefit of the doubt. What the fuck is wrong with you?"

"Watch your mouth, soldier," Red said. "Everything you say in this room is admissible in court. You're the one who agreed to be questioned without an attorney."

Jackson clenched his teeth until his jaw was so tight it felt like the muscles were about to snap in two. "I've changed my mind," he finally ground out. "I want a lawyer. Now."

"We'll have a phone brought in for you. Might as well settle in, Staff Sergeant Hawke. You're going to be here for a while." Pearson smiled, a cold, victorious smile that made Jackson loathe her more than he did already, but not as much as he loathed Harley.

As much as he *should* loathe Harley.

She had conned him, played him, and framed him for a crime he didn't commit, but he couldn't bring himself to hate her.

Not that day. Or the next day, or the next.

But by the time he was sitting in a courtroom in front of a judge pronouncing him guilty of rape, he had begun to hate

Harley Garrett with the same passion with which he'd loved her.

When the judge declared that he would be dishonorably discharged, stripped of all rank and pay, and sentenced to eighteen months in a military prison, the last ounce of his affection for Harley shriveled and died, leaving nothing in his heart except a burning hatred. His hatred was a roaring fire that he would stoke every day he spent behind bars, tempering himself in the flames until he was as heartless and remorseless as the woman who had ruined him.

The woman who had sentenced a man whose only crime had been loving the wrong girl to a fate worse than death.

He would never be the same. He would never love or trust anyone ever again. He would never be the man he was before.

That man was dead.

Harley had killed him and now all that was left was to return the favor.

CHAPTER TWELVE

Hannah

Present Day

*H*er stranger was clearly angry—furious—but Hannah couldn't have stopped the smile blossoming across her face if she'd tried.

It was really him, *him*, the man she'd tried to convince herself she wasn't obsessed with for six long years. The stranger who had laid claim to her body, captured her imagination, and haunted her dreams.

No…he had haunted her awakenings.

In her dreams, one glimpse of his face and she was electrified by pleasure. In dreams she was transported to the heaven of his arms, blessed by belonging to him in a way she'd never belonged to anyone, not even herself. It was waking up and realizing that the one night they'd shared had been a lie and that she would never see him again that was hell.

She'd always known that night was a lie, but now maybe he knew it too.

Maybe *that's* why he'd come for her. Her smile vanished so quickly it sent a flash of discomfort through her cheeks.

Hannah stared up at him, watching his jaw clench and storm clouds roll in behind his dark eyes. She cringed, wishing she could melt through the floor or that she at least had a blanket to pull across her body to shield her nakedness. But the polished hardwood held firm beneath her back and she remained exposed to her stranger, his release cooling on her bare chest as he glared down at her, his hands tightening into fists.

She half expected him to strike her, to drive his fist into her stomach as punishment for the smile she hadn't been able to control.

Instead, he squatted on his heels beside her, moving with a slow, easy grace that sent a chill across her flesh. She felt hunted, but there was nowhere to run. He owned her. He had bought and paid for the privilege of enacting his revenge and now her life was in his hands.

He would decide whether the next month would pass in pleasure or pain.

He would decide how she would pay for her sins and whether she would leave this island alive.

The thought of him beating the life out of her with his large hands made her whimper, even before he brought one of them to her throat. His grip was loose, but his fingers were so long they completely encircled her neck, bringing her claustrophobia surging back with a vengeance, making her blood race and her head spin as he leaned down to whisper inches from her face.

"I will tell you this one time and one time only, so listen closely," he said, his voice thick with rage, but so smooth and controlled it somehow made his next words even more frightening. "I am not the man I was before. There is no softness in my heart for you. There is no heart left to soften. I am beyond your reach. I own you and I intend to break you and nothing you do will change your fate. Do you understand?"

Hannah nodded as she swallowed convulsively, fighting to keep her breath under control as anxiety electrified her nerve endings.

"You can smile while I break you or you can cry," he continued, a smile curving his lips. "But the ending will be the same."

His grip tightened, not enough to hurt, but enough to make Hannah's anxiety creep toward full-blown panic. She was seconds from clawing at his fingers, when he suddenly released her and stood, wiping his hands on his neatly pressed pants, as if touching her had dirtied them in some way.

"Clean up. The bathroom should have everything you need," he said, pointing toward the opposite side of the room. "After you shower, you will stay in this room until granted permission to leave."

He turned to go, but stopped before he'd taken five steps and spun back to face her, making Hannah's slowing pulse lurch back into high gear. "And if I learn you've disobeyed my order—any order I give you while you're here—all the promises I've made to you will be invalidated. Think about that before you try to run. Because I will find you, Harley, and my punishment will make it clear how gentle I've been with you so far."

Harley? Hannah's brows drew together, but she didn't say a word.

She didn't know what to say, what to think. She only knew that she wouldn't be able to organize her thoughts as long as he was in the room. His rage was a fire that sucked all the oxygen from the air and left her gasping, as shocked and confused as a fish dangling from the end of a fisherman's hook.

It wasn't until the heavy door closed behind him and she heard his footsteps moving away down the hall that she dared to drag her trembling body into a seated position. Her movement set his seed sliding down the front of her chest. A wave of self-loathing turned her stomach as memories of their brief time together raced through her head.

He must have thought she was Harley from the beginning. *That's* why he'd kept insisting that she say her name and been so angry when she maintained that she was Hannah North. She'd thought maybe he was one of her family's enemies and wanted confirmation that she was a Mason, not a North, but he'd been waiting for her to confess that she was her sister.

Somehow, he didn't know that her twin was dead and was clearly committed to punishing Harley for whatever sins she had perpetrated against him.

Hannah would have liked to believe her sister was innocent of whatever had turned her commanding, but once beautifully passionate, stranger into a terrifying man bent on revenge, but she knew better. She would always love her sister and grieve the fact that Harley had been taken away from her too soon, but she didn't believe in revisionist history.

Dying hadn't changed the person her twin had been before she was murdered. And Harley had been a spiteful, inexorable, often frightening force of nature. She had played with men's hearts like a twisted child who enjoys torturing animals before putting the poor creatures out of their misery.

Their shared psychiatrist had said Harley's rough handling of romantic relationships was her way of protecting herself from becoming the kind of broken woman their mother had become, but that didn't make Harley's treatment any easier for her victims. Hannah had seen more than one strong man shattered after learning the woman he'd fallen in love with was an illusion and the reality was a sociopath who seemed to gain succor from breaking people's hearts.

Harley had always managed to walk away from the wreckage and disappear before her victim's grief could transform to rage. But now her sister's bad love karma had caught up with Hannah, who had been paid a million dollars to give a man a shot at vengeance.

Hannah couldn't tell her stranger the truth. If she told him that she was Harley's twin, not the woman who'd hurt him, she would endanger her and Sybil's future.

He wouldn't want her if he learned the truth. Obviously a surrogate wouldn't suffice or he would have taken out his frustration on other women years ago. He wanted Harley, the "vindictive, psychotic bitch he'd bought" and no one else would do.

"What did you do to him, Harley?" Hannah whispered as she drew her knees in to her chest, shivering despite the evening sun streaming through the floor to ceiling windows behind her, warming the large room.

Sometimes Hannah would swear she could feel her sister's spirit lingering nearby, not ready to leave until they could go out of the world together, the way they'd come into it, but now the air remained quiet, empty. She was alone, defenseless, and had no choice but to play a dangerous game with a man incapable of compassion.

But maybe Harley didn't deserve compassion. Maybe she'd done something so horrible, so unforgivable that retribution was the only fitting response. And maybe Hannah would have no choice but to pay the price for Harley's mistakes.

As she came to her feet and padded silently toward the bathroom, she hoped she would find a way to survive being shattered by the only man who had ever made her dream about what it would be like to belong to someone—body and soul.

CHAPTER THIRTEEN

Jackson

*J*ackson stormed out of the master bedroom and through the kitchen, where the petite housekeeper with the steel-streaked hair was in the middle of cooking something he dimly realized smelled wonderful.

But he was too angry with himself to pause to register anything good.

He'd come so close to losing it. The first time Harley threw him a curve ball, he'd nearly broken all the promises he'd made to himself.

A smile. A fucking *smile* was all it had taken to set him back to dancing when she tugged his strings. He'd had six years to prepare and she'd nearly broken him two hours in.

But she didn't. You didn't let anger take control. And now you're prepared.

Now, you know better than to think this will be easy.

His thoughts slowed his racing pulse, but he didn't slow his pace toward the front of the house. He kept walking until he was striding down the wooden steps leading up to the lanai and down the gravel trail leading toward the sea. He needed to be alone with nothing but the sound of the waves crashing against the shore. He needed to stare at the place where rocks became sand and remember that steady and relentless wins out in the end.

Rocks may seem more durable than water. But the waves washing in and out, lapping away at stone year after year, eventually wear the largest rocks to pebbles, then to sand, and then to particles so small they might as well not exist at all. He didn't have years, but Harley wasn't a rock. She was slippery and quick, but she wasn't strong. A strong woman wouldn't need to lie, deceive, and shape shift the way she did. Deprived of her usual tools, she would begin to break down much faster than a stone losing its battle against the sea.

He just needed to maintain his focus and keep from getting swept up in any game but his own.

He reached the end of the road where gravel gave way to sand and stood watching the tide come in, the sea air whipping his hair from his face and filling his ears with the meditative rush of wind and waves.

The owners of the property warned their renters that the ocean on this side of the island was dangerous. The shore break was brutal, with waves that slammed into the steep incline where beach gave way to ocean with the force of a wrecking ball.

Even from a few dozen feet away, Jackson could feel the earth vibrating beneath his feet each time the ocean found its target. The first few feet of shoreline was pock-marked and jagged from the constant assault, but the sand farther up the beach remained untouched. It was mounded in peaceful dunes not found elsewhere on the island, where a gradual incline allowed the ocean to creep higher up the shore.

Brutality had its place, but its reach limited and Jackson didn't want to hack away at Harley's protective shell. He wanted to creep past her outer defenses, through the sophisticated diversions she'd erected to deflect focus from her weakness, all the way to the deepest, most secret parts of her. He wanted to find the private places she held sacrosanct and rig the halls with explosives. He wanted to destroy her from the inside out, and for that he would need stealth and strategy, not a hand balled into a fist.

He was mentally running through his list of tactics and strategies, discarding those that seemed too blunt a tool to use now that he realized how quick and clever a viper he'd trapped under a basket, when his cell buzzed in his pocket.

Jackson pulled the slim phone free and glanced down to find a text from his spy—

Hoping you and Miss Hannah made it to your destination safely and will have a wonderful, relaxing vacation. I'll be keeping an eye on Miss Sybil and will make sure she's taken care of. Please give Miss Hannah my best. She's a lovely girl.

Jackson's lips twisted. He tucked the phone into his pocket without bothering to respond.

Harley was only lovely on the outside and he couldn't care less what Hiro did with her aunt. The man had served his purpose and was no longer of any use to Jackson. But the pearl farmer's text did give him an idea...

Harley seemed to truly care about her family. She'd rarely spoken of her father, but when she'd mentioned her mother or aunt, her voice had softened in a way that had made the younger Jackson envious. Fool that he was, he'd wanted her voice to soften that way for him. He'd wanted to be part of her inner circle, to be one of the few people in the world who had touched her heart.

But Harley hadn't let him in that deep. She was selfish and guarded with her affections. Whether she was incapable of romantic love or she had simply hated him too much to find a reason to care about him, Jackson couldn't be sure, but he was positive he could use her love for her family against her.

He just needed to figure out how to sharpen the weapon and where to thrust the blade to do the most damage...

The thought had barely formed before he had his phone in

his hand and Hiro's number on speed dial. When the other man answered Jackson spoke over his bright hello.

"I'd like you to get close to Sybil North and see if you can find out her real last name," he said, turning away from the sea, sensing he had absorbed all the lessons it had to teach for the day. "Become her friend and confidante. I want private details of her life with Hannah, family pictures, stories, secrets they might be keeping, the location of other family members, anything you can find."

Hiro cleared his throat uncomfortably. "I don't know Mr. Hawke. I feel terrible about the lies I've told already. The ladies are good ladies. They are very sweet and gracious and I don't—"

"I'll triple your fee," Jackson said, cutting him off, unable to handle hearing anyone sing the praises of Harley Garrett. "I'll expect your first report in one week or I'll find someone else to do the job."

He hung up without waiting for the other man's response. Hiro would do as he was told. His flash of conscience would fade away in the face of the promise of more money. His family's pearl farm had yet to recover from the global recession and Hiro had three unwed sisters with eight children between them to feed. He would ingratiate himself into Sybil North's life and hopefully report back with information Jackson would be able to use against Harley.

In the meantime, he would do what he did best—get up, brush himself off, and start again. He'd come too far to be thrown off course by a bump in the road. Harley was quick and clever, but he held all the cards.

Now it was just a matter of deciding which one to play first.

CHAPTER FOURTEEN

Hannah

*B*y the time Hannah emerged from her shower that first afternoon, her clothes had mysteriously vanished from the floor and none had appeared to take their place.

After an hour spent pacing the large master suite with nothing but a towel clutched around her breasts, Hannah searched the bureau drawers until she found a flowered sheet she managed to fashion into a toga. It wasn't much to look at —and she wasn't much to look at in it—but it covered her nakedness and stayed put better than the towel.

She expected her stranger to reappear sooner or later—hopefully with something for her to wear since she hadn't been allowed to bring a suitcase—but that first evening came and went without a sign of Mr. X or anyone else.

She woke Saturday morning to the sound of her stomach complaining and watched the sun shorten the shadows of the fruit trees in the expansive back lawn while her belly did its best to digest itself. She was a few minutes from violating the order not to leave her room to go in search of food when a small, nut-brown woman with gray threading through her long black braid pushed into the room carrying a breakfast tray.

The smell of hot buttery croissants, freshly cut fruit, and hot coffee in its own tiny French press was enough to make Hannah dizzy with gratitude. At least starvation wasn't to be part of her punishment.

"Thank you so much," she said, smiling as the woman set the tray down on the low table near the window. "I'm Hannah. Have you worked here long?"

"Eva," the woman replied, her expression guarded. "No English."

Refusing to be deterred, Hannah widened her smile and made her introduction again in French, the language of most Tahitians, but Eva didn't seem to understand that either. Hannah was getting ready to try in Spanish, when a man's voice spoke softly from behind them.

"Mami, tu sabes muy bien que no tienes nada de hablar con esa mujer."

Hannah turned to see the owner of the voice—a tall, slim dark-haired man with expressive eyes and a full mouth—motioning urgently for Eva to exit the room.

"Why aren't you supposed to speak to me?" Hannah tailed the older woman as she hurried across the room. "Please," she said, reaching out a hand to hold the door open after Eva had slipped beneath the man's arm and disappeared down the hall. "Please, I just want someone to talk to. I'm not dangerous."

"But the man we work for is." Up close, the kid looked even younger. He couldn't be more than twenty-one, but there was a dark knowledge in his gaze that made it clear he'd seen more than most men twice his age. "So we'll do what Mr. Hawke says. You will be smart to do the same."

He turned and walked away before Hannah could recover from the excitement of being granted a piece of the puzzle.

Mr. Hawke. She had a last name!

Unless someone else owns this island. Maybe a friend of Mr. X's, who is as dangerous and insane as his houseguest.

The voice of doom had a point, but Hawke fit her stranger. It seemed apropos that he would be named after a bird of prey.

If she'd had a few more minutes with Eva or her son, she might have been able to confirm that her abductor was their employer. She might have even learned his first name, which she would need as soon as she gained access to a computer or cell phone.

She paced back and forth in front of the partially open door, thoughts racing, determined to make contact with the son again at the first opportunity. He was concerned for his mother, but he seemed kind, too. At least kind enough that he had spared the time to give her a word of warning. She sensed that he could be valuable to her if she could gain his sympathy. At the very least he might help her keep from losing her mind.

Hannah didn't want to get anyone in trouble, but she needed human connection. She needed to ground herself in this world via someone other than her stranger. If he was her only contact with humanity, she feared it wouldn't be long before she lost what remained of her composure.

Her shoulders bunching with frustration, she shut the door and crossed back to her breakfast. She ate the two croissants and all of the fruit salad—she didn't know when she would be fed again and it made sense to fill up—but the delicious baked goods and aromatic coffee didn't taste as good as they should have. Anxiety left a bitter flavor in her mouth that tainted every bite.

If someone had asked her yesterday, she would have insisted there was nothing worse than having her stranger standing over her naked body with murder in his eyes. But this...waiting for the other shoe to fall, for the first shot to be fired, for the monster to leap out from behind the trees with claws bared, was so much worse.

She spent most of her first full day on the private island

pacing her bedroom, staring out at the sunny day beyond the back patio off the master suite, growing progressively agitated. She had no work, no books, no television, no radio, not even a pack of cards to keep her mind focused on something other than the fact that she was the prisoner of a dangerous man who intended to destroy her.

Dread was slowly driving her out of her mind, a fact she was sure Hawke—if that was his name—was well aware of. He clearly had no moral compass to prevent him from using every dirty psychological trick in the book to weaken her defenses.

But he'd imprisoned a former psychology student, not a sculptor with a well-documented anxiety disorder. Hannah knew all about Stockholm Syndrome and she refused to fall victim to it. She would not mistake the absence of cruelty for kindness, she would not empathize or identify with her captor. She would remain focused on her deepest sense of self and her right to human decency.

Even if she were Harley and had done something worthy of punishment, she would still deserve that much. Even criminals on death row were allowed to eat, exercise, read, and lift their face to the sun for a few hours each week.

As soon as Hawke returned, she would demand that she be allowed a book and the right to walk outside in the back yard. She would make him see that she deserved a reward for her obedience.

He wants to push you into a breakdown, Hannah. You'll be lucky if you're not tortured, let alone rewarded.

Her thoughts were chilling, but she refused to dwell on them. She had to remain in the moment and face challenges as they arose. If she let herself start imagining all the things he might do to her, she would be doing his work for him and she refused to be complicit in her own destruction.

She went to bed that night determined to stay strong and woke the next morning three times as stir crazy as before. By the time she'd eaten her breakfast and the equally delicious lunch Eva delivered—scurrying in and out of the room so quickly it would have been funny if Hannah didn't know the poor woman's speed was born out of terror—she was near the end of her rope.

Not only was her captivity mind-numbingly boring, it gave her far too much time to think.

For the past six years, she'd been so busy struggling to keep the bed and breakfast afloat and scrambling to recover from one tragedy after another that she hadn't had time to dwell on how empty her life was in so many ways.

But now, with nothing but four silent walls to stare at, she had time to think about the dreams she'd abandoned in the name of survival. She'd never finished her education or opened the children's therapy practice she'd dreamed about since she was eleven years old. She'd never met a man who loved everything about her—the strong and the weak, the sweet and the sour—or started a family. She'd never been able to find out if she would have been a better parent than her cold father or shadow of a mother and now her dreams might never come true.

What if Hawke intended to do more than break her? What if he decided to end her life, here on this island where no one would lift a finger to help her?

And even if he let her live, was she strong enough to survive the kind of mental abuse he had in mind? Would she look back on these long lonely days later and curse herself for being too afraid to run for her life? Should she at least step far enough outside to get a better idea of where she was?

She stood at the sliding door leading out onto the patio, her mouth flooding with saliva and her palms and bare feet itching. She could practically taste how good the sea air would feel on her skin and the cushion of carefully manicured grass beneath her feet. She wanted to go outside so badly her bones ached with the need for freedom and movement and sun on her face, but she couldn't fight the feeling that he was watching and would know the moment she disobeyed his order.

His quiet threat that his promises would be revoked if she violated his commands was all that kept her from throwing open the door and racing across the lawn.

She was as terrified of rape as any other woman, but she was even more terrified of being raped by him, the man who had given her the greatest pleasure she'd ever known. It would be even more heinous and unbearable. It would be seeing something holy and beautiful mutilated and covered in blood.

She was quickly growing to fear Hawke, but she still treasured the memory of that one night and the pleasure he'd given her.

You'd better get over that, Hannah. Fast. You're giving him power he doesn't deserve.

"Easier said than done," she muttered as she paced away from the window, deliberately refraining from looking at the place on the floor where he'd driven her crazy before releasing himself on her bare breasts.

She'd replayed every moment of that encounter at least a dozen times in the past two days, looking for clues to what he had planned for her, but each time all she'd succeeded in accomplishing was making her body long for his touch. He was terrifying, out of his mind, and dangerous, but he was also the sexiest man she'd ever met.

It was sick, but during her shower that night, she couldn't keep from imagining that the fingers slipping between her thighs were his. She craved his touch almost as much as she craved a break from the anxiety soaked air inside her makeshift prison. She craved release, too, but after several long minutes of sliding her fingers through where she pulsed and ached, it became obvious she wasn't going to be able to find it.

Her mind was afraid to violate his order not to make herself come while they were on the island. And her body didn't want her soft touch. It wanted him, his rough hands and commanding voice ordering her to come.

With a soft curse, she shut off the water and dried off with hands shaking from denied satisfaction. She brushed her teeth with her eyes fixed on the marble countertop, refusing to look her pathetic reflection in the mirror, and crept in to curl under the covers fighting the urge to sob.

She had barely spoken more than a few sentences to anyone in two days. It wasn't that long in the scheme of things, but she felt so profoundly alone. She was unraveling faster than she would have thought possible.

For years, she'd been the shoulder her aunt could lean on, and had been Harley's steadying force long before that. She'd thought she was strong, but he was proving how wrong she'd been.

She should hate him for it, for ripping off her blinders and showing her all the cracks in her armor, but she couldn't stop thinking about the last time she'd seen Harley.

Her sister had been up to something, and Hannah's gut had insisted it was something bad. There was a chance that her stranger had been her twin's last victim and had every right to be hurt and angry. But how would Hannah ever convince him that she'd learned the error of her ways if she had no idea what Harley had done to him?

"His name," she whispered to herself, curling more tightly under the covers, her overly sensitive nerve-endings irritated by the feel of the sheets against her bare skin. "Start with his name and go from there."

If she could learn the rest of his name, she'd have something to type into a search engine the moment she had access to a computer. His name was the first step.

That's all she should focus on, taking one step at a time until she found a way to survive this nightmare with her mind intact.

CHAPTER FIFTEEN

Hannah

On the fourth night of her captivity, after more long fear-laced days of monotony and going to bed with tears running down her cheeks, Hannah was awoken by her own groan of relief.

She sucked in a breath and held it, her eyes blinking fast as she peered into the near darkness. For a moment, she had no idea where she was, but then she saw the palm trees waving in the moonlight outside the window, heard the gentle rustle of their leaves in the breeze, and felt big, strong hands hot on her breasts.

Waking up fast, she breathed into the fingers playing with her nipples. Her stranger plucked and teased at her swollen flesh, sending fissures of excitement washing through her. After days of silence and solitude, his touch was a glass of water in the desert.

"You awake, princess?" he asked, his lips moving against her bare neck, sending another rush of awareness sweeping across her skin.

"Yes." She moaned as her bare bottom brushed against where he was hot and hard. He had crept naked and uninvited into her bed in the middle of the night and touched her without her consent. She should be scared or angry, but all she felt was relief and she was too worn down by loneliness to fight it.

Besides, there was nothing to be gained by lashing out. She needed to arouse his empathy, not remind him why he wanted to punish her.

"You feel so good," she said, teeth digging into her bottom lip as he intensified his efforts, rolling her erect nipples until she squirmed in the circle of his arms.

He thrust forward, pressing his thickness between her ass cheeks. "So you've missed me, then?"

"Yes." She arched her back, tilting her hips until her wetness brushed against the base of his erection.

He was as massive as she remembered. His cock was so thick and long she would be afraid he would do her damage if she hadn't already experienced the harmony of how perfectly they fit together. She knew there was nothing better than the feel of him buried to the hilt, filling her up until there was nothing but him, nothing but pleasure so intense it was almost painful.

"You missed this?" One of his warm hands slid down her stomach and between her legs, setting her on fire.

His fingers circled her swollen clit, bringing her body even more fiercely to life. She was tempted to let go and get lost in the bliss he sent cascading through her, but she had to come away from this night with something she could use.

She had to learn his full name. It would give her a reason to hope, something to hold on to as he continued to do his best to break her.

"Yes, sir," she said, heart leaping as he hummed softly in approval. "I'm sorry I smiled."

He grunted. "Is that right? Why are you sorry?"

"Because it made you angry," she said, circling her hips, grinding back against his cock as his skilled fingers drove her higher. "Because it made you leave."

"You're wrong," he said, a smile in his voice. "I set my own course, princess. I've just been too busy to spare time for you. I have a business to run."

"What kind of business?" she asked.

"The kind wrongly convicted criminals turn to after their lives are ruined," he said, pleasantly. "Illegal business. Bad business." He pinched her nipple harder, sending a sharp wave of pleasure pain coursing through her and drawing a gasp from her throat. "Turn over."

Before Hannah could obey—or properly digest the fact that she was in bed with an ex con—he flipped her onto her back and roughly nudged her legs open with his knee. His touch wasn't gentle, but that wasn't what she wanted from him. Her twisted libido craved his rough use.

Fresh heat rushed from her body as he reached down, using his thumbs to spread her sex wide. "I love how wet you get. I love that I can smell how much you want me to fuck you."

"Yes," Hannah said, anticipation making her shiver. "But first I want to give you what you asked for."

"What's that?" he asked, his gaze still directed down at her pussy, though she wasn't sure how much he could see in the dim moonlight drifting through the window.

"Marlena Renee." She gasped as he plunged his thumb into where she ached, but fought to keep her thoughts on track. "That's my name. My parents tried to call me Marley, but I insisted on being called Harley instead."

"Why's that?" he asked, setting a steady rhythm in and out of her body that threatened to destroy her ability to concentrate on anything except how much she wanted him.

"I thought Marley sounded like a dog's name," she said, leaving out that Harley had also been firm in her belief that twins should have names that started with the same first letter.

Harley was only six years old when she'd informed their

parents that she would be Harley Mason from now on and that they should take the steps needed to facilitate the change, including ordering a new monogrammed pillow for her and Hannah's shared princess canopy bed.

Their mother had fought her at first—Marlena was a family name dating back five generations—but Harley had won out in the end. Harley always won in the end, a thought Hannah drew strength from as she tried to channel her twin's cunning.

"What about you?" she asked, lifting into his thrusts. "What was the name on your birth certificate?"

"Jackson Xavier Hawke," he said, but his next words banished the thrill of her small victory. "But you can call me sir. We won't be on a first name basis while we're here, Harley, and you're mistaken if you think stories about your childhood will make me rethink what I plan to do to you."

"I didn't," she said softly. "I just wanted to please you."

"Then you should roll over and get on your hands and knees." He sat back on his heels, watching her calmly, clearly certain that she would obey.

But suddenly Hannah wasn't feeling in the mood to be a good girl. Being a good girl had gotten her nothing except trapped in this room and driven half out of her mind with desire, fear, and frustration.

Compliance was failing her. It was time to see what defiance would do.

"No," she said, scooting back toward the headboard, gasping as he grabbed her behind the knees and jerked her beneath him.

"That word isn't in your vocabulary when you're speaking to me," he said, capturing her wrists in his hands and forcing them above her head, pinning them to the mattress. "Especially when we're in bed. You will say yes sir or nothing at all. Now get on your hands and knees."

"Go fuck yourself." The words sent a giddy rush through

her overheated skin. She had never spoken that way to anyone, but this man brought out all kinds of unexpected sides of her.

"No, I'm going to fuck *you*," he said, dropping his hips and grinding his hot length against the top of her. His erection slid through her slick folds, teasing her swollen clit, but she refused to let the pleasure he sent rushing through her show on her face.

"I thought you were going to make me beg," she said, glaring up at him. "I don't hear any begging, do you?"

"No, I don't," he said with a smile. His lips were so close she could smell the smoky, astringent smell of bourbon on his breath and wondered how much he'd had to drink before he had come to her bed. If he'd had too much, he might not remember his promises, or care about honoring them if he did.

Her jaw tightened and her captive's hands balled into fists as he kneed her legs wider and shifted his hips, bringing the thick head of his cock to press against her entrance. She tensed against him, though she knew that would make it hurt like hell when he pushed inside. He was obscenely long and thick, almost more than she could accommodate even dripping wet and eager, but she refused to make this easy for him.

"Then beg me, Harley," he whispered, nudging ever so gently against her wetness. "Beg me to fuck you."

"I'd rather you go to hell," she said, pushing on before he could respond. "If you're going to rape me, at least use a condom. I'm not on any birth control."

His hands tightened around her wrists until her bones began to ache and murder flashed behind his eyes, but after a moment he lifted his hips, moving his erection away from her entrance. "You think I want to doom an innocent baby to having *you* for a mother?" he asked in a cold whisper. "You think I would do something like that to my own child?"

She swallowed, but didn't know how to respond or how to make sense of the shame that washed through her.

"I have respect for life, Harley. Just not yours," he continued. "I also have a condom on the bedside table. Now shut your mouth and get on your hands and knees or I promise you will be very sorry."

Electricity flashed across her skin and sweat broke out on her upper lip. Her gut screamed for her to obey. If she did, he would keep his promise to make her beg, to make her feel good for a little while before he made her feel bad again. No matter how angry, confused, and frustrated she was, she sensed that she could trust him to keep his promises.

He was angry, but he was in control. It was one of the things that had devastated her the first time they'd made love. He was deliciously in command of himself and his lover, Dominant in a way that made her feel safe giving herself to him completely, trusting him to catch her if she got so lost in pleasure that she couldn't find her way back to her body again.

But he was not the man he'd been the first time they were together. He didn't care about her and she couldn't trust him as far as she could throw him. Which, considering he was twice her size, with muscles on top of muscles and a powerful body chiseled to a cruel kind of perfection, wouldn't be very far.

So instead of rolling over like an obedient mouse, she lifted her chin and whispered, "No."

The moment the words passed her lips, she realized she had made a serious mistake. Because her words made him smile, a dangerous smile that promised pain.

CHAPTER SIXTEEN

Jackson

*S*uddenly the fog clouding Jackson's thoughts burned away and the path forward was perfectly clear.

He'd been going about this all wrong. Isolation and unpredictable, erotic visits at all hours of the night might throw the average woman off her game, but Harley wasn't average. And she wasn't the kind of enemy who could be bested by planning and forethought. Trying to catch her in a trap like that was like trying to swat flies with a fifty-pound cinder block.

She would see him coming and dart away every time. She was too quick, too determined, and too malleable.

Harley's biggest strength was in how swiftly she could read a person and adapt her behavior to get what she wanted from them. Whether it was kindness, hate, fear, or sympathy, Harley was skilled in eliciting the responses she needed. And for some reason, tonight she'd decided she wanted to make him angry, to push him into breaking his promises and taking her by force.

But he wasn't the fool he'd been six years ago. He refused to let her under his skin or allow her to call the shots. He was in control and he was going to make that abundantly clear.

"All right." He rolled off the bed, flicking on the bedside

lamp before reaching for the black silk pajama pants he'd left on the floor when he climbed into her bed. "Then I'll go get your clothes and tell Adam you're ready to leave."

She sat up, clutching the sheet to her chest as she blinked in the glow of the lamp. "What?"

"If you refuse to obey, then you will forfeit the rest of your fee and we'll find another way to settle our unfinished business." He stepped into his pants and pulled them up to his hips, tucking his still raging erection beneath the waistband. He might be putting Harley on a plane and heading to bed with a killer case of blue balls, but he doubted it.

She sat up straighter. "But I don't—"

"One hundred thousand dollars won't save your property. It won't even put a dent in the repairs that need to be done," he cut in as he grabbed the open condom sitting on the box beside the bed and tossed it into the trashcan on the other side of the bedside table. "Especially when I make sure not a single skilled laborer on the island is willing to work for you or your aunt and not a real estate agent who values his or her life will show the property. For any amount of commission."

"You can't do that," she protested, but it was clear she feared he could.

"Money can buy anything," he said with a pointed look. "People are always for sale and usually more affordable than one would think."

"But my aunt is innocent," Harley said, desperation creeping into her tone. "She's done nothing to deserve this."

"I think we've both proven we don't give a damn about guilt or innocence. It will only be a matter of time until your business folds and when it does I'll be waiting for you to end up penniless on the street." He started calmly toward the bedroom door, throwing his parting shot over his shoulder. "And you can trust that my offer of assistance will be much less generous the second time around."

"Wait," she called out. "Please wait…sir."

It obviously pained her to speak the last word, which made her submission all the sweeter.

He paused, but didn't turn. "Yes?"

"I'm sorry," she said. "I'll do what you asked. I'll do whatever you say."

"I'm not sure I believe you." He sighed, keeping his back to her so she couldn't see the satisfied look on his face. "You'll have to show me."

"I will, I promise. Whatever you want, sir."

He turned, electricity prickling across the surface of his skin as he faced his prey. "Whatever I want and exactly when I want it. You will not say no to me again, or the choice to leave will no longer be yours."

He started toward her, closing the distance between them with slow, deliberate steps. "You will obey me and submit to me. And what's more, you will make me believe you enjoy your submission, that you are eager and desperate to service me."

She swallowed, her throat working visibly as she nodded.

"I can't hear you, Harley," he said, stopping inches from the bed, forcing her to tilt her head back to look him in the face.

"Yes, sir," she whispered.

"Yes, sir, what?" he pressed. "What are you going to do to please me, pet?"

"Whatever you say, whenever you say it," she said, the light in her eyes dying a little with every word she spoke. "And I will make you believe that I'm enjoying it."

He smiled as he reached out to cup her cheek in his hand. "Very good."

"Thank you, sir," she said, trembling as he ran his fingers up and down her elegant throat. He was tempted to tell her she was doing a shit job of pretending so far, but he was enjoying her fear too much to play that particular chip right now.

"But if you defy me again, you will find yourself back on that plane faster than you can say lying whore," he said, still smiling as he ran his fingers into her hair and made a fist, drawing a gasp from her throat as he gave her head a gentle shake for emphasis. "Is that understood?"

"Yes, sir," she said, shoulders cringing closer to her ears.

"Good." He released her and pointed toward the bottom of the bed. "Get up. Off the bed, with your feet on the floor and your hands on the footboard."

Harley tossed off the sheet and scrambled off the bed, hurrying to do his bidding so quickly her full breasts bounced as she moved. He enjoyed the show, watching her bend over, assuming the position.

"Feet farther back," he corrected. "And a deeper bend at the waist."

She obeyed, making his cock twitch with appreciation. But it wasn't time for that. Not yet. Not until she'd had her punishment and proved to him how much she enjoyed it.

"Your punishment will be a spanking," he said, slowly circling the bed, admiring the way the submissive posture emphasized the curves of Harley's body.

He wanted to bite the swell where her waist became her ass, to reach beneath her body to pinch and tease her nipples, and finally to plunge his fingers into her wet cunt, stretching her before he replaced his fingers with his cock. But from now on, she would have to earn her pleasure with pain and degradation she would learn to suffer with a smile.

"I'm going to give you the spanking you used to beg me for, do you remember?" He came to stand beside her, running his palm down her right buttock to her thigh.

"Y-yes," she said. "Yes, sir."

"A spanking that will leave you aching and swollen," he continued, caressing her left buttock as well, letting his palms run up and down, warming the soft flesh. "That will leave marks on your skin and make you think of me every time you sit down for the next few days."

She shivered and her muscles tensed beneath his hands, but she didn't speak a word.

"And you are going to enjoy it, aren't you, princess?" he asked. "Because you're getting what you wanted."

"Yes, sir." She sucked in a breath and he suspected she was fighting back tears, but he didn't care. He had no pity for her, not any more than she'd had for him when she'd painted her body to make it look like he'd beaten her black and blue.

The thought gave him a wonderful idea...

"You will keep your hands on the bed until I tell you otherwise and count the blows with me," he said, still stroking her, knowing the gentle way he was touching her now would only make what was to come more shocking. "We will count to fifty, the number of times I would have had to strike you for you to earn all those bruises you faked before you went to the police."

She stilled. "Sir?"

"It's all right." He braced one hand on the baseboard beside hers as he leaned in to whisper in your ear. "I don't blame you." He reached beneath her, rolling her nipple idly between his finger and thumb. "I blame the idiots who were too stupid to tell a real victim from a fake one."

Her breath rushed out. "Well, I...I'm sorry anyway, sir. I really am."

He laughed as he pinched her nipple tighter. "We both know that's not true, but it will be." He captured her other nipple, plucking it once, twice, three times before he added in a whisper. "Besides, I was lying, too. I do blame you, and I'm going to show you just how much."

He stepped back, ignoring her whimper as he kicked her ankles farther apart, widening her stance, baring her pussy to him along with her ass. He was surprised to find a hint of slickness glistening at her entrance, but not displeased. He didn't give a damn if she enjoyed this. Let her. If she got off on being punished, that was fitting, because he was certainly going to get off on delivering the punishment.

He brought his left hand to her waist, curling his fingers around her hip in a tight grip to brace himself. "Count with me. If you stop or lose track, we'll start again from the beginning."

"Yes, s—" Her words ended in a bleat of surprise as his right hand made stinging contact with her right buttock.

"I didn't hear a one," he said, admiring the red handprint already rising on her pale flesh. "So we'll start again."

He let his hand fly, delivering a stinging slap to her left buttock. This time, her cry ended with a strained—

"One!"

He struck her again—hard, with the full flat of his palm and she bleated out, "Two" in the same slightly shocked voice. By the time they reached "Ten" and "Eleven" she was fighting to draw an even breath. By the time she gasped "Twenty-Five" her entire backside was swollen and her knees were shaking as she fought to hold herself upright.

By "Thirty-eight" welts were rising on her flesh and her skin was such an angry red he might have felt a little guilty for assigning such a high number of blows if she wasn't the woman who had sent him to jail.

And if her pussy wasn't so wet he could smell her arousal sweet and salty in the air.

He was hurting her—he had no doubt about that, this was never intended to be a teasing kind of spanking—and she was loving it. Not pretending to love it, not faking a smile or an aroused moan, but dripping down her thighs, swollen and wet and dying for him to fuck her, loving it.

He'd known going into this venture that Harley was disturbed, but even he hadn't expected her to be this messed up. But she was legitimately turned on by being spanked by the man she'd sent to prison.

The only thing more disturbing was how much he wanted to drive his throbbing cock between her flaming ass cheeks. His hand was shaking by the time he reached the fiftieth blow, but it wasn't from exhaustion. It was from the mind-numbing need to fuck her, to get his cock in her dripping cunt as fast as humanly possible.

As soon as the spanking was finished, he shoved his pajama pants down and stepped out of them, leaving the fabric in a pool beside Harley's feet as he headed for the bedside table. He ripped the condom open with his teeth, rolling it onto his cock as he returned to Harley's side. He was so swollen that veins stood out along his length and he could barely force the rubber over the blue head of his cock. He was more turned on than he'd been in years, dying to fuck Harley until she screamed, but he needed to hear two words first.

"Harley, do you want me to fuck you now?" he asked, his balls aching even more fiercely when she arched her back, presenting her wet pussy as she moaned in a low, shamed voice—

"Yes, sir. Please, sir. Please!"

With a savage smile born of beating his fucked up little bitch at her own game, Jackson gripped her full hips in his hands and slammed home.

CHAPTER SEVENTEEN

Hannah

*H*annah screamed as he plunged inside her, forcing his thickness all the way to the end of her channel. The blunt head of his cock collided with the end of her womb, triggering a sharp twinge of pain that made her cry out in satisfaction.

Even though it hurt. Even though it was hurt upon hurt.

God. What had he done to her?

This was so good, so bad, so twisted and sick, but also exactly what she wanted. What she needed.

She was lost in sensation, helpless to control herself. Gripping the base of the bed for dear life, she pushed her stinging, swollen ass backwards as he plunged into her again, filling her with his need, stretching her until her pussy burned. She craved the feel of his lightly furred thighs bumping against her abused flesh. She relished the way his fingers and thumbs bit into the fullness of her hips as he rode her hard and fast, driving them both toward the brink.

She moaned in abandon and spread her legs farther apart, welcoming him deeper, wanting more pain, more pleasure.

When he'd told her how she was to be punished, she'd been afraid, not turned on. She'd had fantasies about spanking before, but never as a way to illustrate that she was beneath a man, beneath his consideration, a whore he would use the way he saw fit. But by the second slap, she'd known there would be no fighting the waves of arousal rushing across her skin, tightening her nipples until they stung.

The blows sent thick, sticky desire spreading through her core, until blood rushed to the places where he struck her, making her engorged sex plump and sensitive. He'd hit her with the flat of his hand, with enough strength to hurt, making it clear this wasn't about mutual pleasure, but it didn't matter. The pain summoned pleasure and together they banished the fear and anxiety that had been plaguing her for days.

For the first time since they'd arrived on the island, she wasn't living half in the terrifyingly uncertain future. She was completely in this moment, this spell-binding, mind-numbing moment, where she was getting fucked so hard her stinging ass rippled with every rough stroke of Jackson's cock. She was soaking wet and her pelvis filled with blood, heat, and that heavy feeling that spread through her core just before release.

But this build was so much more intense than anything she'd ever felt before. This was a sledgehammer swinging straight at her soul, ready to shatter everything that made her Hannah apart. This was more than submission, this was abandon, this was reckless and dangerous and afterward she might never be the same.

As the orgasm crept closer, she began to shake, afraid of the wave of pleasure now that it was so close there would be no escape from it, but she was helpless to hold it at bay. The next time Jackson's cock rammed home she screamed again, her legs buckling as ecstasy unlike anything she'd ever experienced rocketed through her, ricocheting through her body like a bullet fired in a steel room.

She fell to the floor and he followed her, kneeling behind her, his urgent rhythm growing frantic as he pushed through her pulsing flesh, forcing her to accept him even as her pussy clenched down so hard it felt like she might squeeze him in half.

This hurt, too. It hurt and it was perfect. It was wicked and it was wonderful. She didn't know up from down, right from wrong, or anything for certain except that when Jackson grabbed a fistful of her hair and wrenched her head back as he came inside her with a roar, there was nothing to do but call his name as she came again.

The second orgasm was fire licking across her flesh, singeing her nerve endings, leaving scars behind as her soul was forced from her skin and bones by the strength of her pleasure. She would never be the same. She would *never* be the same. Never.

She knew it was true, even before she came back to herself enough to realize that she was muttering the words beneath her breath, while Jackson stroked a slow, easy hand down her sweat-soaked back.

"Never," she whispered, gulping hard as she tried to stop the flow of words and failed. "Never the same."

"Shh," Jackson said gently, still stroking her feverish skin. "You're safe. It's all right."

She shivered. She wasn't safe. She was far, far from safe. She'd just had an out-of-body experience triggered by a hard spanking and a harder fucking from a psychopath. But something in Jackson's tone and that soft touch from his often cruel hand helped her calm down enough to regain control.

"I'm sorry, sir," she finally said, surprised to find tears rising in her eyes.

"Why are you sorry?" He continued to pet her, helping her come back to her body, making her aware of the fact that his softening cock was still buried inside of her.

"I let go of the bed," she whispered.

"You did," he said. "You also came without permission."

"Oh." Hannah risked a glance over her shoulder. "I forgot about that part."

"You're a very bad girl," he said, running his hand over the swollen flesh of her ass as he pulled out and guided the condom off of his cock. "Very bad."

Now that she could see her own skin, she was amazed that the spanking hadn't hurt more. Her bottom was the bright, lobster red of a tourist's sunburn. It was going to ache like hell tomorrow, and there might even be bruises under that enflamed skin, but right now, there was no pain.

Right now she couldn't feel anything but a floating, helplessly satisfied feeling unlike anything she'd felt before. Even with Jackson that night in her sister's bed. She was high on what they'd done and already craving another fix.

"Will you have to punish me again sir?" she asked, shocked by the erotic invitation implicit in her breathy whisper.

She was even more shocked when Jackson smiled, a beautiful, pleased-with-her smile that made her want to please him again. Again and again, no matter what an insufferable maniac he was or how much she feared that pleasing him wouldn't be enough to keep him from driving her out of her mind.

"Yes, I'm going to have to punish you again," he said, sending a thrill of excitement racing through her. "I'm going to have to punish you until you remember to follow the rules. Now turn around, lie down, and spread your legs. We're going to teach you how not to come."

"Yes, sir." Hannah obeyed, fresh heat rushing from her well-used pussy as he brought his hands to the backs of her legs and spread them wide.

CHAPTER EIGHTEEN

Hannah

*H*annah held her breath as she gazed down the landscape of her own body at the gorgeous man kneeling between her thighs, suddenly wishing things were different, wishing this was only a kinky encounter instead of a hopelessly fucked up one.

Jackson was heart-stopping like this, a man in his element, in complete control. If things were different, she could quickly become addicted to this version of Jackson and all the viciously wonderful things he made her feel.

"There is only one rule of cunt licking club," he said, a wicked twinkle in his eye as he lowered his face between her legs.

"What's that, sir?" she asked, clit swelling as she imagined what it would feel like to have his mouth on her.

"You do not talk about cunt licking club," he said, the joke taking her by surprise. "And you don't come until I tell you to."

Before she could say "yes, sir" his tongue was driving so deep into her pussy it made her sex clench and her back arch off the cool floorboards beneath her.

He cupped her stinging ass in his hands, leveraging her

closer to his mouth, banishing the pain that flashed through her abused flesh with the magic he worked with his tongue. Hannah's hands fisted at her sides and her eyes rolled back as he flicked and jabbed, showing her just what she'd been missing with men who were mere tourists in the land of cunnilingus.

Jackson teased her clit with feather light brushes before thrusting into her pussy and curling the thick muscle, caressing her inner walls in a come hither movement that had her pressing her heels into the earth, desperate to get closer to his mouth. She groaned as he pushed deeper, hitting some previously undiscovered place inside her that made her pussy weep for more of him.

"Easy," he murmured, withdrawing his magnificent tongue just as the tension building within her began to peak. "Take slower, deeper breaths."

She sucked in a deeper breath, but slower was much harder. She was already so close to the brink she could feel the hot desert wind of oblivion blowing in her face, tempting her to throw her arms wide and fly.

But this wasn't about pleasure, this was about control and she was determined to show him she had as much will power as he had.

Fingernails digging into her palms she forced herself to blow out through her pursed lips for three seconds and then to sip air in through her nose for another three. But yoga breath only took her so far.

As soon as he resumed his wicked work—kissing and nibbling the quivering flesh on either side of her entrance, his attention to that usually neglected area making her even more sensitive when he brought his tongue back to her clit—she was quickly back at the razor's edge between anticipation and satisfaction, fighting the orgasm she'd usually be reaching for with both hands.

"Pinch your nipples hard enough to hurt," Jackson ordered,

his fingers replacing his tongue, thrusting in and out of her pussy, daring her to come. "Then concentrate on the pain. Concentrate on the pain and fight your way back from the edge until I tell you to let go."

"Yes, sir," she said, her words ending in a ragged gasp for breath as his mouth covered her sex and he sucked all of her into his mouth.

It was a foreign feeling, but an insanely hot one. She pinched her nipples so hard the sting made her jaw clench, but she still wasn't certain she'd be able to hold back for long. He was too good, too intense, so skilled at bringing a woman pleasure she could have come half a dozen times if he'd allowed it.

"Please," she begged, panting as she fought to keep from shattering. But it was so hard to resist succumbing to the deep rhythmic pulls as he suckled her clit into his wet heat even as his tongue undulated inside of her.

"Please, please, please." Her begging became a chant, a prayer for mercy he ignored until she was moaning and writhing on the floor, so close to the edge she felt like she was losing her mind.

Only when she was wild for him, teeth bared in a grimace and nipples bruised from her own abuse did he pull away from her pussy and order in a deep, resonant voice that rippled through her like the first seismic tremor of an earthquake. "Come, princess."

Instantly, she did. She came so hard she literally saw stars, holes in the night that flashed and blinked behind her closed eyes. She came like desert grass meeting a match, like a boulder crashing down a mountain flattening everything in its path. She came screaming and bucking into his mouth and clawing her fingers into the ground because she needed something to hold on to, something to keep her connected to the physical world as she was leveled by the most intense orgasm of her life.

It was epic, beautiful, and so damned intense she knew she'd been ruined for anything less than this highest of highs, the dizzying pinnacle of pleasure on the mountaintops above the clouds, a place she hadn't realized existed until Jackson had taken her there.

It took what felt like forever for her pleasure to be done with her. By the time she finally lay sated on the ground, catching her breath as she stared up at the slowly whirling ceiling fan and her overheated skin cooled, Jackson was on his back beside her.

"That was…" She shook her head, at a loss for words, but feeling like she had to try. "Revolutionary."

Jackson grunted, an amused sound that made her think she'd pleased him. "And the longer you wait, the better it gets."

Hannah's breath rushed out. "I can't imagine anything better."

"You don't have to," he said, his fingertips brushing hers. "I've got enough imagination for the both of us."

Hannah kept her gaze on the ceiling, resisting the urge to turn to look at the man beside her. If she kept her gaze on the spinning fan and the underside of the thickly thatched roof, she could pretend that this was a tender moment with a captivating new lover, not a cease fire in some kind of twisted, erotic war.

As long as she didn't turn to see the darkness in Jackson's eyes, she could look forward to his feats of imagination, instead of fearing him the way she should. It wasn't healthy or sane, but pretending kept her from falling apart when Jackson stood and left the room a few minutes later, without so much as a goodbye.

But then goodbyes were for people, not prisoners, and she had a feeling a lapse in manners would be far from the worst thing that happened to her while she was under Jackson's control.

CHAPTER NINETEEN

Hannah

*H*annah spent the rest of the next day alone in her room, trying to recover from the most intense sexual encounter of her life.

She paced from one side of the large space to another without remembering how she got from Point A to Point B. She stood staring out at the fruit trees, mesmerized by the scenes of the night before playing out in her head, and came back to herself to realize she'd lost over an hour and Eva was already setting her dinner tray down on the glass coffee table beside her.

If it weren't for the ache between her legs and the way her ass throbbed every time she sat down, it would have been easy to dismiss the entire encounter as a dream. Surely no man could make a woman feel the way Jackson had made her feel, especially not a woman he hated, whose mind he was determined to dismantle piece by piece.

But the more clues she gathered about the past, the easier it became to understand why he hungered for revenge.

She couldn't stop thinking about the things he'd let slip last night—about the police not being able to spot a real victim and the bruises Harley had faked—and piecing together how those things could combine to make a man so angry he would dedicate his life to tracking down the woman who had wronged him. Taking into account what she knew about her twin, it didn't take much imagination to guess that Harley had framed Jackson.

Framed him for something awful.

The bruises could have been part of an assault charge, but Hannah's gut said that wouldn't have been enough for Harley. When Harley wanted to punish someone, she went for the jugular. She wanted her vengeance to hurt and to keep hurting for as long as possible.

And what would hurt a man like Jackson the most? A man who had been so crazy about Harley it whispered from his hands, lingered in every word, poured from his soul when he made love?

What would destroy a man who would have died before he laid a hand on his lover in anger?

By the time the sun sank behind the mountains at the rear of the property and birds began to fill the yard, feasting on the insects emerging into the cool dusk air, Hannah was certain that Harley had accused Jackson of rape and that at least a few people had believed her.

What she didn't know was why.

Why had Jackson become Harley's target in the first place? Based on Hannah's one night with him pre-private island, her gut instinct was that he was a good man—intense in the bedroom, but as tender-hearted as he was Dominant. But now she knew that he had a dark side. A black as sin side. She had no doubt that he would destroy Aunt Sybil in his quest for vengeance without thinking twice about it. She also had no doubt that he was a criminal and every bit as dangerous as Eva's son had said he was.

But what had come first? Was he a bad man who had earned Harley's twisted brand of justice? Or was it Harley's lies that had transformed a good man into a person ruled by hate and bitterness?

She didn't know, which was why she had to get permission to leave her room. She would never get to a cell phone or a computer if she was trapped in the master suite all day.

She told herself that's why she was so desperate to see Jackson again, but lying to herself was getting harder with every day she spent in captivity, forced to confront the truth in all its forms.

And the truth was that every cell in her body hungered for Jackson's touch. She longed for his hands on her breasts, his tongue in her mouth, his cock shoving into where she was already sore and aching.

She knew it would hurt to take him again so soon, but she wanted the pain. She wanted the pain and the pleasure and the closeness she'd felt in those few breathless minutes they'd lain side by side on the floor in the dark, their fingertips barely touching.

"What's wrong with you," she muttered as she finished her dinner and turned her teacup over, preparing to pour herself some of the chamomile tea Eva had taken to bringing to help her sleep. But underneath the cup, tucked neatly beneath the tea bag, she found a piece of paper folded into a tiny square.

Tea forgotten, Hannah unfolded the paper to reveal a few words scribbled hastily on the page:

I'm watching. Don't be afraid. I won't let him hurt you. Be strong and wait for my signal. I'll get to you before it's too late. –A friend

Crumpling the note in her fist, Hannah looked up, scanning the world outside her prison. Was this from Eva? From her son? Or was Adam, the pilot, not as obedient as he'd seemed during their flight to the island?

Or maybe this was from Hiro, the man she'd thought was a true friend before he'd helped facilitate her sale to a monster.

Whoever it was, she wasn't sure what they meant by a signal, but she would certainly be keeping an eye out for anything that looked remotely like a sign. It was comforting to know someone was concerned for her, but her less optimistic side insisted that getting away from Jackson wouldn't be so simple.

If there was a traitor in his midst, she had little doubt the man was already two steps ahead of the person who had offered to help her.

Just like he'll stay two steps ahead of you and make sure you never get to that computer to type his name into a search engine.

The thought was depressing, and her tea tasted pungently sweet in her mouth instead of comforting the way it had the night before.

She moved mechanically through her shower and headed to bed not long after dark, but she knew sleep was going to be hard to come by. Her skin felt too tight and every nerve in her body raw and agitated. She tossed and turned for over an hour, shifting from lying on her side, gaze fixed on the door, to flopping the other way to stare out at the patio.

She didn't know which point of entry Jackson had used the night before, but she wanted to see him coming if he joined her again tonight, to be alert and aware instead of waking up already wet and aching and half out of her mind with lust.

Outside, the moon was rising, casting the trees in peaceful blue light. She longed to step through the sliding glass door, to feel the grass cool on her bare feet and the breeze whispering across her feverish skin. It felt like years since she'd been outside and waiting for Jackson was making her feel her captivity even more keenly.

Finally, as midnight came and went and the clock crept closer toward one, she admitted that sleep was a lost cause. She was too on edge, too desperate for contact and the chance to get closer to solving the mystery of the man who owned her.

She flung off the covers, wrapped her toga sheet around her breasts, and padded across the wooden floor. When she reached the glass, she couldn't resist sliding the door open and letting the wind in through the screen door. The villa was one of the few she'd encountered in the islands that had air conditioning, and it had been humming steadily during her entire visit, but Jackson hadn't said that she couldn't open the door. He'd just said that she couldn't leave the room or he would punish her.

The thought sent electricity coursing through her, like lightning dancing across water. It was a beautiful, dangerous feeling and before she knew what she was doing she was reaching for the screen door and sliding it open.

She was about to step one bare foot over the threshold and onto the concrete patio when a voice sounded from outside the door.

"I was wondering how long it would take for you to disobey me," he said, his voice as deep and delicious as it had been last night when he'd asked her if she wanted him to fuck her.

Against all common sense, Hannah smiled. "I haven't disobeyed you. I've only opened the door. I haven't left the room, sir."

"But you were about to," he said, shifting in the padded lounge chair he'd pulled up beside the door sometime between the time she'd gone to bed and when she'd finally given up hope of sleep.

In the soft moonlight, she could make out the outline of his features, but not his expression. She couldn't be sure if he was angry or in the mood to play, the way he had been last night after her spanking, but for some reason she sensed she wasn't in trouble. At least not yet.

But she could be...

She pointed her toe, letting it hover above the unblemished concrete as she circled her ankle. "What will you do if I step outside, sir?"

"Harley..."

Her sister's name was a warning, but she wasn't sure if she wanted to obey or not. To be a good girl or a bad one. It was hard to choose, when he made punishment feel so good.

"I broke a rule last night," he continued softly, his deep voice setting things to stirring inside of her, making her even more anxious for his touch.

"What rule was that?"

"I told myself I wasn't going to fuck you with my mouth," he said. "That it was too good for you. That you didn't deserve that type of pleasure from me."

Hannah brought her foot back to the floor inside, torn between indignation—she wasn't her sister, and she wasn't a foul thing unworthy of his kiss—and empathy. He wasn't the man she'd met that night six years ago and whether she'd had good reason or not, Harley was to blame.

Jackson was profoundly changed, but there was still a hint of vulnerability beneath his merciless exterior, and she wanted to get closer to that soft spot, not farther away. She wanted him to feel in control so that he would loosen the restraints he'd placed upon her and let her out of her cage.

But how could she make that happen when he'd set so many rules for himself? Rules they seemed destined to break as the chemistry between them flared hotter with each encounter?

Finally, she decided she had no choice but to ask and hope he could hear the sincerity in her question.

"What can I do to make things better, sir?"

"Nothing," he murmured. "You have no power here, princess. Remember that. It is the only thing you need to remember."

"I understand," she said, curling her toes into the hard-wood as knowing flickered to life in her bones.

It wasn't a thought so much as a feeling, a certainty that she should trust her instincts. She wasn't an experienced lover, let alone an experienced submissive, but her instincts hadn't led her astray last night. She'd pleased him and she could only hope that following that soft, sure voice inside her would please him again tonight.

"I know I have no power." She released her hold on the sheet, letting it fall to her feet, leaving her naked in the moonlight. "I'm here for your use." She waited until she felt his eyes on her in the near-darkness before she sank to her knees. "So use me, sir."

He shifted slightly in the chair. "Would you like that?"

"Yes, sir," she confessed, knowing she wouldn't be able to pull off a lie when her sex was already slick from the thought of his cock pushing between her lips.

"You'd like me to fuck your mouth?"

She dampened her lips, nerves tingling. "Yes, sir."

"Are you sure?" He rose from his seat, moving closer with that predatory gait of his. He was wearing dark pajama pants and no shirt, leaving his powerful chest and taut stomach bare to her gaze. He was as stunning as he was crazy and just a single look at him was enough to make her pussy wetter. "I won't be gentle. I won't stop when I hit the back of your throat. I'll fist my hand in your hair and force you to take it all, every inch."

She bit her lip, barely holding back a moan of arousal. "Yes, sir."

"I'll fuck you until tears run down your cheeks and spit leaks from your chin." He stopped in front of her, reaching out to tangle his hand softly in her hair, making her ache to wrap her arms around his legs and rub against the silken fabric of his pajama pants like a cat desperate to be petted. "I will use you until you're jaw feels like it's about to snap in two and then I'll come so deep down your throat you'll have no choice but to swallow every drop."

She let her head fall back, not bothering to try to control the way her breasts rose and fell as her breath grew faster.

She wanted him to see what he did to her, how much she

wanted everything he'd just described. She wanted him to take her mouth and then she wanted him to throw her on the bed and claim her body the way he had last night, soothing away the shame of the punishment with pleasure. She wanted his smile between her legs, his face twisting with passion as he labored above her, as lost in the magic they made as she was.

She knew there were no guarantees that she would see Jackson's patient, gentle side again, but it didn't matter. She would take his anger and punishment if that's all he would give her. She wanted him whatever way he would have her and she seemed to have no more control over that than the wind whipping through the trees outside, forcing the limber trunks to bend.

"Have you ever deep throated a cock before, Harley?"

"No, sir. But I want to try."

"It's going to hurt," he warned. "Especially the first time."

"I don't care," she whispered. "Please."

He made a soft, hungry sound low in his throat and his hand tightened into a fist in her hair, sending another shock-wave of arousal coursing through her. "All right, princess. Then sit back on your heels and open wide."

She let her jaw drop and her tongue slip out to cover the edges of her bottom teeth, her body buzzing with awareness as he shoved his pajama pants lower on his hips, freeing his engorged length. Her nipples tightened as his cock bobbed free, seeming even larger from this angel, with the thick, turgid length pointing directly down toward her face.

Her eyes widened and worry that she would choke on him whispered through her, but before anxiety could become fear he guided his leaking head to her lips and pushed inside.

The salty, musky, Jackson taste of him washed over her tongue as he glided in slow, pausing as he neared the back of her throat to adjust the angle of her head with the fist still clenched in her hair. Hannah hummed around his thick head, relishing how soft the spongy flesh of his cock felt against her tongue.

"Relax your neck," he said, murmuring soft sounds of approval as she tilted her head farther back, relaxing into his control. "Good, now your shoulders. Let your shoulders fall away from your ears. That should relax your throat."

She obeyed and fresh saliva filled her mouth in response, easing the way for him to push deeper, slowly easing closer to the sensitive tissue that she feared would trigger her gag reflex.

She tensed instinctively, but he corrected her—

"Don't fight me. Relax. Relax your throat and as you feel yourself about to gag, swallow instead. Just swallow me down." He eased forward and she obeyed, slowly taking more of him, centimeter by centimeter of his massive length slipping down her throat while he whispered encouragement. "Yes, princess. Fuck, that's perfect. Don't worry about drooling. Your spit feels so fucking good on my cock."

She continued to work her mouth farther down his shaft, her breath coming faster as he kept going, sliding deep, deep down her throat.

"Breathe through your nose," he said, his hand gentling in her hair. "Don't panic. You can breathe. There's no reason to be afraid."

She moaned around his cock, wanting to tell him that she wasn't anxious, she was insanely turned on and dying for him to touch her, to pinch her nipples and slide his fingers into where she ached.

Yes, there was something scary about being invaded by him in a way that felt so unnatural. But it was also empowering, to know that her mind was exerting control over her body and insisting that it accommodate her demands. *His* demands.

Right now, they felt like one and the same, and no matter how tough a game he'd talked leading up to this, he wasn't hurting her. He was coaching her, teaching her, the way he had last night. He was insistent, but patient, giving her time and only sliding in that last inch when she was wide open and ready to accept him.

They groaned in mutual pleasure as he sank home, his entire length buried inside her throat and the tip of her tongue resting against his balls. The taste of him flooded her mouth and his scent spun through her head. He smelled like soap and spice and man. *The* man, the one she'd been waiting for, the man whose taste was the best taste and smell was the best smell. The man whose soul hummed at the same frequency as her own and whose touch made her feel safe, even when he was rough with her.

Especially then. She had never felt freer than when Jackson loomed so large in her awareness that there was no room for anything or anyone else.

As he fisted his hand in her hair, sliding out and back in, slowly establishing a rhythm, giving her time to adjust to the way he glided up and down her tongue, she let go of everything. She let go of worry and doubt. She let go of her hopes and fears and plans for coaxing a way out of her cage.

She let go of herself and became nothing but the woman kneeling at Jackson's feet, the source of his pleasure, the goddess who made his breath hitch and this strong, complicated, troubled man come undone. And instead of that giving away making her less, it made her more.

She felt powerful, beautiful, and unashamed of the saliva dripping down her chin as his thrusts grew faster, deeper. The mess was part of the pleasure, and that made it beautiful too.

A beautiful mess.

Like her, like Jackson, and whatever this was growing between them.

She rolled her eyes up to watch his face. Her sight had adjusted to the shadows enough that she could make out his full bottom lip trapped between his teeth and the way his hard features relaxed as he neared the edge. And in that moment he was her stranger again, the one she'd promised herself to the first time he'd taken her in his arms.

He was vulnerable and overcome and as devastated by what was happening between them as she was. It was enough to make her hope again, but then he thrust forward one last time with a groan, his cock jerking deep in her throat, and once again there was nothing but him.

Nothing but the way he owned her every time they touched.

CHAPTER TWENTY

Jackson

*J*ackson came like a steam engine roaring off the tracks, like lava bursting from the center of the earth. His entire body exploded with bliss, not just his pulsing cock or throbbing balls.

He came in his legs and his arms and deep in his chest where his heart swelled to push against the bones that caged it. He came in the fingertips buried in the silken softness of her hair. He came in the lips that buzzed with blood and heat and the longing to replace his cock with his mouth and kiss Harley breathless.

Kiss her until she moaned and begged and confessed every thought racing through her head. Until she laid her secrets bare and finally told him the truth about something other than how much she wanted him to fuck her.

Before he could bring himself to care about breaking another one of his stupid rules, he was pulling his spent cock from between Harley's lips and lifting her up by the hand he'd fisted in her hair.

She moaned as she rose to her feet and fell into him, her arms twining around his neck and her breasts flattening against his chest. Her lips parted and he bent his head, crushing his mouth to hers, pushing his tongue into her heat, tasting sex and submission.

And it was sweet. And filthy. And fucking perfect.

Her tongue sparred with his, giving as good as she got as he pulled her in tight with one arm, drawing her up his body, needing to get closer to her wicked mouth. They kissed like they needed the other's lips to survive, like they were the last refugees of some terrible war.

And Jackson supposed, in a way, they were. Harley had started the war and he would finish it. She had ruined him and he planned to wreck her in return and maybe by the end of it all no one would understand either of them the way they understood each other. They would be broken in the same way, twisted mirror reflections.

He kissed her until his spent cock began to swell between his legs and Harley was making eager little mewling sounds before he finally set her on her feet and pulled back to look into her shadowed face.

"Good, sir?" she asked, swaying slightly, her voice husky and ripe with lust.

"You're a deep throat prodigy," he said, wiping the wetness on her chin away with one hand. "Now put your hands behind your back and interlace your fingers."

She obeyed immediately, her movements bringing her breasts into tighter contact with his feverish skin. Even with the breeze rushing in from the ocean, he was burning up, already dying to have her again not five minutes after he'd come like it was the last, best thing he would ever do.

"You did so well," he said, cupping her breasts in his hands and capturing her swollen tips between his fingers and thumbs. "So I'm going to give you a choice between two rewards."

She held his gaze, breath coming faster as he plucked and teased her nipples. "Thank you, sir."

"The first reward is an afternoon on the beach tomorrow,

all by yourself," he said, cock thickening as she smiled and arched into his touch. "The second is an afternoon spent exploring the island with me, followed by dinner together tomorrow night."

"The second," she said, thighs shifting. "With you, sir."

"Are you sure?" he asked. "I don't promise to be nice to you or give a shit if you have a good time."

"With you, sir," she repeated a pained look flashing across her face. "Please, can I touch you? I want to touch you."

"Why?" He dropped one hand between her legs, sliding a finger through her slick folds. She was already dripping, and clearly hadn't been faking her enjoyment in having his cock rammed down her throat.

"I want to get closer to you," she said, moaning as he began to circle her swollen clit. "I want to dig my fingernails into your shoulders while you fuck me."

"But I'm in charge of pain." He leaned down, kissing her cheek before leaning in to whisper into her ear. "And who said I was going to fuck you?"

"You can't blame a girl for wishful thinking. Especially when you've got your hand between her legs," she said, trapping his ear lobe between her teeth and biting down.

"Good point," he said, plunging a finger between her legs, making her gasp and her mouth open. "But your reward doesn't start until tomorrow afternoon. There's still plenty of time to make you suffer." He pinched her nipple, drawing a moan from low in her throat.

Her head fell back. "I know, sir."

"So what if I said I was leaving you now," he said, the mere thought enough to make his balls ache with grief. "And that you were to go to bed without doing anything to bring yourself relief?"

"That's what I would do," she said, even as she widened her stance, making it easier for him to add a second finger and push deeper inside her. "I don't want my own hand. I want your cock."

"You want my cock, sir," he corrected, though his cock couldn't care less if she added the honorific. His cock just wanted inside her, five minutes ago.

"I want your cock, sir," she amended, her eyes so filled with hunger he wasn't sure he would be able to deny her, even in the name of making her suffer. "I want to be so full of you there's no room for anything else."

"You're a tremendous liar, Harley." His pulse raced as he added a third finger and rammed in deep, making her breath catch. "A fucking master of the art."

"Nothing I've said tonight has been a lie," she said, holding his gaze. "Not a thing. I want you. I've wanted you from the first moment I saw you. You drive me crazy, Jackson, and I—"

He silenced her with another bruising kiss. He couldn't let her keep talking or he'd slap her. Or shake her until her teeth rattled. Or pin her to the wall and howl into her face until she stopped fucking with him and told him why.

Why she did it, why she cheated on him, why she ran away with Clay, why she framed him for a crime he didn't commit, a crime he never would have committed because he was a good man.

Or he had been a good man. Then.

He wasn't now, and she would do well to remember it.

"You will not use my given name again," he growled against her lips as he picked her up with one arm and carried her toward the bed where the bedside lamp cast the rumpled covers in soft yellow light. "Or I will hurt you. And it will not be the kind of hurting you enjoy."

"Yes, sir," she breathed. "I'm sorry, sir."

"Shut up." He threw her onto the bed, where she landed with a yip of surprise that would have made him laugh once, back when he'd loved all her little sounds. Now it just made his jaw clench. "Hands above your head, pinned to the bed. Do not move them from that position or I will stop whatever I'm doing immediately and leave the room."

She scooted backward, watching him warily as she lay down and lifted her hands above her head. "I'm sorry, sir."

"You've said that, but now I want you to be quiet," he said, shoving his pants to the ground and stepping out of them. "I don't want you to make a sound. Not a moan, not a whimper, not a single sound. Do you understand?"

She nodded, eyes widening as he wrapped his hands around her ankles and squeezed.

"Not even when you come," he warned. "If you cry out when you come it will be the last time you come for days and that's a promise."

She pressed her lips together and nodded again.

"Good. Now let's see how you're doing after last night." He pushed her legs up and over her head, until her knees touched her nose and her ass was up in the air. She was as flexible as ever and it was fucking hot, but not as hot as the faint red and blue marks covering her pale buttocks.

He ran a hand over them, gently kneading the flesh. She cringed slightly, but didn't whimper. Either he wasn't using enough force to hurt her or she was simply determined not to make a sound.

One way to find out…

He slapped her ass hard enough to set her flesh to jiggling and definitely hard enough to hurt the parts of her that were already bruised. But still she was silent.

He glanced down between her legs to see her eyes closed and her teeth digging in to her bottom lip. She was so obedient when she wanted to be, so eager to be led, so seemingly effortlessly submissive. If he didn't know better, it would be easy to believe this was the truth and everything else had been the lie. Even his gut was sold. It believed she wanted him and needed this sick game they were playing as much as he did.

But he'd spent eighteen months behind bars for the mistake of believing in Harley Garrett—or whatever the hell her name was—and he wasn't going to make that mistake again. She had always been strong enough not to get swept up in her own deception. Now it was his turn to prove he was her equal.

He would keep pushing until she broke. Sooner or later he'd find her limit, the line she wasn't willing to cross in the name of pretending to be what he wanted and then he would see the woman behind the mask. He would force the real Harley from hiding and then force her to her knees, no matter how long it took.

He'd promised to return her in a month, but she knew better than most that promises were made to be broken.

The thought made his cock thicker and the need to be balls deep in Harley more powerful. Hating her made him want to fuck her as much as love ever had, proving there was indeed a thin line between one and the other.

Holding her legs above her head with one hand looped around both of her ankles, Jackson reached for the box of condoms she'd left on top of the table with the other. The decision had no doubt been a calculated move, one of her many attempts to prove herself willing and eager to please. Like choosing an afternoon with him instead of an afternoon alone on the beach.

But she would regret that decision, sooner or later. Every moment she spent with him was taking her a step closer to her own destruction.

Let her think otherwise. For now. Let her think about the pleasure he gave her and the small kindnesses he showed her and let her think he was weakening. It didn't matter what she thought; nothing had changed and nothing would ever change. No matter how many times she made him come, no matter how she excelled at getting him off, he would never soften or sway. He would stay on course until he was running her over, leaving bits and pieces of her shattered soul littering the road behind him.

Breath coming faster, he ripped the condom open with his teeth and slid it on his pulsing length before returning both hands to Harley's ankles and pushing her legs even farther back, until her face was framed by her muscled calves.

"Look at me," he ordered.

She opened her eyes, worry and lust mixing in the blue depths.

"You said you wanted to be so full of me there was no room for anything else," he said as he brought the head of his cock to her opening and applied the barest teasing pressure. "In this position you will feel every inch. You're going to feel me in your ribs. You're going to feel me in your throat, where you're still sore from taking me there."

She swallowed, but the worry faded from her expression and her tongue slipped out to dampen her lips.

"Does that excite you?"

Her eyes darkened as she nodded.

"It's going to hurt at first," he warned, pushing a little deeper, until the head of his cock eased inside her.

She shook her head slowly side to side.

"It will," he assured her, as excited by the anticipation of the first deep thrust as by her slick cunt gripping the tip of him. "I don't plan on going slow. I'm going to take what's mine."

Holding his gaze, she silently mouthed, "Then take it, sir," and he had no choice but to give her what she'd asked for.

He dropped his hips, plunging inside her gripping sheath with a groan. Even when she was this turned on—dripping and slick for him—they were a tight fit. Her body fought him, unable to adjust to his girth so quickly. He knew it hurt her, could see it in the way she grimaced as he kept pushing, forcing her to take every inch, until his balls were snug against her ass and his head rammed into her cervix.

But by the time he thrust deep a third time, she was bucking into him, eager to be fucked harder, deeper, and he was happy to oblige. He rode her like he hated her—pounding her pussy until he knew she would be even more bruised—and relished the way her slick sheath nearly snapped him in two with the force of her release like he loved her. He hated the way she smiled through the pain he inflicted and loved the way she remained utterly silent as she came a second time, milking his cock into the most intense orgasm of his life.

He came so hard the world vanished, and there was nothing but throbbing bliss and pleasure and the harmony of two bodies that fit together so perfectly.

Twisted and misshapen and perverse, but perfect.

She destroyed him and lifted him up to heights no man could reach alone. And he loved it and hated it and loathed himself for his weakness even as he flipped her over and began to take her again, claiming her from behind until his flaccid cock became hard and he'd fucked a third and fourth orgasm from Harley's dripping cunt and refilled the condom with another gush of pain and pleasure.

Love and hate.

Him and her.

And it was terrible. And wonderful. And by the time he'd worn her out and tucked her limp body beneath the covers he knew it was time to take the next step. He was weakening, but so was she.

Now it was time to push her over the edge, and to show her there would be a price to pay for refusing to fall.

CHAPTER TWENTY-ONE

Hannah

$\mathcal{H}$annah spent the rest of the night in the grips of the worst nightmare she'd had in years. It was one of those un-put-down-able nightmares that sent her surging awake with her heart in her throat only to pick up where it left off as soon as she managed to fall back to sleep.

In the dream, she was one of the Carolina Cult Girls, five young women who had been kidnapped from their homes when they were barely teens and forced to marry into a Doomsday cult deep in the Smoky Mountains. They'd been held captive for years before they were found and were all the news stations could talk about the spring of Hannah's senior year of college.

As a leader in the fields of both child psychology and PTSD, Dr. Patricia Connolly, Hannah's mentor at Duke, had worked extensively with two of the young women after their rescue. Hannah had tagged along to the sessions to take notes, honored by the chance to observe her professor in action and to get an insider's perspective on such a troubling case. She had hoped it would help her in her own practice later in life, but she'd left each session more disturbed than the last.

The first girl, Mary Ellen, was eighteen at the time of her

rescue and had two young children by her much older husband. She'd been the youngest of his five wives and according to her account had been treated like a princess during her captivity. Her husband was an elder in their church, well off in the world of the cult, and besotted with the pretty new addition to his family.

But the moment Mary Ellen was set free, she placed her children in the custody of the state, got a makeover, changed her name, and did everything she could to put her six years of captivity behind her. Despite her best efforts, she was plagued by anxiety and so terrified of losing her autonomy a second time that she lashed out at anyone she perceived as an authority figure, including her therapist. Once, Hannah had been forced to help pin the slim woman to the floor to keep her from attacking Dr. Connolly with a letter opener she'd snatched from the desk.

Three months into her therapy, Mary had started drinking to excess to self-medicate her anxiety. Not long after, she disappeared again, leaving her family even more heartbroken than they'd been before.

They had been so overjoyed to have Mary back, but the girl they remembered didn't exist anymore. She had been broken into a thousand pieces and no one—not even one of the best psychiatrists in the country—was able to put her back together again.

Ella Small, the second young woman, was thirteen when she was taken and sixteen when she was rescued. She'd spent half the time in the cult that Mary had, had no children, and had been married to a younger, less powerful cult member with seven wives and not enough money to feed them all. She'd gone hungry, had a miscarriage brought about by a beating from her sister-wives, and her relationship with her husband had been strained to say the least.

During her sessions she recalled that he would often be kind and understanding about her bigger failings, only to turn around and beat her and lock her in the stocks for public shaming when she forgot to coop the chickens for the night or left the butter out.

But instead of being even more eager than her counterpart to return to a normal life, Ella Small longed for the compound and regretted that she had no children by her cult husband to "remember him by" now that he was going to prison for the rest of his life. She admitted that she didn't love him, but expressed regret that she hadn't been able to make the marriage more successful—the marriage she'd been forced into after being kidnapped from a playground during her little brother's softball game.

Hannah's professor had found Ella's case to be a classic example of Stockholm Syndrome, a form of capture-bonding in which the victim empathizes with and becomes emotionally attached to their tormentor. Dr. Connolly said Ella had subconsciously identified with her abusive husband as a way of protecting herself from the harmful psychological effects of prolonged captivity.

Before those eerie sessions, Hannah had understood Stockholm Syndrome, but only in a textbook way. Coming face to face with an innocent young girl who had been stolen from a loving home, raped for the first months of her "marriage," and forced to live a nightmare for years—but who seemed unable to wake up from the false belief that her cult husband was a decent man who tried his best to provide—was more chilling than she'd expected it to be.

It brought home in a new way the immense power of the human mind.

The mind was innovative, beautiful, and endlessly creative, but it could also be terrifying. Ella's body had been liberated from her prison, but her mind was still locked away, trapped in a dangerous pattern of thinking that allowed the man who had stolen her youth to continue stealing from her long after he was behind bars.

For months after those sessions, Hannah had suffered from horrible nightmares. In her dreams, she'd been working as a therapist, but was unable to get through to the children who had come to her for help. The children were the saddest of sad cases, innocents who had been violently victimized and bore mental and emotional scars that tore her heart in two. She would wake up covered in a cold sweat, her pulse racing, consumed by the fear that she might not be up to the challenge of freeing her future patients from the unhealthy machinations of their own minds.

But when Jackson left her alone in bed—disappearing as soon as he thought she was asleep—Hannah didn't have one of her therapist anxiety dreams. She dreamed that she was one of those lost girls.

She was a teenager trapped in the same shack where Ella had shared a single bedroom with six other women, waiting for her husband to come home. She cooked fried chicken in the nude while her sister-wives watched and laughed when the hot oil leapt out of the skillet to scald her skin.

Later, she waited for her husband on her knees by the door and allowed him to take her on the filthy carpet as soon as he stepped inside. His touch made her sick to her stomach, but she parted her legs and endured it because she knew she had no choice but to obey.

And then the dream skipped ahead and she was pregnant with the man's child and happy, feeding chickens in a threadbare dress not adequate to protect her from the crisp autumn air, daydreaming about how wonderful things were going to be now that the baby was coming. Some part of her mind was horrified by the shift in her thinking, but that part was growing weaker and more distant with every passing day.

Soon, she wouldn't be able to hear it at all.

One morning, she would wake up and no longer see that she was being tortured, degraded, and abused. And on that day she would be as much a captive of her own mind as of the man who had taken her away from the people who loved her.

*H*annah moaned as she sat up in bed, rubbing at the tops of her aching eyes with her fingertips, shivering as she tried to shake off the lingering emotional fog the dream had left behind. She couldn't remember the last time a nightmare had made her physically ill, but right now it was all she could do not to race to the bathroom and be sick.

It had been so real, so horribly real.

Because it is real. The setting is prettier, but the scenario is the same.

You've been taken by a dangerous man, isolated, put under his control, and sooner or later you will bend or you will break.

"No," Hannah mumbled softly to herself, hugging her knees to her chest. She wouldn't end up like Mary or Ella. She wasn't an impressionable, terrified young girl. She was a strong, intelligent woman capable of doing what it took to survive without breaking down or falling under Jackson's dark spell.

She refused to think about how close she'd felt to him last night or how much it had hurt when he'd lashed out and refused to let her say his name.

Last night was last night. She'd been exhausted, vulnerable, and lonely. This morning she was going to keep her eye on the prize—an entire afternoon outside of this damned room— and get her head back in the right place.

An afternoon in the sun would surely help with that. It seemed like she'd been in this cage forever, with nothing but memories of her intense erotic encounters with Jackson to keep her company. A taste of normalcy was all she needed to remember that this would be over soon and she would be back to being Hannah again, with none of her sister's demons haunting her days or owning her nights.

And there was a friend out there somewhere. She couldn't forget that.

Someone on this island was watching out for her and determined to save her before it was too late. Jackson cast a large shadow in her mind, but no man was infallible and there was a chance that her secret friend would escape his notice. She clung to that hope as she made the bed and headed into the bathroom to wash the smell of her tormentor/lover from her skin.

Hannah showered and braided her hair in a loose French braid that trailed half way down her back. She didn't know what Jackson had planned for them, but it was windy outside and she couldn't stand the feel of hair flying into her face. Since moving to the island, her hair practically lived in a ponytail.

She'd been tempted once or twice to cut it short and let it whip into a froth of wild curls atop her head like Eloise, who worked at the sandwich shop in town, but she'd never had a haircut different from her sister's. From the time they were little, Harley had always insisted they cut their hair the same way and Hannah had bowed to her sister's preference for long hair with several tiered layers.

She had a habit of bowing.

The more she thought about her life and her choices, the more clear it became that she had a strong natural inclination toward the kind of sexual relationship Jackson enjoyed. She had always bowed to the more powerful personalities in her life. It made her happier to be of service than to get her own way. She wasn't a doormat and stood up for herself when necessary, but submitting to someone she cared about made her feel useful, productive, and content.

Focusing on someone else's needs aside from her own made her feel safe. To be of service, and to have that service appreciated, *was* her need, and the primary driving force of her personality. But she wanted to serve someone who cared about her and respected her, someone she could trust not to take advantage of her generous spirit.

No matter how much she'd loved Harley, her sister had never been that sort of person. She had abused Hannah's trust and forgiving heart and, if Harley had lived, Hannah knew that they would have eventually come to a crossroads. Either Harley would have had to change the way she did business, or Hannah would have been forced to withdraw from their relationship, no matter how painful that would have been.

Jackson was a lot like her sister, so focused on his own needs that he didn't care about the destruction he left in his wake. She had no choice but to submit to him physically and to let him see how much she enjoyed it, but she had a choice about how far her submission went. She had to keep her heart tightly locked away. There was no room for empathy or hurt feelings where Jackson was concerned. If she let herself get any closer to him than she felt already she might very well end up like Ella, locked in a mental prison of her own making.

"You have to stay strong," she whispered to her reflection. "No matter what Harley did to him, it doesn't make it okay for him to hurt you. Whatever happens today, remember that. If he punishes you for something you didn't do, it's okay to enjoy it, but it's not okay to think you deserve it."

She took a deep breath, meeting her own haunted eyes in the mirror and wishing she looked as strong as she sounded. With a final deep breath and a silent promise to keep repeating her new mantra for as long as it took for it to stick, she wrapped up in a towel and stepped out of the bathroom to find her favorite breakfast—croissants and fresh fruit—waiting on the coffee table.

Even more exciting, however, were the new clothes spread out on the foot of the bed.

At the sight of the khaki cargo shorts and black tank top—with a built in bra, thank God, she was so sick of going without one—her heart flipped over and a giddy grin broke out across her face.

Clothes! Real clothes!

She practically skipped across the room, squealing with delight when she saw the socks and hiking boots on the floor on the other side of the bed.

She was going outside and it looked like Jackson had something active planned! She was so thrilled. After days of stagnantly stewing she was dying for a long hike through the jungle, or up to the bluffs above the sea. Any place where she could breathe deep and feel the eternal, peaceful pulse of nature whispering across her skin.

Where she could feel her blood rush and her skin heat for reasons that had nothing to do with sex or the man who was quickly becoming the seductive black hole at the center of her universe.

She dressed quickly, hands shaking with happiness as she covered her nakedness, even putting the socks and shoes on, though she never wore shoes in the house at home. But if felt so good to have something to wear, to be granted that small privilege. When she was through, she wrapped her arms around herself and held on tight, relishing the way the cotton and spandex of the tank top clung to her skin, helping hold her weakening center together.

If Jackson were here right now, she would throw herself into his arms and hug him until he grunted. She wouldn't be able to help herself. She was just so grateful.

Grateful for clothing, giddy because he's stopped forcing you to walk around in nothing but a sheet, feeling vulnerable and exposed.

Hannah's smile faded and the happy butterflies in her belly died a quick death, falling to the floor of her stomach where they began to fester and rot.

The voice of reason was right. She could enjoy these clothes, but she shouldn't be grateful for them. Jackson didn't deserve credit for easing up on a punishment or for pleasure delivered on his terms. She couldn't afford to start feeling gratitude for anything Jackson gave her except her freedom at the end of this month and the full payment of her promised fee.

With that thought firmly in mind, she sat down to eat her breakfast, determined to keep her head in the right place and make the most of her afternoon of freedom.

CHAPTER TWENTY-TWO

Jackson

*J*ackson asked the cook to prepare a picnic lunch and then deliberately added the cooler pouch with three water bottles and two fruit juices into Harley's pack, simply to add a little extra pain to what promised to be a miserable experience.

For Harley, anyway.

She'd seemed to enjoy their strolls on the beach years ago, but she'd clearly been miserable the one time he'd taken her hiking on his favorite stretch of the Appalachian trail a few weeks before she'd disappeared. She'd complained for most of the six-mile hike and acted like the small camelback water pack he'd brought for her weighed a hundred pounds.

That was the first time Jackson had realized how out of shape she was. Back then Harley had been slim—almost too skinny for his tastes—but she'd maintained her weight by watching what she ate, not exercise. By the end of the trail, he'd been beating himself up for taking her on such a grueling hike. They should have started out slow, to build up her endurance.

Now, he was looking forward to watching her attempt to maintain her "I live to serve" attitude while being forced to hike five miles up hill through a close, humid rainforest and then five miles back down again. By the time they were back at the trailhead, he expected her to be reaching the end of her rope. It would then be a simple business to snip the last few threads tethering her to her self-control and watch her submissive façade melt away.

It was time to force the real Harley out of hiding, before he became any more addicted to the excellent performance she'd been giving in the bedroom. That was another lie, and by tonight he would have the proof snarling and spitting in his face as they embarked on the second phase of their perverse new relationship.

The thought made him smile as he knocked on Harley's door.

A moment later she appeared, flinging open the door with an eager grin on her face, looking refreshed and lovely in the simple clothes he'd had Adam purchase yesterday when the pilot went to the nearest island with a large grocery store and hardware store for supplies.

"Hello again." Her gaze flicked up and down his body and a soft laugh escaped her lips. "You look different in shorts."

He arched one brow. "How so?"

"I don't know," she said, shaking her head. "Less scary, I guess."

"Well, I assure you, I'm still every bit as scary," he said, though he couldn't seem to force the usual gruffness into his tone. He was looking forward to watching Harley's sunny disposition wither too much to channel the full power of his rage today. "And I've got a terrifying afternoon planned for you. Are you ready to go?"

She looked up at him, eyes wide and curious as she searched his features. But apparently whatever she found in his expression wasn't any scarier than his khaki cargo shorts because she smiled again. "You're joking, right? There's nothing terrifying on these islands except the centipedes."

"You'll see," he said, nodding his head. "Follow me. We'll pick up our packs in the kitchen and leave through the garden door."

"All right," she said, practically skipping through the door to follow him down the hall, and into the kitchen. "It's a beautiful day."

"It is," he said, nodding at the cook as he passed Harley the blue backpack and took the black for himself. Black, like his soul, and Harley was a fool to forget that even for a moment.

"Hello, Eva," she chirped to the cook who nodded nervously before retreating to the other side of the kitchen to continue chopping vegetables. "Lots of water. Thank you so much." Harley continued, poking into her pack, seemingly unperturbed by the other woman's less-than-warm response. "Did you remember to pack sunscreen, Hawke? The sun on the islands is intense, even this time of year, and you don't have the base tan I have. You'll get burned faster than you think."

"I have sunscreen," he said, amused by her feigned concern. "But the first part of the trail is in the shade. We shouldn't need it until later."

Harley nodded, not missing a beat as she slung her pack on her back and bounced lightly on her toes. "All right. I'm ready whenever you are."

Her grin was a thing of beauty he couldn't wait to see shrivel as soon as she realized this was no stroll along the beach he had planned, but a grueling ten mile round-trip hike up and down the side of a mountain. Considering she was probably in worse shape now than she'd been six years ago, they would be lucky to make it back to the property before sundown.

But he'd brought a flashlight, too. He was prepared and every bit as eager as Harley to start their day.

"After you." He opened the door for her and followed her

out into the sunny afternoon. "The trail head is at the back of the property. On the other side of the orange grove."

Harley sucked in a deep breath and titled her face to the sun as they crossed the wide lawn. "Thank you for this."

"You're welcome," he said, unable to keep from admiring how beautiful she was with the sun catching the red in her dark braid and a look of such naked pleasure on her face. "I hope you'll still be thanking me by the time we get back to the house for dinner."

She shot him a sideways glance. "Me, too." She bit her lip, but continued after a moment, "I hope it's alright that I haven't been calling you sir. I figured that was only for the bedroom, but…"

"It's fine," he said. "But my given name is still off limits. First names are for equals and that's not something we'll ever be."

"Of course." She nodded and her shoulders wilted, but after a moment her spirits seemed to lift again. As they circled around a fat palm and made their way through the rows of orange trees, the spring returned to her step. But then he supposed it was hard to take anything too seriously on an afternoon like this one, even revenge or captivity.

The smell of flowers and salt water mingled in the air and the sea breeze kept the cloudless day from feeling too warm. The garden was humming with life and exploding with color and when they reached the trailhead the forest seemed to welcome them in with open arms. The feathery leaves of the eucalyptus trees shielded them from the sun and the cool mud beneath their feet smelled pleasantly of earth and the spicy, fermenting scent of plants breaking down to become part of the soil.

For the first half-mile, Jackson shot regular glances Harley's way, waiting for her peaceful expression to grow strained. But by the time they started up the first incline—a slow but steady gain up the mountainside that granted peek-aboo glimpses of the waves crashing on the shore below—he was getting lost in the comforting rhythm of one foot in front of the other.

Whether it was jogging in formation during training drills in the Marines or his daily run each morning, Jackson's mind was never more at peace than at moments like these, when the motion of the body became a soothing meditation, a way to rise above the demons that haunted him. Even before Harley, there had been darkness in his life and a deep surety that he would never feel at home in the world. His father had been a cold, merciless man and his mother far more concerned with her position in society than her husband or only son.

Neither of his parents seemed to consider love or emotion a valuable part of human life. From a young age, Jackson had been plagued by the certainty that there was something deeply flawed within him. He felt too much, too deeply, too often.

He'd been shattered when his dog Petra died when he was seven, so grief-stricken his mother had ordered him to stay in his room until he could stop disturbing the peace with his wailing. He'd spent nearly a week in his room, missing school and having his meals brought to him on a tray by the house-keeper, learning the hard lesson that he'd better keep his pain to himself if he expected to be allowed contact with the outside world.

There had been other hard lessons learned throughout the years, but none as cruel and final as the one Harley had taught him. She had cured him of his fatal flaw, his over-abundance of heart.

If his father could see the cold bastard he was today, he would be pleased.

He will *be pleased, when you deliver Harley to his front door and she confesses the truth.*

And then you will tell Ian Hawke to go fuck himself and prove just how well you've learned your lessons.

Usually thoughts of that final confrontation with his father would send the storm clouds rushing in to darken his thoughts, but the steady sound of his footfalls and the soothing in and out of his breath as the trail grew steeper kept him grounded. His savage beast was so soothed by the walk through the jungle and the stunning view that he and Harley had reached the second mile marker before he regained the presence of mind to realize his companion wasn't complaining.

In fact, she seemed as Zenned out by the hike as he was. Sweat dampened her hairline and beaded between her breasts, but her lips were curved in an absent-minded smile and her breath remained strong and even. And when they stopped at a lookout to soak in the increasingly dramatic view of the sea, she threw her arms open and sighed happily as if she were embracing the world and everything in it.

"Enjoying yourself?" Jackson asked, irritation creeping in to disturb his calm as he reached into Harley's pack for a bottle of water.

"Immensely," she chirped. "Incredibly immensely."

"You're in better shape than you used to be."

"Thanks. I try to hike or swim every day at home," she said, grinning up at him as he took a drink of the cool water. "It helps clear my head."

Wonderful, Jackson thought sourly, but his tone was carefully neutral when he said, "So you've discovered a love of exercise as well as an appreciation for food since we saw each other last."

Harley's happy expression fell, her brows furrowing as she crossed her arms at her chest. "If that's a crack about the weight I've gained, I don't appreciate it. I had enough of starving myself during high school and college. I'm healthy, happy the way I am, and it's ridiculous to think a woman only deserves to feel beautiful if she's a size zero."

"I agree," he said, not willing to stoop to petty insults in his quest to break her. "I like you better this way. Your body is stunning."

She blinked in surprise, her frown giving way to a pink flush that spread across her cheeks. "Well...thank you. I, um..." She glanced down at her feet as she tucked her hands into the back pockets of her shorts. "I don't know how to act when you're being nice."

"I'm not being nice, I'm being truthful," he said, but her words did give him something to think about. She could be faking this awkward moment, but he didn't think so. It seemed like she really was caught off guard by his honesty. And if that was the case, this day might not have to end in failure after all, not if he had the courage to tell the whole truth and nothing but the truth.

"All right," she said, lifting uncertain eyes to meet his. "Then I appreciate your honesty."

He nodded before holding the half empty water bottle up between them. "A drink before we continue? It's another three miles to the top."

"Yes. Thank you." She took the bottle hesitantly, holding his gaze as she took several long swallows.

The way her throat worked as she drank was sexy as hell and part of him wanted nothing more than to tug her shorts down around her ankles and have her against the nearest tree. To show her just how much he appreciated all the tempting new curves she'd developed.

But sex wasn't part of today's agenda. Not in his original plan and not in this new direction he had decided to take. He couldn't afford to have his focus clouded by the increasingly explosive chemistry between them.

Sex had served its purpose. Her defenses were weakening. He could read it in the glances she cast his way as they started up the mountain, feel it in the way she swayed closer to his side than she had during the first leg of their journey.

It made him wonder if she'd truly been faking her feelings

for him all those years ago. Maybe she had felt something, but it simply hadn't been strong enough to compete with her driving need to destroy him. Maybe love and hate could co-exist within the same body at the same moment.

But hate would always win out in the end. He knew that the way he knew that the sun would set behind the mountain tonight and that Harley would end her day much less happily than she'd begun it.

CHAPTER TWENTY-THREE

Hannah

*S*omething was changing between her and Jackson.

Hannah wasn't sure what it was, only that the air seemed easier to breathe after their talk at the lookout. The anger that had been his constant companion since they arrived on the island seemed to drift away in the sweet breeze threading through the trees and the silence that fell between them became a shared thing, not a door slammed in her face.

When she cast furtive glances his way, she found his features soft and relaxed. He looked younger, freer than he had since the moment he removed her blindfold, and so beautiful it was enough to break her heart. *This* was the man she remembered, a man whose sharply angled face and dark eyes were softened by intelligence and thoughtfulness, a man who could be scary but never would be because he knew right from wrong.

She knew it was lunacy to believe a shared love of relaxing walks through the woods and her newer, fuller figure had changed Jackson's plans or her fate. But her gut practically sang with assuredness that something was different and things were going to be better between her and Jackson from here on out. He'd seen something in her, something that he could respect mingled in with all the things he hated.

It didn't mean the hard times were over, but it was a start, enough to make her wish this hike would last forever and they never had to go back to the warped world of the bedroom at the end of the hall.

Liar. You like that world and everything he's done to you in it.

Hannah wrinkled her nose. It was true, she did like what she and Jackson did together in bed, but it would be nice to know that when the games were over she could spend the rest of the night with this man, a person who didn't seem to resent the fact that she was allowed to draw breath.

They reached the summit at a little after two o'clock and spread out the picnic Eva had packed for them on a large flat rock, staring out at the jagged edge of the coastline far below as they unwrapped their toasted cheese, basil, and tomato sandwiches.

"It's nice not to have to worry about snakes, isn't it?" Hannah said, watching Jackson's powerful jaw work as he took his first bite, finding it fascinating to see him doing something as normal as eating a sandwich.

Maybe the man was human, after all.

"When we first moved to the islands," she continued, "I was always worried about running into snakes sunning themselves on rocks, until I learned there aren't any snakes here. Or poisonous spiders."

Jackson reached into his pack, pulling out a container filled with freshly cut vegetables and some sort of dip in a separate compartment. "So I'm the only predator you have to worry about up here, then?"

"I guess so," she said, the teasing note in his voice making it clear he was kidding. Besides, she wouldn't mind being preyed upon right now. It had been far too long since she'd felt his hands on her, and she was curious to learn if this new, easier feeling between them would follow them into the bedroom.

Curious, and a little anxious.

If fear were eliminated from the equation when they were skin to skin, it would be all too easy for another powerful emotion to sweep in and take its place. But she knew better than to think that any affection she felt for Jackson would ever be returned. He would never care about her and anything she imagined she felt for him was the result of a psychiatric disorder.

Better to keep him talking and enjoy the respite from their kinky sexual games as long as possible.

"Can I ask you a question?" she asked, shifting to face him instead of the stunning view. But Jackson was every bit as captivating, especially when he met her gaze with an unguarded look.

"You can," he said. "But don't ask if you don't want an honest answer, princess."

"It's not a serious question," she assured him, not wanting to mar the peace of the afternoon. "Well, maybe a little serious." She bit her thumb, second-guessing herself now that the words were on the tip of her tongue.

"Spit it out," he said, nudging her boot with his. "I won't bite. Not until we're back at the house, anyway."

The thought made an unhealthy wave of longing sizzle across her skin and she was suddenly shy about the nature of her question, but she pushed on anyway. "I was just wondering when you knew you were Dominant?" she asked, keeping her eyes on her sandwich. "Were you always that way or was it something someone taught you to enjoy?"

He hummed thoughtfully beneath his breath as he took another bite of his sandwich. She glanced over to find him gazing out at the sea, seeming to seriously consider her question.

"A little of both I guess," he finally said. "Control was always important in my family. I learned how valuable it was to possess and costly to lose at a young age. But I think the first time I realized I was turned on by it was when I used to play jewel thief with the little girl who lived next door. She would pretend to be a cat burglar and I was an American spy working for the CIA."

He smiled softly to himself. "There was nothing more exciting than catching her with a sack of her mother's jewelry and tying her to a tree."

The unexpected confession made her laugh. "That's cute. A little twisted, but cute."

"There was nothing twisted about it," he said, smile widening. "Laney enjoyed it. I could tell. Even back then."

His words made Hannah's thoughts turn back to the night she'd awoken with her arms tied above her head and Jackson hovering over her in the darkness, smelling like rain, sex, and temptation. The memory made her nipples tighten and a flush of arousal sweep through her.

"I bet you could," she murmured, reaching for the chilled bottle of guava juice, hoping it would cool her off.

"How about you?" he asked. "Did you ever live out those submissive fantasies of yours with anyone else?"

She swallowed the juice, grateful for the extra moment to think. She didn't know how Harley would have answered that —whether she had lovers before Jackson who were Dominant or not—but she figured she was safer sticking to her own truth. "No. There hasn't been anyone since we moved. At least, nothing serious. I dated a couple of men a few years ago, but I've been too busy for that kind of thing."

"Too busy for a fuck buddy?" He lifted one brow. "I find that hard to believe."

"It's the truth," she said. "Seems like we're both into honesty today."

He met her gaze and something flickered behind his eyes.

"What are you thinking?" she whispered, even though she knew she shouldn't push. She shouldn't crave the intimacy of knowing his thoughts any more than she should crave his touch. He was the enemy, but it was hard to remember that on such a seemingly normal afternoon, when she felt more like she was on a first date than enjoying a brief break in her captivity.

"I am very interested in honesty today," he said, his voice rough with an emotion she couldn't decipher. But it wasn't anger and whatever he was feeling made it impossible to pull her eyes away from his. "But this isn't the place for it. We should finish up and start back soon so we'll have time to clean up before dinner. The cook is making something special."

"Her name's Eva," Hannah whispered, feeling it needed to be said. Names were important. Names helped strangers become friends.

If only she could tell Jackson her real name.

She wondered what would happen, if maybe he would understand why she'd lied...

"I know," Jackson said, leaning closer. "But she wasn't supposed to tell you her name. She wasn't supposed to talk to you at all."

Fear whispered through Hannah's chest. "She was just being polite. She didn't say anything else, except that she didn't speak English. Please, forget I said anything. I don't want to get her in trouble."

Jackson reached up, grabbing the back of her braid and giving a gentle tug, forcing her to tilt her head back, bringing her lips closer to his. "If I didn't know better I would think you cared."

"I do care," she said, heart racing as Jackson's mouth moved closer and the spicy, masculine smell of him swept through her head.

"Maybe," he murmured. "Maybe you do."

Hannah's pulse stuttered and her lips burned. She was so certain he was going to kiss her—and so eager for the feel of his tongue stroking against hers—that when he suddenly pulled away her fluttering heart plummeted into her stomach, making it clench.

"You should eat," he said, motioning toward the lunch forgotten in her lap. "I don't want you giving out halfway down the mountain."

She reached for her sandwich with an unsteady hand. "It would take more than a missed meal. I'm tougher than I look."

"That's one thing I've never doubted," he said, the mixture of frustration and admiration in his voice making her unsure how to respond.

So she said nothing. She turned her attention to finishing her sandwich and juice and watching the waves curl into the rocks far below.

Silence fell between them once again, but it wasn't the same as the comfortable silence they'd enjoyed before.

This silence was electrified, simmering with potential. Something had been set in motion, something was going to happen that would change both of their fates. Hannah wasn't sure what it was, but she sensed it wouldn't be long before she found out. This might not be the place for honesty, but they would find that place soon and then truths would come out.

Maybe the entire truth.

Slowly but surely, being hated by the man next to her was becoming as unbearable as the thought of her and Sybil ending up on the streets. There was always a chance that with a mixture of hard work and a little luck that she could claw her way to a better life for her tiny family of two.

But if she waited too long to tell Jackson that she wasn't the woman he'd hunted, there would be no redemption for either of them. There were some things in life that couldn't be forgiven or forgotten, paths taken deep into the woods from which there was no way back.

Now Hannah had to decide whether it was time to come clean before it was too late.

CHAPTER TWENTY-FOUR

Jackson

*I*t took less time to get down the mountain than it had to hike up. Harley tried to strike up a conversation several times, but each attempt died a swift, sudden death.

Jackson couldn't stomach small talk, but he couldn't start his honesty experiment until they were back at the house. If they started talking here in the woods and her answers didn't satisfy him, there would be no one to keep him from wringing her neck and burying her body in a shallow grave beside the trail. The servants wouldn't lift a finger to stop him if he decided to strangle her on the dining room table, but knowing there were other eyes and ears close by would help him exercise restraint.

He didn't want to hurt Harley—at least not to the point of killing her—but his control was fraying fast. She was making him feel things again, things he was certain he was incapable of feeling for any woman, let alone the woman who had ruined his life.

He hated her, but he had enjoyed her today. He enjoyed her smile and her laugh and the way she looked at him with that wistful expression, as if she were wondering what could have been, if things had ended differently six years ago. It was insane, but those damned looks of hers and everything else that had happened between them in the past week had him wondering if maybe there was some sort of explanation.

Maybe she'd been forced into her deception. Maybe she'd fallen in with bad people and ruining him had been her only way out. Maybe the thing with Clay had been a way to keep her sanity, soothing herself with one man while she prepared to destroy another, and his death was purely accidental.

He knew people who forced others into situations like that now. Drug dealers who forced their girlfriends to become drug mules. Bookies who cut off a little girl's fingers, one by one, when her father failed to pay his debts in a timely fashion. Fathers who sold their own daughters into sexual slavery to solidify an alliance with a rival cartel.

He had no idea where Harley had come from or who her parents were—not even the best intelligence men had been able to pinpoint her origins—but there was a chance she'd come from a rough home life. She could have been born into some dark vendetta against his family and had no choice but to play her part.

Six years ago Jackson hadn't been the kind of man who ended up on a hit list, but his father certainly was. Ian Hawke had more than his share of enemies, from former business partners he'd ruined, to politicians he'd blackmailed, to women he'd used and discarded with no concern for the hearts he'd broken. And if someone didn't know his father well, they might have thought the best way to get to Ian was through his son. Most parents would take on any amount of suffering if it meant sparing their children pain, and Ian Hawke did a decent imitation of being that sort of man when there were witnesses around to observe.

In truth, Ian was more concerned about the embarrassment of having a son in prison than the fact that Jackson had been convicted of a crime he didn't commit. Ian hadn't even bothered hearing Jackson's side of the story. As soon as the arrest hit the news, he'd publicly disowned his son and Jackson knew if he hadn't already reached the age when his trust fund was in his control, Ian would have confiscated that as well.

And without that start-up money, Jackson would never have been able to capitalize on the connections he'd made in prison or become the self-made criminal he was today. There would have been no way out for him, no future but scraping by working the kind of jobs convicts were allowed to work, lingering on the fringes of decent society.

Maybe Harley had been in a similar situation. Maybe she'd had no choice, no other way out. Maybe he at least owed her the chance to explain herself and say something more than "I'm sorry."

But even if she had an explanation and was truly sorry, did that go anywhere close to excusing what she'd done?

She'd framed an innocent man and gotten away with it. The fact that Jackson wasn't innocent anymore didn't matter. She had redefined his life and turned him into something the polar opposite of the rule-following, honor-bound, decorated Marine he'd once been.

Was there any way to get past that?

He didn't know, but it was time to put the games aside and cut to the heart of the matter. He would give her the chance to be honest and if she failed the test, they would move forward with a new set of rules, one that involved no kindness, no dignity, no rewards, and no mercy.

They arrived back at the house just as the sun was setting. Jackson walked Harley to the sliding glass door to her room, but stopped on the patio, not following her inside.

"Are we still having dinner?" she asked, gazing anxiously up at him, making it clear she could sense that the unresolved shit between them was swiftly coming to a head.

"We are," he said, his voice scratchy with disuse. He hadn't spoken a word in well over an hour. He'd been too lost in thought. "You'll find a dress and new shoes in your closet. Meet me in the dining room when you're ready."

"All right." A smile flickered across her face only to disappear just as quickly. "Then I'll see you soon."

Jackson nodded before spinning on his heel and circling around the side of the house, heading toward the servants' quarters. He needed to speak with Adam before things went any further with Harley. He needed to be sure the alternative lodging arrangements for his prisoner were ready if they were needed.

There was a chance that he and Harley would both be sleeping in her big bed tonight, but there was an equal chance that she would end the evening in accommodations more fitting for a monster.

Monsters didn't deserve clean sheets, a soft mattress, or second chances.

Monsters deserved pain and a strong cage to contain them while they suffered.

CHAPTER TWENTY-FIVE

Hannah

*H*annah showered quickly, but took the time to blow dry her hair and curl the ends into ringlets with the fat curling iron she found under the sink.

In addition to the stunning strapless red maxi dress, with layers of chiffon over-skirting she knew would become something magical in an ocean breeze, she'd found delicate gold sandals in just the right size and a bag of high-end make-up waiting for her in the closet. She wasn't sure who had chosen the clothes and cosmetics, but the dress fit her like a dream and the bronze and pink hues were the perfect shade for her skin.

By the time she was finished dressing, she barely recognized the woman staring back at her in the mirror. She was stunning, every bit as beautiful as Harley had ever been, but with a vulnerable look in her eyes that betrayed her swiftly softening heart.

It was time to face the truth. She wasn't her twin and she would never be hard enough or clever enough to pull off this kind of deception. Even if she could figure out exactly what Harley had done to Jackson, there was no guarantee she could find a way to make amends or help him heal. And she wanted to help him heal. The more time she spent with him, the more certain she became that he hadn't deserved what Harley had done to him, and it wasn't a side effect of Stockholm Syndrome to want to help a victim recover.

Sometime between this morning and tonight, she'd become certain that closing herself off wasn't the answer. She could fight the connection she felt to Jackson tooth and nail, but the end result would be the same. She was going to keep falling for him, and continue to crave his touch until the day they put her in the ground. Her best chance of surviving with her heart and soul intact was to tell him the truth, the whole truth, and throw herself on his mercy.

He still had some left inside of him. There was a good man buried beneath the hardened mercenary. She had glimpsed it today and a dozen other times since they'd arrived on the island. Now she just had to hope there was enough of that good man left to forgive her for lying to him.

"All you can do is try," she whispered as she started down the hall from the bedroom. She walked through the now empty kitchen and into a stunning great room with vaulted ceilings, plush couches and chairs arranged in cozy conversational groupings, with a pool glittering at the center of the room.

It was a gorgeous space and for a moment she couldn't help imagining how much fun she and Jackson could have in a room like this if all the ugliness between them could be put away. Images of her kneeling at Jackson's feet by the pool, both of them naked in the water, or entwined on one of the soft couches flashed through her head, but she pushed the erotic images away. She had to keep her wits about her and dwelling on how much she wanted to be with Jackson—really be with him, not as Harley, but as herself—was the kind of distraction she didn't need.

Following the scent of something grilled and lovely smelling, she found her way into the dining room, but the large polished wood table was empty and the bay doors leading onto the front lanai were open. Outside on the redwood decking a table draped in white linen was set for two, with a gently sweating bottle of champagne, a water carafe filled with lemon slices, fresh flowers, and two silver dome covered plates.

But she couldn't focus on the lovely table for long, not when something far more beautiful stood on the other side, framed by two flickering tiki torches fitted into the lanai railing.

Jackson was facing the sliver of sea visible at the end of the lane, his broad shoulders relaxed and the wind ruffling his still damp hair. His white dress shirt and gray suit pants fit him perfectly, accentuating the power of the body beneath the elegant fabric. The contrast of the civilized clothing and the dangerous man who wore them was the sexiest thing she'd ever seen, reminding her that there were more barriers to a way forward for the two of them than the ugliness of the past.

This man was a criminal, an unrepentant predator, maybe even a killer.

But even as the thought flitted through her head, she dismissed it. She couldn't imagine Jackson killing. He'd said that he had respect for life. Just not hers.

Or not *Harley's*.

She pulled in an anxious breath, ready to get this over with, to scatter Jackson's expectations and see if there was anything left worth saving between them once he realized the truth. She crossed the freshly stained planks to stand at his elbow, feeling very small beside him. She barely came up to his shoulder. She hadn't noticed the height difference that much until now, when so much was riding on her being strong enough to find a way to get him to understand.

Swallowing past the lump in her throat she parted her lips to speak only to have Jackson turn to her and bring one finger to press against her mouth.

"Not yet," he said. "We'll get to that part, but first we're going to enjoy the food Eva prepared."

Holding his gaze, marveling at how much deeper she could see into his soft brown eyes, she nodded. They were going to tell the truth, both of them, but something unmistakable had already been confessed.

He felt the pull between them, too. He felt it, and perhaps once her true identity was revealed, he wouldn't feel the need to fight it.

"You're beautiful," he said, setting her nerves to tingling as he moved his hand from her mouth and stepped back to let his gaze drift up and down her body. "Perfect."

"You too," she said, shivering, amazed at how much he could make her feel with just a look.

"Cold?" He nodded toward the house. "We can go inside if you'd rather."

She shook her head. "No. I'm not cold. It's lovely out."

"Then we should eat while the food's warm," he said, leading the way to the table and pulling out her chair.

She settled in, the back of her neck prickling with awareness when Jackson's hands lingered on her bare shoulders for a moment before he circled around the table. On the way to his chair he plucked the silver cover from her plate and then his own, revealing a perfectly cooked medallion of filet mignon, surrounding by freshly grilled potatoes and vegetables.

At the sight of the steak she smiled. "I had a feeling you were a red meat kind of man."

"I thought we deserved something decadent." He sat, reaching for the champagne and pouring her a glass. "And this is part of your reward, after all. I assume you enjoy still-mooing meat as much as you used to."

She hesitated, torn between continuing the ruse for a little longer and dropping her bomb now. But Jackson was right, they probably wouldn't have much of an appetite after the truth came out, at least not for a while, and she was starving, even if she had always preferred fish to red meat.

"Steak is perfect," she said. "Thank you."

"Then bon appetit, princess." He draped his napkin into his lap, claimed his silverware, and proceeded to dig into his meal with the grace of a man who was accustomed to eating in high-class restaurants with civilized people.

He was such an odd and compelling mixture of conflicting traits. It made her want to ask questions, get to know more about him.

And why shouldn't she? She was too close to sharing her secret to worry about giving herself away by asking things Harley should know.

"I know we're not talking about anything too serious until after dinner," she said, as her knife eased into her steak like the meat was made of melted butter. "But I'd love to know more about what you were like growing up. What did you enjoy aside from playing jewel thief and CIA agent?"

Jackson shot her a skeptical look as he chewed, but when he'd swallowed his first bite, he replied more frankly than she'd expected. "I enjoyed soccer, football, chess, and staying out of my parents' way as much as possible. My mother didn't have much interest in parenting and my father and I didn't care for each other. That's why I applied to military boarding school as soon as I turned thirteen. And from there I went straight to West Point."

Her eyebrows lifted. "You went to West Point?"

"Graduated top of my class, and was one of only two graduates to be commissioned into the Marines instead of the Army." He frowned. "I'm sure I told you that the day we toured Quantico."

"I'm sorry, it must have slipped my mind," she lied, impressed. And even more confused. West Point and service in the Marines.

How had he gone from there to here?

"What about you," he said, stabbing another bite of steak. "What were you like as a child? Aside from determined to change your name?"

She glanced down at her plate, cutting a slice of grilled zucchini in half. "Quiet. My sister did the talking for both of us. She was a natural leader and I was happy to follow. I guess I've always had that side of me. The part that prefers to let someone else lead." She glanced up at him through her lashes, as she added, "Though I can't say following my sister's charted course was always enjoyable."

He cocked his head, seemingly interested though his gaze was more guarded than it had been a moment before. "And why's that?"

"I got hurt a lot when I was following her orders," she said. "When I was younger I assumed she didn't think far enough ahead to realize the potentially dangerous consequences of her actions. But as we got older, I realized she just didn't care."

She lifted a shoulder as she reached for her glass of champagne, needing a little liquid courage as she skated closer to the truth. "I mean, I had it better than the friends or boyfriends who got in her way, but she was only protective of me to a point. After that, I was on my own."

"And where is she now? Still out there somewhere causing trouble?"

"She's dead." Hannah studied his expression, but his gentle nod gave nothing away.

"I'm sorry," he said. "I hear losing family can be hard."

"It is," she said, her tongue slipping out to dampen her lips. "It's even harder when they leave unfinished business behind. Messes you're left with that you can barely understand, let alone know how to clean up."

His brows drew together, but before he could respond something buzzed in his lap. He shifted his weight, pulling a cell from his front pocket and glancing quickly at the screen before he pushed his chair away from the table. "Excuse me, I have to take this. Business. But keep eating, no sense in both our dinners getting cold."

"Of course," Hannah said, heart thudding in her ears with a mixture of frustration and relief as Jackson disappeared though the doors leading into the dining room. She heard him say hello, but his next words faded away as he retreated deeper into the house.

Adrenaline pumped through her system, making her hands shake as she set her silverware down beside her plate. For a second, she'd thought he was about to put the pieces together, and a new fear had sliced through her head like a laser.

What if he didn't believe she was telling the truth about being Harley's identical twin? Considering everything he'd been through, he might be more inclined to think her "explanation" was just another lie. And how on earth would she prove otherwise? She had no pictures of her and Harley together, no birth certificate except the forgery she'd brought with her to Tahiti.

And what would he do to her then? When he was certain he couldn't trust a word out of her mouth?

She sensed it would be bad, and that she would suffer more for having made her way past his first line of defenses. He'd let her in today, more than he ever had before. If she betrayed what little trust he'd given her, he would make sure she suffered for it.

She had to make a decision. Right now. She might not get another chance to exercise her free will before Jackson took it away from her again.

As if summoned by her fearful thoughts, she caught sight of Adam on the far side of the lawn, emerging from one of the small huts she guessed were the servant's quarters. He had a phone pressed to his ear and was carrying a hefty kennel, the kind used for Labrador Retrievers or other large dogs.

But there were no large dogs on this island, no dogs at all as far as she knew. And certainly no reason for Adam to be carrying that kennel around to the back of the house—to where she had slept since she arrived on the island —except one.

The cage was for her.

For some reason—whether it was to be part of her and Jackson's "play" or something more serious—that cage was being taken to her room. Jackson didn't know that she suffered from claustrophobia and might not care if he did. It would all depend on whether she was speaking to kind Jackson or heartless Jackson and there were no guarantees which she would get.

They had no safe word, no contract drawn up to encourage him to respect her limits, and the man had contradicted himself more than once when it came to what she could expect if she resisted his control.

Once, he'd threatened to send her home on the next plane without another penny. But before that, he'd threatened to make her suffer if she tried to run. And why would he make a threat like that if he was truly willing to set her free?

It was suddenly starkly clear that she should be worrying far less about whether Jackson would believe her story and far more about whether she believed his.

The difference in focus could mean much more than the loss of a lover; it could mean the difference between life and death.

CHAPTER TWENTY-SIX

Jackson

*H*iro's call came at the perfect time. Jackson needed a moment to clear his thoughts and refocus his intentions. He'd known Harley would be beautiful in that dress, but he hadn't been prepared for the sucker punch of desire that had nearly leveled him when he'd turned to see her standing next to him, looking up into his eyes like all she wanted in the world was to rewind the clock and go back to when they first met.

To go back and make things better, to give them a shot at having more than some intense hate fucking on the way to hell and back.

She'd taken his breath away. He'd wanted to take her right there on the lanai, shove her dress up and rip her panties down and fuck her from behind with the wind blowing that dress around their joined bodies as he made her come, screaming his name loud enough for the servants to hear. He wanted to fuck her until there were no more lies left between them, just the truth of how hot they were together, electric like nothing he'd ever known.

But instead, he'd forced himself to sit down and get something in his stomach before things got ugly.

And things were going to get ugly, he had no doubt about that. Nothing Hiro might have managed to learn in the past week would change that.

Jackson and Harley were on a collision course. The crash was inevitable. The only question that remained was whether there would be anything worth salvaging among the wreckage when it was over.

"All right, talk," Jackson said, closing the door to his bedroom behind him. His room wasn't as large as Harley's, but it was big enough to provide plenty of room to pace while Hiro filled him in on the fruits of his first week of spying.

"Sybil is very reluctant to talk about Hannah or the rest of the family, and shuts down whenever I push the subject," Hiro said. "I can't be certain, but I believe they've suffered a great loss and may even be in hiding from people who wish them ill."

Jackson's brows drew together, but he supposed it wasn't such a strange thing to hear. He might not be the only former victim of Harley's out looking for revenge.

"What else?" he demanded.

"Sybil has nightmares," the pearl farmer said, affection and pity clear in his voice. "Her medications make it difficult for her to come fully awake during the night and leave the nightmares behind. She's called out several names during her sleep, but so far nothing that would aid in the discovery of another last name. If there is one."

"There is one, I'm certain of it," Jackson said, pacing back toward the bedroom door. "Is there anything else or should I look for someone who will make sure I get what I pay for."

"Don't send anyone else," Hiro said, pitch rising. "I'm making progress, I just need more time. I found a letter Hannah wrote as a child and an old photograph yesterday. I took pictures of them with my phone so I could send them to you. There may be more keepsakes that will offer clues, but Sybil woke up from her nap before I could find them."

Jackson fought the urge to curse. It wasn't Hiro's fault. He'd had private detectives on retainer who had found out less than the farmer had. Sybil was every bit as secretive and mysterious as her niece. "Fine, send me the images and look harder this week. I'll have Adam make a deposit to your account."

"I don't need the deposit," Hiro said, cutting in before Jackson could hang up on him. "I'll help so that you won't have to hire some stranger to bother Sybil, but I don't want any more of your money. I don't want to have that hanging over my head. She means something to me."

"Congratulations," Jackson said, but his sneer wasn't as pronounced as it would have been a week ago.

All the more reason to finish this call and get back to Harley. He had to know if she was making a fool of him all over again or if there was something real growing between them, no matter how twisted its origins or tangled its roots.

Jackson ended the call with Hiro and waited for the text to come through—wanting to review all the information before he returned to Harley—but he didn't expect a child's letter or the picture to offer any real insight. It wasn't until the image flashed onto his screen that he realized what was wrong about Hiro discovering a letter "Hannah" had written when she was a child.

There was no Hannah, not until six years ago when Harley Garrett became Hannah North.

Or at least that's what he'd thought...

He gazed down at the faded picture of the two little girls in front of a sparkling lake, his stomach turning as the truth of what he was seeing penetrated.

The brown-haired, ponytailed girls were maybe ten or eleven years old. The slightly smaller, skinnier one stood with her foot propped up on a beached canoe and her hands fisted on her hips, silently daring the world to prove she wasn't the master of all she surveyed. The more solid of the two, stood slightly back from her sister, watching her other half with a big grin on her face. She was so caught up in enjoying whatever joke had just been told that she didn't seem to notice the camera, which only made the image more poignant.

Both of the girls were lovely—mirror images so alike he doubted their own mother could tell them apart without looking very closely—but the second girl's smile made her loveliness something more. Something sweet and touching and terribly familiar.

He'd seen the same smile beaming up at him for half the hike this afternoon.

A moment later, a shot of the back of the photo came through with "Harley and Hannah Grade 5" scrawled in looping script, but by that point he'd already sorted out the truth.

Harley had a twin sister. A twin.

And Jackson had most likely spent the past week alternatively tormenting and fucking the wrong woman.

A thousand questions dumped into his head all at once— Why had she lied? Why had she allowed things to go so far? Was she protecting Harley? Was Harley even still alive?

Or had the past five years been a wild goose chase that ended now, with him realizing he'd committed the same sin he'd hated Harley for?

Had he been punishing an innocent woman for a crime she didn't commit?

No one is innocent.

But looking at that little girl's smile the words didn't feel as true as they did even a week ago.

He didn't take the time to read the letter scrawled in a child's handwriting that appeared on the screen after the front and back of the photo. He turned and stalked across the room, hurried through the open living area where the softly whirring fans above his head seemed to mock him for being a fucking fool, and took the five steps up into the dining room at a run.

But when he stepped out onto the lanai, Harley— Hannah's?—chair was empty and her napkin blowing across the wooden planks in the ocean breeze.

She was gone.

But she wouldn't get far.

Pulse leaping in his throat, Jackson jabbed Adam's contact profile on his phone, issuing orders the moment the other man picked up. "Our guest decided to make a break for her freedom while I was inside taking a phone call. She doesn't have more than a ten-minute head start. Fetch the gardener and start looking down toward the beach. I'll check the road back toward town."

"Yes, sir," Adam said, hanging up without bothering to say goodbye.

Slipping his phone back into his pocket, Jackson turned and started walking up the road toward town, carefully scanning the ground for signs of which way his prey had run.

He was going to find her, and then, one way or another, he was going to force the truth out of her pretty mouth and find out everything she'd been hiding.

To be continued…

Jackson and Hannah's story continues
in DESPERATE DOMINATION

DESPERATE DOMINATION

Bought by the Billionaire
Book Three

By Lili Valente

CHAPTER TWENTY-SEVEN

Harley

Six years ago

*B*efore you embark on a journey of revenge, you should dig two graves.

Or so Confucius said.

Harley Mason had never been the type to put stock in conventional wisdom. She resented authority figures—even those who had died thousands of years ago—and didn't believe anyone in the unjust, uncaring, fucked up world had answers to the big questions. People were crazy and the ones who considered themselves sufficiently enlightened to dispense wisdom to the masses were usually the craziest of all.

She preferred to trust in her gut, her wits, and the sharp-toothed creature deep inside of her that demanded debts be paid. She'd learned at a young age that life wasn't fair, but she refused to believe it had to stay that way. The cheaters could be caught, the untouchables brought low, and the wicked crushed beneath the boot of her uniquely heartless brand of justice.

The man who had destroyed her mother deserved to suffer.

Not long before Harley's ninth birthday, Emma Mason had disappeared, leaving nothing behind but a note saying, "The heart wants what it wants." Harley and her twin sister, Hannah, had suffered through the usual stages of grief after a traumatic loss and resigned themselves to living without a mother when, early one morning nearly a year after Emma had vanished, she'd reappeared at the front gate, a half-starved, anxiety-riddled shadow of the woman she'd been. Their mother's body had come home, but her spirit had never returned.

Before, Emma had helped with homework after school and sent the staff home early so she and her daughters could make dinner together, choosing recipes from her favorite French cookbook. After, she abandoned Harley and Hannah to the care of their nannies during the school year and their Aunt Sybil during the summers. She acted as if it pained her to set eyes on her children, but Emma was too relentlessly miserable for Harley to take it personally. Her mother also shunned walks in the garden, good books, charity work, her sewing room, afternoons in the kitchen making coq au vin, and almost everything else that had once given her joy.

No, Harley didn't blame her mother for being broken. She blamed the person who had broken her. She swore to herself that someday she would make the man pay, and finally, after years of searching for clues to the stranger's identity, she'd learned his name.

Ian Hawke.

And so she had launched her summer of revenge— intending to shatter Ian's son and teach the bastard what if felt like to see someone you love ruined forever—and she hadn't regretted a moment of it.

Until now.

Now, as the car rolled down the side of the mountain, each horrifying revolution seeming to last forever as Harley realized she was about to die, she wished she could take it all back. She wished she could go back to the beginning of the summer and spend it in Paris instead of on the Virginia shore. She wished she'd never met Jackson Hawke or tricked him into loving her. She wished she'd never filed the false report with the military police or doctored evidence to make sure Jackson would be found guilty of a crime he hadn't committed.

But most of all, she wished she'd never seduced Jackson's best friend. She wished she'd never met Clay, never loved him, and never agreed to run away and get married this weekend. If she could take it all back, she would, and then Clay wouldn't be dying in this car beside her.

Should have dug three graves.

Three graves. One for her, one for Jackson, her enemy's son, and one for Clay, the only man Harley had ever loved.

"I love you. I'm so sorry," she sobbed, reaching for Clay's arm as the car's roof bounced off the ground and they spun upright once more. But the sound of metal screaming, as it caved in around them, made it impossible to hear her own voice.

Later, when she came to, hanging upside down by her seatbelt with Clay dangling beside her, his eyes wide and death stiffening his handsome face, she would regret that most of all. He hadn't heard her say that she loved him one last time, and he didn't know that she was sorry.

"I'm so sorry," she sobbed, tears streaming up her forehead to run into her hair, stinging into a cut on her scalp. "It should have been me. I wish it were me, Clay. I'm so sorry."

She cupped his face in one shaking hand, leaving a mark behind on his cool cheek. In the moonlight streaming in through the crumpled windows, the blood smear looked black. Harley stared at it, strangely mesmerized by the thickness of it and the slow drip, drip, drip as the cut on her arm leaked onto the roof below her.

She was still hanging there, tears flowing the wrong way and her pulse slowing to a dangerous—*thud...du-dud....dud*—

when a hand punched through the web of crinkled glass on the passenger side, making her flinch and cry out.

"It's Dominic," came a low, lightly accented voice. "Are you hurt?"

"Clay's dead," she whimpered, not turning to look at the dark-eyed boy her father had hired to follow her around this summer.

Dominic was allegedly part of a security team hired to protect her—her father said he'd been receiving threats from an old business rival—but Harley suspected Daddy was simply using that as an excuse to spy on her. She'd come by her sneaky streak honestly and had learned not to trust her father around the same time she'd learned to walk.

Any other summer, she would have had an affair with Dominic, just to piss off dear old Dad—he hated it when she fucked the help—but she'd been too busy ruining two men's lives to have time for the slim Puerto Rican boy with the kind eyes.

"I'm sorry," Dom said as he reached for her seatbelt. "Let me help you out."

"Stop." She shoved at his hand as it fumbled near her waist. "Go away. I won't leave him."

"We have to go, Harley," Dom insisted. "This wasn't an accident. I saw the truck that pushed you off the road. It was the same one that's been parked outside the bar for the past two weeks."

"What?" Harley's question became a moan as Dom succeeded in releasing the seatbelt. She slumped down onto the dented roof, every bruise on her body crying out in protest.

"It was the man in the camo hat," he said, helping her shift onto her back. "The one who was watching you at the bar. He was at your apartment complex tonight and followed you when you left. I tried to call your cell to warn you, but there was no answer."

"I had the ringer off," she said, lips moving numbly. She'd always turned her ringer off when she was with Clay, just in case Jackson called. She hadn't wanted to explain why she was still taking phone calls from a man she claimed frightened her.

When she'd told Clay that Jackson had hit her, he'd been devastated, his usually smiling blue eyes filling with so much pain that, for a moment, she had wished she could reel the lie back between her lips. But back then, hurting Jackson's father had mattered more than sparing the best man she'd ever met. Back then, she'd been too stupid to realize that she'd finally found a love bigger than all the bitterness and hate.

If only she'd laid down her weapons and walked away before it was too late.

"We need to get you somewhere safe," Dom said with a sigh. "If this guy is a professional, he'll want to make sure you're dead before he reports back to whoever he's working for."

Dom pulled her through the window, dragging her spine against the twisted metal of the crumpled frame. Every inch of her body throbbed with distress, the wounds she'd inflicted to fake her police report providing a dull background agony to the wail of new injuries. She'd lost a lot of blood and when Dom helped her to her feet, the world spun in great looping circles.

"Lean into me." He grunted, tightening the arm banded around her waist. "I need you to stay awake, Harley."

"I'm awake," she mumbled as she staggered along beside him, following a narrow trail through the woods.

She was awake and alive and Clay was dead.

Clay was dead.

Clay was *dead*.

The horrible mantra thrummed through her thoughts, drawing a sob from deep in her chest. She didn't want to get to safety; she wanted to lie down next to Clay and wait for someone to send her to the other side to find him.

She'd never believed in heaven or hell, but the way she loved Clay made her hope this wasn't the end. It couldn't be, not when they were just getting started, when she'd finally realized that there was something more important than revenge. There was love, blue eyes filled with laughter, and a man whose kiss softened the once impenetrable walls around her heart.

But now those lips were cold and she would never kiss them again.

Her knees buckled as she went limp with grief, sliding down the side of Dom's wiry body.

"Stand up," he ordered, hitching her higher. "I can't carry you up the side of the mountain, Harley. I need you to walk."

"I can't." She sobbed, her head bowing over her chest. Clay could have carried her. Jackson too. She'd had two brave, strong men devoted to her and she'd destroyed them both. Clay was dead and Jackson would wish he were dead—sooner or later—and it was all her fault.

She was poison, just like her father, just like Ian Hawke. She was a predator who had taken pleasure in other people's pain and now she would pay for it a thousand times over. She would never know peace or an end to the crushing guilt of knowing she had killed the man she loved.

"If you don't start walking, they're going to find us," Dom whispered, his fingers digging painfully into the bruised flesh at her hip. "And then we'll both be as dead as your boyfriend."

He was right. Someone was coming. The hairs at the back of her neck stood on end, warning that the hunter had become the hunted.

Swallowing hard, Harley forced strength back into her knees and began to put one foot in front of the other. She didn't care if she were murdered, but Dominic didn't deserve to die this way. He was only trying to do his job and if she'd answered his call, Clay might be alive.

Dom wasn't to blame. She was in this mess because of her

stubborn insistence that those who'd wronged her should pay for their sins a thousand times over.

A thousand times a thousand times a thousand.

*I*n the years that followed, as fate ensured there was no way to forget the horrible things she'd done, Harley paid the price for that one terrible summer again and again. Every morning she woke with the reminder that Clay had died too soon staring her in the face, and every night she went to bed wondering if she would ever stop aching for the man she'd destroyed.

And then, one night the past caught up with her, and she learned that no matter how high a price you've paid, there is always something left to lose.

CHAPTER TWENTY-EIGHT

Hannah

Present Day

*F*aster, Hannah! Run faster. Faster!

Hitching the red chiffon of her dress up around her knees, Hannah sprinted as fast as she could down the road toward what she hoped was civilization. But her legs still ached from the six-mile hike earlier and she'd only choked down a few bites of food. She was exhausted, running on empty, and there was no way she would make it to safety before Jackson tracked her down. The jungle on the left side of the road was too thick for her to penetrate and the shore-line to the right offered little to no cover. If she stayed on the road, it wasn't a matter of *if* Jackson would find her, but when.

Unless she found a way to escape that he wouldn't suspect…

With a quick glance over her shoulder to make sure no tall, terrifying men had appeared on the road, Hannah darted off the gravel and across the dunes toward the beach. The sand ended a few feet from the ocean, replaced by a line of jagged black rocks that seemed to grimace at the sea, daring it to take its best shot. The tide was low, but fierce, slamming into the stones with a ferocity that made her shiver.

If she didn't jump far enough or swim hard enough, she would be tossed back toward the shore and dashed to pieces on the rocks long before Jackson or anyone else could find her. She was a strong swimmer, but she didn't know this stretch of shoreline. She didn't know the tide patterns or the reef nearby or what kind of ocean life claimed this part of the island as their territory.

Back home, she knew which beaches were her best bet for observing giant sea turtles, which were good for snorkeling or boogie boarding, and which to avoid because of dangerous rip tides.

Or sharks.

There was a bay to the far north of the island where shark attacks were quadruple the number of anywhere else in the region. It was their feeding ground and anyone with sense knew to stay out of the water. Even the tourists knew, their guidebooks containing strongly worded warnings about the likelihood of shark attack and grisly stories of the people who had lost their lives in the bay over the years.

Looking out at the churning water, where sea foam frothed pink in the setting sun, Hannah couldn't see anything beneath the water except occasional dark patches indicating coral formations. But that didn't mean there was nothing to see and dusk was a dangerous time to swim. Sharks hunted from dusk until dawn and as soon as she hit the water, she would be prey.

You're already prey, fool.

Hannah swallowed hard. Her inner voice was right. She was Jackson's prey and she had no idea what he would do to her if he caught her. He might lock her in that cage she'd seen Adam carrying to the back of the house or something worse. And at least with a shark she knew how to fight back.

Sharks preferred easy prey. If you managed to get a few

solid punches in to their nose and eyes, most would swim away looking for a less feisty food source. Jackson, on the other hand, would take pleasure from overpowering her while she struggled, showing her who controlled her, body and soul.

"No," she said aloud, her hands fisting at her sides.

She was in control now and she had to stay that way. No matter how much a part of her wanted to believe that she could trust Jackson, she couldn't gamble her life on it. She'd made the choice to run and now she had to see it through.

Without letting herself think too much about the things lurking beneath the water or the vicious crash of the waves as they pounded against the shore, Hannah toed off her sandals and unzipped her dress. The fabric fell to her feet, leaving her in nothing but her strapless bra and panties. It wasn't a swimsuit, but it would leave her body at least partially covered so that she wouldn't have to approach a potential rescuer buck-naked.

The cool ocean breeze whispered across her skin, raising gooseflesh on her arms and legs as she picked her way across the dark rocks, getting as far from the shore as she could without being sucked into the waves. As she reached the outer most point, just before the rocks dropped away into deeper water, she exhaled long and slow, her fingers wiggling at her sides as she waited for the perfect moment.

As soon as the next wave crashed against the shore and began its rush away, she jumped, leaping into the churning froth. The ocean closed around her, cool and shocking, but she didn't waste time allowing her body to adjust to the water temperature before bobbing back to the surface and pulling hard toward the open sea.

She made it a good ten feet out before the next wave bore down hard upon her, trying to toss her back the way she'd come. Diving beneath the curl, she slipped beyond the reach of the strongest onshore current and turned left, swimming parallel to the shore. Thankfully, the current seemed to be on her side, drawing her south toward the other end of the island.

Ignoring her racing heart, Hannah established a rhythm with her strokes and did her best to keep her breath under control. She was used to swimming a mile or more every morning before bustling around the bed and breakfast cleaning and taking care of guests. If she kept calm and used her body efficiently, she could easily swim five miles or more and hopefully come across some sign of life along the shore.

The island was small, but surely there had to be some indigenous population. She would look for boat docks or cleared beaches and be ready to head back in toward land when she spotted them. She would find help and she would get off this island in one piece. She had to stay positive and focused or fear would swallow her whole.

Over the past week, she had convinced herself that Jackson wasn't as frightening or cruel as she'd thought at first. She'd convinced herself that he cared and that she wasn't in any serious danger. But the moment she'd started down the road away from the house where she'd been held captive, those pretty lies had vanished in a wave of terror.

Now, when she imagined Jackson finding her, it wasn't the man who had touched a soft finger to her lips that she saw in her mind's eye. It was the man who had balled his hands into fists when she'd smiled at him, the one who had promised to break her and looked like he would enjoy doing it.

Just keep swimming, she thought, trying to talk her heart down from her throat. *Just keep swimming.*

She sounded like that fish from the Disney movie, the one she'd gone to see when she was in high school even though Harley had said they were too old for cartoons. But even back then, when she was fifteen and discovering boys while learning to drive, Hannah had known she would never be too old for cartoons. She would never be too old for anything that brought her joy.

There was no reason to outgrow simple pleasures. There was no reason to shut out the things that made her happy because she was growing up. She didn't have to be like her parents.

There was too much magic in the world to become bitter and jaded and growing up didn't have to mean growing old. She had always believed that and secretly thought that holding on to childlike wonder would make her a better mother, the kind who understood what her children were going through because she'd never let go of the child inside of herself.

But after a week under Jackson's control, a good deal of it spent in isolation with nothing to occupy her thoughts or distract her from taking a hard look at the state of her life, she realized she would never be a mom. She would never have a husband or children because she was going to spend the rest of her life addicted to the touch of a man who didn't care if she lived or died.

Jackson didn't love her—he didn't even know her true identity—but she would crave his touch until the day they put her in the ground. He'd summoned a darkly sensual part of her to the surface and there would be no putting it back to sleep. She would always long for his firm hand and the erotic bliss of being under his control.

She might escape him today, but he would haunt her forever, no matter how far or how fast she ran.

Her thoughts were depressing to say the least, but that wasn't why she sank lower in the water, her head dipping below the surface before she bobbed back above the waves. It was the pain that made her falter, a sharp agony knotting low in her legs.

Hannah winced, crying out as another wave of suffering flashed through her calf muscles. The cramps were so intense they soon rendered her numb from the knees down. Fighting the urge to panic, she strained harder with her arms, trying to compensate for her suddenly useless legs. All she wanted to do was stop swimming and dig her thumbs into her aching calves, but if she stopped pulling with her arms, she would drown.

While she struggled, willing her thrumming muscles to relax, a larger wave swept in, taking her by surprise. She sucked in a breath at the wrong time, taking in a mouthful of seawater as she was rolled beneath the curl. She broke the surface again in the trough, coughing up ocean, fighting to catch her breath before the next wave hit, but she barely had time to clear her lungs before she was swept under again.

Chest aching with the need for oxygen, Hannah tumbled through the dark, the muffled thunder of the churning water above her roaring in her ears. As she revolved, she became aware of a sucking sensation tugging at her torso, drawing her farther from the shore, out into the wilds of the open sea.

In some still, quiet hall inside her mind, a sober voice announced that she was caught in a rip current and would likely die before she made it back to shore. If she had the use of her legs, she might be able to fight her way free by swimming parallel to the beach until the current let her go, but without her legs this was most likely a lost cause. Chances were that she was about to drown. Her body would be lost to the ocean and her Aunt Sybil left alone in the world, with no idea what had happened to her niece.

Jackson wouldn't know what had become of her either.

The thought shouldn't hurt, but it did. She'd run from him tonight, but deep down she'd expected to see him again, somewhere, someday. She'd never imagined it would end this way, with her dead and him forever haunted by his unanswered questions.

The thought made her soul howl with regret. She didn't want to go out like this. She didn't want to lose her life in the middle of running from her problems, the way she always had. She was tired of running, tired of being afraid. She wanted to face her fears—to face Jackson—and come away a better person for proving that she was stronger than anyone gave her credit for.

She might be submissive, but she wasn't subhuman. She didn't deserve Jackson's contempt or abuse. She should have stayed, told him the truth, and insisted he believe her. She should have stood up to him and shown that she could be every bit as persistent and stubborn as the man she was falling in love with.

He inspired so many conflicting feelings, but love was there, threading through the fear, a ray of light in the darkness.

But if she didn't get back to shore, he would never know that one of the Mason twins had truly cared for him and wanted nothing more than to give him pleasure and ease his pain.

Drawing strength from her thoughts, Hannah pulled hard to the surface, managing to get in three long strokes before another wave bore down on her, forcing her beneath the water. She dove down, ears ringing and legs stinging with soreness, but she refused to let terror take over. As soon as she was able, she resurfaced and flipped over onto her back to float. If she could draw in a few easier breaths and get her racing pulse under control, she would have the strength to keep fighting.

She was in the midst of her second smooth inhalation— and silently congratulating herself on keeping her head in the midst of a crisis—when an arm wrapped around her chest, banding beneath her armpits. Surprised, she flinched, but the arm only tightened its inexorable grip around her ribs.

A moment later, Jackson's ragged breath warmed her ear. "Lie still and let me help you. Fight me and I'll drag you back to shore unconscious."

With a shudder of relief, Hannah relaxed into him, going limp to make her body easier to tow out of the rip tide. Clearly sensing her surrender, Jackson kicked hard beneath the water, his powerful legs sending them gliding toward the beach on the crest of the next wave. She could feel the current tugging at her thighs, but it was still hard to believe that Jackson was fighting the full force of the ocean to get them both to safety. He was, as ever, in control of himself and all he surveyed.

The immense strength and power of the man hit home long before they reached the shallow water and he pulled her into his arms, carrying her out of the waves like she weighed nothing at all. But it was the moment he laid her down in the sand—gently, carefully—that impressed her the most.

Any man could bulk up until he was the biggest beast in the jungle, not any man could communicate with a touch that he believed the world was a better place with you in it.

"You almost died," he growled as he swiped water from his face, his voice a low rumble that threatened an impending storm. "If I hadn't seen your dress blow into the road, you would be dead right now."

Hannah stared up at him, still breathing hard. "Maybe not. I was fighting. I might have made it."

Heat flashed through his eyes as he braced his hands on either side of her shoulders. "Or you might be dead. You might be at the bottom of the ocean because lying to me is more important to you than your damned life!"

"Lies are the only things you'll believe," she shot back, refusing to be cowed by his anger. "You wouldn't recognize the truth if it walked up and slapped you in the face, Jackson Hawke."

"You don't have permission to—"

"I will call you what I want, when I want," she barreled on, tears rising in her eyes. "I don't want to be your property; I want to be your friend. Because I c-care about you. Even if you are mean and dangerous and probably out of your damned mind."

"You care about me," he echoed, his expression going blank in that way he had, the way that made her unsure whether she was going to earn pleasure or pain from his hands. But right now she was too fresh from near-death to be afraid of the consequences of her frank speech.

"Yes, I care about you." She blinked faster, trying to keep her tears from slipping down her cheeks "But I'm probably as crazy as you are you big, stupid, arrogant—"

Jackson's lips found hers, silencing her with a kiss. His tongue slipped into her mouth, mating with hers, sending electricity searing across her chilled skin and a roar of approval thundering through her every cell. She relaxed her jaw, welcoming his invasion with a moan as she wrapped her arms around his neck.

She clung to him, each press of her fingertips into his muscled shoulders a promise that she would never let him go. He might be mean and dangerous and crazy, but he cared about her, too. She could feel it in the way he pulled her close, rolling her on top of him as he claimed her with his kiss.

CHAPTER TWENTY-NINE

Jackson

*H*e didn't know up from down or right from wrong. All he knew was that he needed her. He needed to be inside of her, to prove to both of them that she was still alive.

Thank God she was still alive. If he'd lost her…

If he'd been forced to watch her die…

He couldn't think about it. He wouldn't think about that or anything else.

Driving a hand into her wet hair, he fisted the other in her panties, ripping them away with one swift jerk. She cried out against his lips as the satin tore, but when he tugged at the back of her thigh, guiding it to the outside of his hip, she spread her legs without resistance. He smoothed his palm over her ass, tracing the seam of her buttock until he dipped his fingers between her legs, finding where she was already slick and hot.

"No more lies," he said, shoving two digits deep into her pussy, summoning another moan from low in her throat. "From now on, you tell me the truth or I will show you how mean and crazy I can be. Do you hear me?"

"You don't scare me," she said, nipping his bottom lip

between her teeth hard enough to send pain coursing through his jaw.

"You don't scare me, sir," he corrected as he delivered a stern swat to her bare ass, falling back into the game.

He understood the game. The game had rules and a logic that was easy to follow. He didn't know what to do with this woman when she refused to play by the rules, when she told him she cared about him in that sweet, sad voice that made his heart want to believe her, even if his mind knew better.

"Yes, sir," she said, easing the tension in his chest. "You don't scare me, sir."

"I should." He released the close of her bra and tossed it away. Her breasts fell heavily onto his chest, making his cock throb. He cupped her fullness in his hands, pinching her nipples until she cried out and her hips began to squirm, restlessly seeking the friction of his erection between her legs.

"Because I don't love you," he continued in his hardest voice. "I told you, the man who cared about you is dead. Even if I wanted to, I could never love you, or anyone else, ever again."

"I thought you said no more lies," she said, arching her back, pressing her breasts more firmly into his palms.

"I'm not lying." He kneed her legs apart and bowed upward, lifting her into the air as he pressed his cock against her through the drenched fabric of his boxer briefs. "I don't love you, and I don't want to make love to you. I want to fuck you until you scream and realize what a stupid decision it was to run from me."

"Then fuck me until I scream, sir," she said, a flush spreading from her breasts up her throat to her gently parted lips. "Fuck me until I know who I belong to."

God *damn.*

He didn't want to give her the upper hand, even for a second, but there was no way he could resist an invitation like that.

Clenching his jaw tight, he reversed their positions, rolling her beneath him as he shoved his soaked boxers down his thighs. He kicked the fabric free and reached down, spreading her outer lips with his thumbs, revealing the slick, swollen flesh of her pussy.

His pussy. She was his and he was going to make sure that every time she sat down for the next three days she remembered it.

He positioned the dripping head of his cock and shoved home with a brutal thrust that wrenched the promised scream from her lips. The sound was part pleasure, part pain, and so fucking sexy he couldn't have held back if he'd tried.

With a groan of surrender, he braced his arms on either side of her pretty face and rode her hard. He fucked her until her breasts bounced against his chest and the sound of their bodies connecting made a dull thudding sound audible over the crash of the waves against the shore. They were both going to be sore as hell tomorrow, but he didn't care. He needed her to feel him, every inch of his cock filling her up, staking his claim.

Her pleasure and pain belonged to him. *She* belonged to him.

"You're mine," he said, biting his bottom lip as he fought for control, for the strength to hold on until he felt her go. "You belong to me. Even if you kill yourself, even if you kill me, you will always belong to me."

"Oh God, Jackson, please!" Her nails raked down his arms, leaving stinging trails behind that he knew would fill with blood.

But he didn't care. Let her mark him. Let her bleed him, so long as she came begging him for more.

"Please what?" He shifted the angle of his thrusts until her breath caught on a gasp of pleasure.

"Can I come?" she asked, voice rising as she writhed

beneath him, fighting to hold back the wave mounting inside of her. "Please, sir, can I come? Please? God, Jackson, please!"

"Come," he commanded, shoving into her one final time. She cried out his name and he roared something incomprehensible into the soft curve of her neck as her pussy clenched tight around his cock, triggering an orgasm so intense he lost time.

For a moment, he existed outside of reality, in an alternate dimension where there was nothing but warmth and pleasure and the smell of this woman all around him. And it was sweet, so sweet he thought maybe he could die a happy man as long as he died with the smell of her thick in his head, the taste of her on his tongue, the feel of her arms and legs locked around him, holding him close to her heart.

He came and came, pleasure having its way with him for what could have been hours before he finally collapsed on top of her, fighting to regain his breath. Between the battle with the ocean and the erotic battle with his newly recaptured prisoner, he was too spent to move, even when he realized that he hadn't pulled out. He'd come inside her, spilling every drop into the slick heat of her pussy.

He cursed himself but didn't roll away. It was too late for pulling out to do a damned bit of good and he wanted to stay joined with her a little longer, with his softening length buried inside her and the sticky heat of their pleasure binding them together. He didn't want to think about what came next, or what he would have to do if she lied to him again.

"I'm sorry I ran," she finally whispered. "I saw Adam carrying a cage around to the back of the house and I lost it. I...I was afraid it was for me."

"It was for you." He didn't bother to add that it still might be, depending on her answers to his questions.

"But why?" she asked, her voice breaking. "I thought we had a good time today. I thought we were connecting in a way we hadn't before."

"I agree." He drew back until he could take in her flushed cheeks and blue eyes, still glittering with passion. "That's why I trusted you to remain alone on the porch while I took a phone call. And you rewarded that trust by running away and nearly killing yourself."

Her brows drew together. "And if I hadn't, you would have put me in a cage. What kind of reward is that?"

"I said the cage was for you; I didn't say I was going to put you in it. It was a possibility, not a foregone conclusion."

"Can't you just give a straight answer for once?" she asked. "Is that so difficult?"

"The only thing I've promised you is that I will break you," he said, capturing her wrists and guiding them above her head before pinning them to the sand. "I never promised you truth or affection or anything else."

She held his gaze, her bottom lip trembling. "You're right. You're impossible, but you're right."

"I'm not impossible," he said, shocked to feel desire whispering through his core as she shifted beneath him, her hips sinking deeper into the coarse beach. He wanted to fuck her until he was hard again and they both had more sand in uncomfortable places, but the time for pleasure was through.

He needed answers and he intended to get them. "I'm going to give you a chance to make this better," he said softly. "If you please me, you will sleep in your bed tonight. If you displease me, you sleep in the kennel."

CHAPTER THIRTY

Jackson

*H*er eyes widened. "No. I can't. Please, I'm terrified of small spaces."

"Then I suppose you'd better answer my questions honestly." Jackson leaned in until his face hovered inches from hers, close enough for him to see the starbursts of gray surrounding her pupils.

Had Harley's eyes turned into tiny blue and silver suns at their centers? He didn't think so. Not exactly like this, anyway. If he were a gambling man, he would bet this was her sister, Hannah, but he needed to hear it from her own lips.

And then he needed her to tell him why she'd lied.

"What is your name?" he asked, his fingers tightening around her wrists as he relaxed more of his weight on top of her. He wanted her to feel just how vulnerable she was. Vulnerable, exposed, and completely at his mercy.

"My name," she echoed, searching his face. "We're back to this?"

"We are," he said. "But this time I want the truth."

She pulled in a breath and held it for a moment before releasing her words in a rush, "What if you don't believe me?"

"I'll believe you. If you're telling the truth."

"How will you know?"

"I'll know." He would. She had no reason to suspect that he'd discovered her secret. If she confessed the truth now while staring up into his eyes with her body slick around him and the steady thud of her heartbeat echoing through his chest, he would believe her.

"All right, I…" Her tongue slipped out, dampening her lips. "My name is Hannah. Hannah Elisabeth."

He swallowed, keeping his expression impassive, trying not to think too much about all the things he'd done to this woman while laboring under a case of mistaken identity. "Harley is your twin sister."

She nodded, fear and uncertainty swirling in her eyes. "Yes."

"And where is your sister now?" He moved his hands away from her wrists, granting her that slight freedom as a reward for her honesty.

"She's dead," she whispered. "She died in a car accident six years ago."

He closed his eyes. If he didn't, there would be no way he would be able to hide his response. She was telling the truth. Harley was dead and he'd wasted six years of his life hunting a ghost.

Six *fucking* years.

And now here he was, buried balls deep in a stranger he'd been hate fucking for a week, treating her the way he would only have treated his worst enemy.

Throat so tight it felt like it would collapse, Jackson pulled out and rolled away from the woman beneath him. He sat back on his ass in the sand, propping his elbows on his bent knees and dropping his face into his hands, his thoughts worming into such a wicked knot he couldn't pluck a single logical thread from the tangle.

"I'm sorry I lied," Hannah said, the direction of her voice leading him to believe she'd sat up beside him though he still couldn't bring himself to look at her. "I was afraid you wouldn't want me if you knew I wasn't Harley and my aunt and I are in a really hard place. We need the money badly, but after a while I..."

She sighed. "It started to feel so wrong to lie to you, no matter how much is riding on this job. I was going to tell you the truth tonight, at dinner, but when you left the table, I realized I had no way to prove that I had a sister. No pictures or birth certificate or anything. And then I got scared that you wouldn't believe me, so when I saw the—"

"The cage," he supplied numbly. The cage he'd bought for the monster who had slipped through his fingers. Harley was probably rolling around on the steamy floor of hell right now, laughing her ass off at his failure.

But that was all right. He would hunt her there, too. Eventually.

"I'm not sure what she did to you," Hannah said in a careful voice, "but I'm sorry. I'm sure you didn't deserve it. I loved Harley, but I knew her better than anyone. She could be so cruel. She hurt a lot of people who didn't deserve to be hurt. Especially men."

"Why men?" Jackson asked, keeping his eyes closed and his face in his hands. His reality was falling apart, but he wasn't about to let Hannah see him crumble. She might not be his sworn enemy, but he didn't trust her. He didn't trust anyone related to the viper who had put him behind bars.

"I don't know for sure," she said. "I think it was her way of protecting herself. My mother was miserable in her marriage. She had an affair when I was a kid. She was gone for almost a year, and when she came back, Daddy was horrible to her. He treated her like a prisoner, but she never fought back or tried to leave. It was...painful to watch. It scared me and I think it scared Harley even more. She was so afraid of becoming like Mom that she became like Dad, instead, taking what she wanted and hurting before she could be hurt."

Hurting before she could be hurt.

He would *never* have hurt Harley, not back then. And he certainly wouldn't have set off a nuclear bomb in the center of her life the way she had his. The explanation didn't make any sense, but he could tell Hannah was telling the truth as far as she knew it.

But that didn't mean her psychoanalysis of her sister was the entire story. There had to be more to Harley's plot to ruin him, and Hannah was going to help him discover the secrets her sister must have been keeping.

Taking a deep breath, Jackson lifted his head and opened his eyes. Hannah was mirroring his position, her legs curled to her chest and her arms wrapped around her knees, concealing most of her nakedness. They'd spent the past week having boundary-pushing sex and he'd just had her so hard his balls still ached, but he felt like he was looking at a stranger.

He didn't know how to talk to her or be with her and he was too fucked up to cross that bridge just yet. It was better not to think too much about what to do with Hannah, at least not until he had the information he needed.

"Hannah Elisabeth," he said, even her name softer and sweeter in his mouth than Harley's. "Pretty."

Her lashes fluttered as her gaze fell. "Thank you."

"So what is your last name, Hannah Elisabeth?"

She glanced up sharply before dropping her eyes back to the sand and hugging her legs tighter to her chest. "I'd rather not say. If that's okay."

"It's not. I need to know Harley's last name. I already know Garrett, the one she gave me, wasn't it."

Hannah shook her head, her damp, tangled hair moving heavily around her shoulders. "I'm sorry. I can't tell you. My family has enemies. That's why my aunt and I are in hiding. I haven't told anyone my real last name in years."

"What kind of enemies?" he asked, wondering if maybe Hannah wasn't so innocent after all.

"The kind who kill people," she said, her face paling. "Harley's accident wasn't an accident. Someone drove the car she was in off the road. There was reason to believe I would be next so...we ran. It's been just Sybil and me ever since."

"Why would someone want you and your sister dead?"

"I don't know for sure. I have theories, but I'm not ready to share them," she said, her mouth set in a stubborn line. "All I can tell you is that it was nothing Harley or I did. She might not have been innocent, but she'd done nothing to earn her way onto a killer's hit list."

"I understand not being ready to share your secrets with me," he said in a patient voice. "But what you don't understand is that if you don't tell me your last name, you're going to make a new enemy. And I'll be able to get to you a lot easier than anyone else who means you harm."

Hannah's lips parted in shock. "Are you threatening me?"

"I'd rather not, but if you won't give me what I need..."

"B-but I'm not Harley," she sputtered.

"I believe you, and I don't want to punish an innocent woman any more than I have already," he said, muscles tensing, ready to spring after her if she decided to run. "But I need to know the truth. Give me a name and we'll be finished with questions. For now."

Her clever gaze darted to the right before returning to his. She was going to run. He almost hoped she would so he would have something to do with all the frustrated rage coursing through him.

"I can't tell you," she said with another shake of her head. "If it were only me, it wouldn't matter, but I have to think about Aunt Sybil. I can't put her at risk."

"She won't be in danger," he said. "I won't tell anyone anything about you or your aunt. I just need to know Harley's last name."

Hannah went still, holding his gaze in the fading light. "I can't. Please ask me something else."

"I thought you said you cared about me," Jackson said, unable to keep the hard edge from his voice. "Aren't you supposed to trust the people you care for?"

Her eyes narrowed. "I also said I thought you were out of your mind. So until you prove otherwise, no, I don't trust you. And if you hurt me because I refuse to answer this question, then I will trust you even less and you will *never* get what you want from me."

"Now you're making threats?" he asked in a low, dangerous voice, some primitive part of him gnashing its teeth in rage that she dared to threaten him now, when his entire world had been ripped apart.

"It's not a threat," she whispered. "It's a promise."

He shifted forward, but before he could stand, Hannah sprung to her feet and raced back toward the ocean. He leapt after her, eliminating her brief head start in three large strides. Grabbing her hips, he spun her around and bent low, tipping her over his shoulder.

"Let me go!" she screamed, driving a fist into his back. "Put me down!"

Jackson responded by securing one arm around her thighs, banding them tightly together as he turned and started back up the beach.

He'd given her the chance to play nice.

Now they were going to play his way.

CHAPTER THIRTY-ONE

Hannah

*a*ll the way back to the house, Hannah beat Jackson's back with her fists as hard as she could, but it was like his skin had turned to stone along with his heart.

His heart was always stone.

You were a fool to think differently and a fool to let him know you care. He'll just use it against you, another weapon in his crazy, senseless war against a dead woman.

"I'm not Harley!" Hannah sobbed as Jackson walked around the side of the house, cutting through the garden. She hated the tears filling her eyes. She wasn't sad, she was livid, but apparently her stupid body didn't understand the difference. "I didn't do anything to you! You have no right to punish me."

"I don't need a right. You sold yourself to me," Jackson said in an infuriatingly cold voice. "I can do what I want with the things that I own."

"I'm not a thing, you bastard," she said, delivering another hard punch to his muscled back that, again, seemed to have absolutely no effect. "I'm a person. An *innocent* person."

"No one is innocent," he said, flipping her upright so suddenly the world spun and her knees buckled.

Before she could even attempt to regain her balance, Jackson's strong hands gripped her hip and the back of her neck, bending her in half and shoving her forward. She fell onto her hands and knees, knowing as soon as she felt the hard plastic beneath her fingers where she was.

The cage. She was in the cage.

She spun in time to see Jackson slide the lock home and wailed at him through the bars, "No! Let me out! You can't leave me in here!"

Jackson stood and turned, walking away with that slow, predatory gait of his, as if he couldn't care less that he'd locked a woman he had just made love to in a dog kennel.

"Stop!" she screamed as he crossed the patio. "I'm not a criminal! I'm not an animal. I don't deserve to be treated this way!"

He paused with his hand on the sliding glass door and turned, glancing over his shoulder with a pitiless expression on his face. "No one gets what they deserve, Hannah. If you didn't realize that before, you certainly will now."

And then he opened the door and stepped inside, ignoring her shouted, "Wait!"

She sucked in a breath, frightened by the sound that emerged from her parted lips. It was half whimper, half growl, and all crazy. If he left her in here for any length of time, she was going to lose her mind. She could already feel the narrow plastic walls tightening around her, the thin metal web of the bars digging into her skin, slicing her sanity into pieces.

"Let me out," she moaned as she wedged herself into the corner of the kennel, her knees tucked to her chest. "Please, let me out. Please."

But there was no one to hear her beg. The garden beyond the patio was quiet and empty. The only sounds breaking the silence were the wind through the leaves and the insects buzzing and clicking in the soft blue light.

Dusk had fallen on the journey back to the house. Before

long, it would be dark and she would be alone until morning. She knew Jackson wasn't coming back for her any time soon. There would be no one to plead with for her freedom until Eva brought her breakfast tray in the morning and for all she knew, she might be denied food until she gave Jackson what he wanted.

"I hate you," she growled, her foot shooting out to kick the opposite wall, sending a shudder through her prison. "I hate you, Jackson! I hate you! Do you hear me? I hate you!"

She screamed until her throat was raw, her eye sockets throbbed, and tears streamed down her cheeks. She screamed until she could have sworn she'd used up all the air in her prison and her head felt light enough to float off her body. She screamed and screamed until darkness fell and the moon rose over the black hulk of the mountain and she was too weak to do anything but curl into a ball on the floor of the cage and cry herself to sleep, pitifully mumbling promises to herself.

She was going to hurt him. She was going to make him sorry he'd done this. She was going to show him that sometimes people *did* get what they deserved and that he wasn't the only one who could become a monster.

By the time she finally began to drift off to sleep—still feeling the full-body crawl of terror only a claustrophobic could fully understand—she had nearly convinced herself that she didn't pity Jackson, let alone love him.

How could she be in love with a man who would hurt her this way?

Nothing he'd done in the past week had been as awful as this. Before today, he hadn't known he had the wrong woman and there had always been pleasure at the end of the pain. The most mind-blowing, heart-wrenching, explosive pleasure of her life, unlike anything she could have imagined until Jackson took her by the hand and led her down his dark path.

But maybe he didn't want to give her pleasure or pain anymore.

She wasn't Harley. She wasn't the woman he wanted. Maybe now that he knew Harley was truly beyond his reach, he wanted answers and nothing more. And maybe, if she broke down and gave him what he was asking for, he'd send her home to Sybil.

The thought should have been a sliver of hope to cling to. Instead, it summoned fresh tears that slid down her already hot, swollen cheeks. She didn't want him to send her away or even to simply let her out of her cage. She wanted him to care the way she cared.

"So stupid, Hannah," she mumbled to the darkness. "You're so fucking stupid."

She'd always heard that love was blind, but apparently it was dumb, as well, and lacking in even the most basic sense of self-respect.

She still loved Jackson, even now, curled on her side with hard plastic digging into her bones, her head full of cotton, and her mouth filled with the sour taste of terror. She still ached for his touch and the feel of his body joining with hers, promising with every brush of skin against skin that she belonged in his arms, and she sensed she would only stop loving him when she began hating herself.

"First thing in the morning," she whispered as her eyes slid closed. She would start to work on hating herself first thing in the morning.

Right now she was too tired for love or hate or anything in between.

CHAPTER THIRTY-TWO

Jackson

*J*ackson locked himself in his room, turning the stereo to a classical station to drown out the sound of Hannah's distant screams. He took a long hot shower, doing his best not to think about anything in particular as he scrubbed the saltwater stickiness from his skin. Afterward, he dressed in silk pajama pants and a cotton tee shirt and sat down to decode a message encrypted on the website his underground contacts used to negotiate prices for his shipments.

If Hannah was still screaming that she hated him an hour later, he couldn't hear it over the soothing piano music, but he would swear he could feel her contempt stinging across the surface of his skin. The hair at the back of his neck stood on end, his jaw ached from being clenched for too long, and his stomach had solidified into a granite slab that weighed down the center of his body. Working was challenging and eating was unthinkable.

When Eva brought him a tray a little after eight, he sent her away, opting for a tumbler of scotch on the rocks instead. He hoped the drink would dull the edges of his anger. But two tumblers later, all it had accomplished was to make it impossible to stop thinking about Hannah, the woman he'd locked in a cage for the crime of not giving him what he wanted.

He was behaving like an infant king, a tyrant given power far greater than his capacity for compassion.

Her sister destroyed your capacity for compassion and Hannah's purpose is to give you what you want. It doesn't matter that she isn't Harley; you're still paying for her obedience. She knew the rules and she knew she would be punished for disobeying them.

She brought every bit of this pain and suffering upon herself.

That line of defense held until eleven o'clock, when he turned off the lights and slipped between the sheets, only for his mind to stubbornly replay the events of the evening over and over again, keeping him awake and riveted by remembered fear.

He kept seeing Hannah struggling in the waves, reliving the terror that had flooded through him as he realized he might lose her until his heart thudded faster and his arms ached to hold her. All he wanted to do was to press her tight to his chest and assure his anxious mind that she was safe and alive. But she wasn't safe and he doubted any amount of money could convince her to come willingly into his arms. She hated him. As she should. As she should have from the very beginning.

But she didn't. She cared. And you paid her back with cruelty.

With a curse, Jackson flung the covers to the end of the bed and rose to pace back and forth on the cool hardwood. A part of him wanted to go to her, to try to make this better, but it was too late. It had always been too late.

Maybe if he'd met Hannah first instead of Harley. Maybe if he'd never become a criminal or learned to take what he wanted and damn the consequences, maybe then he and Hannah could have been something other than enemies. But as things stood, the situation was too fucked up for it to ever be put right again. Harley had made sure of that.

Jackson snatched his phone from the bureau, thumbing

back to the picture of the two girls by the lake, feeling something painful flash through his chest at the sight of Hannah's smile. It was the same smile she had as an adult, that sweet, open smile he'd seen in the moments she felt comfortable enough to let down her guard. It was the smile that had made him wonder if there was some way forward for him and Harley, as twisted and crazy as the path might be.

But Hannah wasn't Harley. Harley was dead and Hannah was a stranger he'd known for barely a week.

She's not a stranger. She's yours.

"Fuck me until I know who I belong to." The memory of her words was enough to make his cock stiffen, but he ignored his body's response. Hannah didn't belong to him and she never would. She deserved better than what he could give her. A broken man was good enough for the woman who had broken him, but he would never be good enough for anyone else.

Ignoring the odd rush of melancholy inspired by the thought, Jackson flipped forward to the letter he hadn't had time to read earlier tonight. Upon closer inspection, he realized it was written in colored pencil and that the contents of the missive weren't as childlike as he'd first assumed. The looping cursive was awkward, but the thoughts the words communicated were unexpectedly eloquent.

Dear Aunt Syb,

I miss you so much! I dream about the lake house every night and wake up sad that I'm not there with you. I wish it were already next summer. Don't tell them I told, but Mom is still as sad as when we left and Dad is always at work. Sometimes I wonder if they wish they didn't have kids, but I'm probably wrong. I guess I'm just cranky because Nanny Hammond is awful.

She punishes us BOTH every time Harley does something bad!

Harley says it's because Nanny is too dumb to tell us apart, but I think she does it to try to make Harley feel guilty so she'll stop getting into trouble. But Harley never feels guilty and at this rate I'm never going to get to go to my rock-climbing lesson again. It's always taken away as a punishment.

It almost makes me want to break the rules just so there's a reason for being punished, but my heart gets all jumpy just thinking about doing things I'm not supposed to do. The closest I got to being bad was sneaking into Nanny's room and putting leaves in her underwear drawer. When Harley found out, she teased me for being a baby. She said she would have put mice or cockroaches in there instead. And she probably would have.

She's so angry all the time, Aunt Syb. She's not the same as she is when we're at your house. So when we come home I miss you and *her, even though she's right here beside me.*

Does that sound crazy?

I hope not. Sometimes I'm scared of ending up like Mom. Nanny says depression is a disease, so we can't blame Mom for it. And I don't, but sometimes, when I'm sad, I wonder if I'm catching depression, too.

But I know I wouldn't catch it at the lake house, Aunt Syb. I know I would be happy and could grow up to be a good person, like you. I just want to be happy and good and not to be scared or sad all the time. That's why I'm writing to ask you to please, please, please ask Daddy to let me come live with you. I know he'll say yes if you ask.

And then I could go to school there and help you whenever your arthritis is giving you trouble. I promise I will be the very best kid ever and never let you down. Cross my heart and hope to die!

Much love and hoping to see you soon,

Hannah

Jackson set the phone back on the bureau, his head bowed and his throat tight. It had been a long time since he'd felt anything close to this fierce sense of empathy and he wasn't sure what to do with the emotion swelling inside of him.

No child should have to feel so scared and alone. His childhood home had been cold and loveless, but at least he hadn't been constantly punished for a sibling's misbehavior. And he'd gotten out, scheming his way to freedom when he wasn't much older than Hannah had been when she wrote this letter.

It made him want to reach through time, scoop up that lonely, neglected little girl, and find a way to get her to the aunt who loved her.

But he couldn't rescue the child Hannah had been. The best he could do was save the woman she'd become.

Before he'd made the conscious choice to move, he was through the bedroom door, striding through the darkened great room and down the hall toward the master suite. Inside, the air still smelled like Hannah, a sweet and sexy smell he knew would haunt him long after she was gone, but he didn't pause to draw it in.

Now that he'd made the decision, he couldn't get to her fast enough.

He was already going to be too late. Too late to spare her another ugly memory of being punished for her sister's crimes, too late to reward her loyalty to the aunt she loved so much or to show her that he wasn't completely rotten inside. There was still some healthy tissue hidden away in the diseased corridors of his heart. She had shown him that, but unfortunately for the both of them, the discovery had come too late.

CHAPTER THIRTY-THREE

Jackson

*O*utside on the patio, Jackson glanced down through the web of bars on the roof of the kennel to see Hannah asleep, curled into a pitiful ball in one corner of her cage. A sharp, slightly sour smell rose from her body, sending a fresh wave of self-loathing oozing through his chest.

He knew that smell. It was the smell of terror and captivity, made familiar from his first days in prison when his clothes had been constantly damp with sweat despite the chill in his cell. It had taken a week for his body to adapt to living in a cage, but his mind had never adjusted. Once you've known what it's like to have your freedom unjustly taken away, it's impossible to recover. Trust, faith, hope, and all the other fragile things that give life deeper meaning become impossible, locked away in a room inside of you that has no key.

He knew from experience something like this could never be undone. Hannah would never forget being caged for the crime of trusting the wrong person. She'd only been in the kennel for a few hours, but she would bear the scars of this encounter for the rest of her life.

Bracing himself for the worst, Jackson knelt to peer into the cage, where Hannah's skin glowed like moonlight reflecting on the ocean. She was beautiful—the curve of her hip poetry in the darkness that surrounded her—but he still wished he'd given her clothes. It was warm enough that she shouldn't be cold, but her nudity added to the cruelty of her punishment. He could imagine how vulnerable she must have felt in those moments before she fell asleep when she was lying naked and alone inside a cage meant for a dog.

She'd told him that she cared about him, and in exchange, he'd treated her like an animal. She was right to hate him. Hatred was all he deserved.

"Hannah," he said, knowing putting this off until morning wouldn't make it any easier. "Hannah, wake up. I'm here to let you out."

She moaned and shifted in her sleep, but her eyes remained closed.

"Hannah," he repeated in a firmer voice. "Wake up, Hannah."

She woke with a start, her head snapping up, sending her tangled hair flying. With her curls obscuring her features he couldn't see her face, but he knew the moment she saw him. She cringed away with a sound of disgust, pressing herself against the wall of the kennel and drawing her knees to her chest.

"What do you want?" she asked, her voice low and hoarse from screaming.

"I'm here to let you out." He flipped the latch, letting the gate swing open, but Hannah didn't move. She remained in her corner, making it clear she'd rather stay in the dog crate than move a centimeter closer to him.

"What do you want?" she demanded again, voice rising sharply. "*Why* are you letting me out?"

"I thought you might want a shower," he said as he backed away from the kennel, knowing it was the wrong thing to say when a bark of laughter burst from Hannah's lips.

"A shower," she repeated as she crawled through the gate

and stood shakily, her arms clasped across her chest. "You thought I might want a *shower*."

Jackson sighed, but she cut him off before he could find something less ridiculous to say.

"No, I don't want a shower." She lunged forward suddenly, sobbing as her palms struck his ribs. "I want to hurt you, you twisted son of a bitch!" She shoved him again, sending him staggering back a step. "I want to lock you naked in a cage and let you know what it feels like to have the walls closing in and your skin crawling off of your body."

Jackson lifted his hands into the air, the gesture of surrender resonating in some deep, primal part of his brain.

He suddenly realized there was only one way to show Hannah how profoundly he regretted what he'd done. Slowly, he reached for the bottom of his shirt, pulling it over his head before letting it fall to the ground.

"What are you doing?" Hannah edged back a step, wariness in her tone.

"You said you wanted me naked." He could sense where her thoughts were headed and how little she wanted him to touch her, but this wasn't about sex. It was about being as vulnerable as she was, something she'd realize when she saw his cock limp between his legs.

He shoved his pants to the ground and stepped out of them before kneeling on the hard stone at her feet. "There's a crop in the bedside table drawer. You should get it. If you beat me with your hands, you'll hurt yourself."

He watched her bare toes curl against the stone, but didn't lift his eyes from the ground. He couldn't stand to look at her right now. Seeing how close she was to a breakdown and knowing he was the one who had driven her there was even more painful than he'd imagined it would be.

"You want me to beat you?" she asked.

"I'm too big to fit in the kennel," Jackson said practically. "A beating would be a reasonable substitute, but if you'd rather punish me some other way, that's up to you. Whatever you decide, you have my full cooperation."

"Why?" she said. "Look at me, Jackson."

He kept his chin tucked close to his chest. "You know why."

"Jackson, look at me," she repeated. "Let me see your face."

Slowly, he tilted his head, meeting her gaze in the dim light. The moon was hiding behind the thick clouds that had moved in not long after sunset, but there was enough illumination to see the way her eyes glittered with a mixture of rage and suspicion. It was clear that she would never trust him again, not even the small amount that she had before.

The knowledge made his chest feel heavy and his voice flat when he said, "Because I deserve it."

"What did you do to deserve it," she pressed, refusing to let him off easy. "Tell me what you did wrong."

"Once I knew who you were, the ugliness should have stopped," he said. "I never should have fucked you on the beach or dragged you back here against your will. And I sure as hell shouldn't have put you in the kennel."

"Then why did you?" she asked, shaking her head as if he were a puzzle she would never be able to make sense of.

But there was no puzzle. He was a simple creature, a simple monster, and after all he'd put her through she deserved to know his creation story.

"Because I'm a twisted son of a bitch. Like you said. And I'm never going to be anything else." He took a deep breath. "It started six years ago when your sister filed a report with the military police accusing me of rape."

He let the rest of the story spill out, every detail of that summer that had started out golden and ended in a nightmare he couldn't wake from, no matter how many times he'd insisted that he had never touched Harley in anger.

"I don't know how she did it," he continued. "In the video

of her interview with the police she was covered in bruises, but the last time I saw her she was fine. There wasn't a mark on her. I saw every inch of her." He swallowed hard. "We slept together and I told her that I loved her for the first time. She said she loved me, too, and…I believed it. I believed her."

His lip curled, disgust for the fool he'd been making his skin crawl. "Later, I found out that she'd been killed later that same night, on her way to elope with my best friend, days after framing me for a crime I didn't commit. I was sentenced to eighteen months in a military prison and dishonorably discharged from the Marines. My family hasn't spoken to me since I was taken in for questioning."

Hannah's breath rushed out. "Jesus." She sat down across from him, her arms still folded at her chest. "I thought it was something like that, but I never… I had no idea that you'd gone to prison. Or that the man who was in the car with her was your friend."

"Don't pity me," he said in a brittle voice. "That's not why I told you the truth. I told you so you'll understand that I have nothing to offer you except the chance to even the score. Now go get the crop."

"I don't want to get the crop," she said, sounding exasperated. "You know, there's such a thing as an apology, Jackson. Where you say you're sorry for something you've done and the other person says you're forgiven."

"I don't deserve to be forgiven."

Her gaze softened. "Then I guess this time it's lucky for you that people don't always get what they deserve." She reached out, laying a hand on his arm. "I believe that you're sorry. And I forgive you."

He shook his head, fighting to swallow as a wave of emotion tightened his throat. "You can't."

"You don't get to tell me what to do," she said stubbornly. "That's not the place we're in right now. I want to forgive you, so I will. And I hope you'll forgive me, too."

"There's nothing to forgive," he said, sitting back on his heels, the knot in his throat even worse than it had been before.

"Yes, there is." She moved closer, taking his hand in both of hers. "I played my part in the confusion you've been feeling for so long. I didn't realize it, but..." Her fingers tightened around his palm. "That wasn't Harley you were with the night you climbed through her window, Jackson. It was me."

He glanced up but was too stunned to form a response.

"I tried to tell you," Hannah said, anxiety creeping into her tone. "But you thought I was playing along with the game. And then, after the first time we were together when I had the chance to tell you it had all been a horrible mistake, I...I didn't want to."

Her gaze fell to their joined hands. "Because it wasn't horrible. It was wonderful. And that's why I smiled when you took the blindfold off. Because I'd been hoping to see you again for so long, even though I knew it was wrong, and that it was Harley you cared about, not me."

"I...I can't..." He trailed off, still not knowing what to say, only that so many things finally made sense now. Not just the bruises, but the way Harley had seemed so naturally submissive that night, almost like a different person.

It was because she *had* been a different person. She'd been Hannah. It was Hannah who had made him believe he and Harley had a future. It had been Hannah all along.

"Can you forgive me?" she asked.

"There's nothing to forgive," he repeated, hoping she could tell that he meant it. "I should have known the difference. If I hadn't drunk half a bottle of scotch before I came through Harley's window, I would have. It was my fault as much as yours."

"Not really," she said, her lips lifting on one side. "But thank you."

"God, Hannah, don't thank me." He tried to pull his

hand away, but she held tight. "I'm glad you told me the truth, but I'm not that man anymore. I couldn't be, even if I tried."

"I don't believe you." She drew his hand toward her, guiding it to rest, palm down, on her chest.

His fingers fit neatly between her bare breasts and the feel of her soft, warm flesh had the usual effect on his body. His cock didn't care that he hated himself. His cock only cared that he could have Hannah's breast cupped in his hand with a shift of his wrist.

But he refused to indulge the urge. Sex was no longer an option, not if he were truly sorry for the things he'd done.

"Don't do this to yourself," he said, his voice rough. "I'm sorry for what I did tonight and all the other nights, but I can't promise I won't do something like that again." He grimaced. "Or something worse. I'm not safe for you."

"Who said I wanted safe?" she asked, leaning closer. "I'm not a fool, Jackson. I know you're dangerous and I'm not looking for any big promises. All I need is one thing."

"What's that?" Her nipples brushed against his chest, sending heat spreading through his core. He clenched his jaw, fighting to keep from reaching for her.

"Tell me that you care," she said in her soft, sexy voice. "Even if it's only a little. Because if you can care a little, then you can learn to care a lot. And maybe someday you'll even learn to let yourself be happy."

Jackson pressed his lips together, but it did nothing to stop the ache spreading through his chest. He didn't deserve this; he didn't deserve her, but he couldn't hide from how much he wanted what she was offering. He was broken and twisted and wrong inside, but when Hannah touched him it felt right, *he* felt right in a way he hadn't in so long. Not since that night in Harley's bed when he'd unknowingly slept with the wrong sister.

"Tell me you care, Jackson," she whispered, kissing first

one corner of his mouth and then the other. "I know you do. And I know you want me as much as I want you."

"I want you so much," he said, his eyes sliding closed. "I want you like my next breath, but I'll hurt you, Hannah. I know I will and I don't want to."

"Why don't you want to?" she asked as she reached down, her cool fingers closing around his erection, stroking him with a gentle insistence that sent longing and grief flooding through him in equal measure.

She had him right where she wanted him. He couldn't deny her though he knew this wouldn't end well. It never did when Beauty fell in love with the Beast.

"Because I care about you." His eyes opened as his fingers closed around her wrist, stopping her mid-stroke. He stared deep into her big eyes, willing her to see what a bad idea this was. "But this isn't a fairy tale. In real life, the monster doesn't get better. In real life, the monster drags you down to hell with him and you burn there."

"You make me burn, that's true." Her lips twisted in a wry smile. "Which reminds me that I have a favor to ask, sir."

"What's that?" he asked, not sure whether to feel grateful or terrified that she was taking them back onto familiar ground.

Things between them would never be the same. She could call him "sir" a thousand times, but he was vulnerable now and they both knew it. They might be using the same pieces, but this was a whole other game, one he wasn't sure he remembered how to play.

"I would like a safe word," she said. "People like us usually have those, right?"

"They do," he said, mesmerized by the feel of her fingertips teasing across his palm. "Though I'm not sure there are other people exactly like us."

She shrugged one shoulder. "That doesn't have to be a bad thing."

He made a non-committal sound. This was all bad, but it was hard to concentrate on good and bad when she was naked in the moonlight, looking up at him like he was all she needed to get through the night. "So what's your safe word, sunshine?"

She cocked her head. "No more princess?"

"Sunshine suits you better."

She nodded, her lashes fluttering as she swallowed. "See? You can be sweet," she said, pushing on before he could assure her that he was as far from sweet as a man could get. "And my safe word is cheese biscuits. I'd like to see you stay mean and growly when I'm shouting cheese biscuits in your ear."

Against all odds, a smile stretched across his face. "Cheese biscuits? Those are the words that make you feel safe?"

"What's safer than a fluffy biscuit, covered in melted cheese?" she asked with mock seriousness. "That's practically the definition of safety."

"You're funny," he said, warmth spreading through his chest.

"I'm not funny." She shifted her weight as she shook her head slowly back and forth. "I'm a very serious person, and I've got a serious problem."

He lifted a brow. "What's that?"

"I think it's best if I show you, sir." She held his gaze as she guided his hand between her legs. As his fingers slid through the slick folds of her sex, a ragged sigh escaped his lips.

When he'd come out here, he'd been certain he would never touch her this way again. And he wouldn't have if she weren't the person she was, a generous, gentle, unbelievably strong woman who had looked into the darkest corners of his soul and refused to be scared away. And because she was who she was, he could be something better, at least for the night.

"You won't need your safe word this time," he said,

pressing one finger deep into the well of her heat, relishing the way she spread her thighs, welcoming him in. "There won't be any games tonight. It will just be you and me."

"Should I still call you 'sir'?" she asked, anxiety flickering across her features.

"Don't be afraid," he said. "I can't make you any promises about the future, but I swear there won't be any pain tonight."

"But sometimes pain is easier, isn't it?" she said, proving she understood the game far better than most people who had only just begun to play.

"It can be," he agreed, withdrawing his fingers from her slickness and taking her by the hand. "Pain gives you a place to hide. But I can't hide tonight. I'm not in the right head-space. So if you'd rather go to bed alone, I understand."

"That's the last thing I want." She squeezed his hand. "Take me to bed, Jackson. If you're not afraid, I'm not, either."

Who said I'm not afraid?

He *was* afraid. So afraid. Of her, of himself, of the trust in her eyes and the affection in her touch. He would betray her trust and affection. He was certain of it, but still he held on tight to her hand as he led her through the sliding doors toward the bed.

He held tight because somewhere deep inside of himself, a voice whispered that maybe it wasn't too late. He could never go back, but maybe there was a way forward, as long as he kept his eyes on this woman who believed that he could be something more than a monster.

CHAPTER THIRTY-FOUR

Hannah

*P*ulse racing with a heady combination of desire and fear, Hannah stretched out on the bed, waiting with bated breath for Jackson to lie down beside her. This shouldn't be more frightening than being spanked, punished, or locked in a cage, but it was. The look in his eyes, as he gazed down at her, was the scariest thing she'd ever seen.

He was so vulnerable, adrift and directionless, with all his carefully constructed armor falling away. He reminded her of a wounded predator, made more dangerous by the knowledge that his defenses were weakened. But he was also utterly captivating.

For the first time since she'd come into his keeping, she glimpsed the man she'd met that night in her sister's bed, the man capable of trust and affection. He'd been wounded by betrayal and smothered by rage, but he was still there, nearly within her reach, and she didn't want to do anything to scare him away.

As Jackson eased onto the mattress beside her, she was shocked to realize that she felt like the Dominant one tonight. The responsibility for his emotional well-being lay heavy on her shoulders, but she could handle the weight. She was stronger than she'd imagined she could be. Jackson had taught her that. He'd shown her the strength in submission and the core of steel that ran through her softness.

And tonight she would use her strength to begin leading him out of the darkness before it was too late.

"You're beautiful," he said, his palm skimming up her stomach to cup her breast reverently in his hand. "Have I told you how beautiful you are?"

"Yes. I think stunning was another word you used," she said, knowing it was exactly the word he'd used. She would never forget a single word he'd said to her, this man who had captured her imagination, her heart, and everything in between. "You're pretty stunning yourself."

"I'm glad I please you," he said, rolling her nipple between his fingers, sending a sweet ache flooding through her core.

"You do more than please me." She pushed gently at his shoulders until he rolled onto his back. "You drive me crazy." She leaned down, holding his gaze as she pressed a kiss to the center of his chest. "I've never wanted anyone the way I want you."

She moved higher, trailing kisses up his neck until she reached his mouth, where she let her lips hover a whisper above his. "Am I allowed to kiss you anywhere I want now?"

"Anywhere you want, sunshine," he said, the pet name making her heart turn over. The way he said that word spoke louder than any promise. When he said *sunshine*, she heard *I love you.*

Someday soon, she hoped he would hear it too, and realize maybe they weren't so far from the fairy tale, after all.

"Everything is going to be okay," she said, cupping his scruffy cheek in her hand as she addressed the unspoken doubt in his eyes. "It will, Jackson. I promise."

And then she kissed him and he kissed her back, his tongue slipping into her mouth and his arms wrapping tight around her. The kiss was as hot as any they'd shared, but it was also richer, deeper, an exploration of new territory and an offering of something more than their physical bodies. There was more than hunger in his touch as he cupped her breasts in his hands, kneading and caressing her sensitive skin until she was dizzy. There was more than a desire for release in the way he urged her thighs apart and pressed his erection tight to the slickness between her legs.

She could sense the emotion simmering beneath his touch and the longing for a union that thrummed through his veins. It was the same longing that swelled inside her, filling her with warmth, crowding out the last of her fear.

"I need you so much," she mumbled against his lips. "I need to feel you inside me."

"Condom." He reached for the bedside table, but she took his hand, guiding it back to her breast.

"No, I want you bare," she said, grinding her slickness up and down his rigid length. "It isn't the right time for a baby and we've already gone without a condom once today. Once more won't hurt."

"I know we did," he said, pinching her nipples. "But I didn't realize it until after. I wasn't thinking." He groaned softly as she circled her hips, coating his cock with more of her wet heat. "That's what you do to me, Hannah. You make me forget to think."

"Good." She reached between them, positioning him at her entrance. "You think too much."

She dropped her hips, taking him inside her, inch by glorious inch. She'd never been on top with him before and relished the new way he filled her. His engorged erection took up every inch of space until there was a hint of pain as she sank down the final inch, fitting her hips to his.

But it was sweet pain, the kind that only drove her desire higher.

She moaned as she began to move, gliding up and down

his shaft as he lifted his head, suckling her nipple into his mouth. His hands squeezed her hips, sending fresh waves of need coursing through her body and a ringing sensation vibrating through her cells. She felt like a tuning fork finding the perfect pitch, a meditation bell summoning the chaos of the world into perfect harmony, and was suffused with a sense of rightness that swept away the last clinging cobwebs of doubt.

There was no longer any question in her mind—this was where she was meant to be. She belonged with this man. She was born to share his bed, warm his heart, and climb out of hell by his side. It was as close to a moment of utter truth as she'd ever experienced, and she had to know if he felt it too.

"Wait. I need to see you. Please." Fighting the pleasure cresting within her, she squirmed until he released her nipple and lay back, his breath coming fast.

"Just don't ask me to stop," he said, thrusting sharply into her core, his cock stroking so deep it drew a gasp from her throat. "I can't stop. I need you so much. So fucking much." A pained expression flashed across his face that she understood completely.

It was painful to get this close, so close there was nothing but a fraying thread keeping you from losing yourself and being eaten alive by need for the person in your arms. It was heaven and hell mixed together, but better for it.

Darkness made the light shine brighter, pain made pleasure that much sweeter, and what was the point of angels if not to save beautiful devils like Jackson Hawke.

"I won't give up on you," she whispered, holding his gaze as she caught his rhythm, riding him with sensuous rolls of her hips, building the fire already raging between them. "I won't ever give up."

His grip on her hips tightened until his fingertips dug into her flesh. "Hannah."

It was only her name, but it carried so much. It bore his

fear, his sadness, and his pain. It held his certainty that they were doomed to fail and the fragile hope that maybe his heart wasn't dead and buried after all.

"It's not too late." She leaned down until her hair fell around their faces, providing a safe place to say dangerous things. "I love you. Every part of you."

He answered her with a kiss, groaning into her mouth as he fisted a hand in her hair and rolled them both over, reversing their positions. As soon as he took control, he made the most of it, grinding against her clit until she was trembling all over and gasping into his mouth.

"Yes," she breathed, eyes sliding closed as he took her higher. Higher and higher until there was nothing but light and bliss and the heaven of finding where she fit. Just right.

"Come, Hannah," Jackson said, his teeth scraping against her throat. "Come for me, beautiful."

She obeyed with a ragged cry, her inner walls pulsing around him as he gripped her hips and thrust into her clutching heat, stroking into her with deep, languid thrusts that threatened to send her tumbling over a second time. But she clenched her jaw and clung to his shoulders, fighting the second wave, not wanting to go again without his permission. They weren't playing games tonight, but her pleasure still belonged to him.

Every part of you belongs to him. For better or for worse, you're his. Only his.

"I'm yours," she gasped, threading her fingers into his hair. "Yours. God, yes. Please. Please!"

Jackson's tempo grew faster until he was driving inside of her with a wild abandon that let her know how close he was to the edge. "I'm going to come," he said, his voice strained. "Come with me. Come with me."

"Yes," she said, wrapping her legs tighter around his waist as his rhythm faltered. "I'm coming. Right...now."

She groaned as his cock jerked inside of her, the feel of his heat scalding her inner walls sending her spiraling a second time. She clung to him as the waves of bliss swept across her skin again and again, wringing sensation from her body until movement was impossible and she and Jackson lay tangled together on the sweat-damp sheets, his body pinning hers to the mattress as they remembered how to breathe.

He was heavy, but she loved the feel of him relaxed on top of her like this. In the quiet moments after release, Jackson was finally at peace. It didn't last long, but maybe someday it would.

Maybe one night, not too long from now, they would fall asleep with their bodies entwined and wake up in the morning with nothing between them but shared happiness. The road to that place wouldn't be smooth or easy, but right now, with the feel of his heart beating in time with hers making her bones hum with contentment, she believed they could get there.

As Jackson rolled onto his back and drew her into his arms, clearly intending to spend the night, she began to believe a little more. And when he kissed her forehead and said, "Sweet dreams, sunshine," her chest filled with so much hope that her heart ached with a fierce, sweet wanting.

The sins of the past didn't matter. They would find a way to put it all behind them and move on. She was sure of it.

CHAPTER THIRTY-FIVE

Hannah

*H*annah drifted into a sleep more peaceful than any in recent memory and dreamt of an afternoon on the beach with Jackson. They made love in the shade of a palm tree and fed each other slices of pineapple before running into the ocean and making love again amidst the waves.

It was such a lovely dream that she woke up smiling, determined to make her dream a reality.

She rolled over, blinking in the early morning light, a little disappointed to see the rumpled covers beside her empty. But wherever Jackson had gone he would be back. And when he returned, she would talk him into spending the day at the beach with her. It would be like a first date.

The thought made her smile, a goofy grin she was glad Jackson wasn't around to see. She knew he still had his fears and doubts, but after the way they had made love last night, she had a hard time holding on to her own. Still, they would have to move forward slowly, and it was too early in the process for love struck grins and humming on her way to the bathroom.

But as she padded into the bathroom to wash up, she couldn't stop an airy tune from vibrating up her throat to her lips. And when she emerged wrapped in a towel to find her clothes from yesterday freshly washed and laid out on the bed, she let out a blissful sigh, startling Eva, who was depositing her breakfast tray on the table by the window.

"Good morning, Eva," she said, dancing across the room. "Isn't it a beautiful day?"

"Good morning," Eva said with a shy smile. "Mr. Hawke ask for me to bring these special. For you. Special breakfast from him."

"Thank you so much." Hannah glanced down, warmth spreading through her as she realized what was on the tray. On the delicate china plate sat two steaming biscuits, each cut in half and topped with a different kind of cheese.

Cheese biscuits. He'd had her safe word delivered for breakfast.

It was funny, sweet, and weirdly romantic, and she could barely contain the giddy cry of delight threatening to burst from her lips. She was so touched that it took a beat for her to notice the piece of paper with her name written on it tucked beneath the edge of the plate.

It took even longer for her to make sense of the message written inside.

Dear Hannah,

I never thought I'd experience something like last night again. You touched parts of me I was certain no longer existed, but there are other parts that are unreachable, even by a spirit as lovely as yours. That's why I have to leave.

I am not now, nor will I ever be, worthy of your affection. I could try for a hundred years, but I would still fall short of what you deserve. I can't be the man you want me to be. I am incapable of love, but I do care enough about you to do what's right.

Adam will fly me to my destination this morning and return this afternoon to take you home. The remainder of your fee will be deposited in your account by close of business today.

Thank you for your goodness and your forgiveness. Both mean more than you know.

Yours,

Jackson

She read the note through three times before the truth penetrated. When it did, she dropped the paper and spun toward the bed, dropping her towel and pulling on her clothes, heedless of the fact that Eva was still in the room to see her naked.

A glance at the clock on the bedside table said it was only six fifteen. If she hurried, she might be able to catch Jackson before he left. She couldn't let him slip away without a fight, not when they were so close to finding forever.

On some level, he must know they were meant to be or he wouldn't have signed the note the way he did. Subconsciously, he knew that he belonged to her and she belonged to him. Now, she just had to convince the rest of the stubborn man she loved that the last thing he should be doing is running away.

As soon as her hiking boots were tied, Hannah stood and turned to pin Eva with a stern look. "I need to go to Mr. Hawke. Is there someone who can drive me to the airstrip?"

Eva shook her head, but before she could respond a deep voice spoke from the door.

"I'll take her, Mama." The dark-eyed boy who had warned her about Jackson motioned for her to follow him. "They left a few minutes ago. We can catch up if we go now."

Hannah hurried toward the door, skin prickling with relief. "Thank you so much. I promise you won't get in trouble. I won't let him punish you."

"I'm not worried about being punished," the man said, starting down the hallway toward the front of the house. "My name is Dominic."

"Hannah," she said, then shook her head. "I'm sorry, you

know that. I'm just… I'm a little flustered this morning. I can't believe he left like this."

"It might be for the best," Dominic said, slowing as they reached the great room and turning back to face her. His almost black-brown eyes flicked to check the corners of the room before he added in a whisper. "I can have a plane here in an hour to get you out. I've got a pilot waiting on Moorea. All I have to do is make a phone call."

Hannah blinked in surprise, but her mind quickly connected the dots. "You're the one who sent the note saying that you would help me."

Dominic nodded, continuing in a low voice, "I work for your father. He's sent money to help you get resettled. As soon as we're on board the plane, I'll make contact with your aunt. She can meet us at the airport. That will give you about an hour to decide where you want to go next."

"Where to go next," Hannah repeated, her heart beating faster. "You mean where to hide next."

"I can't say for certain, but your enemies might already know where you are," he said, confirming her fears. "And if they do, they will come for you. Soon."

"So Jackson isn't one of them," she said, relief coursing through her when he shook his head. She hadn't thought Jackson was one of the people hunting her family, but it was good to have confirmation of the fact.

"No," Dominic said. "But that doesn't mean he isn't dangerous. The sooner you're away from him, the better."

"Do you know who wants to hurt my family?" she asked, ignoring his advice. "Who are they? And why do they—"

"Who and why doesn't matter. All that matters is that they want you dead." The matter-of-fact way he said the words made them even more chilling. "You and every other heir to your father's fortune and they won't stop until the job is finished."

Hannah shook her head, the need to get to Jackson warring

with her fear. And mistrust. That was there too, bubbling beneath the surface. Dominic was saying all the right things, but he could be lying. He could be a wolf in sheep's clothing, pretending to be her friend until he had her isolated on a plane with nowhere to run.

"How do I know I can trust you?" she asked, eyes narrowing on his face.

"I've worked for your father for almost ten years," he said, proving, if he were telling the truth, that he was much older than he looked. "I've been watching you for the past three years and you never knew I was there. If I'd wanted to hurt you, I could have done so a thousand times. I could have killed you while you were sleeping in your yellow canopy bed or while you hiked by the waterfalls behind your house or when you went to pick lemons with your friends at the grove up the side of the mountain."

Hannah took a step back, his intimate knowledge of her life at the bed and breakfast making her skin crawl. He really had been watching her, but that didn't prove he was one of the good guys, especially considering who he was working for here on the island.

No matter how much she cared about Jackson, or how much she believed he could change, she knew what he was. He was a criminal who had intended to do bad things to her and he had been careful to hire people he could trust not to interfere with his plans. People who wouldn't lift a finger to help her when she screamed for help or begged for mercy and somehow Dominic had found his way onto that list.

"How did you get this job?" she asked. "You and your mother? If she is your mother."

"She is," Dominic said. "But I'm not at liberty to reveal more information."

Hannah smiled, but she was far from amused. "So I'm just supposed to trust a man who's working for an admitted criminal, no questions asked?"

"You trust *him*," he said, gaze hardening. "You're ready to chase down the man who locked you in a cage and beg him to stay with you. You think that's a better idea?"

"You don't miss much, do you?" she muttered, glancing toward the lanai, where she and Jackson had almost had a lovely meal.

But they hadn't. Instead, she'd run from him, he'd pursued her, and she'd spent the next twelve hours swinging from intense hatred of the man to confessing her love for him as their bodies came together in the dark. But between love and hate only one had felt true and now only one decision felt like the right one.

It didn't matter if she was crazy; she had to go to Jackson. She had to see him again and convince him that it wasn't time to say goodbye.

"I'm going to the airstrip to see Jackson, and I'm going alone," she said, turning back to Dominic with her fists balled at her sides, ready to fight him if he tried to stop her. "How do I get there?"

"There's a golf cart parked in the driveway with the keys in the ignition," he said, not seeming surprised by her decision. But then, Dominic didn't seem like the type of person who was surprised by much. "Follow the road until it forks and take a left. You'll see the airstrip about four miles down on your right."

Hannah moved to go but stopped when Dominic called after her—

"Are you going to tell him who I am? If so, I need to get my mother to safety before you get back."

She turned, cocking her head as she studied his guarded expression. "Do you trust my word that much?"

His eyes softened. "I told you. I've been watching you. I know who you are, Hannah. I know you're a good person and that you deserve better than a *canto cabron* who has to hurt his lover to feel like a man."

Hannah frowned but didn't bother contradicting him or trying to explain the way Jackson could make pain feel like pleasure. It was none of Dominic's business and she didn't have time to waste with explanations. Besides, she didn't care what Dominic or anyone else thought of her or Jackson; she only cared about getting to the man she loved before it was too late.

"I won't tell him anything about you or your mother," she said. "I give you my word."

"And I give you mine that I'll do my best to protect you until you're ready to leave," he said. "Let me know when you decide to get out. If I'm not able to help you, I'll find someone who can."

"Well, thank you," she said, backing toward the front door. "I appreciate that."

"I'll do my best, Hannah," he said, his brow furrowing with concern. "But I can't assure your safety here. Watch yourself. If you see something suspicious, run first and ask questions later."

She shivered, the fear in this no-nonsense man's voice bringing the danger she was in home in a visceral way. If she valued her life over all else, she would run now, and figure out a way to reach Jackson once she was safely hidden away.

But she had learned that there were more important things than safety. She would rather spend a year living dangerously with Jackson than another twenty years in hiding, watching the world pass her by.

She was done hiding and waiting for her life to begin. From now on she would fight for what she wanted, no matter what or who stood in her way.

CHAPTER THIRTY-SIX

Jackson

*J*ackson leaned back in the cool leather seat, watching through the jet's window as Adam and the attendant who manned the field's small tower during daylight hours made their way down the tar-streaked pavement, dragging fallen limbs and other debris from the airstrip. The sad state of the runway was costing him precious time, but for once he didn't mind. The delay allowed him to continue to breathe the same air she breathed for a little longer, to spend another twenty minutes replaying every moment of his time with Hannah.

Once the plane took off, he would put her out of his mind and move on, but for now he indulged himself, drifting from one memory to the next, summoning an ache deep in his chest. It was like pushing on a bruise—hurtful, but strangely gratifying. For the first time in years, he was capable of feeling something other than hate. He felt pain, regret, and a sad, hopeless affection for the woman he'd left sleeping so peacefully in the early morning light.

Her face had looked childlike this morning, her features so relaxed it was clear she didn't have a care in the world. And that's why he had to care for her. Leaving was the best—the only—way to do that, but he couldn't help wishing things were different. He wished that he could promise her something other than pain or at the very least have said a proper goodbye.

But he hadn't trusted himself not to weaken. Just the smell of her was enough to make him want to stay. She wouldn't have had to say a word.

For a moment, he thought his memory had conjured up the salt and honey scent of her, sending it drifting through the plane's open door, overpowering the smell of jet fuel and jungle, but then he heard footsteps on the metal stairs leading up to the cabin. A moment later Hannah appeared in the doorway, backlit by the early morning light, her hair wild around her shoulders and her breath coming fast, making him wonder if she'd run all the way here.

He wouldn't put it past her. She was stubborn, determined —a force to be reckoned with. He knew all of that about her. He knew her better than he'd known anyone in years. He also knew that this goodbye was going to be even harder than he'd imagined.

"Tell me you didn't run all the way from the house," he said because he didn't dare say anything else. He couldn't apologize for leaving or give her any reason to believe his resolve was weakening.

"I found a golf cart with the keys in the ignition and I stole it," she said, arms braced on either side of the entrance. "I read your note."

"Then why are you here?" he asked, his tone cool.

"Because that note is bullshit." She stood straighter. "And you know it. I don't need you to protect me from you or anything else. All I need is you. With me. Please, Jackson, I—"

"That's why you nearly drowned yesterday? Because you don't need protection from your own bad ideas?" He turned back to the window. "Go back to the house, Hannah. This is over."

"No, it is not over." She moved to stand in front of him, but he feigned great interest in the work of the men outside. "I love you. And I know you love me, even if you're too scared to admit it."

He glanced up at her, keeping his face fixed in an indifferent mask. "I don't love you; I'm scared for you. But as soon as this plane takes off, I won't be scared of anything. I will cease to think of you and by the end of the month, I doubt I'll remember your name."

Hurt flashed behind her eyes, making him hate himself a little more, but she didn't back away. "You don't mean that. That isn't what you really feel. What about last night, and the note this morning? You admitted that you care."

"I was trying to let you down easy," he lied. "But clearly you're too stubborn to go along with what's best for you."

"Don't do this." Her bottom lip trembled. "Don't pretend to be awful so you can shut me out. I'm strong enough to make my own decisions and I know what I feel for you is real."

"You think you're in love with a man who hate fucked you for a week, Hannah," he said, his voice hard. "You're either out of your mind or have absolutely no sense of self-worth. Whichever it is, you're in no place to make grand declarations and even if you were, I don't want what you have to offer."

"What's that?" she asked, tears filling her eyes. "Love? Passion? Someone who cares about you for exactly who you are? You don't want any of that?"

"Vanilla sex with a vanilla woman." He let his eyes flick up and down her body, affecting disdain for her simple clothing. "I think you know I have more exotic tastes."

"So you want to fuck me like you hate me again?" she asked, a challenge in her tone. "Is that it?"

"I don't want to fuck you at all."

"Now I know you're a liar," she said, reaching for the bottom of her tank top. In seconds, she'd whipped the fabric over her head, baring her gorgeous breasts, which bounced lightly as she unlaced her boots and reached for the close of her shorts.

"Put your shirt on," he said, struggling to keep his eyes from drifting to her nipples, which were pulling tight in the cool air of the cabin. He wanted his mouth on her tits and his cock between her legs, but that wasn't going to happen. Fucking her again would only make this harder.

"You want me, and I want you," she shot back, wiggling her shorts over her full hips and pushing both shorts and panties to the floor. "So why don't you bend me over that desk in the corner?"

She kicked her boots and clothing to the side as she sank to her knees in front of him. "Or maybe you'd rather I take your cock down my throat. All the way in, until I'm choking on you while you fuck my mouth."

Shit. Jackson clenched his jaw, but there was no fighting the sudden surge of blood to his groin.

She leaned in, her hands coming to rest on his knees as she tilted her head back to look up into his eyes. "And don't you dare tell me you don't want any of that because I can see that you do."

Her hand slid toward his crotch, where his cock had become a hard ridge straining the close of his pants, but he stopped her, his fingers wrapping tightly around her wrist.

"Are you sure you want to play?" he asked. "I don't promise to be nice."

"I don't want to play, sir," she countered. "I want you to fuck me."

"Turn around," he said, grinding the words out, fighting the urge to push her onto her back and take her hard and fast. "Face on the ground, ass in the air."

She held his gaze for a moment before she nodded. "Yes, sir."

She turned to assume the position, giving him an excellent view of the swollen lips of her pussy and the cream filling the well between her legs. She was so fucking beautiful, so strong and obedient, demanding and submissive, all at the same time.

"Reach your hands between your knees," he said as he stood, crossing to the desk where the cloths he'd used to blindfold Hannah on the flight in sat curled in the top drawer. "I'm going to bind your wrists and ankles together. And then I'll decide whether I want to fuck your ass or your pussy. Do you remember your safe word?"

"Yes, sir." She shivered as he knelt beside her and began to wind the fabric around her ankles and then her wrists. "I've never done that before, sir."

"Are you afraid?" He finished with the last knot and brought his hands to the mounds of her ass, smoothing his palms across her soft skin before using his thumbs to spread her lips wider, revealing the hard pink nub that strained toward him.

"No, sir," she said. "I know you won't hurt me."

"You don't know that," he said, plunging one thumb into her heat before bringing the slick pad to her clit and rubbing in slow circles, drawing a low moan from her throat. "I could rip you in two. I could make sure you limped off this plane bleeding, wishing you'd never met me."

"You could, sir," she said, arching into his attentions. "But you won't."

"You won't speak again until I tell you to." He reached for his belt buckle with his free hand, jerking the leather free and shoving his pants and boxers down around his thighs as he took his cock in hand. He stroked his already engorged length, suddenly desperate to be inside her. "Spread your legs. Wider, Hannah. Show me every inch of what's mine."

She obeyed, spreading her thighs as wide as she could with her ankles tied together, sending a rush of need surging through him so fierce it made his head spin. By the time the world stopped reeling, his cock was at her entrance and he was shoving into Hannah's pussy, spearing through her swollen walls, feeling her inner muscles clench around him as he sank into her all the way to the hilt.

"I'm going to make you come," he said, bringing his fingers around to tease her clit as he began to thrust in and out. "And when I feel you go, and my cock is slick with your heat, I'm going to take your ass."

Hannah's breath hitched, but she didn't speak. She only squirmed beneath him, welcoming the flicks of his fingers between her legs.

"You aren't to speak until you're given permission, except to say your safe word," he continued, the thought of fucking her in a way no man ever had making his balls ache and his erection swell even thicker. "If I hear your safe word before you come, I'll stop and untie you. If I don't, I'm going to fuck your ass. You'll take every inch of me, even if it hurts."

Her breath rushed out, but she didn't speak. The only response was a gush of heat around his cock that made him ride her harder, fighting the urge to come. She made him want to lose control like no woman ever had.

Which made rising to the challenge of topping her that much more intoxicating.

"You're almost there," he said, fingers flying back and forth across her clit as her inner walls tightened around him. "I want you to tell me when you come. I want you to scream my name and tell me you're coming."

She whimpered, her hips undulating wildly as she sought what she needed to go and he plunged into her again and again, until her pussy was a vice squeezing his cock in two and he knew he could only hold on a few more seconds.

He was about to lose it when she arched beneath him and cried out—

"Jackson, I'm coming!"

With a groan, he pulled out. Smoothing the slickness from her pussy up to her second hole with shaking hands, he got her as wet as he could before giving in to the need screaming through his veins. Fitting his aching cock to her ass he pushed slowly inside until his plump head popped through the tight outer ring into where she was even tighter. So tight he was afraid he was going to hurt her if he tried to move.

"Breathe, Hannah." He groaned, fingers digging into the flesh of her hips as he forced himself to hold still, giving her body time to adjust. "Breathe and relax."

"It burns, sir," she said, her breath coming faster.

"That's because you're fighting me," he said, teasing her with the shallowest of thrusts as he ran one hand back and forth across the small of her back, urging her to let go of the tension tightening her lower body. "Stop fighting and let me in. Just breathe and let me in."

"I don't know if I can," she whispered, her thighs trembling.

"Then use your safe word," he said as he slid a centimeter deeper. "That's what it's for."

"No, sir," she said, her breath rushing out. "I don't want to give up. I want to take you there. I want all of you."

"Then we'll go slow." He reached down, freeing her wrists from the cloth before guiding her onto her side and lying down behind her. "You should be able to relax in this position. Let go, relax every muscle, one by one."

He ran a hand up and down the side of her body, from her ribs to the curve of her hip and down to her thigh. "Start with your jaw. Let it go, let the tension melt and disappear. Now focus on your neck, feel the places where you're tight and give the muscles permission to stop working."

As he talked his way down her body, urging her to relax, muscle by muscle, he smoothed his palm down her stomach and between her legs, finding her clit and applying the barest pressure.

By the time he reached her middle and lower back, she was relaxed enough to allow him to glide into her another two inches. By the time he reached her thighs and knees, her breath was coming faster and his cock was almost all the way in. By the time he talked her ankles and arches into a state of softness, she was mewling softly low in her throat and arching her hips, giving him permission to move.

He slid out and back in again, burying his face in the sweet skin at the back of her neck as he fought for control. "God, I love fucking this ass, Hannah. My ass. Only mine."

"Yours," she echoed. "And you're mine and you're not leaving."

"You're not giving the orders right now, sunshine," he said, punctuating his words with a sharper thrust of his hips, making her yip in surprise. "Your only job is to take me inside you and don't come again until I tell you it's time."

"Yes, sir," she said, spreading her thighs slightly, giving his fingers more room to move.

He welcomed the distraction from how insanely good it felt to be driving in and out of her tightness. He played through her slick folds, teasing her aroused flesh, coaxing her back to the breaking point as he gradually picked up speed. He held on until she was arching into him, her breath coming in frenzied little gasps, and he knew he wouldn't last more than a few seconds.

"Now, baby," he groaned as the dam began to break. "Come for me, sweetness. Now. Now!"

Hannah cried out, coating his hand with fresh wetness as he began to pulse inside her and the world turned upside down the way it always did when he was with her. She fucked the soul from his body, the sense from his head, and left him wanting nothing but more of her. All of her. He wanted to devour her, possess her, and fuck her until she couldn't remember that she'd ever been with any man but him.

Even more frightening, he wanted to stay with her, and forget all the reasons he would never be good enough or gentle enough or man enough for this woman who had given him the greatest gift any person could give: the gift of her entire self, body and soul.

"Sorry," she whispered, pressing his hand to her chest, where her heart thudded heavily against her ribs. "I'm still learning the rules."

"It's all right," he said, his own heart still racing. "But in the future, once we start to play, you follow orders, you don't give them. Save the bossing me around for after I've finished fucking you the way I need to fuck you."

"Okay." She was silent for a moment before she added in a softer voice, "Does that mean you're going to stay?"

He pressed a kiss to the place where her neck became her finely muscled shoulder. She was stronger than her sister in every way, mentally, physically, and emotionally. If there was ever a woman who could survive him, it was Hannah, but he didn't want her to simply survive.

"I want better for you than this. Than me," he confessed, finding it easier to tell the hard truth when she was facing away from him. "I don't know how to love anymore. Maybe I never did. I want you more than I've ever wanted anyone, but I want to possess you, consume you. It's not the same thing."

"I like being possessed and consumed," she said, her fingers playing through the hair on the back of his arm. "If that's all you can give, I'll take it."

"It isn't enough. Eventually, you'll want more."

"Maybe I will, maybe I won't," she said, glancing over her shoulder. "But neither of us will ever know what we want, or how good this could have been if you run away."

He propped up on one arm, staring down into her blue eyes. "How much of yourself are you willing to give up, Hannah? How much are you going to let me take before you draw the line?"

She smiled, seeming sincerely amused by the question. "You don't take anything from me, Jackson. You give me so much. I've never felt more beautiful or powerful or special than I do when I'm with you."

He blinked, surprised though he supposed he shouldn't be. The deeper the game and the more intense the power exchange, the more the lines began to blur. He was the Dominant in their relationship, but only because Hannah was brave enough to abandon control. Power was a two-way street. The more she gave him, the more he was indebted to her and the more she owned him every bit as much as he owned her.

"But I would like some clothes to keep in my room and permission to call my aunt and check in on her," she continued, granting him respite from his heavy thoughts. "And I'd like to know that I don't have to worry about you running away again. At least for a little while."

He lifted his hand, running his knuckles down her cheek to the tip of her chin. "Ten days."

Her eyebrows lifted. "Ten days until…"

"I'll stay ten days," he said. "At the end of that time I reserve the right to renegotiate."

Her lips quirked, but her eyes remained serious. "All right. Ten days sounds fair. Any thoughts on clothes and phone calls?"

"I have clothes for you," he said. "You can have them when we get back to the house and you can call your aunt whenever you wish. There's a phone in the kitchen and in my bedroom, where you're welcome anytime."

"That sounds nice." Hannah sighed happily. "I like being welcome in your bedroom."

"You're welcome anywhere in the house," he said. "The business portion of our relationship has concluded. From now on, consider yourself my guest."

She wrinkled her nose. "That sounds awfully formal."

"My friend, then," he amended softly. "With benefits."

She smiled. "And rules? Can we make a list of those? I'd

like to avoid making any more newbie mistakes if I can manage it."

"No rules outside the bedroom. I'm not a full-time Dominant," he added, smoothing a hand down her thigh. "I like control when we're naked. The rest of the time, you're free to do as you please."

"Free to boss you around?" she teased.

"You can try," he said with a gentle swat on her butt cheek. "But I'm nearly as pig-headed as you are. Expect to have your work cut out for you, sunshine."

"I'm not afraid of hard work," she said, pressing a kiss to his chest that melted something deep inside of him. "But I would like a shower before any more bossing around. The events of this morning have left me feeling adventurous, but also—"

"Like you had a cock up your ass?"

She laughed as a flush crept across her cheeks. "Yes, Jackson. Exactly like that. How did you know?"

"I have a sixth sense when it comes to your body," he said with a wink. "Are you sore? I've got ibuprofen in my suitcase. I can have Adam fetch it before we get back into the car."

She shook her head, her smile fading. "No, I'm not. You were very gentle and patient, the way I knew you would be."

"Smug doesn't look good on you," he lied.

Lying next to him with her skin dewy from making love and her eyes glowing, she was the most beautiful thing he'd ever seen. And she was his, at least for the next ten days.

He knew he should be ashamed of himself for weakening, but he couldn't seem to feel anything but relief. It wasn't until he had given himself permission to stay that he'd realized how miserable he'd been to leave her.

"Then I'll try to keep the smug to a minimum," she said, brow furrowing. "How about smug on Saturdays until noon and every other Tuesday?"

He leaned down, capturing her lips for a long, slow kiss

because she was simply too cute to resist. "Get dressed," he whispered against her mouth. "I'll tell Adam there's been a change of plans."

"All right," she said, then added in a soft voice. "Thank you for staying."

"Hopefully you'll still be thanking me in ten days," he said as he stood, adjusting his pants.

"I hope that too," she said. "Very much."

CHAPTER THIRTY-SEVEN

Hannah

*B*ack at the house, Jackson put Adam to work alerting the staff to the change of plans while they retreated to their separate bedrooms to clean up. Hannah was disappointed that Jackson didn't consider joining her in the large shower in her room, but she didn't show it.

He'd come a long way in a single morning, but he was still far from embracing their new relationship with open arms. She wasn't surprised when he elected to keep his distance for a little while and when it was Eva, not Jackson, who brought a small stack of clothes with the tags still attached to her room after she emerged from her shower.

As she spread the dresses and sports clothes out onto the bed, Hannah tried to catch Eva's eye—wondering if she'd spoken to her son and if she too was working for Hannah's father—but the cook kept her gaze on the floor and retreated as soon as Hannah assured her that she had everything she needed. Dismissing the mystery of Dominic and her family's enemies from her mind for the time being, Hannah slipped into a black and white striped, two-piece bathing suit that made her look like a 1940s pin-up and a semi-sheer black gauze cover-up with embroidery on both sleeves and went in search of breakfast.

It felt strange to leave her room without permission and even stranger to pad barefoot around the empty kitchen, opening drawers and cupboards and otherwise making herself at home. But by the time the oatmeal was simmering on the stovetop and she'd chopped up fruit and almonds for topping, she was beginning to relax. Giving the bubbling pot one last check to make sure the heat wasn't too high, she crossed to the phone on the counter.

A few seconds later, Sybil's voice crackled to life on the other end of the line. "The Mahana Guesthouse. How may I help you?"

"It's me, Syb," Hannah said, her throat tight with emotion. It felt like ages since she'd heard Sybil's voice and so much had happened since she'd said goodbye, none of which she could tell Sybil about. "The phone was installed this morning so I wanted to call and check in."

"Hannah! Sweetheart, it's so good to hear from you." Sybil's smile was practically audible, and Hannah could imagine the way her aunt's kind eyes were crinkling with plea-sure. "I know you said you might not be able to call, but I was still worried. Are you enjoying the job? Is the family nice?"

"Yes, I am, and yes, the family is very nice," she said, only feeling the faintest twinge of guilt as the lie slipped from her lips.

She'd told her aunt that she was going to be working as a nanny for a wealthy family while they spent a month deco-rating their new home on a private island. It had seemed like the kindest choice at the time—if Sybil knew her niece had sold her body to save their home she would be devastated—and it seemed the best choice now. At least until she and Jackson decided that their relationship was going to last for longer than the next ten days.

"So when do I see you?" Sybil asked. "Are you still staying the entire month?"

"Actually, the remodel is going better than expected. I might only be another ten days. I'll let you know when the plans are firm," Hannah said. "So tell me all the news. Have you been able to find anyone to start on the repairs?"

"I have," Sybil said. "Hiro's been an amazing help. We found a father and son team to work on framing the new cottages and I got a bid from the roofers on the other side of the island that's half what our old company quoted. Hiro says they do extraordinary work."

"That's great. I'm glad he's been there to help out," Hannah said, stomach souring at the way her aunt's voice caressed the pearl farmer's name. Before Hannah had learned that Hiro had been Jackson's spy, she'd encouraged her aunt to think about something more than friendship with the man, but now...

"Just be careful, okay," she added. "Hiro seems great, but we really don't know him that well. Sometimes there are ulterior motives with these kinds of deals, and the trusting third party loses out in the end."

"Oh, I doubt it, Hannah," Sybil said before adding in a softer voice. "And I know Hiro much better than I did. We've been seeing each other. Romantically."

Hannah winced as her fears were confirmed. "Really? And it's been...good?"

"It's been wonderful," Sybil gushed. "He's such a gentleman and so kind and thoughtful. You were right. I should have given him a chance a long time ago."

"That's great, Syb," Hannah said, grateful for the hiss of the stove as the oatmeal pot threatened to overflow. "I'm about to burn the kids' breakfast, so I've got to go, but I'll call soon. Take care of yourself, okay?"

"You too, darling," Sybil said. "And call me soon."

Hannah promised to call tomorrow and hung up the

phone. She reached the oatmeal pot in time to rescue it from bubbling over and stood scowling at the stove, wishing she'd said something more pointed to her aunt.

She'd promised not to tell Jackson about Dominic, but she hadn't promised to keep secrets from her aunt. Still, there was a chance that Jackson had tapped the phone. It seemed a little paranoid, but he *was* a criminal used to watching his back and a control freak to boot.

And that's the man you want to live happily ever after with, Hannah. A criminal who you can bet wouldn't like learning that you're keeping secrets from him.

Especially a secret like a man in his employ secretly working for someone else.

"You should have asked Eva to make that for you."

Being careful to keep her thoughts from showing on her face, Hannah looked up to see Jackson standing in the doorway to the kitchen.

CHAPTER THIRTY-EIGHT

Hannah

*G*od, he was beautiful, sexier than any man she'd ever met or imagined. In gray suit pants and a white linen shirt that emphasized the bronze of his skin, he looked more like a businessman than a criminal, not to mention good enough to eat.

She smiled, refusing to let stress of any kind ruin their first semi-normal day together. "No, I shouldn't have. I'm perfectly capable of making oatmeal on my own."

"I'm sure you are." He moved to stand on the other side of the island, facing her across the stove. "But I don't want you to have to do anything that makes you frown."

"I wasn't frowning because of the oatmeal," she said as she turned off the burner and pulled the pot away from the heat. "I was just thinking."

"Always a dangerous thing." He held her gaze, his dark eyes boring a hole through her skin and straight into her soul, making her certain he could read her thoughts. "What were you thinking about?"

"Your job," she said, impulsively. It was at least partly the truth and she didn't like keeping secrets from Jackson if she didn't have to. "I was thinking about how dangerous it must be. It worries me."

"You don't have to worry. I know what I'm doing." He threaded his hands together into a fist as he leaned his forearms on the counter. "But I've decided to take some time away from my work. There's nothing that can't keep until after the holidays and I figure I have enough on my plate at the moment."

Hannah glanced up from the pot, her spoon stilling. "You mean me?"

"I mean you," he confirmed, sending a shiver of awareness across her skin. "I find you take up an inordinate amount of my focus."

She fought a smile. "Well...good."

His eyes narrowed even as his mouth curved. "I thought you were only doing smug on Saturdays and Tuesdays."

"Isn't it Saturday?" she asked, deciding she enjoyed flirting with Jackson almost as much as she enjoyed being naked with the man.

"Thursday."

"Oh, well then. Sorry about that." She lifted one shoulder and let it fall. "Guess my focus has been off, too. I seem to have lost all track of time. Do you want some oatmeal? I have almonds and fruit to put on top."

"Sounds good," he said. "Thank you."

She turned back to the cupboards, chuckling softly to herself as she fetched two bowls.

"What's funny?" he asked when she returned to the stove.

"Nothing," she said, still grinning. "You're just cute when you do normal things like say thank you for your oatmeal."

"I wasn't raised in a barn, either, you know," he said, sliding onto a stool on the other side of the island. "And I'm not cute. Ever."

"I have to disagree, Mr. Hawke." She sprinkled chopped

almonds, berries, and pineapple on his oatmeal before placing the bowl and the honey pot in front of him. "There are times when you are adorable."

His smile faded. "And there are times when I'm a nightmare. Don't forget those, Hannah."

"I won't," she said, keeping her tone light. "But it's too early for Broody McScary to come out to play. So be sweet and eat your oatmeal and then we can decide what to do with the rest of the day."

He arched one brow. "You do have a bossy side."

"I know," she said with a wink. "I never claimed to be submissive all the time, either, you know."

He studied her as he reached for his spoon. "I wonder if you're a switch."

"A switch?" She frowned. "What does that mean?"

"A submissive who enjoys taking her turn as the Dominant or vice versa."

She frowned. "I don't know, but I don't think so. I don't like the idea of tying you up." She took a bite, humming beneath her breath as she added more honey to her bowl. "No, I take that back. I do like the idea of tying you up, but not for sexual reasons. Just when you make me angry. There are times when you'd be more manageable tied up."

"And times when I more than earn a spanking?" he asked, eyes sparkling.

"Of course." She licked honey off the tip of her spoon, not missing the way Jackson's eyes followed her tongue. "But that wouldn't be sexual either. In a bedroom situation, I prefer to be the one being spanked."

"And I prefer spanking you," he said, his voice husky.

"So maybe I shouldn't follow the rules all the time," she said, hips swaying back and forth as she leaned her palms onto the counter. "I do enjoy being punished now and then."

"Eat your oatmeal," he said, the intensity in his gaze making her blood rush faster. "Or you'll be eating it cold."

"Why's that?" she asked though she already knew exactly what was going through his head. There were times when Jackson was a mystery, but there were also times like these when she swore she could read every thought flitting through his beautifully dirty mind.

"Because if I hear one more word out of that pretty mouth, I'm going to have you for breakfast."

Hannah's tongue slipped out to dampen her lips before she whispered, "One word."

Jackson's spoon clattered into his bowl. A moment later he was around the island, pulling her into his arms as he lifted her onto the counter and reached beneath her cover up. As soon as her swimsuit bottom hit the floor, he knelt between her legs, his lips finding where she was already wet and his wicked tongue working its magic. He brought her over twice—once without honey and a second time after drizzling a sticky spoonful across her clit and licking her clean—before he stood and reached for the close of his pants.

"You should put on swim trunks," she panted, hands shaking as she helped push his boxer briefs over the firm mounds of his ass. "Easier access."

"You should stop making me want to fuck you every ten minutes."

Her response died on her lips, becoming a moan of satisfaction as Jackson's cock drove inside her, pushing through her already pulsing flesh. Cupping her buttocks in his big hands, he rode her hard and fast, the urgency in his thrusts making it clear how much it had turned him on to bring her pleasure.

"Yes, Jackson," she said, gasping as he shoved deeper. "God, yes."

"Come for me again," he growled as he claimed her mouth, sending the taste of her own salty heat rushing through her mouth as he kissed her. "Come for me, sunshine."

She obeyed with a ragged cry, her pussy contracting with an intensity that was almost painful. She wasn't sure her body was built to withstand three orgasms in such rapid succession, but she wasn't about to complain, not when she was flooded with such mind-numbing bliss.

Jackson pulled out this time, groaning into her mouth as he pressed his cock between them and came on the fabric of the cover up bunched at her waist. She would have to change again, but who cared?

Not her. She didn't care a bit about cold oatmeal or changing clothes or anything but how perfect it felt to be wrapped in Jackson's arms, catching her breath as they both drifted back to earth.

"Looks like you were right about the timing," he said, kissing her forehead. "I'll have Adam pick up supplies for you when he goes to the market this afternoon."

Hannah's brow furrowed until she glanced down and saw the blood on Jackson's still semi-erect length. "Oh my God," she said, embarrassment rushing through her. "I'm so sorry. I knew it was close to time, but I—"

"Why are you sorry?" he asked, reaching for the dishtowel beside the stove. "There's no reason to be sorry."

"I'm sorry because it's gross," she said, blushing as he cleaned himself and began to wipe away the red smears on her thighs.

"It's not gross. It's part of you and no part of you is gross."

Hannah's lips parted, but before she could think of how to respond to something so sweet, Jackson continued.

"It also means that we've dodged a bullet. If we don't want to use condoms we need to figure out an alternative soon." He knelt down, plucking her swimsuit bottom from the floor and dropping it into her hands. "Maybe an IUD? I can find a doctor to make a house call if you think that's a good option."

She nodded as she eased off the counter, suddenly feeling shy. "That would probably be best. Birth control pills would take too long to work, so...yeah. Let's do that."

He studied her face before asking in a softer voice, "Are you all right?"

"I'm fine," she said, stepping into her suit. "Just a little embarrassed."

"Don't be embarrassed." He squeezed her shoulder gently. "I'm a grown man. I stopped being bothered by things like this a decade ago."

"I believe you," she said with a nervous shrug. "I don't know. I guess it's the birth control talk, too. It makes this seem so much more real."

"I thought that's what you wanted?"

She lifted her gaze. "It is, but that doesn't mean it's not scary." One side of her mouth lifted in a crooked grin. "You're like fire, Jackson. Beautiful, but a little intimidating to get close to."

"I understand." His thumb brushed across her bottom lip. "I feel the same way about you."

"I'm not intimidating," she said with a breathy laugh. Her skin prickled in response to his touch, her body already wanting him again. She felt like she would never get enough of him, not even if their ten days turned into ten thousand.

"No, you're terrifying," he said. "Like a tropical storm, coming to sweep away everything I've worked to build."

"Well, you can always rebuild," she said, strangely flattered by the comparison. "Start fresh from the ground up."

"Maybe I could," he said thoughtfully.

"I called my aunt," Hannah said, sensing that they both needed a change of subject. "She already has a team in place to frame the new cottages."

His hand dropped from her face. "Good. I'm glad she was able to find someone. I know skilled workers can be in short supply on the islands."

As they washed up and ate their now-cold oatmeal, they continued to chat about safer topics, but Hannah's mind was never far from Jackson's words.

Maybe she was his tropical storm. But maybe a tropical storm was what he needed in order to have a shot at turning his life around.

CHAPTER THIRTY-NINE

Jackson

Six Days Later

*B*ack when Jackson had been on active duty in the Marines, there never seemed to be enough time. He was always busy with work and when he wasn't, he was playing as hard as he could, determined to live hard and go to his grave with no regrets.

But since his time in prison, he'd lost awareness of the passage of time. Fueled by rage and obsession, months had faded into years without any change of heart or mind to mark them. Still if anyone had asked, he would have said his days were full. But by the start of his seventh day of his new beginning with Hannah, he had realized that before he'd met her, time had been standing still.

With her, hours were devoured in an instant, a day here and gone in the blink of an eye. It seemed he'd just awoken with her in his arms and already it was dusk and they were wandering along the beach in the sunset light, talking about their plans for tomorrow.

He'd heard that time flew when you were having fun, but it

had been so long since he'd experienced anything even close to "fun" that it took a few days for him to recognize the light, pleasantly expectant feeling that filled him when he woke up each morning. Finally, sometime between picking oranges in the grove with Hannah Saturday afternoon and going for a morning sail around the island Monday morning, it hit him that he was having fun.

Simply sharing a day with her was enough to make it feel like he was on a permanent vacation from the evil in the world, and there was always something to look forward to. There was another moment in her company, another smile, another brush of her lips against his, and the touch of her hand reaching for him between cool sheets.

By Wednesday morning, he already knew he was going to need more than ten days. If time kept flying by at this rate, he might need a hundred.

It was a sobering thought, and one that made him keep to himself more than he had since the morning Hannah pulled him off the plane. He ate breakfast alone in his room and worked on answering email and paying bills until nearly ten o'clock. When he finally emerged, Hannah was nowhere to be found, but there was a note on the kitchen counter saying that she'd gone to the beach and that if he wanted to he should come join her.

Of course he wanted to. All he wanted was to be with her, but taking too much time off from work could wreck his business. If he was out of the loop for an extended period of time, his connections would find new places to buy and sell their weapons, and he would be out of a job. He had a good amount of money stored away, but not enough to continue living the way he had for the past several years.

But you don't have to live that way anymore. Harley's dead. You can let the detectives go, call off the hunt, and start thinking about what you want to do with what's left of your life.

As Jackson stepped outside and started down the road to the beach, he began to imagine again what it might be like to let go, to let Hurricane Hannah finish destroying the man he had been and see what sort of creature would arise from the ashes. Maybe it wouldn't be a monster or a man who felt uneasy when a day passed more perfectly than expected.

Maybe it would be someone new, someone who would know how to take proper care of the beautiful woman rocking back and forth in the hammock in front of him, so absorbed in her book she didn't notice him until he leaned against the palm tree near her feet.

"Oh my God," she said, flinching so hard her book tumbled to the ground as she started laughing. "You scared me. I was just getting to the good part."

He knelt, picking up her paperback and shaking the sand off before glancing at the cover. "Another murder mystery?"

"Adam bought it for me yesterday when he was in Moorea." She scooted back on the hammock and drew her legs into her chest. "I don't know why I'm so addicted to them. I usually prefer something with a happy ending and a lower body count."

He returned the novel before easing into the hammock across from her and holding the netted rope out to one side to make room for her legs. Closing the book she stretched out, curling her toes beneath his ribs. Despite the warmth of the day, he could feel her chilled skin through his tee shirt.

But then, her toes were always cold. It was one of the many things he'd learned about Hannah since he'd become incapable of thinking about anything else for more than a few minutes at a time.

"Maybe my dark side is rubbing off on you," he said, capturing one of her feet and warming it between his hands.

She smiled. "I don't think so. It's the puzzle aspect that's appealing. I have a few puzzles I'd like to solve." Her smile faded. Her toes wiggled against his palm before she added in a softer voice, "That's why I've decided to tell you my last name."

His hands stilled, but before he could decide whether he wanted the information she was offering, she pushed on—

"It's Mason. My father is Stewart Mason. He won a senate seat in North Carolina a few years ago so you might have heard of him."

"The name's familiar," he said, his throat dry despite the coconut water he'd downed with breakfast. "Your family is wealthy."

"Very," Hannah said bluntly. "My mother's family had more money than God and my father's side made hers look two steps from the poor house." She smiled, but it didn't reach her eyes. "*Fortune 500* magazine covered their wedding. An aerial shot of the estate where I grew up made the cover."

Jackson grunted as he dug his thumb into the arch of her foot, massaging her instep. There went his theory that Harley had grown up on the wrong side of the tracks and been forced into what she'd done. An heiress wasn't the kind of person who was easily pushed around; she was more the kind to do the pushing.

"That's all you're going to say?" Hannah prodded his ribs with her free toes. "Ugh?"

"So you've decided I'm not crazy?" he asked, lifting his gaze to hers. "Or at least not too crazy to trust with your secret?"

"No, I don't think you're crazy." Hannah cocked her head, shooting him a wry look. "You've been very well behaved the past week."

"Not the entire week," he said, lifting her foot to his mouth and biting her big toe, making her squeal.

"Stop it." She tried to tug her leg away, but he held on tight. "I'm serious, Jackson, that's disgusting. Feet don't belong in your mouth."

"I put all your other parts in my mouth," he said, biting her little toe right where the flesh peaked in the center. "Some much more exotic than your sweet little toes."

She flushed. "I don't walk on the dirty ground with any of those parts."

"Is this a hard limit?" he asked, his mouth hovering above an as-yet-unbitten toe. "If it is, you should let me know now."

After a moment she shook her head, her breath rushing out with a sigh. "No, it's not. What are you going to do?"

"If it's not a hard limit? I'm going to keep biting your toes."

"Not about that," she said, refusing to let him off the hook. "About the other. What are you going to do now that you know Harley's last name?"

"I don't know," he said honestly. "Now that I know she's really gone…"

He brought Hannah's foot back to rest on his chest and wrapped his hands around her toned calf, simply because it felt good to touch her. "Even if she were alive, I'm not sure I'd know what to do. I won't lie, I would still want to hurt her. But I wouldn't want to hurt you in the process."

Hannah sat up and leaned in to place her hands gently over his. "If she were still alive, I'd make sure she paid for what she did to you myself."

His lips curved. "I believe you would."

"I'm not joking," Hannah insisted. "I'm very fierce when it comes to the people I love."

Jackson held her fathomless gaze and slowly forgot how to breathe. It wasn't the first time she'd said it, but it was the first time in the past few days. The first time since he'd started to feel incomplete when he wasn't within touching distance of this woman who affected him like no other.

The first time since he'd begun to suspect that maybe his heart wasn't twisted beyond repair.

"I…" He swallowed the words before they could find their

way out into the air. It was too soon. Once those words were out, there would be no going back and he didn't trust himself to make promises. Not yet. "I was wondering if you'd stay a little longer," he said, hoping he'd covered the awkward moment.

Hannah's eyebrows lifted. "But we're not at the end of the ten days."

"I don't need the full ten days to know that I want more," he said, loving the obvious pleasure that bloomed on her face. "Would you stay and spend the holidays with me? I called my associate who owns the island. It's available through January second if you're free to stay."

"Yes," she said, her megawatt grin fading only a watt or two when she added, "though I might need to fly home for Christmas Day to visit Sybil. We've never been apart on Christmas."

"She could come here," he said. "I'm sure Eva could make something appropriate for a celebration."

"No way. I could make something and Sybil could help. The staff should have the holiday off." Hannah hesitated, doubt creeping into her shining eyes. "But do you really mean it? You'd be okay with her coming here? Meeting you and finding out about...us?"

Us. Even a few days ago he would have told her there was no such thing as "us", but now...

"Assuming we can come to an agreement about how to label the relationship before she arrives, then yes. I'd like to meet her. And I promise to be on my best behavior."

Before he realized she was moving, Hannah's mouth was on his. He returned the kiss, humming appreciatively as the salt and honey taste of her filled his mouth.

"What was that for?" he asked when they came up for air, both of them breathing faster.

"For you. For this." She settled on top of him, setting the hammock to swaying gently. "For making me happy."

"You make me happy, too." He ran his palms down her spine to cup her ass. "Thank you for telling me about your family. I won't betray your trust."

"I know you won't," she said with a confidence that touched him. "You have your bad points, but you're not a betrayer."

"What bad points?" he asked as he silently wondered if she were right. He'd been a smuggler for years, but he'd never cheated a contact or double-crossed a connection. He played rough, but he played fair.

Maybe Hannah saw that. Maybe she saw him more clearly than he gave her credit for—his good points as well as his bad ones.

"You're stubborn as a mule and twice as nasty when your temper's up," she said, finger drifting slowly down his throat. "But you're slow to anger so the temper is bearable. And the stubborn part I'm willing to forgive since I suffer from a similar condition."

He smiled. "Pig-headed-itis."

"Something like that," she said, kissing her way down the trail she'd drawn with her finger. "Your skin tastes so good."

"Not as good as yours." His fingers slipped beneath the band of her swimsuit bottoms, tracing the curve of her ass cheek. "Have you ever had sex in a hammock?"

She laughed, her breath warm on his throat. "No. And I don't think we should try. We'll tip over and kill ourselves."

"No, we won't," he said, tugging her swimsuit lower on her thighs. "I won't let you fall."

"You can't promise things like that," Hannah whispered. "Some things are beyond your control. Like gravity. And my klutzy side."

"You're not a klutz." He slid one finger into her slickness. "You're unspeakably elegant. Help me get these off."

"I think you may be seeing me through rose-colored glasses," she said, but she shifted to one side, allowing him to pull her bottoms down to her ankles and toss them away.

"I see you as you are," he said, opening the Velcro at the front of his trunks, freeing his erection. "Beautiful." He gripped her thighs, urging her to move, spreading her slickness along his shaft. "Sweet." He reached between them, parting the lips of her sex. "And sexy as hell."

He drew her down, impaling her on his cock, groaning as her body fought to slow him down. She was wet, but she wasn't completely ready to take him. In the past week, they'd discovered a mutual love of this moment, the initial erotic battle as he demanded entrance and her pussy struggled to adapt, and then the sudden bliss as a gush of slickness eased his way and tension became sweet friction.

It was one of the many things he'd learned about Hannah. And now, he knew her last name.

But he wasn't thinking about that as he fucked her in the hammock, making her come twice before he shot himself inside her clutching heat. He wasn't thinking about family history when they washed the stickiness from their lovemaking away in the ocean and spent the next hour floating in and out on the waves. And during their lunch on the lanai and walk through the woods after, all he was thinking about was how much he enjoyed her company.

It wasn't until after dinner, when they were settled on the couch reading—a history of Tahiti for him and the murder mystery for her—and Hannah fell asleep in his lap, that he began to think about the Masons. He sat watching her sleep, wondering how a family who had raised the extraordinary human being drooling on his leg could have also created a monster. He wondered and wondered until the wondering compelled him to pick up his phone and type a quick text to the detective he still had on retainer.

Harley Mason was the daughter of Stewart Mason. Find out everything you can.

Later, he would look back on that moment and wonder what would have happened if he'd resisted temptation, if he'd allowed his love for Hannah to be stronger than his morbid obsession with her sister. But at the moment, he hadn't admitted that what he felt was love or realized how easy it would be to lose the precious thing he'd found.

CHAPTER FORTY

Hannah

Three Weeks Later

What did a woman buy for her Dominant lover for Christmas?

Jackson had told her that Adam would pick up anything she ordered at a postage box near the airport the same morning he flew to pick up Sybil for their Christmas Eve celebration. But faced with an Internet filled with holiday offerings, she kept coming up empty.

A collar seemed too over the top, a paddle too blatant, and the tiny diamond earrings that spelled "His" too presumptuous. She *was* his, but he had yet to stake a formal claim. They'd agreed to tell her aunt that he was related to the family she'd worked for and that they'd started dating during his visit to the island and decided to stay on for a few extra weeks of personal time after the rest of the family returned home.

It was a decent story, but one that could create problems down the line.

What if she and Jackson decided to settle down? Wouldn't Sybil wonder, sooner or later, why his sister and her children never came to visit?

Of course, she hadn't mentioned her concerns to Jackson. It would only scare him and he would withdraw into one of his moods, hiding out in his bedroom until noon, wasting half a precious day they could have spent together.

"For a Dominant man, he's very delicate," she mumbled to the laptop, smiling when a grunt sounded from the other side of the bed.

"I'm reading," Jackson said dryly. "I haven't gone deaf."

"You *are* delicate," she said, wrinkling her nose in frustration "And very difficult to buy for. Can't you give me some idea of what you want?"

"I already have what I want." He pulled the laptop off of her thighs, clicking it closed before setting it on the bedside table with his book on top. "All I want for Christmas is you, wearing nothing but a bow tying your hands behind your back. Preferably, you'll be bent over the end of the bed Christmas morning, waiting for me to wake up and redden your pretty ass."

She grinned, pulse spiking as he rolled on top of her. "But I've been so good. You have no reason to spank me."

"I'm sure I can come up with something," he mumbled into her neck as he kneed her legs apart. "Pull down your shirt. I want your nipples in my mouth."

Hannah hesitated for a moment before deciding she didn't want to wait for Christmas Day for her spanking. Sybil would be in the house then and she didn't trust herself not to make sounds that would carry to the guest bedroom. Besides, she and Jackson hadn't played in several days. Sex was amazing with him, no matter what, but she still craved the game.

"No," she said, deliberately omitting the honorific. "I don't feel like being kissed there tonight."

He arched a brow. "Who said I was going to kiss you? Maybe I planned to bite, instead."

She shivered, arousal spiking at she imagined what it

would feel like to have his teeth on her sensitive tips. "I don't want to be bitten either."

"Then what do you want, sunshine?" He dropped his hips, pressing his erection between her legs so tight she could feel his cock pulse through her thin satin panties and his pajama pants. "Do you want me to remind you why your pleasure belongs to me?"

She nodded slowly, holding his dark gaze as currents of anticipation zipped back and forth between them, charging the air.

"Because it does. Your pleasure and your pain. They both belong to me." His fingers slipped into her hair, the touch gentle until suddenly it wasn't anymore.

She gasped as his hand fisted tightly at her scalp. Before she could say, "Yes, sir," he was off the bed, dragging her with him. It didn't hurt—he had too large a handful of her hair for there to be any strands torn from her scalp—but it made her keenly aware of how strong he was, how powerful, and how easily he could bend her will to his, with or without her permission.

But her permission was what made it hot, not scary, when he opened the sliding door, propelled them both across the patio, and tossed her onto the grass in the darkened garden. She fell onto her hands and knees, but before she could even think about crawling away, he was in front of her, shoving his pajama pants low on his hips, baring his cock. It bobbed free—long, thick, intimidating, and so gorgeous her mouth watered for a taste of him.

She sat back on her heels, anticipating being told to open her mouth and take him down her throat. Instead, he fisted the base of his length in his hand, guiding his pulsing erection down one side of her face and then the other. His skin was burning hot against her cheek and so soft all she wanted to do was kiss him. She wanted to lick the pre-cum from the tip of his shaft and suckle his plump head into her mouth, but she stayed still, nerves sizzling as she waited to see what he had planned for her.

"Have you ever had a man come on your face, Hannah?"

"No, sir," she said, heat rushing onto her panties at the thought.

"What about your tits? Have you had a man shoot his cum on your tits?" he asked, leaning down far enough to grab the top of her black camisole with his free hand. A second later, he jerked hard on the fabric, tearing it in two.

Hannah swayed on her knees, fear and arousal rocketing through her as her breasts were freed to the night air. Her logical mind knew this was the game, but her primitive mind insisted any man who would rip away her clothes with such violence was dangerous.

The result of the war between the two sides of herself was lust so intense her pussy began to pulse like a second heart, thudding between her thighs.

"Answer me, Hannah," Jackson said. "Don't make me wait."

"Y-yes, sir," she stammered. "You did. That first day. You came on my tits."

"I'm the only one?" He cupped her breast in his hand, his thumb tracing the outer edge of her nipple, close enough to make her ache for contact, but not close enough to trigger sensation.

"Yes, sir," she said, arching into his touch. He answered her unspoken plea by slapping her breast hard enough to set it bobbing back and forth and to send a sting of pleasure-pain coursing across her skin.

"You don't make demands," he said. "Not even silent ones. You aren't in charge. The only thing you control is your safe word and whether or not you say it. Now turn around and present your ass."

She hurried to obey, swallowing a bleat of surprise when Jackson reached down, tearing her panties in half before she'd made it all the way onto her forearms. She bit her lip, fighting the urge to press her thighs together. He would know she was seeking relief from the desire making her clit swell and her pussy slick and he wouldn't be pleased.

"If you're obedient, you will be rewarded with release," Jackson said in a low voice as he knelt behind her. "If you are not, I will come and you will spend the rest of the night with your hands tied to the headboard, wishing you could get a finger between your legs, sobbing because you so desperately need to get off. Do you understand?"

"Yes, sir," Hannah said, muscles tightening as his palms settled on her ass, warming the skin.

"Good." He stroked her flesh with a gentleness that sent her fear spiraling higher. A soft start didn't mean anything. She knew that from the last time he'd reddened her ass. "Now I'm going to show you what happens when you forget who you belong to."

Before she could properly brace herself, he'd delivered two sharp swats to the insides of her thighs. The speed and the unexpected location made her flinch in surprise. Surprise that he could move so quickly, and surprise that being spanked on her thighs was even more arousing than on her ass. He slapped her again in the same places, the stinging sensation seeming to flow directly up her leg to coil around her entrance, making her body burn.

But not with pain, with longing.

By the time Jackson had reddened her thighs and moved on to her ass, Hannah was trembling all over, her pussy so swollen and wet her arousal had begun to run down the inside of her legs. Slowly, as his rhythm grew faster and the blows harder, the need building in her core became the center of her world.

She was no longer Hannah or even a woman kneeling before a man, she was a hurting, aching, frantic void. She was a stinging, grieving, exposed nerve so desperate for contact, for relief, that tears ran down her cheeks. By the time Jackson told her to start counting to fifty, her throat was so tight with misery and wanting she could barely force out the words, but she did.

It was almost over. God, *surely* it was almost over.

She couldn't take much more. She was so near the edge her voice sounded foreign to her ears, a strained, high-pitched yelp that echoed through the garden, scaring all the other night creatures away.

"Keep counting," Jackson demanded as his hand continued to torment her flaming cheeks, his blows coming so fast she could barely keep up.

But she did and finally, when she cried out, "Fifty!" Jackson delivered her promised reward. He gripped her hips and positioned his cock, telling her to come at the same moment as he drove inside her.

And come, she did. Her pussy began to contract before he'd rammed home the first time and kept clenching and releasing, clenching and releasing, as he fucked her so hard his hips slammed into her ass, making it feel like the spanking continued. She came until her entire body was in the midst of one long, never-ending orgasm, until her abdominal muscles ached and her lips went numb and her limbs dissolved into boneless appendages too weak to hold her upright.

By the time pleasure was finally finished with her and she came back to her body, Jackson was carrying her into the bedroom and laying her on the bed. She sniffed hard, reaching up to swipe the tears from her cheeks, but he captured her hand and laid it gently on her stomach.

"Let me," he said, reaching for a tissue from the bedside table. He dabbed her tear-streaked cheeks and upper lip before positioning the tissue beneath her nose and ordering her to, "Blow."

And so she blew, her mind still so deep in the scene she

didn't consider disobeying him. It was only after he'd wiped her nose that she flushed with embarrassment.

"I can blow my own nose," she said, her voice thick and rough.

"Not right now you can't," he said, grabbing another tissue. "Right now I'm taking care of you. Blow."

She blew, studying his expression as he continued to clean her face. He looked so relaxed and happy, the skin around his eyes no longer pinched and his full mouth resting in a lightly curved position.

"If it makes you this happy to blow my nose, you can do it all the time."

His smile widened. "It's you who make me happy." He cupped her face in his hand, staring deep into her eyes. "Do you know how perfect you are?"

She blinked, emotion making her throat tight though she wasn't sure why. "I don't know."

"It's okay to cry," he said softly. "After an intense scene a lot of feelings can come up. And when that happens, you'll need after care from me and kindness from yourself."

"After care?" Her brow furrowed.

"It's when I help you transition out of the scene. No more power exchange, no more game, just me telling you how beautiful and perfect you are and how much I love you."

Her eyes widened and her breath caught in her throat, but he gave no sign that something momentous had been said. He only leaned down to kiss her forehead and whispered, "I'm going to go run you a bath. I'll be back in a few minutes. Just relax."

"Okay," she said, sucking her lips between her teeth until he'd crossed the room and disappeared into the bathroom. Only when he was out of sight did she allow her smile to burst wide open like a firework exploding across the sky.

He loved her. He *loved* her!

She'd felt love in his touch for weeks, seen it in his eyes

when she looked up to find him watching her while she read or gathered pretty shells from the beach, but to hear it…

To hear it was pure magic. The trembling at the center of her bones was banished by a giddy rush of happiness and gratitude so intense she wanted to run naked through the garden, howling her delight up at the moon. Instead, she rolled over onto her stomach and pressed her face into the mattress to muffle her squeal of celebration.

He loved her! He loved her!

The three words thrummed through her head like some mystical tattoo, filling her with strength. She bounced off the bed, carried across the room by an adrenaline rush so strong it felt like her heart was going to burst through her chest. She danced around the table where Eva laid their breakfast each morning and spun in a circle with her arms held out wide, coming to a stop facing the door.

If she hadn't, she wouldn't have seen that the door was cracked or that someone stood on the other side.

Her hands flew to cover as much of her nakedness as she could—one arm across her breasts and one hand darting down to shield her sex—as she backed away. She was about to call for Jackson when Adam stepped into the room, holding a phone out in front of him.

"Dominic sent me." He kept his eyes on the floor, making it clear he wasn't interested in her nudity. "You have to leave now. A helicopter landed on the other side of the island. The men sent to kill you will be here within the hour."

"I have to tell Jackson," Hannah said, her adrenaline rush transforming to a frantic, hunted feeling. "He has to come too."

"He's the reason they found you. Look at his messages," Adam said, gesturing for her to take the phone.

Dread flooded through her, transforming her stomach into a hard knot. With a quick glance over her shoulder to make sure that the entrance to the bathroom was still empty, she took the phone. It didn't take long to see what Jackson had done, but she still didn't want to believe.

She didn't want to believe that he'd lied to her or betrayed her trust and she really didn't want to believe he'd done something like this. But the proof was right there in the two final messages.

The first was a question from someone called Titan beneath a photograph of a woman Hannah never thought she'd see again. It was Harley, older, with her hair bleached blond and sadness tightening her features, but Harley, no doubt in her mind.

She knew her sister was alive even before she read the message confirming her suspicion—

I've tracked Harley Mason—now Baudin—to a small village in southern France. I.D. is 100% certain via image and DNA analysis. How do I proceed?

The last text was a response from Jackson—

Kill her.

The phone clattered to the floor and a sound rose in her throat—half cry of shock, half wail of grief—but she stifled it with a fist pressed tightly to her mouth.

"Hannah? Are you all right?" Jackson called over the sound of the bathwater.

"I'm fine," she called back, but she was anything but fine.

Her sister was alive. *Alive.* But maybe not for much longer.

Because Jackson had given the order to kill her. To kill a member of her family, her *sister*. All his talk about loving her and not wanting to hurt her had been a lie. He was a liar and a killer and she'd been a fool to let herself believe anything else.

The realization made her feel like her heart was being ripped out of her chest, but there was no time to grieve the death of the man she'd thought Jackson was, not if she wanted to leave the island alive. Heart racing, she spun and hurried to the closet, grabbing the first dress she laid hands on and pulling it over her head as she crossed back to Adam.

"Let's go," she whispered. "He'll be out any second."

Adam nodded and motioned for her to lead the way. "There's a golf cart out front. I've disabled the car and the other carts. He won't be able to follow us except on foot."

Hannah broke into a run in her bare feet, racing silently through the house and out the front door. Outside, the world brooded in an ominous bluish-yellow light, the sickly moon hanging in the sky coloring everything in shades of ugly. It was a night for death and betrayal, but she was going to escape. She would get off this island, away from Jackson, and she would find some way to save her sister's life.

Harley might be a monster, but she was *her* monster, and she didn't deserve a death sentence.

"Hold on." Adam slid onto the golf cart seat beside her. Hannah gripped the metal bar on her right, squeezing tight as the wheels churned through the gravel and the cart zoomed away down the road.

The house was nearly out of sight when she heard Jackson roar her name. "Hannah! Hannah!"

Tears filling her eyes, she set her jaw and kept her eyes on the road in front of her. There was nothing to gain from looking back.

She had nothing else to say to Jackson Hawke. Not even goodbye.

CHAPTER FORTY-ONE

Jackson

*A*s soon as he emerged from the bathroom, Jackson knew something was wrong. The sheets were empty and his cell was lying on the floor halfway between the bed and the door.

Stomach clenching, he quickly crossed the room, his pajama pants whispering ominously in the silence. Whatever this was about, it wasn't good. He'd deliberately left his phone in his room when he'd come to bed, not wanting to risk Hannah seeing something she shouldn't.

At least not yet.

If the Titan agency's trip to southern France proved fruitful—if Harley truly was alive and in hiding—then he would tell Hannah what the detectives had uncovered. Until then, there was no point in upsetting her. Or in getting her hopes up.

Hannah hated what Harley had done to him, but the woman was her twin. They shared a bond and Hannah still loved her. No matter how many crimes Harley had committed, Hannah would be thrilled to learn she still had a sister.

He knew there might come a time when he would have to choose between his love for Hannah and his hate for Harley.

He also knew that, if that time came, the choice had already been made.

Hannah was all that mattered. She was his heart and soul and the reason he'd returned from the dead. Before her, he might as well have been six feet under. He'd deluded himself into thinking his life had purpose, but a lust for vengeance wasn't purpose, it was a disease that ate away at your soul, leaving you blind. Before Hannah, his existence had been solid darkness. She'd brought him back to the light and reminded him that there were a hundred thousand things in the world more important than revenge.

There was her smile and her kiss and the way she touched him first thing in the morning, with that hint of hesitation, as if he were a beautiful dream she couldn't quite believe was real. There was her laugh and her sweet spirit and the way she gave herself entirely into his keeping. Her trust humbled him, her heart transformed him, and her happiness was the only thing that mattered.

She was all that mattered and now she was gone. He knew it the moment he picked up the phone.

His conversation with the Titan group was pulled up on the screen, including two new texts. One that confirmed Harley Mason was still alive and a second that issued a kill order, an order he sure as hell hadn't given.

"Hannah!" Jackson dropped the phone and ran, his bare feet slapping on the cool wood floor as he hurried through the darkened house, his heart in his throat and the terrible certainty that Hannah was in danger crawling across his skin.

He emerged into the soft humidity in time to hear a golf cart puttering away from the house.

"Hannah! Hannah!" He screamed her name as loud as he could, but there was no answer. By the time he fell silent, the soft rumble of the cart's engine had faded and there was only the wind, shushing through the palm leaves.

Fighting the urge to chase after her in his bare feet, he

sprinted to where the car was parked beneath a wide overhang near the entrance to the kitchen, but a glance at the slashed tires was all it took to assure him he wouldn't be getting anywhere in the Cadillac. Cursing, he cut across the grass to where the other golf carts were parked in the equipment shed.

He was halfway to the staff cottages when he heard a woman cry out, followed by a rapid stream of Spanish.

Shifting direction, he circled around Eva's bungalow. On the other side, he saw the cook sitting on the ground in the soft pool of light from the bulb above her door, cradling her son's bloodied head in her lap.

"Mr. Hawke," she said, reaching a hand toward him. "We need a doctor. Please, we have to get Dominic to a doctor."

"I don't need a doctor, Mama." Dominic sat up with a groan, gently pushing his mother's hands away. "Head wounds bleed a lot. It's not as bad as it looks."

He turned to Jackson, body weaving slightly as he pressed one palm to the flowing wound near his hairline. "Adam's not who you think he is, Mr. Hawke. I believe he means to hurt Hannah. We need to put a guard—"

"Hannah's gone, but I think I know where she went. I heard a golf cart leaving the property," Jackson said, hands balling into fists and the need to run after her becoming almost irresistible. "Tell me what happened. Quickly."

"I was coming to check on my mother," Dominic said, swallowing hard. "Adam stopped me before I could knock on the door. He said he knew I'd been hired to keep Hannah safe, but that I was going to fail. We struggled. I was close to taking him, but he's working with someone. I was hit on the head from behind and didn't come to until a few minutes ago."

At least two men, Jackson mentally catalogued. At least two men he had to destroy before they hurt Hannah. That was all that mattered. He could grill Dominic on the rest of his story—especially that part about being hired to protect Hannah—at a later date.

"Stay here," Jackson ordered. "Watch the house. If she comes back detain her somewhere safe until I get back."

"Take my gun." Dominic reached down, pulling a small revolver from a holster hidden beneath his jeans. "If Hannah is still alive, she might not be for long. I believe these men were sent to kill her. If you get a clear shot at them, take it."

Jackson's throat threatened to close as he took the gun and quickly checked to make sure it was loaded. "I don't have time *not* to trust you right now, Dominic. But if you've kept something from me and it leads to Hannah being hurt..."

"I want to keep her safe," the shorter man said. "I swear it."

"For your sake, I hope that's the truth." Without another word, Jackson hurried on to the equipment shed only to find the remaining golf cart had been tampered with. Given thirty minutes with a few wiring tools, he knew he could correct the problem, but he didn't have thirty minutes and neither did Hannah.

Abandoning the shed, he ran back toward the main house. Underneath the lanai, where the beach chairs and umbrellas were stored, sat two lightly rusted bikes. Shoving the gun in the back of his pants, he grabbed the larger of the two, swung onto the seat, and began pumping hard down the road leading away from the estate.

Years of pushing his body to the breaking point had given him thigh muscles of pure steel. He could bike around this entire island twice before he gave out. He would be able to catch up with the cart, and when he did, he wouldn't hesitate to shoot first and ask questions later. The men in front of him had given up their right to mercy when they'd laid hands on the woman he loved.

He loved her. He loved her so much, but he'd only said the words once.

He wanted to say them a hundred more times, a thousand. He needed Hannah safe in his arms more than he needed his next breath and by the time he reached the fork in the road and turned instinctively toward the airfield, his heart was threatening to punch a hole through his ribs.

He'd tested the edge of his endurance nearly every day of his adult life, but terror had never been a part of his daily runs or workouts. After he'd been released from prison, he'd assumed he was immune to this kind of fear—a man without a soul doesn't have much to be afraid of—but that was before Hannah. Before her love and before she'd given him something priceless to lose.

He swore beneath his breath, jaw clenching as he pumped even harder.

He told himself the rumble he heard wasn't a plane engine purring to life. Then he told himself that he would reach the field in time to stop the plane from taking off. But he knew he was grasping at straws, knew it even before he saw an unfamiliar aircraft lift into the sky, flying low over his head as he leapt from the bike near the airfield's entrance.

Jackson's head snapped back, but it was too dark to see much of the plane aside from the breadth of the wings and the red stripe running from the nose down toward the belly, illuminated in the spill of the headlights. He didn't know who owned the plane, but he would bet his fortune that Adam was flying the aircraft, which meant his own plane was useless.

He couldn't fly a plane or follow the men who had taken Hannah. He couldn't do anything but stand and watch the aircraft move farther away from the island, heading north before veering slightly to the east and gradually disappearing from sight.

When the sky was empty once more, he did a sweep of the small, shuttered outbuildings and the field, finding two golf carts parked by the gate in the glow of the lamp lighting the area, but there was no sign of Hannah. There was no sign of a struggle either, simply the imprints of her bare feet in the dust next to Adam's larger ones. There was another set of prints, too, slightly smaller than Adam's that tapered at the toe and had no pattern on the bottom of the shoe. A dress shoe, he guessed, which told him nothing.

He had no idea who Adam was working with, why his most trusted employee had betrayed him, or what he planned to do with Hannah. He only knew that he had never felt more helpless than he did right now, not even on the day he was led away to a cell and locked away for a crime he hadn't committed.

"I'm going to find you," he said softly, staring up at the star-flecked sky in the direction where the plane had flown away. "I'll find you and if they've hurt you, they will pay for it. I swear it."

The vow helped calm the impotent rage burning in his gut. If there was one thing he was good at, it was tracking down people who didn't want to be found. He would find Adam, and the man would pay the price for betrayal. He would pay in pain, suffering ten times the torment for every mark he left on Hannah's skin.

CHAPTER FORTY-TWO

Hannah

*S*omeone else was flying the plane, but Hannah didn't know who it was. She supposed in some part of her mind, she had assumed it was Dominic. Adam had said that Dominic sent him, after all, and Dominic was the first one to approach her about the dangerous people who might be coming to the island.

But when the aircraft reached cruising altitude and Adam slipped into the cockpit to take over the controls, it wasn't Dom's dark head that ducked through the door leading into the cabin. It was an enormous, silver-haired man with broad shoulders, a strong jaw, and the most familiar pair of brown eyes in his lightly tanned face.

They were Jackson's eyes, but so much colder. Colder even than the day he'd pulled off her blindfold and glared down at her with a ferocity that had made his contempt for her abundantly clear.

Hate was a terrifying thing to see in another person's eyes, but at least it meant that the person still had the capacity to feel deeply. Love and hate were opposite sides of the same coin and shared far more similarities than differences. They both came from the heart and the heart could be reasoned with, appealed to, even changed from time to time. The heart knew how to forgive, and as long as forgiveness was a possibility, hope was never beyond reach.

But this man's eyes were...empty. The windows to his soul had been blown out and any mercy he might once have possessed had escaped into the ether, never to be seen again.

One look at him and Hannah's gut sensed the approach of an enemy. It was all she could do not to cringe in her chair as the terrifying man began to speak.

"Hello, Miss Mason. I'm Ian Hawke. I've come to take you to your sister."

A sudden surge of delight streaked through her fear, but it was gone in an instant, excitement at the thought of seeing Harley too fragile to survive the terror swelling inside her.

Jackson had betrayed her trust in the worst way, but not everything out of his mouth had been a lie. She believed his stories about his father, the cruel man who had never given his son the love a child deserved and had abandoned Jackson without bothering to find out if the charges against his son were true or false. No matter what Ian Hawke said next, she knew the fact that Jackson's father was here wasn't a good thing.

"Why?" she asked. "Why are you taking me to Harley? What do you want?"

The older man smiled, but it was nothing like Jackson's smile. There was no light or joy in it. He was simply baring his teeth, the smile an implied threat that made her pulse speed faster. "You're clever, but not as clever as your sister. We had to drug her to get her onto the plane. She knew better than to trust anyone but herself."

Adrenaline dumped into Hannah's bloodstream, her most primitive instincts screaming for her to run, but there was nowhere to run to. She was trapped in a plane above the ocean with a man who made Jackson look like a teddy bear in comparison, and there would be no escape.

"As for what I want," Ian continued, settling onto the small leather couch next to her seat. "I want your father to pay his debt. If he does, you will be allowed to live."

The tension fisting in her middle eased a bit. If Ian wanted money, her father certainly had enough of it, and he wouldn't hesitate to pay her ransom. For all his faults, Stewart Mason valued her life as much as he valued his fortune. She was about to tell Ian as much when he spoke again.

"I think he'll choose you, anyway," he said, smiling that terrible smile. "You're the good girl, aren't you? The one who always did as she was told? I understand your sister was his favorite once, but when he realizes he can only keep one daughter, I suspect he'll see the wisdom in sparing your life instead of hers."

Only keep one daughter. Only one.

He was taking her to her sister, but she might only have hours with Harley before one of them was murdered.

Acid surged up Hannah's throat. A moment later she was bent double, retching on the floor of the private jet whisking her away to meet the fate she'd been running from for six long years.

Jackson and Hannah's story concludes in DIVINE DOMINATION.

DIVINE DOMINATION

Bought by the Billionaire
Book Four

By Lili Valente

CHAPTER FORTY-THREE

Ian Hawke

*T*he kid didn't stand a chance.

That's what people said about Ian when he was a little boy, growing up in the projects of inner-city Chicago, hiding under the bed while his mother turned tricks to keep the heat turned on and a needle in her arm.

That's what they said when he came to school wearing the same dirty sweater for months. When the lice infestations got so bad the school nurse was forced to shave his head. When he grew more and more withdrawn until most of his classmates couldn't remember his name.

But what no one realized was that Ian was different than the other lost and forgotten children. He was special, the one in a million person who could live without love or kindness and who bounced back stronger every time the world knocked him down.

Later on in his life, the words "sociopath" and "psychopathic tendencies" would be bandied about by social workers and one of his more astute commanding officers, but Ian only accepted one label—survivor. He was a survivor and he was going to come out on top or die trying.

When he was still too young to go to school, Ian lay on the filthy floor beneath his mother's bed while she entertained her clients. He studied the delicate legs of the dead bugs littering the ground beneath the ancient four-poster, tuning out the sound of the squeaking mattress as he imagined the house he'd have when he grew up. It would be a mansion with a hundred rooms and a flock of servants to clean them. And if he discovered dust under a bed or a dead bug curled in a corner, he would punish the housekeeper responsible until she understood that Ian required excellence from everyone and everything associated with Hawke Manor.

His mansion would be like Wayne Manor, Batman's house, but even bigger, without any stuffy butlers bossing him around or bat caves hidden beneath it.

Ian didn't want to save humanity or even Gotham City. He just wanted to be bigger, meaner, and richer than anyone else and he wanted the entire world to know it. Once he was grown and richer than Batman, no one would look at him with pity in their eyes. They would look at him with respect or fear or they wouldn't look at him at all.

He didn't mind being invisible. There were times when he preferred to fade into the background, becoming part of the shadows until the moment he chose to make his presence known. It was an art he'd mastered before he learned to walk, a necessary survival technique growing up in a home with a short-tempered mother and an endless stream of johns who were never happy to see a kid hanging around.

By age three, Ian was a master of camouflage. By age six, he'd learned to use his ability to blend in with a crowd to hunt for the things he needed. At first he hunted food—stealing from the local bodegas and then the fancy grocery stores downtown, acquiring a taste for the finer things he wouldn't have known existed without his swift, clever hands.

As he grew older, his criminal proclivities expanded. He learned to hunt for wallets and expensive clothes and pretty girls, the kind who wouldn't give him the time of day if they knew where he'd come from and all the terrible things he'd done. He hunted drugs to sell, weapons to defend himself, and enough money to escape the neighborhood and make his dreams come true.

But then, days after his eighteenth birthday, Uncle Sam stepped in and changed the course of his life, drafting him into his first tour of duty in Vietnam. Uncle Sam put an even bigger, better gun in Ian's hand, money in his pocket, and, most wonderful of all, gave him free rein to kill.

And kill he did.

Ian slaughtered the enemy with impunity and was happier in the dark, bloody jungle than he had ever been before. He was finally at home, in a place where monsters like him could run free. He loved war the way some men loved women or booze and by the time Stewart Mason was drafted into his platoon, Ian had served two tours of duty and advanced to the rank of Sergeant of his own squadron.

Mason was the softest of the new recruits, the son of a billionaire. He'd never held a gun before basic, let alone had to defend himself against the horrors of the world. His daddy's money had always done that for him.

The other higher-ups gave the kid two months, tops, but Ian saw something in Mason. The boy was soft and inexperienced, true, but behind his pale blue eyes lurked a devil waiting to be born.

In the humid jungles of Vietnam, Ian helped to birth Mason's darkness, awakening a blood lust in the other man that confirmed they were similar creatures. He taught Mason to hide, to hunt, and to kill with a ruthless efficiency that left entire villages decimated in the blink of an eye.

For the first time in his life, Ian had a true friend, a brother-in-arms and a brother of the soul. Mason understood what it was like to look out at the world and realize there was nothing to be afraid of. They were the predators, the top of the food chain, the masters of their blood-soaked kingdom.

But nothing beautiful lasts forever.

Children grow, love dies, and wars end.

Mason was pulled out in 1973, near the official end of the war. Ian followed two years later, escaping in one of the last helicopters during the fall of Saigon. He'd served six tours of duty without serious injury, but as the helicopter lurched into the sky he took two bullets in the leg, the shots fired by someone in the mass of South Vietnamese crowding around the embassy, desperate to be evacuated before the North took over.

*H*e was recuperating in a military hospital in D.C., mourning the loss of the life he'd known and wondering if he would ever find a place as perfect as his terrible, wonderful jungle, when Stewart Mason walked into his hospital room.

Mason's father was dying and soon the family's estate would pass to the next generation. Stewart had three older brothers—Aaron, Ezra, and Matthew—as well as a much younger sister, Sybil. Each of the boys was slated to inherit one-fourth of their father's fortune while Sybil would inherit the summer house on the lake and a smaller trust fund.

"She isn't Dad's." Stewart's lips curved in a wry smile as he re-crossed his legs for the fifth time. He seemed to find the hard wooden chair beside Ian's bed as uncomfortable as his lone other visitor, the hospital psychologist. "But she's never been well and he's too soft to cut her out of the will."

Ian grunted. "I would have cut her out the moment I knew she wasn't mine. Right after I kicked her mother out of the house without a penny."

"No, you wouldn't." Stewart laughed. "You've got too much pride. You would have found another way to deal with the problem." His smile faded and a new tension crept into his voice, signaling that they were getting down to business. "And that's why I'm here. I have a proposition for you."

Ian searched Mason's face, not surprised to see the devil dancing behind his friend's eyes. "I'm listening."

"You know my brothers hate me," Mason said, keeping his voice low so as not to be overhead by the patients on either side of Ian's tiny partition. "If they inherit three-fourths of the estate, they'll stick together and shut me out. They'll ignore my advice and squander everything Dad fought so hard to build. If I don't do something now, in fifty years there won't be anything left. I've seen it happen before. No one is too rich to lose it all, not even us."

"So you want to find a way to have them written out of the will?" Ian feigned ignorance, resisting the urge to smile when Mason shot him an incredulous look.

"No, I don't want them written out of the will," he said in a harsh whisper. "I want them out of the picture. Permanently. And I want you to be the one to do it."

"Why me?" Ian asked, keeping his expression neutral. "Why not keep it in the family? We both know you're capable."

"I'll also be the first person the authorities will suspect. My alibi has to be airtight. While you're getting the job done, I'll be attending parties in the city, skiing upstate, and making sure I'm never near my brothers and never alone."

"But if I'm caught, it could still lead back to you," Ian said, his mind already clicking through possible assassination methods. "I wouldn't say who hired me, but we served together. There are records."

"You won't be caught. That's why I'm here. Because you're the best." Warmth softened Stewart's usually cool blue eyes. "You're my real brother. And if you help me, I'll make sure you never want for anything for the rest of your life."

Ian studied his friend, his brother, a part of him wanting to take the job with no more questions asked. But he knew Mason as well as he knew himself and realized the other man didn't appreciate anything that came too easily.

"I'll think about it." He relaxed back onto the too-thin pillows propped beneath his shoulders. "Come see me next week and bring your best offer."

"I'll give you my best offer now," Mason said, leaning closer. "I said you're my brother and I meant it. Do this for me and you'll have fifty percent."

Even Ian, a master at controlling his emotions, couldn't hide his surprise. "Half. Of everything?"

"Half of everything," Mason confirmed. "Half of three billion is a lot more than the twenty-five percent I'll be getting if my brothers inherit. I'll still be coming out on top, and I'll have a partner who understands that sometimes we have to make hard choices to make the most of our lives."

Ian concentrated on his breathing, drawing in long slow breaths and letting them out to the count of five. It was everything he'd ever wanted, handed to him on a silver platter, but he couldn't start counting the money or building his mansion yet.

He had to stay calm, stay smart, and make sure this went off without a hitch.

"I'll need time to heal," he said. "I can't start something like this with a bum leg. And I'll need information on all the targets. Everything you can get me."

"I'm already working on that." Mason cast a glance over his shoulder as one of the floor nurses bustled by with a tray of water glasses. "We have some time. Dad should have a few months left, maybe more. The disease is progressing rapidly, but he has the best doctors money can buy."

The best that money can buy.

Ian had never had the best that money could buy. He'd had the best that he could steal, snatching riches away from the people who hoarded them and running like hell before they could snatch them back. He couldn't imagine what it would be like to know he had all the money he would ever need, all the power he'd ever dreamt of.

And all he had to do was snuff out a few lights.

He'd already snuffed out hundreds, maybe thousands. He'd lost track of his tally by this third tour of duty, but he was undoubtedly an efficient killing machine unimpeded by remorse or regret. There wasn't a man or woman alive who was truly innocent. Innocence was for very small children and even they were simply seeds waiting to open, holding their potential for evil tight inside of them until it grew large enough to burst free.

Ian didn't believe in the sanctity of life. He believed in his own survival and his right to do as he pleased. He spared no one and he trusted no one…not even his best and only friend.

"All right," he said after a long moment. "But I'll need half of the money up front."

Mason's eyes flicked to the right, gazing over Ian's shoulder through the filmy window that overlooked the parking lot below. "I can't do half, but I can have an untraceable, fully laundered two million in the account of your choice by tomorrow morning. The rest will have to wait until I inherit. I won't have access to that kind of capital until then."

Ian cocked his head. "Most people look to the left when they're lying."

"I'm not lying." Mason shifted his gaze back to Ian, his face an expressionless mask. "And I won't be back next week. Take the deal now, or I'll find someone else. I'd rather be partners in this, but I don't have time to waste. I'm not going to let everything I deserve slip through my fingers because you aren't sure you can trust me."

And why should I trust you? Ian thought.

Mason was planning to have his family members murdered so that he wouldn't have to learn how to share. No matter how much Ian admired Mason's predatory instincts or how many times they'd saved each other's skins in combat, he would be a fool to jump into this without some serious thought.

Mason was dangerous. But he also wasn't the kind to make idle threats. If he said this was Ian's one shot, it was his one shot, and he wasn't about to piss away his chance to have everything he'd ever wanted.

"I'll call you with the bank account information this afternoon," Ian said, not missing the way Mason's shoulders relaxed away from his ears at the news.

Maybe his friend was sincere about wanting a partner. Or maybe he was simply relieved not to have to seek out another monster to get the job done. Truly excellent monsters—the kind who are crazy enough not to care about society's rules, but sane enough to cover their tracks—are few and far between.

Mason rose from his chair, reaching out to clasp Ian's hand tight. "Thank you, brother. You won't regret this."

Ian nodded. "And neither will you, as long as you keep your word."

Mason smiled, a hard curve of his mouth. "I'm ambitious, but I'm not a fool. You'll get everything you've been promised and more."

"I don't need more," Ian said. "Half is enough."

*A*nd it would have been. One point five billion dollars would have made his wildest dreams come true.

But on the cold December morning when Mason was named the sole heir to his father's vast fortune, the money never came. Ian's bank balance remained steady—not a penny more, not a penny less.

At three o'clock, he called Mason, but there was no answer, only a busy signal that droned in his ear, summoning the rage bubbling inside of him closer to the surface. At five o'clock, he drove by the row house in the elite part of D.C. where Mason had lived since he began his work as a lobbyist, but the house was empty. A glance in the windows revealed that the furniture was gone and the floors bare.

Even before Ian returned home to find an envelope slipped beneath his door, he knew he'd been cheated.

The message the missive conveyed confirmed it—

If you talk, you'll go to jail, and you'll go alone.

There is no paper trail, no money trail, nothing to prove you weren't acting on your own. This is your chance to walk away. Take what you've been given, make a life for yourself, and don't attempt to contact me again.

If you do, you die. I've hired security and they've been instructed to shoot on sight.

Goodbye and good luck.

The note was typed with no signature, nothing to point to Mason. Ian wasn't surprised. Mason was as careful as he was greedy and had enough money to hire a small army to protect him. If Ian tried to take his revenge now, it would be a suicide mission. It would take time for his former friend to drop his guard, time that would be best put to use in planning and preparation.

Ian was a patient man. He was also a determined one.

He might have lost the battle, but he would win the war. By the time he was finished with Stewart, cheating a Hawke would be his greatest regret.

*A*nd now, just days from his sixty-fifth birthday, his moment had finally arrived. He'd failed once before, but now he had his hands on the only things Stewart truly cared about.

He had one of Mason's daughters locked away in a remote location in the Florida Keys and he had the other on his private plane looking up at him with frightened blue eyes the exact shade as her father's.

"As for what I want…." Ian settled onto the small leather couch next to Hannah Mason's seat, close enough to smell the grass and perfume scent drifting from her body. "I want your father to pay his debt. If he does, you will be allowed to live."

Hannah swallowed and her taut features relaxed, making it obvious she had no clue that he was talking about so much more than money.

No amount of money could right Mason's wrongs. There was only one way to even the score. Mason would pay his debt with the blood of his children, the keepers of his legacy.

What good was an empire, after all, without someone to pass it on to? Money could be replaced; not so little girls.

And Hannah and Harley were the last living Masons of their generation. Ian had already taken care of their cousins, those tragically unlucky men and women he'd orphaned when they were so very young.

"I think he'll choose you, anyway." Ian smiled at the pretty thing peering up at him, not surprised his son was smitten with her.

Hannah was beautiful, with a sweet heart that shone in her eyes and a brightness of soul found only in the very young and very breakable. She was one of the fragile, gullible, victims of the world fools like Jackson couldn't resist taking under their wing. He had assumed Jackson had learned the dangers of caring too much after the other sister had ruined his life, but apparently his son was a glutton for punishment.

"You're the good girl, aren't you?" Ian continued, knowing that she was. He knew everything about her, from the hobbies she'd enjoyed as a child to her grade point average when she graduated from college. "The one who always did as she was told? I understand your sister was his favorite once, but when he realizes he can only keep one daughter, I suspect he'll see the wisdom in sparing your life instead of hers."

Ian paused, watching the color drain from Hannah's face and her hands begin to shake. She seemed to be getting the message loud and clear, a fact she confirmed when she bent double and was sick all over the floor.

He watched, taking pleasure from her pain, determined to relish every moment of his hard-won, long-awaited revenge.

CHAPTER FORTY-FOUR

Jackson

*J*ackson had killed before—in combat and once when negotiations with a Mexican drug cartel had gone awry and he'd had no choice but to kill or be killed—but he had never experienced anything like the blood lust pulsing through his veins as he steered the abandoned golf cart he'd found at the airstrip back toward the villa.

When he got his hands on the men who had kidnapped Hannah, he was going to rip their hearts, still beating, from their chests and stuff the organs down their throats. He was going to pull them limb from limb and toss the pieces of their mutilated bodies into the sea. Or maybe he'd leave them out for buzzards to pick at and maggots to writhe inside.

Every fate he imagined for the men was more horrible than the last, but no amount of terror, pain, or desecration seemed sufficient punishment for the sin of taking Hannah away from him.

And if Dominic were correct, and the men intended to kill her...

Jackson swallowed hard, forcing down the gorge rising in his throat.

They would beg for death by the time he was through with

them. They would *beg* for it. Jackson had no doubt he could deliver enough suffering to make Hannah's kidnappers sorry they'd ever heard her name, but that wouldn't bring her back. Once she was gone, she would be gone forever—and his heart and soul along with her.

He had to get to her before it was too late for both of them.

He parked the cart by the lanai and took the steps up to the villa two at a time. He found Eva and Dominic in the kitchen talking animatedly in Spanish, but their conversation cut off abruptly when he entered the room.

"I was too late." Jackson aimed himself at the phone, where Hannah had called her aunt nearly every day for the past month, trying not to think about the way her sweet laughter had filled the room as she chatted with the woman who was like a mother to her.

He would hear that laughter again. But first he would hear the screams of the men who had taken her away from him.

"They left on a small private plane," he continued. "The jet is still here, but I can't fly it. I'll have to hire a charter and see how fast they can—"

"We can take my jet," Dominic said. "I've already put in a call to the pilot in Moorea. He should be landing soon. And I've got a tech team hacking into a surveillance satellite orbiting the area. Hopefully, they'll be able to get a visual and tell us where the plane is headed."

Jackson slammed the phone back into the receiver before turning to shoot Dom his most threatening look. "Who are you? Who are you working for and why should I trust you when you knew Hannah was in danger and failed to protect her?"

"I'm working for her father, Stewart Mason," Dom said, as his mother angled her body in front of his, clearly intending to protect her son from Jackson, even if her employer was twice her size. "I've been working for Mr. Mason for years, trying to keep Hannah safe from those who mean her harm."

Dominic paused, eyes narrowing as he shook his head back and forth. "And then you showed up. At first, I thought you were part of it. But you really have no idea, do you?"

"No idea about what?" Jackson growled.

"About your father," Dom hurried on, clearly sensing Jackson's mounting frustration. "He's the one who killed Hannah's cousins. He's trying to take out all of Stewart Mason's heirs."

Jackson's brows drew together so sharply it sent a flash of pain through his temples. "My father is a real estate developer. He's a cold hearted bastard, but he doesn't kill people." He frowned harder. "And even if he did, why would he give a shit about Mason's money or his heirs? My father is a wealthy man. The last thing he needs is more money."

"Story too long," Eva piped up, waving a hand at Jackson before turning back to her son. "Is too long and Hannah in trouble. You work together. Help her. Then you fight."

The seemingly sincere concern in the older woman's voice reminded Jackson of his other source of information, the one person he trusted wanted nothing but the best for Hannah. "I'm calling her aunt." He snatched the phone up with one hand as he pointed at Dom with the other. "Get my cell from the floor in Hannah's room. As soon as I'm finished with this call, I have to place another one. Then we'll talk."

He should probably call the Titan group first. He doubted Alexander Titan would initiate an execution based on a text message—especially since they'd never discussed the price for murder on demand—but Hannah was his first concern.

He would do what he could to keep Harley safe, but only after he found out who had Hannah and was on his way to getting her back.

Sybil answered on the third ring, saying, "Hello, darling, is everything all right?" in a sleepy voice.

A glance at the clock above the stove revealed it was nearly midnight. Jackson had been so terrified he hadn't even noticed the time.

"No, Sybil, it's not. This is Jackson, Hannah's friend," he said, wincing at the last word. He was so much more than her friend, but her aunt had never met him or seen him and Hannah together. She might not trust him enough to open up about their family secrets, but he had to try, for Hannah's sake. "I'm sorry to be the one to tell you this, but something terrible has happened. Hannah's been taken. By two men, one of whom I thought I could trust with my life."

"Oh my God," Sybil whispered.

"I realized she was missing and followed them, but it was too late," he continued, knowing he didn't have time to waste explaining all the finer—and crazier—details of Hannah's abduction. "I got to the airfield in time to see their plane take off. My plane is still here, but I don't have a pilot so I couldn't follow them."

"Hannah's been taken," Sybil said, speaking to someone on the other end of the line. "And her friend can't fly the plane. Do you think—"

"There's a man here who claims he works for Hannah's father," Jackson broke in. "He says there's a plane on the way that we can use to go after her, but I don't know if I can trust him."

"Well, you don't really have a choice, do you?" Sybil's voice was surprisingly strong and steady. "You have to get to her as soon as possible, Jackson. If they took her alive, she won't be alive for long. I've already lost three brothers and four nieces and nephews to this nightmare. I can't lose Hannah, too. She's like a daughter to me."

Jackson leaned against the kitchen counter, fear prickling across his skin. Could Dominic be right about his father?

"The man here said that someone is killing the Mason heirs," he said, deliberately keeping things vague to see if Sybil would confirm Dom's claim. "Do you know why? It might help me figure out where they've taken Hannah."

"It has something to do with my brother, Stewart," Sybil said after only a moment's hesitation, evidently deciding to trust him. "Over the years, he's received threats from an old business partner. But when I've pushed for more information about the threats or the partner, he refuses to speak about it or to go to the authorities for help. He has deliberately kept the assassinations of our family members a secret while concealing the other man's identity and I... Well, I believe I know why."

"Why?" Jackson pressed, his thoughts racing.

Was his father the old business partner? It was easy to imagine Ian bending the law to crush a rival, but murder wasn't part of the tax code. As far as Jackson knew, his father had never even had a parking ticket. He was a decorated Marine, a self-made man who had married into one of the oldest families on the eastern seaboard. He wasn't a mob boss for God's sake.

You were a decorated Marine, and look how far you've fallen. Maybe you inherited more from dear old dad than height and the color of your eyes.

"I think Stewart had something to do with what happened to our brothers," Sybil said in a pained voice. "He's always been different and they bullied him terribly when he was small. I was the only one who was kind to Stewart and I am the only one who didn't meet with an unfortunate accident in the fall of 1975, just weeks before our father's will was set to be read."

She sighed, the sound making it clear how heavily her suspicions had weighed on her. "I've had too much time to think to believe that's a coincidence. I was spared because Stewart told the person he'd hired to kill the others to let me live. But then, I assume something must have happened to make the killer turn on him." She paused before continuing in a haunted tone, "And now Stewart has spent the past forty years defending his family from a nightmare that he set in motion, knowing his connection to the murderer would be obvious if anyone ever learned the man's name."

"You could be right," Jackson said, his throat tight. "I'm going to look into a few things, Sybil. I'll call you back."

"I'll come to you," Sybil said. "My friend Hiro is a pilot. He says he can borrow a plane and get us both there in ninety minutes. When you figure out where they've taken Hannah, we'll come with you."

Her friend, Hiro. Jackson was tempted to tell the woman her trust was grossly misplaced but resisted the urge.

Hiro had been his spy, but he'd also said he cared about Sybil and sounded like he meant it. If there was one thing Jackson had learned from his time on the island, it was that people could change. Even the hardest heart could soften in the hands of the right person. Hannah had transformed him, given him back his soul and a reason for living. If Sybil had done the same for Hiro, Jackson wouldn't do anything to ruin the happiness they'd found.

But he would do what it took to keep Sybil safe. It's what Hannah would want.

"No," he said. "Pack what you need for a week or two and have Hiro fly you somewhere no one will think to look for you. You can give me his cell number and I'll call you as soon as I have any updates on the situation."

"But I—"

"I know you want to help find Hannah," Jackson interrupted gently. "But the people who have taken her are dangerous. Hannah loves you more than anything. If I brought you into a situation that would put your life in danger, she would have my balls for breakfast."

Sybil's laugh ended in a soft sob. "Sounds like you know her well. Most people think she's a pushover. They don't see how strong she really is."

"I see her," Jackson said roughly. "And I love her and I swear to you I will get her back or die trying."

"Don't die," Sybil said. "There's been enough death and Hannah needs you. She loves you very much, too, Jackson. And I'm sure she knows you're doing everything you can to reach her."

"I hope so," he said, falling silent as Sybil gave him Hiro's familiar number and he pretended to write it down.

He hoped that Hannah believed he loved her. Or that he'd at least have the chance to explain that he hadn't given the kill order she must have seen on his phone.

He didn't care enough about Harley to want to kill her. Not anymore. His hate had faded to a two-dimensional emotion, one that could be folded and put away in a box inside of him and left to quietly decompose. The only passion he felt now was for Hannah, for her safety, her love, and the chance to build a life with the woman who had made him believe in miracles.

She was his miracle, his savior, his heart, and he was going to find her. He couldn't be too late. He couldn't have come so far out of the darkness only to lose his light.

CHAPTER FORTY-FIVE

Hannah

*T*he first thing Hannah felt was the sun warm on her face, then the cool breeze blowing across her bare arms and the gentle rocking of the boat beneath her.

They were lovely, lulling sensations, but none of them were the source of the desire pooling in her belly, making her blood feel hot and sticky. The source was the tongue swirling around her belly button, sending sizzles of awareness rushing through her and setting a hungry pulse to throbbing between her legs.

"Hmm…" She hummed lazily, opening her eyes to see Jackson's dark head bent over her stomach as his mouth made love to her navel with a singular focus that made her nipples bead tight beneath her damp bikini top.

"Are you finally awake?" he asked, his voice vibrating against her sun-warmed skin.

"I didn't know the belly button was an erogenous zone," she answered, reaching down to thread her fingers through his thick hair. She loved his hair. Its softness, its sealskin color, the way it slid silkily through her fingers unless she fisted it in her hand and hung on for dear life.

"Silly woman." His tongue thrust deeper into the soft flesh, summoning an answering twinge low in her body. "In the right hands, all of your zones are erogenous zones."

She bit her lip, breath catching as Jackson's hand smoothed up the inside of her thigh. "Is that right?"

"Take your clavicle for example." Jackson kissed his way up through the valley between her breasts to the skin just below her neck. He kissed the place where her throat became her collarbone before letting his tongue trace a path across it to her shoulder. "If I wanted to, I could make you come just from kissing you here, again and again."

"Fascinating," she said with mock awe as she shivered, feeling his tongue in a hundred different places as he traced a line back the way he'd come.

He hadn't kissed her in any of the ways she usually associated with making love, but she was already wet and aching for him. Despite a healthy anti-foot-fetish, if Jackson told her that he could make her come from nibbling on her toes, she would believe him.

But that didn't mean it wasn't fun to tease...

"But I have to confess I have doubts about clavicle-induced orgasms," she said, as his tongue circled the hollow at the base of her throat, making her already tight nipples sting with the need for contact. "Are you sure you aren't being hyperbolic, Mr. Hawke?"

"You know I hate that word." He nipped at her neck, the feel of his teeth against her skin ratcheting her desire up another notch. "I'm many things, sunshine, but I'm not a liar."

"Hyperbole isn't a lie." She fought the urge to squirm as he turned his attention to the other side of her collarbone and fresh heat pooled between her legs. "It's an exaggerated statement never intended to be taken literally."

"I appreciate the grammar lesson," he said, dryly. "But I wasn't exaggerating. Do you want me to prove it?"

"No," she said, tightening her grip in his hair. "I'd rather you fuck me, sir. If that's all right with you."

He laughed softly as he moved on top of her, spreading her legs with a nudge of his knee before settling between them, pinning her against *the warm wood of the deck.* "I think I could be persuaded to fuck you. If you're a good girl."

"Or a bad one?" She lifted her hips, grinding into the hard, hot ridge of his cock, still trapped behind his swim trunks.

He cursed against her mouth as their lips met in a long, slow, sultry kiss. "Either works for me. Choose your own adventure, sunshine, but choose quickly or I'll choose for you."

"I'll be good, but I want it a little rough," she whispered, a thrill zipping through her as the words left her lips. "I can't stop thinking about last night when you had your hand in my hair. It made me so wet, sir."

"Then roll over." Jackson pulled away, his volume dropping, the way it did when they started a scene. It was his "I'm in charge now" voice, the one that held such incredible power over her body that she suspected there would come a day when he would be able to make her come with his voice alone, no touch required. "Now, Hannah. Don't make me ask again."

"Yes, sir." She hurried to obey his command, rolling over onto her stomach before pushing up onto her hands and knees on the beach towel she'd spread on the deck after their swim, her thighs already trembling with anticipation.

But she should have known Jackson wouldn't want her in the same position as last night. Her love wasn't only sweetly skilled and wonderfully wicked; he was creative.

"Swimsuit off and on your belly. Arms in front of you and legs spread." As she hurried to obey, Jackson crossed to the other side of the boat, collecting something from the banquet where they'd had lunch before returning to her side. "Lift your hips."

Hannah curved her spine and Jackson slipped a small pillow from the seating area beneath her pelvis before setting a hand on her bottom, signaling for her to relax.

"Now you're ready." He pressed a kiss to her shoulder as he tied her wrists in front of her with her discarded sarong. "Now I'll be able to fuck you without leaving bruises on your pretty hip bones."

"I don't mind a bruise or two." Hannah held her breath as he moved behind her, holding himself up in a push-up position, hovering close enough for her to feel the heat of his body, but not the brush of his skin against hers.

"Well, I do." He kissed her other shoulder, making her ache for the feel of his weight settling on top of her. But he held himself away, taking his time trailing kisses up the back of her neck. "No bruises today. You're too beautiful. All your sun-warmed skin and that white tan line on your ass. I've been dying to get you out of your swimsuit all day."

"You should have said something sooner," she whispered, shivering as his fingers wrapped gently around her throat, urging her to tilt her head back and push up on her forearms. "There's no one around to see. We could have gone sailing naked."

"Sometimes delayed satisfaction is the best kind." His fingers trailed down her throat to skim the top of her breast. "Don't you think?"

"How are you holding yourself up with one arm?" she asked, breath coming faster as her nipples pulled tight, aching for his touch. "I want to feel you."

"I want to feel you, sir," he corrected, but there was amusement in his voice. "And the answer is skill, sunshine. Patience and skill. Arch your back more. Yes, like that. Perfect." He captured her nipple between his fingertips, pinching with the barest teasing pressure. "Now I want you to hold absolutely still. Don't move, don't squirm those pretty hips, don't even let your shoulders rise and fall too fast as you breathe. Do you understand?"

"Yes, sir," she said, pressing her lips together as soon as the words left her mouth, sensing that obedience was going to be a battle.

Even with his warm fingers barely touching her nipple, it felt like her nerves were being set on fire. Electricity hummed from her sensitive tips to knot between her legs. As he transferred his attentions from one nipple to the other—continuing to hover above her body in a one-armed push-up position that she couldn't believe even he could sustain for this long—her clit swelled and the pulse between her thighs picked up speed.

"I love your breasts," Jackson whispered, kissing the place where her neck curved into her shoulder. "I love how your nipples get so tight for me."

Hannah squeezed her eyes shut and dug her teeth into her bottom lip, fighting to stay still as he pinched and teased her nipples and her breath came faster, making her stomach flutter against the towel beneath her.

"I love the sounds you make when I bite them," he said, trapping a mouthful of the top of her shoulder between his teeth and biting down, making her groan as a primal wave of lust rocketed through her.

"Yes, bite me again, sir," she whispered, her entire body beginning to tremble. "Please. Please bite me again."

"Not yet, sweetness," he said, returning his teasing attention to her breasts, plucking first one nipple and then the other until it was pure hell not to move and a soft whimper escaped her lips. "You're doing so well, but I know you can give me more. Spread your legs wider."

She obeyed, so relieved to be granted permission to move, even just a little bit, that she danced a few feet away from the razor's edge, regaining enough control that she was able to remain still when Jackson brought the tip of his cock to her entrance. It rested lightly at her opening, enough for her to feel how hot and hard he was, but not enough to grant her even the slightest bit of relief.

All she wanted was to lift her hips and shove backward, impaling herself on his erection. She wanted it so badly her inner walls pulsed and her body gushed wetness onto the blunt head of his cock, desperate to ease his way. But instead of pushing forward, he rocked his hips slowly from side to side, teasing first one side of her opening and then the other, while his fingers continued to twist and pluck at her nipples and Hannah slowly went out of her mind.

"God, please, Jackson," she panted, tears rising in her eyes as she fought the overwhelming urge to move. "Please, please, please."

"Please, what," he demanded, tongue teasing back and forth across the place where he'd bitten her, where she was dying for him to bite her again. "And please, who?"

"Please fuck me, sir," she practically snarled, so desperate for relief she couldn't decide if she loved him or hated him. "Please, I can't take any more. I can't."

"Yes, you can." The strain in his voice indicating that he was nearing the edge of his own control was the only thing that kept her from breaking. "Just another minute, sunshine. You can do anything for one more minute. Sixty, fifty-nine, fifty-eight…"

As he counted down his touch grew rougher, harder, until he was twisting her nipples in painful, blissful circles and she was panting for breath and making desperate, unfeminine sounds low in her throat.

But she didn't care. She was beyond caring about what Jackson thought of her. All she cared about was relief from the pressure mounting to a previously unfathomable peak inside of her. She was so high on lust there was no air to breathe.

Higher, higher, he took her until the world spun and her head felt too light for her body.

For a moment, she was afraid she would suffocate on her own desire and pass out before Jackson decided to end his erotic torture. But then he bit her again, hard enough to send pain flashing through her nerve endings, and dropped his hips, shoving all the way to the end of her.

Her cry of pain became a high-pitched keen as Jackson wrapped a bracing arm around her ribs and slammed all the way to the end of her, triggering an orgasm so intense it was like an atom bomb had been detonated in her core.

Hannah clawed at the deck beneath her as the world went white and she was blinded by pleasure. Euphoria spread from her center out to bathe every inch of her body in bliss, the release so sweet that pleasure became pain and then swung back around to pleasure again in a seemingly endless feedback loop while Jackson fucked her so hard she felt him everywhere.

Everywhere. In her belly, in her ribs, in her throat, filling her up until there was no place he hadn't touched and there was no awareness of what was his and what was hers. There was only pulse and throb, hunger and satisfaction, love and the communion of two hearts beating in perfect harmony.

Hannah was dimly aware of Jackson finding release and rolling onto *his back, pulling her on top of him while he freed her hands, but she was still too lost in that other world they'd found together to pay too much attention to her body. She was at ten thousand feet, soaring weightless, not certain she would ever come down.*

She had no idea how long she lay on top of him, catching her breath, only that when she finally opened her eyes the blue sky was stained with sunset light and the sea air had grown cooler.

"I wonder if that's what heroin is like," she rasped, her voice rough.

"If so, no wonder it's so hard to quit." Jackson's fingers played gently up and down her stomach. "How do you do it?"

"Do what?" She turned her head, meeting his eyes over her shoulder, her heart flipping when she saw the vulnerable, open expression on his face.

"Make me want you more every day?"

She lifted her hand, cupping his scruffy cheek in her hand. "Dark magic."

He smiled, and her flipping heart turned a cartwheel. "I believe it. There's no other explanation."

But there was another explanation. It was love. Once-in-a-lifetime, only-gets-better, love-you-more-every-day-until-they-put-me-in-the-ground love. She'd known that for a while now and someday soon, Jackson would know it, too.

She didn't doubt it, not even on those mornings when he stayed in his room until well after breakfast, hiding from her after a night when close had become too close for his comfort. There would come a day when he would realize that there was no need to hide and nothing to be afraid of.

He was safe with her. He could let his guard down and be the man he truly was, the man who was as sweet as he was Dominant, as gentle as he was controlling. She would never take his love for granted or betray his trust.

Never. No matter what.

"No matter what," she said aloud, her brows drawing together as something ugly whispered through her subconscious. It was like a foul

smell drifting through the air, familiar, but horrible, something she knew she didn't want to recognize.

Once she named it, there would be no denying the existence of the filth smeared across the walls or the body rotting beneath the floor.

Once she remembered, she would never forget again.

"What's wrong?" Jackson asked, his voice going deep and dangerous as the orange sky darkened, black and blue creeping in to bruise the undersides of the clouds. "Cat got your tongue, Harley?"

Before she could reply, or tell him that she wasn't Harley, Jackson's hands were back around her throat.

But this time, his touch wasn't gentle. His fingers tightened like a vice and pain blossomed through her forehead, the pressure building suddenly, fiercely, until it felt like her eyes would burst from their sockets.

Panicked, she clawed at Jackson's arms, desperate for breath, but his grip only tightened.

"You're going to die, Harley," he growled against her throat as the world went black. "I will end you if it's the last thing I do."

CHAPTER FORTY-SIX

Hannah

*H*annah woke with a startled groan, hands flying to her neck. She gasped for breath, her throat still tight from the terror of the beautiful memory turned nightmare.

She swallowed slowly and blinked, willing herself to remember the way that day on the boat had really ended, with her and Jackson sailing home under the stars. She'd snuggled in his lap as he'd steered with one arm wrapped around her waist, holding her close to him with a gentleness that made it clear that she was precious to him.

Her heartbeat was nearly under control when the world pitched. A moment later, the plane touched down with a rough bump.

Startled, Hannah turned to look out the window, where pale light glowed on the horizon and unfamiliar palm trees—more sparse and scrubby than the ones back home—streaked past the window. For a moment, she couldn't remember where she was, but then it all came rushing back—Adam in the doorway, the miracle of learning that her sister was alive, the pain of realizing Jackson planned to kill Harley, and then the terror of grasping that she had much bigger problems than a broken heart.

She had been kidnapped by Jackson's father and he was going to kill her. Or Harley. But first, he was going to make her father choose between the daughters he'd sacrificed so much to protect.

Depending on how things played out, this could be the last sunrise Hannah would ever see.

No. He won't get away with this. You'll find a way out and you'll take Harley with you.

Hannah swallowed hard. Ignoring the lingering taste of her own sickness in her mouth and the acrid scent rising from the blanket she'd thrown over the puddle of vomit, she glanced around the cabin. Jackson's father was nowhere in sight. He and Adam must both be in the cockpit, landing the plane, which meant she was alone for a few precious moments and she meant to make the most of them.

Flicking open her seatbelt, she lurched out of her seat, clinging to the back of the seat behind her, fighting the drag of the g-force as the plane continued to decelerate. She pulled her way to the rear of the cabin to a large desk that occupied most of the space near the bathroom and snatched the slim gray phone from its cradle, sagging with relief when she heard the buzz of the dial tone.

She'd noticed the phone last night, but under Ian's watchful eye there had been no opportunity to attempt a call for help. Now, she had at least a minute or two before the men finished landing the plane.

Hopefully, it would be enough.

Quickly, she punched in the familiar phone number and waited with held breath as soft clicks drifted from the receiver, signaling that the call was trying to connect. She rubbed the sleep from her eyes with her free hand as her brain sparked and hummed, waking up fast as adrenaline dumped into her system.

She couldn't believe she'd fallen asleep with Ian sitting across from her, watching her like an animal he couldn't wait to slaughter. It must have been a defense mechanism, a way to cope with the stress induced by sharing air with a predator.

Whatever kindness Jackson possessed, he'd clearly inherited it from his mother. Based on their few hours of acquaintance, Hannah was willing to bet that Ian Hawke was a prototypical psychopath—a creature utterly without empathy or remorse—but she didn't intend to stick around to confirm her diagnosis.

She was going to get away from Ian, even if she had to reach out to one monster to be saved from another. She couldn't believe that Jackson had anything to do with her abduction. The tortured note in his voice as he'd called after her had been too real.

Finally, after several more clicks and a long, vibrating silence that made Hannah's stomach sink with dread, the phone rang just as the plane slowed to cruising speed. Hannah's fingers tightened around the receiver as she spun to look over her shoulder, praying that Jackson would answer before his father came back through the cockpit's door.

He picked up halfway through the second ring. "Who is this?"

Unexpected tears surged into Hannah's eyes, her throat locking tight as a wave of relief and longing swept through her. No matter what he'd done, it was so fucking good to hear Jackson's voice.

"It's Hannah, but I don't have much time," she said, sucking in a panicked breath. "Adam is working for your father. I'm on his private plane right now. We just landed somewhere with palm trees, but a long way from Tahiti. We were flying all night and the sun is just now coming up."

"I'm coming for you. Can you see anything outside?" Jackson asked, getting right down to business though the strain in his voice made it clear he was worried about her. He was fine with killing Harley, but it seemed he still cared whether she lived or died. "Are there any identifying landmarks or an airfield name or—"

"Nothing. Just the palm trees." Hannah leaned down to stare out one of the rear windows as the plane made a slight turn to the left, revealing a stunning view of the ocean and a tiny island off the coast. "No, wait. There's a little island next to the airstrip. It has a beach, a small dock, and bright red hammocks hanging in the trees. There's no one there now, but it looks like some kind of tourist destination. Maybe that will help?"

"Maybe, but keep looking, and if we're disconnected know that I'm close," Jackson said, making Hannah's knees go weak with relief. "The last satellite image had you near the Florida Keys. We're only a couple of hours behind you. We'll figure out where you've landed and I'll get to you before he hurts you. I promise, Hannah. I swear it on my life. Just hold on."

"I will, but hurry," she said, sniffing hard as tears filled her eyes. "He's going to kill me, Jackson. Me or Harley. I know you don't care about her, but I—"

"No, you don't understand, baby. I never—"

With a click and an ominous sounding whine, the line went dead. Stifling a panicked cry, Hannah jabbed at the switch hook, trying to get back to an open line and call him back.

She needed to hear his voice again. She needed him to finish what he'd been about to say. Maybe there had been some kind of horrible misunderstanding. Maybe he hadn't betrayed her, maybe there was—

"Just like Romeo and Juliet." A low voice from behind her broke into her panicked thoughts.

Hannah whirled to see Ian seated on the small sofa, his long legs crossed.

"Two households, alike in dignity," he continued, a smirk

on his face. "An ancient grudge that lingers on, souring the hearts of both young and old…"

"You have no heart," Hannah whispered, letting the phone slip from her hand. "Jackson told me all about you."

Ian's brows rose. "I doubt *all* about. My son and I have never been close. I don't tell him my secrets." He lifted one shoulder and let it fall. "I don't tell anyone my secrets. That's the best way to keep them, don't you think?"

Hannah leaned against the desk as the plane continued to taxi toward some unknown destination, wishing she had tried to open the cabin door when she had the chance. Now Ian sat between her and a possible break for freedom and there was no chance of overpowering him. He looked like he was well into his sixties but was in excellent physical condition, nearly as powerful and intimidating as his son.

"Unfortunately, Jackson is closer to sorting out our destination than I anticipated," Ian continued. "I'd hoped my contacts at the Titan group would be able to steer him in the wrong direction, but it looks like he's decided to take matters into his own hands."

Hannah frowned. "The Titan group. Those are the people who texted Jackson the picture of Harley."

"Yes." Ian stood, shaking out the front of his gray slacks. "I asked Alexander to wait to send the image until the timing was right for Adam to extract you from the island."

"Adam's the one who sent the text telling them to kill Harley, not Jackson," she said, feeling like a fool. She should have questioned the text, and Jackson's right-hand man, the moment she saw the kill order.

Deep down, she'd known that wasn't who Jackson was. Not anymore. He loved her—madly maybe, but truly. She should have trusted in that love instead of letting fear send her running into the hands of her enemies.

Ian nodded, amusement curving the edges of his mouth. "Trust is such a fragile thing, isn't it," he said as if reading her mind. "So hard to gain and so easy to lose. You didn't even stop to think he might have been framed, did you?"

Hannah dropped her gaze to the floor without bothering to reply. Obviously she hadn't stopped to think or she wouldn't be here right now.

"It's all right," Ian continued. "If anyone should understand how hard it can be to build trust, it's my son. I'm sure he'll forgive you. Perhaps one day you two will be together again. Assuming you're the sister lucky enough to walk away."

"You don't get to do this." Hannah glared at him, rage sweeping through her like a hot wind, banishing her fear. "You don't get to decide whether Harley or I live or die!"

"But I do, sweetheart," Ian said breezily, as the plane pulled to a stop. "And there's nothing you or my son can do to stop me. By the time Jackson finds out where we are, one of you will already be dead."

Adam emerged from the cockpit and Ian turned to him with a wave of one hand. "Escort Hannah to see her sister and then meet me in my office. We're moving up the timetable. I want to have this finished before lunch."

Hannah balked at the words. The man wanted to get the murdering out of the way so he could enjoy his noon meal. If she'd had any doubts that Ian was a psychopath—or beyond the reach of appeals for mercy—they would have vanished at that moment.

A wave of sickness tightened her throat, but there wasn't anything left in her stomach. She hadn't had so much as a drink of water since boarding the aircraft. She'd been too traumatized to think about asking for food or drink.

But now, as Adam led her from the plane and across a wild, overgrown lawn toward a mansion that made her father's look reserved in comparison, she wished she'd at least asked for a bottle of water. She didn't want to die with the taste of her own sickness ripe in her mouth. She didn't want to face down a gun or a knife or whatever Ian had planned for her feeling weak with thirst.

If she was going to die, she wanted to die with dignity, standing tall and strong, meeting Ian Hawke's cold gaze and letting him know that he hadn't won. He could take her life, but he would never break her spirit.

The only person who could ever break her was Jackson because she'd loved him too much to hold him at a safe distance.

Loved him so much you turned on him at the first sign of trouble.

What kind of love is that? You should have talked to him, the way you were always insisting he talk to you.

Her inner voice was right, but there was nothing she could do about it now. As Adam led her into the tomblike silence of the giant home and up a curving staircase, Hannah just hoped she would live long enough to learn from her mistake.

CHAPTER FORTY-SEVEN

Jackson

*S*omewhere over Mexico, minutes after the line went dead without him knowing if Hannah had heard that he hadn't given the kill order, Jackson forced himself to lie down. He was so wired and scared for Hannah that he knew rest wouldn't come easy, but he had to try.

He couldn't face his father burned out and exhausted.

Ian was always five steps ahead of everyone, but Jackson wasn't the same relatively naïve kid he'd been growing up in his father's house. He'd learned his share about outthinking his enemies, and this time he was fighting for something more important than a shipment of illegal arms or a good price on his latest black market investment.

He was fighting for Hannah's life, and her sister's, too.

If his father killed Harley, Hannah would never forgive him. He had to make this right. He had to think six steps ahead and be waiting for Ian when he turned the corner.

He was off to a good start—he'd already learned that Stewart Mason, his father, and Alexander Titan, of the Titan Group, had served in the same squadron in Vietnam. Therefore, he also knew that he couldn't trust the intelligence he'd received from the Titan Group or hold on to his previously held beliefs about his father.

The realization had led him to dig beneath the surface, deeper into Ian's past.

Turns out, Ian Hawke wasn't the last living member of a Texas oil family, the way he'd led everyone—including his wife —to believe. He was a thug who had grown up in a Chicago slum and, before he was drafted, been well on his way to living a life of crime.

Yes, he'd been awarded his share of medals during his service, but he'd also been written up for insubordination dozens of times. If he'd been serving at any other time than during the least popular war in modern history, Ian would have been discharged before his second tour of duty.

Armed with nothing more than an Internet connection and better-than-average hacking skills, Jackson had unearthed a dozen skeletons in his father's closet. It made him ashamed of himself for not looking behind the mask years ago. But Ian was good at pretending to be something he wasn't.

He was also good at eliminating possible threats before they became *probable* ones.

Jackson had to assume that Ian would know he was on his way so they'd made plans to land at an airstrip on the opposite side of the island from the mansion his father's subsidiary company had purchased last June. Jackson wanted to keep the news of their arrival from Ian as long as possible and hopefully gain entrance to the house unnoticed.

He refused to think about what would happen if his guess were wrong and the home was empty. He wouldn't think about how much time that would waste or what might happen to Hannah while he was scrambling to locate whatever snake hole his father had crawled into.

He had to trust the intelligence he'd gathered and have faith that he was on track to saving the woman he loved.

But faith was harder to hold on to when he was alone.

With Hannah, it had begun to feel natural to wake up in the morning believing he would continue to become a better man, one worthy of her good heart.

Now, as he drifted into a fitful sleep, he wasn't sure what he believed. The only thing he knew for sure was that if his father killed Hannah, hers would be the last murder he would live to commit.

*J*ackson slept, dreaming of a sweltering battlefield where he hunted his father through a blood-soaked jungle and down a hole in the ground that smelled of death and decay. He dreamt of screams and pain and rats that burrowed into the bodies of wounded men, and he woke covered in sweat in time to hear Dominic's half of an ominous sounding phone call.

"Tell him to stall as long as he can," Dom said, his troubled gaze trained out the window. "We'll land in half an hour and be at the house not long after. If he can put it off for even an hour, we'll be there in time to intervene."

Dominic sighed, shaking his head at whatever the person on the other line was saying. "I don't know, Peter. I'll figure something out. You just make sure Mr. Mason doesn't make contact until he absolutely has to."

He ended the call with a jab of his thumb and tossed the phone angrily onto the seat beside him, catching Jackson's eye as he moved. "You're awake," he said, the frustration fading from his features, replaced by a carefully neutral expression that made Jackson wish he were on this plane with someone he knew he could trust.

"I am." Jackson sat up, running a hand through his hair as he pushed the light blanket to the end of the couch. "Who's stalling and why?"

"Your father made contact with Mr. Mason and told him he

had the girls." Dominic plucked his phone from the seat, tucking it into his front pocket. "Stewart was told to get to a secure computer and prepare for a Skype call in twenty minutes."

Jackson's hands balled into fists. "Do you think Hannah was right? Is Ian going to make Mason choose between them?"

"I don't know," Dom said, the muscle in his jaw leaping. "But nothing good is going to come from taking that call. The longer Stewart can put it off, the better. My associate, Peter, is trying to find someone in our network close enough to Key West to offer backup, but there's a good chance they won't get there in time. We may be on our own."

"We should plan on it," Jackson said. "There are already enough unknown variables. We shouldn't go in counting on someone who won't be there."

Dom turned, pinning Jackson with a hard look. "And what about you? Can I count on you?"

Jackson's expression darkened, but Dom pushed on before he could respond.

"I'm not trying to be an asshole. I believe you care about Hannah, but this man is your father. If it comes down to a choice between him and her, are you going to be able to do what needs to be done?"

"Hannah is all that matters," Jackson said, holding the other man's gaze. "I will do whatever it takes to get her out of there alive."

"And Harley?" Dom pushed. "Because I'm not going in to save just one of them."

"If I can save Harley without risking Hannah, I will. If not, I won't," Jackson answered honestly. "Like I said, Hannah is what matters. I'd rather spend the rest of my life begging her forgiveness for failing to save her sister than hating myself for letting Hannah die."

Dom studied him for a long moment, doubt clear in his

dark eyes. "The rest of your life, huh? You're serious about that?"

Jackson fought the urge to snap that it was none of Dom's business what he was or wasn't serious about. Like it or not, Dominic was the only ally he had, and they didn't have time to waste bickering amongst themselves. "I am. If she'll have me."

"You don't think you'll get bored," Dom said in a cold voice. "Once you've smacked her around for a year or two."

Jackson's jaw clenched, but he refused to move—or speak —until the wave of anger summoned by the other man's words had faded. "The things Hannah and I do together are consensual. Not that it's any of your business, but more often than not, she's the one who instigates a scene."

"Right," the other man sneered.

"For the past month, she remained on the island with me of her own free will," Jackson snapped, unable to believe he was being forced to waste time justifying his and Hannah's sexual preferences when her life was in danger. "Clearly, she doesn't feel that she's being abused."

"Yeah, well things can get confusing for victims," Dom shot back. "I've seen it before. They get beaten down so low they confuse the absence of pain with pleasure."

Jackson leaned forward, no longer making any attempt to hide the heat in his gaze. "Hannah is one of the strongest people I've ever met. I haven't beaten her down; she's lifted me up. I am not a perfect man, far from it, but she makes me want to be. I love her and I would die before I would willingly hurt her again."

He paused, making sure Dom was paying attention before he added in a harder voice, "You can choose to believe that or not, but don't you dare call her a victim again. You're insulting her strength and intelligence, and not much makes me angrier than that."

Dominic's eyes narrowed, but after a moment, he shrugged. "Fine. I'll keep my mouth shut. And assuming we get them both out alive and Hannah chooses to stay with you, I won't try to interfere."

"Good."

"But I won't sit by and watch it happen, either." Dom pushed his armrest up with a rough shove. "Assuming she's still in need of protection, I'll ask for someone else to be assigned to her detail. I can't watch a sweet woman like her flush her life and free will away. It's too fucking depressing."

Jackson sighed, the fight slowly going out of him.

Dom was obviously one of the many people in the world who would never understand the kind of relationship he and Hannah both craved. There were few people who did, which had always made it hard for him to imagine finding happily ever after.

Even back before Harley had made sure romance was the last thing on his mind, he'd been cautious when it came to love. He'd learned from experience that he wasn't going to find long-term happiness with a vanilla woman, no matter how beautiful, funny, or likable she might be. He craved the thrill of Domination too much, needed the rush when his top came out to play with a woman who could handle everything he could dish out.

But she needed to truly be able to handle and *enjoy* it, to be tough enough to meet him as an equal in the game.

That's what so many people didn't understand: that a submissive can be every bit as strong as her Dom. Her strength simply manifests in different ways. He had never met that uniquely resilient, yet submissive, woman in his younger years, and even Harley had only pretended to want the same things he wanted. He had never believed he could find that forever kind of happiness with a woman until now.

Hannah was one in a million, the strong, sensitive, beautiful, clever, kinky-as-hell lover he hadn't believed existed until she'd swept into his life. She was his hurricane and his touchstone. She was an endless adventure and the home he never thought he'd find.

She was…everything, but he hadn't told her all the things that were in his heart. And now, if he failed her today, she might never know that she was the answer to everything, even the questions he'd been too stupid to ask.

"Listen," Jackson said, his voice rough with emotion. "You do what you have to do. But right now we need to focus on saving two women's lives. Can we put aside our differences and concentrate on that? Because I need Hannah alive a hell of a lot more than I need you to agree with my lifestyle choices."

Dom's nostrils flared, but after only a moment he nodded. "There will be a car waiting for us at the airstrip and I found a blueprint of the house." He reached into his pocket, pulling out his phone. "I've marked the places where I think they're likely to keep prisoners and where we've got the best chance of getting in undetected. But why don't you do a once over, too. See if there's anything I've overlooked."

Jackson took the phone from Dom's outstretched hand, surprised to find their argument had made him more confident in depending on the other man for backup.

Stewart Mason could be paying this man more money than God for all he knew, but money couldn't buy loyalty. Adam had taught him that. Knowing that Dominic cared about Hannah enough to start an argument with someone nearly twice his size made him trust that the man would do whatever he could to get Hannah to safety.

Now they just had to get there in time for him to eliminate the threat to Hannah once and for all.

Dom didn't have to worry; Jackson was ready to do what needed to be done.

As long as Ian Hawke walked the earth, Hannah would never be safe. It didn't matter that her father had likely committed a crime worthy of a heaping helping of vengeance. The moment Ian had started killing innocent people in his quest for revenge, he'd proven that it was time for him to be put down.

It wasn't something Jackson was eager to do, but he had no other option. As he'd told Dominic, Hannah was his first priority and he would do whatever it took—including killing his own father—to keep her safe.

CHAPTER FORTY-EIGHT

Hannah

*H*annah was too busy memorizing the layout of the house and looking for possible avenues of escape to have time to anticipate what it would be like to see Harley for the first time in six years.

When Adam paused to shove open the bolt on the door at the end of a long hallway on the third floor, she was watching the mechanism slide and wondering if there was a way to force it open from the inside. She wasn't thinking about reunions or the fact that somewhere beyond the door her long lost sister was waiting for her.

And then, Adam pushed her over the threshold and suddenly she was inside with the door closing behind her, staring into the eyes of her missing piece.

Hannah's breath caught and pain flooded through her, leaving her entire body feeling bruised. There she was, rising slowly from the window seat on the other side of the room, the sister who had once been like a part of her own body and soul. With her hair bleached blonde and her skin a pale, creamy shade that bore testament to how little time she must spend in the sun, Harley looked different, but there was no doubt it was her.

Hannah held her sister's troubled gaze, her gut twisting with love and regret and a fierce, bittersweet nostalgia, but the familiar rush of affinity never came.

This woman was no longer her other half. Jackson was her other half, and if she hadn't come into his life when she did, the man she loved would never have found his way out of the hell Harley had consigned him to.

"I'm sorry," Harley said, her eyes shining. "I'm so sorry, Hannah."

"For what?" Hannah asked, not taking another step into the room, not ready to get any closer to Harley than she was already.

"I should have found a way to let you know I was alive." Harley's lashes swept down, sending the tears in her eyes sliding down her pale cheeks. "Dad told me I couldn't because it would put you in danger. But I knew losing me would kill you, the way losing you killed me. I've missed you so much, moo." She pulled in a breath, pressing her lips together as she swiped the wet from her face with her fist. "Please tell me you'll forgive me. If I die here, I don't want to die with you hating me."

"I don't hate you." The lump in Hannah's throat grew a size or three, making it hard to swallow, but her eyes remained dry. "Though I should. I know what you did to Jackson Hawke."

Harley blinked, her brow furrowing as if she were having trouble placing the name.

"Don't you dare pretend you don't remember him," Hannah said, her hands balling into fists at her sides. "Don't you dare because then I will hate you. Forever. No going back."

Her sister swallowed, her thin throat working. "No, I do remember, I just... I wasn't expecting to hear that name. Especially from you."

"I understand." Hannah's lips curved in what she was

certain was an ugly smile. "I wasn't expecting Jackson to come looking for me, either. I was totally unprepared. So was he. He had no idea you had a twin sister. He thought I was you, the woman who had betrayed him and ruined his life."

"Oh my God," Harley whispered, a trembling hand coming to cover her lips. "Are you okay? Did he hurt you?"

"Not as much as you have," Hannah said, knowing now wasn't the time to go into how she'd ended up on a private island with Jackson or how long she'd felt compelled to pretend to be her sister. They didn't have time to waste catching up; they had to find a way out.

But she had to know one thing first. "Why did you do it?" she asked. "Why did you frame an innocent man?"

Harley crossed her arms at her chest, pulling the thin gray sweater she wore tighter across her shoulders. "God, Hannah, I don't know. It was all so messed up. If I could go back and undo it, I would. I swear I would."

"That's not what I asked," Hannah said, her voice cold. "I want to know *why*. Did you even have a reason, or did destroying a man just seem like a fun way to spend the summer?"

Her sister flinched. "I know I deserve that, but I promise you, I'm not that person anymore. I hope I have time to prove that to you and to prove how sorry I am." She wiped the last of her tears away with her sleeve. "As far as the other, I convinced myself ruining Jackson was fair play. An eye for an eye, someone I loved for someone he loved."

Hannah frowned. "Jackson loved *you*. I don't—"

"Not Jackson, his father," she said. "Ian Hawke was the one who took Mom away, Hannah. He's the one who broke her."

"What?" Hannah frowned but understanding clicked into place before Harley could respond. "You mean he was the man Mom had the affair with? When we were kids?"

She nodded. "Now I know seducing Mom was all part of Ian's obsession with evening an old score with Daddy, but I didn't back then." Harley paced toward the two leather couches in the middle of the room and stared into the empty fireplace. "I just knew he was the man who'd ruined our family so…I decided to ruin his."

Hannah shook her head. "That isn't justice, Harley. Jackson was innocent. Completely. At least Mom went with Ian of her own free will, Jackson was just—"

"I know that," Harley said, her pitch rising as she spun to face Hannah. "Believe me, Hannah, I know. I fucked everything up and ruined people's lives and proved I was every bit as evil as that man who plans to kill one of us."

She stepped closer, until only a few feet separated them, before continuing in a softer voice, "And I swear I would give my own life if it would make it all right again, but it won't. The only thing I can do is move forward trying not to do any more harm." Her tongue slipped out to dampen her lips. "And that's what I've done and why I have an enormous favor to ask you."

"A favor." Hannah's breath huffed out. "Considering I might die today, Harley, I don't think I'm in a place to make promises."

"You're not going to die," Harley said, a resigned look in her bloodshot eyes. "I've had a few days to think about this and I seriously don't see Daddy choosing me. He knows you deserve mercy more than I do, and I think a part of him would like an excuse to bring Jasper to live with him."

Hannah's brow furrowed, but Harley pushed on before she could imagine who Jasper might be.

"He thinks it would be better with a boy, easier, or something, but he's wrong." Harley's lip curled. "He'd get tired of Jasper the same way he got tired of us, and I can't stand for my son to grow up that way."

Hannah leaned back against the door, her knees suddenly unsteady.

Harley had a child? A little boy, who would be left without a mother if their father chose to spare Hannah's life instead of hers?

Harley threaded her hands together in front of her. "That's why I want you to take him, Hannah. I don't know if you have kids, but—"

"I don't," Hannah said, the admission sending another wave of pain through her chest. Her dreams of love and family had disappeared along with her other dreams, on the day her sister had died and she'd learned she was a hunted woman.

But they'd come back. With Jackson, for a stolen moment in time that was likely all she would ever know of romantic love.

Harley's expression softened. "Well, I have no doubt you'll be an amazing mother. And I know you would love Jasper like he was yours. He's such a good, smart, sweet kid, just like you were when we were little. And I've told him all about you so he won't be shocked to see someone who looks like me."

She paused, tears rising in her eyes again before she added, "I think it would give him comfort, really. And maybe someday he wouldn't even remember the difference between his first mom and his second one."

"Jesus." Hannah closed her eyes, sagging more heavily against the door. Her thoughts raced even as her pulse slowed until her hands felt like lumps of ice at the ends of her arms.

"Please, Hannah," Harley begged, her voice even closer now. "I know it's a lot to take in, but—"

"Dad's not going to choose me," Hannah said, forcing her eyes open. She couldn't fall apart now, not when Harley had basically confirmed that the only way she was getting out of here alive was if she managed to escape before Adam returned. "He won't take Jasper's mother away from him. If it comes down to making a choice, you'll be the one walking away from this."

Harley shook her head. "Have you forgotten who our father is? He's not going to care about taking me away from Jasper. He'll convince himself it's for the best. If I'm dead, then Jasper won't have to hide. He'll be able to come back to the States and live like a prince and start kindergarten next fall where the kids speak English. It's everything Dad's wanted for the past five years."

For the past five years. Hannah's gut churned as she quickly did the math. Harley's son was five years old, getting ready to start kindergarten, which meant she must have gotten pregnant that summer six years ago, which meant...

Jasper might be Jackson's. Jackson could have a son.

It was a painful realization—she didn't want to think about Jackson having children with another woman, especially her sister—but it was also a reason to love the little boy even more. Jasper might be more than her nephew; he might also be a piece of the man she loved.

"If something happens to you, I will take care of Jasper," Hannah promised, knowing it was the right decision as soon as the words left her lips. "I will love him like he's my own and do everything I can to give him a happy life."

Harley's shoulders sagged. "Thank you, moo. Thank you so much."

"But let's make sure nothing happens to you. Or to me," she said, motioning toward the window as she crossed the room. "How do things look outside? Are there guards who will notice two women climbing out a window?"

"I haven't seen any guards," Harley said, following her. "But there's nothing in here to use for a rope. I took the covers off the couch cushions and tried to tie them together, but the leather is too thick. And even if we could find a way to connect the pieces, they wouldn't reach far enough anyway. We're three stories off the ground."

Hannah opened the window, letting in the cool, but muggy, Florida winter air. She leaned forward to press her face against the screen, taking in the sheer drop down to the grass below. There was nothing to hold on to and a fall from this far up would likely kill them. It would definitely leave them too hurt to run, and then they would end up right back where they were now.

But Harley was right, there was nothing in the room except bookshelves and the two leather couches, no bed sheets or clothes or anything else they could use to make a rope.

"But there are two of us now," Hannah murmured, gaze shifting left and right, trying to get a better idea of how far up they were.

The bottom floor had a vaulted ceiling—she'd noticed that on the way through the foyer to the stairs—but the next two floors seemed fairly standard sized. She guessed they were about thirty feet up. Cut that number in half and one of them would have an excellent chance of surviving the drop without being any worse for wear.

She spun back to Harley, gaze skimming up and down as she took in her sister's clothing. The gray sweater wasn't very thick, but it looked strong. If they used the sweater to tie them to something heavy…

"Let me see your sweater," she said, holding out her hand.

Harley frowned, but obediently stripped off the sweater, revealing the tight gray tee shirt she wore beneath. It hugged her sister's torso, showcasing the ribs clearly visible beneath the fabric. She was even smaller than she used to be and her arms were thin, but soft, without a hint of muscle tone.

Still, Harley ought to have enough strength to hold on to Hannah's hands until it was time for her to drop to the ground.

"With my sweater, your dress, and my pants we've got maybe eight feet of rope," Harley said, proving she could still read Hannah's mind. "That still doesn't get us close enough to the ground and we'll be in our underwear when we run into the swamp."

"It's warm enough that exposure shouldn't be a problem and *we* won't be running anywhere," Hannah said, eyeing the couch and deciding it looked plenty heavy to serve her purpose. "*You're* going to be running into the swamp. We'll have eight feet of rope, five and a half feet of me once I tie the rope to my ankles, plus the length of our arms extended when we're holding hands. That will take you halfway to the ground. As long as you land with bent knees and roll across the grass you should be fine."

Harley's eyes widened. "And what happens to you after this circus trick?"

"I pull myself back up into the room," Hannah said, trying to act like the thought of dangling headfirst from a third story window didn't scare her half to death. "Ian wants to make Dad choose between us. He can't choose if I'm the only one here."

"What if he decides he doesn't care about making him choose," Harley said. "What if you fall?"

"I won't fall." She pushed on, talking over Harley's next argument. "And even if I do, I would rather die trying to escape than sit here waiting for Ian to kill one of us. Jackson's on his way to try to help, but his dad knows that and he's moved up the timetable. He could come for us any minute."

Harley blinked. "Jackson? Is on his way here?" She blinked again. "And he's coming to help *us*, not to help his father kill me?"

"It's a long story. I'll tell you as soon as we're somewhere safe," Hannah said, then added quickly, "but if you end up seeing Jackson before I do, tell him that I'm sorry I didn't trust him the way I should have. And that I love him and I always will."

Ignoring her sister's bug-eyed expression, Hannah waved her toward the couch. "Come on. Help me move the couch. We'll secure the rope to the legs."

They had the couch pulled up beside the window, the screen shoved out onto the grass below, and had just finished ripping Harley's sweater into two long strips they were securing to the couch legs when the door opened.

Hannah turned to see Adam step inside, a gun in one hand and strips of long black fabric in the other.

CHAPTER FORTY-NINE
Jackson

*T*he driver who met them at the airstrip took them immediately to a marina nearby, where Mason's people had hired a speedboat for their use. Within ten minutes of touching down, they were on the water, racing around to the other side of the island, the salty wind in their faces making conversation impossible.

They were moving fast, but Jackson had no idea if they would be fast enough. And when the hulking shadow of the mansion appeared around the next bend in the coast—a behemoth crouched on the top of a small rise, casting a dense blue shadow in the hazy winter light—the sight gave him little comfort.

The house looked abandoned, the windows dark and the yard overgrown.

His stomach clenched, but a moment later, the island Hannah had mentioned came into view on their right side. The snack bar was closed and the tiny dock empty, but red hammocks hung from the trees. A little farther along the coast, the palms on the opposite shore opened up, revealing a small private airstrip.

The plane with the red stripe down the nose sat at the end of it, only yards from the mansion's expansive lawn.

Dom motioned forward with two fingers, signaling that he was going to continue around to the other side of the house. They'd agreed that they shouldn't pull up to the beach within sight of the home—his father likely wouldn't be expecting them to have acquired a boat so quickly and wouldn't pay attention to a boat as long as it didn't stop near the house. Still, a part of Jackson wanted to take the wheel and aim them straight for the mansion's private dock.

Time was running out. He could feel it. The invisible tether connecting him to Hannah was being strained. Soon, it would snap. His gut kept screaming that he was minutes away from losing her and that every second counted.

The thought was barely through his head when a loud pop sounded from inside the home, echoing out across the water.

It was a gunshot, followed quickly by a second and a third.

Hannah

*A*dam blindfolded them before pushing them out into the hall. There, they were forced to fumble along with their hands on the wall and then to cling to the wooden handrail as they descended the stairs.

They were halfway to the first landing when Hannah heard Harley stumble behind her and turned to snap at Adam—

"We've already seen the house. I don't see the point in the blindfolds unless Ian's decided he wants us to die from falling down the stairs."

"Mr. Hawke wanted you blindfolded," Adam said in his usual low, disaffected voice.

"You always do what the Hawkes tell you to do?" Hannah asked, not afraid of the gun in Adam's hand. He wouldn't shoot them. Not until his master gave the signal, anyway.

"I do what the highest bidder tells me to do. Your father had the chance to pay up and make this go away, but he thought I was bluffing."

"We can pay," Harley piped up from behind her before Hannah could figure out what to make of Adam's claim.

If he were telling the truth, what did that mean for her and Harley? If Ian wanted money in addition to one of their lives, would their father give it? Stewart had always been generous when it came to his daughters, but maybe blackmail changed things.

"We've both got trust funds," Harley continued, "and I've made money on my artwork. Just let us go, and I'll give you everything."

"Too late for that," Adam said with a sniff. "But I'll do what I can to make it painless. Whichever one your father chooses."

"You're a fucking prince, Adam," Hannah sneered, shocked by how much she wanted to wrap her fingers around the man's neck and squeeze the life out of him with her bare hands.

He let forth a grunt of amusement, the closest she'd ever heard him come to laughter. "You used to be such a lady. Jackson's been a bad influence. Watch the last step."

"This is a mistake, Adam," Hannah said as she stepped down onto the ground floor, her bare feet tingling as they touched the cold, slick hardwood. "If you hurt me, Jackson will destroy you. You know I'm right. If I were you, I'd let us both go right now and run like hell."

"I'll be gone before he gets here. And as long as your dad chooses you, I should be okay." Adam took her arm. "He wanted the other one dead anyway."

Harley whimpered softly. Hannah reached back, fumbling until she found her sister's hand and squeezing tight, silently promising that she wouldn't let her die, not if she could do anything to stop it.

It didn't matter what Harley had done in the past. What mattered was that she had a little boy who needed his mother. Hannah didn't want to die, but she couldn't live with herself if she orphaned an innocent child.

She knew what that felt like, how devastating it was to lose the person you loved most in the world. There had been times, after her mother had first gone away, when she'd been certain she would never be happy again. No matter how bright and sunny the day outside, her world had been a dark place. She wouldn't consign her nephew to that kind of darkness. Losing an aunt he'd never met wouldn't hurt him; losing his mother would destroy something sweet and sacred inside of that little boy that would haunt him forever.

She held tight to Harley's hand, walking straight and tall as Adam led them into another room and abandoned them in the middle of a thick, padded rug that scratched the bottom of her feet. She didn't know if her father was watching, but if he were, she wouldn't show fear or give him any reason to doubt her when she told him to choose Harley.

"Welcome, ladies." Ian's voice oozed from somewhere in front of them. "I regret to have met you under such grim circumstances. Unfortunately, your father gave me no choice."

"I'm here, girls." Their father's voice sounded tinny and distant as if he were on speakerphone. It had been years since Hannah had heard his voice and even longer since she'd heard him sound so hopeless.

In fact, she'd only heard that particular sad resignation once before, on the day he sat her and Harley down to tell them that their mother had left the family. Maybe forever.

"Don't be afraid," Stewart continued. "I'm going to find a way to make this better. I promise, I won't—"

"Not this time," Ian cut in, a squeaking sound following the words. It was the squeak of a chair giving under someone's weight, but Hannah couldn't tell if he was sitting down or standing up. "You'll honor your obligations this time, Mason. And to make it clear how very serious I am about the choice you're about to make…"

His words ended with a thunderous *boom! boom! boom!* that echoed off the walls, the gunshots deafening in the enclosed space.

Harley screamed and Hannah ripped the blindfold from her eyes, no longer caring about obeying the rules. If Ian had shot Harley, all bets were off. She would save her sister if she could and run if she couldn't.

Or maybe she'd hurl herself at Ian and see if she could claw his eyes out before he managed to kill her, too.

She spun, blinking at the sudden rush of light, to see that Harley had pulled her blindfold off, as well. Her sister's breath came fast and shallow as she backed away from the body beginning to bleed out at her feet.

Hannah swallowed, eyes flicking from Adam's paling face to the red stains spreading across his shirt. She fought to think past the horror clutching at her throat, struggling to figure out what this meant.

Ian had shot his accomplice. Adam was dead—or dying fast—and soon either she or Harley would follow.

Or maybe he'd shoot both of them, no matter what he'd told her father.

She hadn't had any experience in a hostage situation before, but her gut said that if Ian had his way, he would be the only one leaving this room alive.

Jackson

*T*he moment Dom pulled the boat within five feet of the dock, Jackson jumped out and ran.

He wasn't worried about stealth or secrecy anymore.

Gunshots had been fired. Three of them. Harley and Hannah could both be dead.

Or maybe Harley, Hannah, *and* Adam.

If Jackson knew his father, he wouldn't allow a traitor to live. It didn't matter that Ian couldn't have taken Hannah without Adam's help or that his father had committed enough sins to thoroughly blacken his own soul. Ian had no tolerance for betrayal.

That was why Hannah was here. Her father had dared to betray a Hawke and now he was paying the price for it.

No, she's here because of you. You led Ian right to her.

If you hadn't been such a vengeful bastard, Hannah would still be safe on her island with her aunt.

Vengeful bastard. Just like his father.

As Jackson ran around the side of the house, bent double to stay out of sight of the ground floor windows, he cursed himself for growing up too much like Ian Hawke. If he hadn't been a madman bent on revenge, his father wouldn't have the woman he loved held at gunpoint right now.

He had to believe that Hannah was still alive. He couldn't admit that he was probably too late or he would start screaming and never stop. He couldn't lose her. Not now, not because he was five fucking minutes too late.

He was rounding the front of the house when he heard his father's voice and froze. He glanced over his shoulder, motioning for Dom—who was quickly gaining on his head start—to stay quiet before jabbing a finger at the open window above him.

"Now that you understand how serious I am, Stewart." Ian's voice sounded like he was facing away from him, but Jackson couldn't be sure. Slowly, he moved closer to the window, ears straining.

"You have two minutes to decide which of your daughters will live," Ian continued. "At the conclusion of one hundred and twenty seconds, I will make the choice for you."

Jackson's heart lurched into his throat. Hannah was still alive, but in less than two minutes she wouldn't be. There was no time for the diversion he and Dom had planned or to chart another course of action. He had to take advantage of the element of surprise and hope he could take his father down before he killed Hannah.

Pulling the gun from his pants, Jackson met Dom's eyes and nodded toward the window. Without missing a beat, Dom motioned back around the house before drawing his own gun and hurrying back the way he'd come. Dom would cover the window on the other side of the room. If Jackson missed, hopefully, the other man wouldn't.

Slowly, Jackson stood up far enough to peer into the room, his stomach clenching when he saw Hannah and Harley on the other side of a large wooden desk. His father stood in front of the desk, his back turned to Jackson and his attention directed down at the open laptop beside him.

"Please, just give me a few more minutes." Stewart Mason's voice emerged from the computer. "I haven't spoken to either of the girls in years because of you, Ian. At least give me time to say goodbye."

"One hundred seconds," Ian said, proving his utter lack of compassion.

But then, he knew he was on a timetable and he wasn't one to waste time indulging other people's emotions. *His* emotions —his rage, his jealousy, his avarice—were all that mattered, all that had ever mattered.

Still, when Jackson stood up, aiming the gun at the back of his father's head, he couldn't help but hesitate for the barest second. He'd spent the past six years imagining the look on Ian's face when he realized that his son was innocent. He hated his father, but some part of him, that child buried deep inside of the hardened man he'd become, still craved his approval, his love.

But there was no love inside Ian Hawke. He was beyond redemption and it was past time for him to die.

Jackson was squeezing the trigger when his father suddenly turned and fired at the window, aiming right between his son's eyes.

CHAPTER FIFTY

Hannah

*I*t all happened so fast.

One second, her father was pleading for more time from the laptop screen; the next, Ian had turned and fired at the window behind him.

Hannah cringed, her shoulders hunching toward her ears as the glass shattered with another *boom! boom!* and a crystalline ringing that sliced through the air. Ian staggered backward, clutching his chest just as a third shot sounded from the other side of the room.

Acting on instinct, Hannah tackled Harley to the ground, rolling across the carpet as the window near the fireplace exploded.

"Run!" she shouted as they untangled themselves, urging Harley toward the entrance to the room. She had no idea who was shooting at the house, but they needed to get out of the room before they were caught in the crossfire. "Stay low, find somewhere to hide. I'm right behind you."

Harley scrambled out of the room on her hands and knees. Hannah was following when she caught a flash of movement out of the corner of her eye. It was Ian, lurching toward the window with his gun in hand, aiming at something outside.

She came to her feet in the shelter of the doorway, standing on tiptoe until she could see the lawn outside and the wounded man sprawled on the grass.

She couldn't see his face, but she recognized the shape of Jackson's body instantly.

Her heartbeat stuttered and the blood in her veins turned molten as something primal inside of her responded to the sight of the blood staining his shirt with a roar of fear and rage. He'd been shot! His father had shot him in the chest. And now, unless she did something to stop him, Ian was about to finish the job of murdering his son.

The realization hit; a second later, Hannah was in motion.

She surged back into the room, her thoughts racing even as time seemed to slow, giving her a few precious seconds to think. As she rushed toward Ian, she snatched her discarded blindfold from the floor, wrapping it tight around her hands as she closed the last of the distance between them and leapt into the air.

She landed on the desk, skidding across the smooth surface on her knees to collide with Ian just as he lifted the gun and fired. His arm jerked down, sending the shot intended for Jackson burrowing into the baseboards. Before he could take aim again, Hannah wrapped the blindfold around his neck and pulled backward with all the strength in her body.

Ian thrashed and spun away, dragging her off the desk, but she held on, gritting her teeth and squeezing her hands into fists so tight her joints screamed in protest.

But she didn't let go. She clung to the fabric, using her body weight to her advantage. She let her knees go weak, sagging toward the ground, dragging Ian down with her. After a few more heavy steps, he bent backward, hanging halfway between the ceiling and the floor for a seemingly endless second before he collapsed on top of her, his torso pinning her hips and legs to the ground.

Panting for breath, Hannah kicked his bulk to one side and

struggled free, her makeshift garrote at the ready and her eyes glued to Ian's face, which looked strangely peaceful now that he was unconscious.

The moment she knew Ian was out cold, the old Hannah would have jumped up and run to Jackson. But the new Hannah understood that you can't always run from your problems. Sometimes you have to fight for your life and the lives of the people you love. Now, that fighter inside of her insisted it would be dangerously stupid to leave this wounded predator alive. Ian would only wake up more determined to finish what he'd started.

As long as Ian Hawke was alive, none of the people she loved would be safe and she was tired of living in fear and being hunted for the sin of being Stewart Mason's daughter. Ian's revolver lay on the floor beside him, but she'd never shot a gun in her life and wasn't sure she could hold a weapon to a man's head and fire.

But she could finish this the way she'd started it.

Jaw clenched and a dark determination rising inside of her, Hannah straddled Ian's chest and brought the blindfold back to his throat. She was leaning forward, drawing the fabric tight across his windpipe when a hand touched her shoulder, making her spin and lash out.

By the time she recognized Dom's face, her fist had already connected with his stomach, making him double over with a groan.

"I'm sorry," Hannah said, her voice soft and surprisingly steady. "I thought you were one of his people."

"I'm not," Dom said, grunting as he fought to catch his breath. "I'm on your side. Jackson's on the front lawn. He's been shot. It doesn't look fatal, but I need you to go apply pressure to the wound until your father's cleanup crew gets here."

Hannah glanced toward the laptop, but the computer was closed. The realization made her arms begin to shake. She hadn't even thought about her father or who else might be watching her murder a man.

Not that it would have changed her mind...

"Go check on Jackson," Hannah said, turning back to Ian. "I have to finish."

Dom's hand landed lightly on her shoulder again. "You already have, Hannah. He's not breathing, and I'm not going to administer CPR."

Hannah blinked down at the man beneath her, unable to believe she'd been sitting on his chest for nearly a minute and hadn't realized that he wasn't drawing breath.

"Oh." She rolled off of Ian, her stiff fingers relaxing their grip on the blindfold as her hands began to shake.

He was dead. She'd killed a man. She was a murderer.

The knowledge should have done more than make her shake, but aside from her trembling hands she felt very calm, almost peaceful. She suspected she was going into shock, but she didn't have time to worry about it. She had to get to Jackson.

She stood, weaving slightly as the blood rushed into her legs.

"Are you okay?" Dom put a steadying hand to her back. "I can go to Jackson if you need a minute."

She shook her head, but before she could speak, a voice sounded from the foyer.

"Hannah! Hannah where are you?"

She turned to see Jackson round the corner and lean heavily against the doorway, clutching his right shoulder. He was grimacing and pale, with sweat beading on his forehead and blood streaming through his fingers to form tiny rivers that flowed down his left forearm, but he was alive.

He was alive and the most beautiful thing she'd ever seen.

She hurried to his side and tucked herself beneath his uninjured arm, gratitude rushing through her when he hugged her close with his usual strength. "You shouldn't be standing up."

"You're okay?" he asked, his pained gaze scanning her face. "He didn't hurt you?"

"I'm fine," she said, swallowing hard. "But your father's dead."

Jackson's eyes flicked to where his father lay on the hardwood floor, a small puddle of blood forming beneath his left shoulder.

"Your shot started it, but she finished it," Dom said, subtext in the words Hannah couldn't understand, but that Jackson seemed to.

"Good." He met the other man's gaze before turning back to her. "He would have killed both of us if you hadn't. Don't doubt it for a second. You only did what you had to do."

"We need to get the bleeding stopped," Hannah said, anxiety pricking at her skin as blood continued to seep from the wound near Jackson's shoulder, soaking his shirt. "Come on. Let's get you settled in the dining room."

"I'll find Harley," Dom said. "She has her pilot's license. She might be able to get us out of here before the cleanup crew."

"That would be great." The thought sent a wave of relief rushing through Hannah's chest. She wasn't surprised that Harley had acquired another exotic skill set. Her sister had always been a fan of acquiring new hobbies, especially ones that cost obscene amounts of money. "The sooner we can get Jackson to a doctor the better."

"We'll land at the airstrip near your father's house," Dom said, moving away down the hall as Hannah guided Jackson into the dining room. "He'll have a doctor waiting who won't ask questions."

Hannah's breath rushed out with a curse.

"Are you really okay?" Jackson asked softly.

"I'm understanding what a cleanup crew is correctly,

right?" she asked, suddenly acutely aware of the acidic taste flooding her mouth. "People who clean up murder scenes so the bad guys don't get sent to jail?"

"Except this time they're cleaning up the murder scene so the good guys don't go to jail." Jackson grunted as he sat down on the edge of the heavy oak table and let Hannah help him lift his legs so he could lie down on top of it.

"Or the good woman, anyway," he added, paling as she wadded the blindfold into a ball and pressed it to his bullet wound. "You don't deserve to go to jail or even trial for this. It was self-defense."

"I wasn't thinking about myself," Hannah said. "When I saw you lying on the ground and your dad going in for the kill shot, I just...lost it." She shook her head, the dazed feeling still hanging around her head like a protective fog. She was grateful for the way it softened the edges of what she'd done, making it okay to push the sight of Ian's slack features from her mind. "I didn't even think about what I was going to do, I just did it."

"I understand. You were protecting what's yours."

Hannah held his gaze, her throat tightening as she searched his eyes for a sign that everything was going to be okay. "Are you? Still mine? Even though I ran away and nearly got us both killed?" She rushed on, cutting him off before he could speak. "I know you didn't give the order to kill Harley. I know it was a trick now, but I should have suspected that from the beginning."

Jackson's lips curved in a humorless smile. "It's not your fault. I didn't tell you that I'd put my people back on her trail. I should have." He paused, finding her hand with his. "The same way I should have told you that I love you long before last night."

"Yeah?" The lump in Hannah's throat swelled until she could barely breathe.

"Yes." Jackson squeezed her cold fingers. "I love you and it shouldn't have taken almost losing you to make me realize I never want to let you go."

Tears rose in her eyes and the numb feeling began to fade, replaced by an overwhelming mixture of fear and relief that made her voice break as she asked, "Never?"

"Never," he said, without a hint of hesitation. "I'm yours. For as long as I'm on this earth. And I hope you'll be mine."

"Of course. Of course, I will." She smoothed his hair from his forehead before pressing a kiss to the sweat-damp skin. "I can't wait to be away from all this and know you're going to be okay."

"I'm going to be fine." He shifted, wincing as he moved his injured shoulder. "Don't worry. I've been in worse shape than this. Lots of times."

Hannah swallowed, willing her tears away, trying not to show how much the blood soaking the cloth scared her. "Well, hopefully, Dom will be back with Harley soon and we can get going." She nibbled her lip, dread knotting in her stomach as the reality that Jackson and Harley were about to set eyes on each other for the first time in years fully penetrated.

"I know you're still angry and you have every right to be," she continued, "but I talked to Harley and I believe she's changed. That doesn't excuse what she did, not even a little bit, but I—"

"It doesn't matter," Jackson said with a small shake of his head. "I don't care about her. You're all that matters. You and me."

Hannah's mouth trembled, caught between a smile and something guiltier. "Well, anyway. I believe she's sorry at least. For what she did to you."

Because she had a child—maybe your child—and it changed her.

Love changed her, the way loving you has changed me.

She knew she had to say something to Jackson—warn him that Harley had a bombshell to drop—but she couldn't make her lips form the words. She told herself that she didn't want to upset him while he was wounded, but she sensed the truth was she didn't want to upset herself. After everything she'd been through in the past twelve hours, telling the man she loved that he could be the father of her sister's baby might be the straw that broke the camel's back.

Still, she was trying to put together a few coherent sentences, something she could say to ease tensions on the off chance that Harley brought up Jasper on the way to the plane, when Dom appeared in the doorway.

He was alone, a grim look in his eye Hannah didn't understand until she heard the faint drone of a plane engine flying low over the house, heading away to the east.

Her next breath emerged with a huff as she realized who must be flying the plane. "She left us. That's Harley, isn't it? Flying the plane? She left us here."

Dom dropped his gaze to the floor. "Looks like it. There's no one else on the property and I couldn't find her anywhere."

Hannah cursed, while Jackson laughed, a humorless sound that transformed to a groan. "Fuck, it hurts to laugh."

"Then don't," Hannah said, her voice sharp with rage. "There's nothing to laugh about. And if you die because she ran away and left us, I'm going to hunt her down and kill her myself."

Jackson tightened his grip on her hand. "No. No more hunting. No more revenge."

She glanced down at him, her anger fading a few degrees when she saw the love so clear in his eyes.

"We're going to get out of here," he continued, "I'm going to heal, and then you and I are going to make a life together away from all the crazy people in our lives."

"Yes," she whispered. "That's all I want."

Hannah leaned down to kiss his forehead again, silently willing the cleanup crew to move faster. The sooner she and Jackson were away from this place of fear and death and moving toward their brighter future, the better.

CHAPTER FIFTY-ONE

Jackson

*J*ackson did his best not to pass out, not wanting to scare Hannah, who he suspected wasn't holding up as well as she was pretending to for his sake.

But by the time the two burly members of Stewart Mason's cleanup crew arrived with a stretcher to carry him to the private jet, he was so lightheaded he couldn't fight the urge to sink into something deeper than sleep.

*H*e blinked out and when he flickered on again—coming to staring at a vaulted ceiling in a room that smelled faintly of roses—he had no idea where he was, how he'd gotten there, or how much time had passed since he'd been shot.

Shot.

He'd been shot and his father was dead.

The memories came in a cold flood, making it hard to draw a deep breath.

He shifted on the crisp sheets beneath him, becoming aware of the IV in his arm—evidently the reason he wasn't desperately thirsty or suffering from more than a dull ache in his chest—and the woman asleep in the recliner in the corner. It was Hannah, in black spandex pants and a soft-looking red sweater, curled up with an afghan she'd wadded beneath her head to use as a pillow. Her hair was tangled, her face pale, and it looked like she might have been drooling on the blanket sometime during the night.

She was beautiful, so perfect and precious his heart lurched, sending an ugly sensation coursing down his right arm.

He grunted softly as the pain came and went. As soon as the sound rumbled through his throat, Hannah bolted upright, blinking sleepy blue eyes in his direction.

"You're awake." She slipped out of her chair and crossed the room to his bedside, taking his hand as she perched carefully on the mattress beside him. "How do you feel?"

"All right," he said, his voice rough with disuse. "Pretty good really, considering. How long have I been out?"

"Almost two days," she said, worry clear in her eyes. "You lost a lot of blood. Thankfully, my mother was a match so the doctor was able to do a transfusion not long after we landed."

"I'll have to thank her." He glanced around the room, not sure how he felt about recovering in what he assumed was Stewart Mason's home. Stewart's money and connections had no doubt saved his life, but if Sybil's suspicions were correct, the man had also hired Ian to kill his own brothers.

"No, you won't," Hannah said, her tone brittle. "She wasn't happy about it. She wanted to let you die, but I convinced her to do it. For me."

His brows lifted and fell. "Well, I guess I'm lucky she loves you, then."

"I guess so." Hannah sighed, her gaze falling to their joined hands. "Or lucky she feels guilty or whatever it is that goes through her head when she looks at me."

She ran her free hand through her tangled hair. "I don't

think it was really about you. Apparently, she had a thing with your father and it ended badly. She was never the same after the year she spent with him."

"What?" Jackson frowned. "You're kidding."

She laughed softly. "No, I'm not. That's why you became Harley's target. She wanted revenge against your father. So she decided to ruin his son in exchange for ruining our mother."

He relaxed back onto the pillows, strangely comforted by the revelation.

"You don't seem surprised," Hannah said, peering at him through her lashes.

"I'm not. I mean, I'm surprised to hear about Ian's relationship with your mother, but I'm not surprised I was a target because of something he'd done. I'd thought of that before, that one of his enemies might have assumed the best way to ruin my father was to destroy his only child."

He glanced down at his wounded chest, his lips curving in a bitter smile. "Harley obviously didn't realize that Ian couldn't have cared less if I lived or died."

Hannah brought his hand to her lips and pressed a kiss to his knuckles. "I can't wait to get out of here." She glanced over her shoulder, before adding in a softer voice, "I don't trust Dad. He's been nothing but helpful and sorry, but it's clear he's not a fan of our relationship. And I can't shake the feeling that there's something he's not telling me."

"About what?" he asked, wondering if Hannah knew about Sybil's suspicions. He didn't imagine so, or she wouldn't be able to speak her father's name without horror in her voice.

She shook her head. "I don't know. I feel like it's something about your dad. Or your dad and my mom, something that happened while they were together maybe, but I know better than to push. If I do, he'll shut down and disappear and we'll be left alone with Mom and the maids."

"Might not be so bad," he said. "I'm not in any hurry to meet your father."

Hannah's lips pursed to one side. "Oh yeah? You're not planning to ask him for permission to court me?"

"I don't need his permission," Jackson said, holding her gaze. "I have your permission."

Her expression softened. "You most certainly do." She squeezed his hand. "Dom told me to tell you he's sorry for the things he said on the plane, by the way. He didn't give me specifics. He just said that you were right and I was stronger than he'd given me credit for."

Jackson grunted. "He should have apologized to you, not me."

"He did," she said, her smile fading. "And then he left to go find Harley. She's given Dad's people the slip and disappeared."

"Why?" The mention of her sister's name sent nothing but a vague irritation flashing through his chest, proving that his lust for revenge was truly dead and buried. "My father's gone. The danger's over."

Hannah ducked her head. "Yeah, well, maybe she doesn't know that. Maybe she thinks he's still out there. Which means…"

"That she left without knowing you were safe," Jackson supplied with a sigh. "I'm sorry, Hannah."

She shrugged but didn't speak again for a long moment.

"Maybe it's for the best," he added gently. "I know you were happy to find out that she's alive, but she's not the kind of person you need in your life."

"I know I don't need her in yours," Hannah mumbled, keeping her gaze on the flowered quilt covering his legs.

"You don't have to worry about me." Jackson shifted his head, trying to catch her eye. "Look at me, Hannah." He waited until she reluctantly lifted her gaze. "I meant what I said. I'm not going to do anything to Harley. And I'm not going to go looking for her, either. Not anymore. I'm ready to let it go, to let go of everything except you and me."

"You promise?" Her eyes began to shine. "Even if you found out she'd done something else? You would still want to let it go?"

"Something like what?" he asked, brow furrowing.

She shook her head as she tilted her chin down, sending her tangled curls falling into her face. "Nothing. I don't know anything for sure. I didn't ask enough questions. I thought there would be time to talk later. But instead she ran away."

She laughed, a strained sound that ended in a soft sob. "I feel so stupid. I actually believed that she was sorry. I bought her lies all over again, the way I did when I was a kid."

Jackson studied her for a moment, unable to shake the feeling that there was something wrong.

Something more than you being unconscious for two days, her father being a criminal, her mother loathing her new lover, and her sister running off without bothering to make sure Hannah survived, you mean?

It was true. Hannah had been through hell and now wasn't the time to push her about Harley or anything else. If he was going to prove to her that he was ready to let go of the past, actions would speak louder than words.

"Can you get me a new cell phone?" he asked, inspiration striking. "Something I can be sure my father's people didn't have traced?"

Hannah nodded. "Of course. I'll go to the store this afternoon."

"You should go now," he said, releasing her hand. "If I can reach the right people before noon, we should be able to fly out tonight."

Her eyes widened. "Fly where?" she asked eagerly, betraying her excitement before she shook her head. "No. You can't fly. You're hurt and you've been unconscious for two days."

"I'm fine to fly," he said. "But if you're worried I can make sure wherever we end up has a doctor on call."

She pegged him with a hard look. "A doctor who won't mind treating a gunshot wound without blabbing about it? I don't think so. We have to lie low, Jackson. My father said you're being investigated by the CIA."

Jackson snorted. "They've been investigating for years. If they haven't found enough to arrest me by now, they never will."

"Well, you'll forgive me if I'd rather we not put your hubris to the test." She closed her eyes and took a deep breath. "I just got you back. I don't want to lose you again to a prison sentence."

"You're not going to lose me," he said, hating that he was the reason for the pinched, exhausted expression on her face. "I'm sorry."

Her eyes blinked open. "For what?"

"For coming to you with so much baggage," he said. "I'd undo it if I could, but I can't. All I can do is promise you that it ends here. From now on, I'll be conducting business strictly above board. Legal channels only."

Hannah smiled, a beautiful, hopeful smile that made Jackson swear he'd do whatever it took to keep it in place. "You don't know how happy I am to hear that."

"I do." He reached up to cup her cheek in his hand. "It's all over your face, sunshine."

She pressed her lips together. "For a while, I wasn't sure I'd hear you say that again. The past few days have been… pretty terrible."

"I'm sorry about that too," he said, scooting over to make room for her on the bed. "Come here, lie down with me."

"I'll hurt you," she said, but she was eyeing the empty space beneath his arm with a hunger that made it clear how badly she needed to be held.

"You will not." He clenched his jaw as he waved her onto

the bed, refusing to show her how sore his other side still was. "And even if you do, you know I like a little pain."

She rolled her eyes. "Now's not the time for that."

"It's the perfect time," he said in a close approximation of his Dom voice. "So get your ass in this bed. Right now."

With a laugh, she climbed onto the bed and curled against his side, her head on his good arm and her palm resting lightly on his stomach. And even though it hurt, he hugged her closer. Pain and pleasure had always been tangled up with her, this woman he loved beyond all reason.

"I'll rest today, but tomorrow we're getting on a plane," he said, kissing the top of her head. "We'll find a peaceful place to celebrate the holiday and plan our next move."

"Our next move. I like the sound of that," she said with a wistful sigh. "Speaking of the holiday, I talked to Sybil yesterday. She and Hiro are back on the island. She said to give you her love and thanks when you woke up."

"I'm glad someone approves of our relationship."

"Yeah, that's nice, isn't it?" She sounded more amused than troubled by the fact that most of her family would be happier in a world without Jackson in it. "I told her it was all over and she was free to come home, but she's decided to stay. Hiro's going to help her fix up the bed and breakfast. Apparently he's moving in this week."

"You didn't tell her the truth?"

Hannah snuggled closer to his side. "No, I didn't. She's so happy and in love. And I figured that's Hiro's call. I believe he cares about her. If he's decided it's kinder to let the lie of why they met stand, I'm going to trust he has a good reason for it. I know honesty is important, but maybe sometimes it's kinder to give the person we love the gift of ignorance."

"Maybe you're right," he said, thinking about Sybil's suspicions about her brother, which she'd apparently kept from her niece for her entire life.

Maybe Sybil had come to the same conclusion that Hannah

had, that sometimes it was kinder to keep the truth from the people we love. There was nothing to be gained from Hannah knowing that her father might have ordered the murder of his brothers. She obviously already knew that she couldn't trust the man. Learning that he was even more of a monster than she'd assumed would only hurt her and make her wonder how much of that DNA had made its way into her own genetic makeup.

Jackson knew what that felt like. He didn't know if he'd ever look in the mirror again without seeing the shadow of his father's sins written in the lines of his face. Hannah didn't deserve that baggage. She deserved happiness and peace and a life where the future was wide open.

Which compelled him to ask a question he wished he could avoid.

"What if I can't come all the way back, Hannah?" he asked, running his fingertips lightly up and down her arm.

She shifted, frowning up at him. "What do you mean? You're going to make a full recovery. The doctor said there wasn't any major damage."

"I don't mean that," he said, lifting his gaze to the ceiling. "I mean back from the things I've done. I'm not worried about a few days here and there, but I can't settle permanently in the States while I'm on a CIA watch list. And I don't know if that threat is ever going to go away. Your options will be limited because of me. After everything you've been through I wouldn't blame you if you needed some time to decide if that's what you really want."

Hannah propped herself up on one arm, bringing her face even with his before she said in a soft, but firm voice, "Don't even try it, Hawke."

He studied her, admiring the strength in her pretty eyes. "Try what?"

"To get away from me," she said seriously. "You're where I want to be. The rest of it is just geography."

An unexpected stinging sensation pricked at his eyes and his voice was hoarse when he said, "You're where I want to be, too."

Hannah's lips trembled into a smile. "Are you going to cry?"

"No," he said, with a sniff. "My arm's hurting. That's all."

She made a cooing sound, kissing his cheek before she whispered against his skin, "You're the sweetest man in the world. Do you know that?"

Jackson grunted. "If you knew the dreams I was having about you while I was out you would know just how wrong you are."

"Oh yeah?" She pulled back, her eyes sparkling. "Were they dirty dreams?"

"Filthy." His cock stirred, the foolish thing too stupid to know he would hurt himself if he tried anything more than talk right now. "I had you tied up in a swing with your knees in your armpits and you were so fucking wet and begging me to take you. There were clamps on your nipples and—"

"Miss Hannah," a feminine voice called from out in the hall, making Hannah flinch, "are you ready for your breakfast tray, ma'am?"

"Leave it in the hall, please, Miriam," Hannah called out, holding Jackson's gaze as her hand slipped lower, sliding beneath the waistband of his pajama pants. "And bring another tray for Mr. Hawke, please. He's finally awake."

"Wide awake," Jackson whispered as Hannah gripped his erection and began to stroke him slowly up and down.

"Yes ma'am," Miriam said. "That's wonderful news."

"It is," Hannah agreed, tightening her grip until Jackson couldn't stop a groan from escaping his lips.

He lay back, focusing on keeping his heart from pounding through his chest as Hannah expertly worked his cock until he came so hard his vision blurred, smudging the sharp edges of the tray ceiling.

"Good?" she asked, kissing his throat, where his pulse still beat faster.

"Amazing," he murmured, running a palm over her hip. "My turn."

But before he could slip his hand down the front of her pants to return the favor, she'd squirmed away and slid off the edge of the bed.

"No, you're hurt," she said, reaching for tissues from a box beside the bed. "You need to rest and get your strength back."

"I don't need to rest." Jackson shifted higher on his pillows, ignoring the pain that flashed through his shoulder as he put weight on his injured side. "I need you to come on my hand."

She shot him a stern look. "No. You'll make your shoulder worse. I can tell you're in pain. I'll go call the doctor and ask if you can take something for it after breakfast."

"I'd rather have you for breakfast." He grudgingly took the tissues she offered, capturing her fingers and holding tight when she tried to pull away. "I could arrange to lie very still while you sat on my face."

Hannah rolled her eyes, a blush creeping up her neck. "You're impossible."

"I'm not impossible," he said, running a suggestive finger down the center of her palm. "You're irresistible."

"So it's my fault, is it?" she asked, letting him draw her closer to the bed.

Jackson nodded. "All your fault. Now get back into this bed and let me finish what we started."

Hannah leaned toward him. For a moment, Jackson was certain he was going to have his way, but then another voice sounded from outside the door. This time, it was a man's voice, and there was little doubt in Jackson's mind who it belonged to.

"Hannah, I need to see you. It's urgent," Stewart Mason said, sounding much more self-assured than when he had been begging for more time to say goodbye to his daughters. "There's a letter here for you. I think we should open it together."

Hannah sighed, the happy light in her eyes flickering out as she called over her shoulder, "I'm coming. Just let me get Jackson settled with his breakfast tray."

"I'll meet you in the study." A moment later, Stewart's footsteps retreated down the hall.

"And a good morning to you too, sir." Jackson's lips curved in a rueful smile. "He seems excited to hear that I'm awake."

Hannah grimaced. "I'm sorry."

"It's not your fault," Jackson said. "None of this is your fault."

"I know, but I wish things were different. I kept hoping..." Hannah trailed off with a shrug. "I don't know. I guess all the time apart tricked me into thinking my parents were better people than they really are."

"Absence makes the heart grow fonder."

"Absence makes the heart grow stupid," she said, tossing the tissues into a small trashcan near the bedside table.

"You're not stupid," he said in a firmer tone. "I don't want to hear you talk about yourself that way."

Hannah looked up, a smile curving her lips. "Yes, sir."

"Go see what he wants," Jackson said gruffly, shocked to find himself stirring again, simply from hearing those two words tumble from her lips. "And then bring me a secure phone so I can start plotting our path to freedom."

"Yes, sir," she said again, with a little salute.

Jackson growled. "Don't tease me, sunshine. Or you'll be sorry. I'm not going to be a gimp forever."

She winked. "I'm terrified, sir. Truly."

He couldn't help but smile. Smile and tell her again, that he loved her.

"I love you, too," she said, her playful mood vanishing as

she crossed to the door, opening it to reveal an older woman in a simple gray sweater and khakis holding a breakfast tray.

"Perfect timing, Miriam." Hannah scanned the plates and bowls artfully arranged on the tray. "And you made sure these are from the list of foods approved by the doctor?"

"Yes, ma'am." Miriam nodded. "Mr. Hawke can start with broth and if that settles well, I've got oatmeal and toast with honey."

"Wonderful, thank you so much, Miriam." Hannah turned over her shoulder, shooting him a tight smile as she stood back to make way for the maid to enter the room. "I'll be back to check on you soon."

Jackson nodded. "All right." He resisted the urge to tell her to hurry back, instead focusing his attention on Miriam, thanking her for the tray she settled gently across his lap.

He was already an invalid. He wasn't going to start acting like one of those needy bastards who couldn't stand to be separated from his other half for more than ten minutes at a time. And he wasn't going to let himself get sucked into creating problems where none existed.

Everything was fine. Hannah was safe, the danger to her life had been eliminated, and they had agreed to share their life together for the foreseeable future. All they had to do was get out of this house and away from her parents and things would go back to normal.

As normal as they ever had been, anyway. But he wasn't going to let that bother him, either.

He and Hannah might not be normal, but they could and *would* be happy together. He refused to contemplate the thought of anything else.

CHAPTER FIFTY-TWO

Hannah

*H*annah took the envelope from her father, frowning at the broken seal. "I thought we were going to open it together."

"I couldn't wait. I was too worried." Stewart leaned in, templing his fingers as he watched her pull the letter from the envelope. "And it seems I was right to be. It's from your sister."

Hannah glanced up at him, fighting a wave of irritation. "Are you going to let me read it, Dad? Or should I just ask you what it says?"

Stewart's brows crept higher on his broad forehead. "I apologize," he said in a tone that made it clear he thought he had nothing to apologize for. "As I said, I was worried." He motioned toward the letter. "Please. Read. I'll wait until you're done and we can discuss it together."

She took a deep breath as she turned her attention back to the letter, determined not to let her emotions show on her face as she read.

No matter how much she wanted to believe the danger had passed and she was finally safe to relax her guard and reestablish a relationship with her father, she couldn't shake the "off" feeling that made her nerve endings itch whenever she was in Stewart's presence. Her gut said that her father still had secrets, dangerous secrets that might threaten the peaceful future she yearned for.

Dearest, sweetest, bravest Hannah, she read, resisting the urge to sneer at the effusive address.

It seems I'll never come to the end of asking your forgiveness, but I do hope you'll forgive me for leaving without saying goodbye. I waited to make sure you were okay, but then I had to leave. It was my one chance to get away and get to Jasper before Dad's people figured out where he was. We worked out a special hiding place years ago and I knew he would be there, waiting for me, and we would finally have the chance to start a life away from all the sins and miseries of the past.

Some of those sins are mine, but most of them are Dad's.

I'll leave it up to him how much he wants to tell you. I would tell you everything, but I know it would cause you pain. And I'm sure Dad will intercept this letter before you're allowed to read it—Hello, Dad, and goodbye, you sick son of a bitch—and my truth-telling would do no good. He would destroy the letter without passing it on and I would never get to tell you how much I love you.

And I do love you, so very, very much.

You are still my Jiminy Cricket, moo. You're my conscience and the voice that leads me to all the best and brightest places. It's your voice I've listened to for the past six years as I've fought to be the kind of mother Jasper deserves. And it is because of Jasper—and the Hannah voice in my head that insists his welfare must come first, no matter what—that I have to disappear again. He deserves to grow up happy and safe, with none of the ugly past shadowing his future.

I hope there will come a day when it's safe for us to be a family again, but until then, know that I am out there somewhere in the big wide world loving you with all my heart and wishing you happiness. If you've found that with Jackson, then I wish you both well. But don't let him make you pay for the things I've done, moo. You are your own person and a better one than I could ever be. The similarities between us are only skin deep, as you know better than anyone.

Take care and may the years ahead of you be happy ones, my sister friend.

Never ever,

Harley

Hannah pressed her lips together, fighting to regain control of her emotions. The letter left her torn between being touched and suspicious, hurt and saddened that she'd lost Harley all over again.

But more powerful than any of those feelings was the certainty that her father was hiding something. Something bad, that Harley had known would cause Hannah pain. Something that had made her sister call the father she'd once idolized a "sick son of a bitch."

Once upon a time, Hannah would have talked around that line, but when she looked up to find Stewart's face set in his usual "master of all he surveys" mask, she couldn't think of a valid reason to let him off easy.

"What did you do?" She set the letter on the table beside her wingback chair, suddenly cold despite the fire roaring in the fireplace near her feet.

Stewart sighed wearily as he pinched the bridge of his nose between two long, thin fingers. "Aside from do everything in my power to protect you and your sister? And nearly have a heart attack when I thought I was going to lose one of you?"

"Yes," Hannah said, not buying the worried father act for a moment. "Aside from all that."

He glanced up, studying her with his shrewd blue eyes. "I did what had to be done. It wasn't gentle, but it was necessary. Your sister discovered a small part of an ugly, old story and rushed to judgment. If she'd given me the chance to explain, she would have understood that I did the best that I could. Considering the circumstances."

Hannah didn't bother trying to pick that tangle of words apart. She simply squeezed her lids closed, her features scrunching into a tight wad at the center of her face.

"There are things you don't understand, Hannah." Her father sighed again, a more put upon sound this time. "Will you stop making faces and look at me, please?"

She opened her eyes, pinning him with a cool glare. "Are you going to tell me what those things are? Are you going to explain what you did to make Ian Hawke your enemy? Or what Harley found out that made her think the only way to keep her son safe was to run away and hide in a place where you could never find her or Jasper?"

He sat up straighter, a new stiffness creeping in to tighten his jaw.

"That's what I thought," Hannah said, rising from her chair. "Jackson and I are leaving tomorrow, Dad. If you change your mind and want to be honest with me, then I'd love to have an adult conversation about this. If not, don't bother contacting me again. And don't send any spies or people to protect me. I don't want or need your kind of help."

Stewart made a grumbling sound. "You absolutely do need protection. As far as most people are concerned, you're the last living daughter of one of the richest men in the world. That will make you a target, Hannah. Ian wasn't the only person after my money or willing to hurt my children in order to—"

"You don't have children anymore, Dad." She ignored the pained look that flashed behind his eyes. "You have me. For now. But if you insist on lying to me, you will lose me too. I can forgive a lot, but I can't forgive being kept in the dark about things that could endanger my life and my family."

"*I'm* your family." Stewart stood, spreading his arms in a gesture that insisted he had nothing to hide.

A gesture that was just another lie.

"Jackson is my family," she said firmly, needing him to understand that she wasn't making idle threats. "I'm going to build a life with him and I hope someday we'll have children. Children I will love and do everything in my power to keep safe because nothing will be more important to me than their health and happiness."

"That's what I've done, Hannah. God, can't you see—"

"No, Dad, that's not what you've done," Hannah said, refusing to back down. "If my safety were truly your first priority, you would tell me the truth. I need the truth. I can't protect myself from something I don't understand."

"You don't need to understand, you need to trust your father."

Hannah's breath rushed out in an exasperated huff. "Maybe when I was a child, Dad, but I'm not a child anymore. I'm a grown woman, who has lost years of her life hiding away from the world, all to help you protect your secrets. Because your secrets are the most important things in your life, not me or Harley or Mom or anyone else."

Stewart balked but didn't say anything for a long moment, long enough for Hannah to notice how gray his hair had become and the way his eyes sagged at the edges. Her father didn't have smile lines. He had creases in his stony face, marks caused by gravity, not by the soul contained within his body.

Suddenly, that seemed like the saddest thing in the world, to have lived over sixty years and bear so few signs of a life filled with love or laughter.

Finally, he spoke, his voice rougher than it had been before. "I'm leaving you everything, Hannah. The fortune, the estate, the businesses, everything. You can look at my will if you don't believe me. I have a copy in the desk drawer."

It wasn't what she'd been expecting to hear, but it wasn't what she needed to hear either. "I don't care, Dad," she said, fighting to keep her frustration from her voice. "I don't care about the money. I never have, don't you know that by now?"

"I've been in touch with Sybil. I know your business is in trouble." Stewart folded his arms, scowling down his nose at her in that way that used to make her shake in her shoes when she was a girl. "I could make your problems go away. Or I could cut you off without a penny, and let you see how hard the world can be without money to smooth your way."

Hannah stood up straighter, meeting his scowl with a hard look of her own. She wasn't a little girl anymore, and she wasn't the fragile, bendable daughter her father had known, either.

"Go right ahead, Dad," she said, feeling like she'd shrugged off a lead weight from around her shoulders. "I'm capable of making my own money. I'm also capable of surrounding myself with people who understand the difference between love and manipulation."

She turned to go, but her father called out for her to wait. She turned back, eyebrows raised, waiting for him to give her a reason to stay.

"I...I don't know what to do," Stewart said, his arms falling limply to his sides. "I don't want to lose you. I just...I don't know how to make you stay."

Her chest flooded with a tender, wounded feeling, pity and anger swirling inside of her until finally both emotions faded away, leaving her as confused as the tired old man facing her across the room.

"I'm not a chess piece, Dad," she said wearily. "I'm your daughter. I'm a person and I'm willing to listen if you're willing to talk."

He blinked, his features softening in a way she had never seen before. But it wasn't regret or love that gentled his expression; it was hopelessness, helplessness, the barren look of a man who had finally realized that the war was over and he had lost the final battle.

No matter how much he might want her to stay, he couldn't, or wouldn't, let her in. He was trapped inside a fortress of his own lies and he would remain there—safe, but desperately alone—until the day he died.

"I did what I had to do," he said in a voice not much louder than a whisper. "There's no point in talking about the past.

It's too late for regret. Or forgiveness. You couldn't forgive it all, anyway. No one could."

Hannah nodded, tears stinging into her eyes as Stewart settled back into his chair by the fire, clearly resigned to letting his daughter walk away.

To the outside world, her father appeared to have it all—money, power, influence, a beautiful, well-bred wife, and a shot at the presidency if he played his cards right. But looking at him now, all Hannah saw was the shell of a man, a lonely, suffering warning that every dream came at a price.

The price her father had paid had been too dear, and it had left him all alone. He would rule his kingdom from a dusty, empty tower room, knowing that everything beautiful in his life had withered and died in the shadow of the dark bargains he had made.

Tears slipping silently down her cheeks, Hannah turned to go, wondering how high a price she would pay for her own dreams.

She waited until she was down the hall, nearing the garage on the south side where the servants parked before she pulled her cell from the band of her sports bra, where she'd had it tucked since last night. Dominic said he would call as soon as he had news, but she couldn't resist punching in his contact number and hitting send.

The phone rang four times before forwarding to voice mail. For a moment, Hannah considered hanging up without leaving a message, but if she was in for a penny, she was in for a pound.

It was time for Dom to know just how serious she was about getting the information she needed.

"It's Hannah," she said after the beep. "I took some samples of Jackson's hair last night while he was sleeping. I'm overnighting them to the post office box address you left so you'll have them as soon as you're ready. Hopefully, finding

Harley and Jasper won't be as difficult as my father seems to think it will be and we can have this settled soon."

Hannah hesitated a moment before adding. "And Dom, don't forward any information to my father. I know we agreed that you work for me now, but I want to make it clear that I don't want Dad to know where Harley and Jasper are. She had her reasons for wanting out from under his thumb and I respect them, whatever they are. Talk soon."

She hung up and stood in the dim light at the end of the hallway, squeezing the phone tight, wondering when she had become the kind of person who has spies on retainer. Or the kind who collects hairs from the pillow of her unconscious lover, proving she was as concerned about her own peace of mind as she was his precious life.

She didn't know, but she knew she couldn't back down now. She had to know the truth. Then she would decide how much to tell Jackson and whether or not she could live with keeping his son a secret from him for the rest of their lives.

CHAPTER FIFTY-THREE

Jackson

*T*hey landed in Jackson Hole, Wyoming four days before Christmas and barely made it to their cabin on Granite Ridge before the snow began to fall. By midnight, the gentle drifting flakes had become a madly swirling blizzard and Hannah spent half the night crawling in and out of bed, making sure the power hadn't gone out and taken the heat with it.

No matter how many times Jackson assured her that he was firmly on the mend, he knew she was concerned about the isolated state of the cabin and worried about what would happen if his health took a turn for the worse. He also knew that he should be grateful for her love and concern, instead of frustrated by the constant reminder of his own vulnerability, but he couldn't help wishing she would stop worrying.

He was just so damned grateful to have her back and safe. He wanted to enjoy loving her and let things between them go back to normal.

But worry seemed to be Hannah's new default setting and things remained far from normal. She still refused to do anything but sleep in their shared bed, insisting she was too afraid of hurting him to make love gently, let alone anything else. Jackson intimated that there were games they could play that had nothing to do with rough stuff, but Hannah acted as if he'd suggested she punch him in his bullet wound so he'd let the matter drop.

They had time. There was no need to rush or push Hannah to drop her guard before she was ready.

They spent the next three days reading by the fire and watching the snow cover the valley below their window, but the energy between them wasn't the same as it had been on the island. Before, they'd enjoyed easy silences. Now, something lived in the air between them, an unspoken fear Hannah refused to name. Every time he asked her what was bothering her, she would smile and insist that everything would be better as soon as she knew he was really going to be okay.

He wanted to believe her, but couldn't shake the feeling that something had changed, something that might not be as easily mended as his flesh and bone.

By the time the snow melted enough for them to drive into town for supplies on Christmas Eve day, Jackson was going stir crazy and desperate for a chance to prove to Hannah how rapidly his health was improving. They had breakfast at the Four Seasons and then drove to the town square.

There, the fresh snowfall made the Old West style buildings look like something out of an antique Christmas card and strings of brightly colored lights lit up the archway of elk antlers marking the gateway to downtown. Jackson had never been a fan of the holidays—any holiday—but as he and Hannah stepped out into the brisk morning air, he found himself looking forward to exploring and picking out a few surprises for Christmas morning.

"So where do we want to go first?" Hannah asked, looping her arm through his and huddling close to his side though he knew it was more to offer him support than to absorb his warmth. In her heavy white wool coat and white rabbit skin hat, she was more appropriately dressed for the weather than he was in his thick black sweater. "The art gallery looks interesting."

"It does," Jackson agreed as he gently detangled her arm from his. "But *we* aren't going anywhere. *I'm* going to need a little time alone to buy presents."

Hannah scrunched her nose, but he could see the smile she was trying to hide. "You don't have to get me anything."

"I know I don't have to," he said. "I want to. Let's meet at the Cowboy Bar in an hour. We can have another coffee and check out the gallery after."

"An hour," she repeated, nibbling on her bottom lip.

"Do you need more time?"

"No, I don't need more time." She reached up, adjusting the tension on his sling for the third time this morning. "I'm just worried about leaving you alone for an hour. You only have one arm."

"One arm is sufficient to get my wallet out of my pocket and put it back in again," he said dryly. "I don't plan on buying any souvenir antlers so I'll be fine to carry the packages, too."

Her frown remained in place. "But what if you get tired? Or what if something happens and you need my help?"

"Nothing's going to happen." Jackson forced himself to smile. "I'm fine. The pain is manageable, the wound is closing well, and I haven't had any fever in five days. It's time to relax."

"But you've been resting for the past five days," she said. "You haven't been traipsing around all over the place shopping and exhausting yourself in the dead of winter wearing nothing but a sweater."

"The sling wouldn't fit with my coat and I'm not going to be traipsing, I'm going to be walking at a sedate pace."

"But—"

"I've never traipsed a day in my life," he pushed on. "I wouldn't know how to traipse if I tried and shopping is hardly in the same league with the amount of exercise I'm used to doing on a daily basis."

"You don't usually have a bullet hole in your chest on a daily basis," Hannah grumbled, but he could tell that she'd realized it was time to cut the apron strings. Or at least let them out a little.

Thank God. As sweet as her concern was, he was starting to feel suffocated.

"Fine, go shop," she said with a sigh. "But call me if you get too tired or need my help. And make sure you're at the Cowboy Bar in exactly an hour or I'm going to come looking for you. And I'm not going to be happy when I find you."

You aren't happy now. The thought flashed through his head unbidden, leaving him feeling the cold for the first time this morning.

She *wasn't* happy and he couldn't help feeling like it was something more than his injury causing the sparkle in her eyes to dim.

As he kissed her goodbye and crossed the street, bound for a local crafters' store and the jewelry store beyond, he decided it was time to put an end to the weird dynamic between them before things got any worse. And he suddenly had a good idea how to start bringing them back together.

Hannah was a strong woman who had proven how brave she was, but she was also submissive. *His* submissive.

She'd given him so much trust in such a relatively short amount of time. She'd abandoned herself to him, trusting in his strength and control, and then he'd been shot, proving that he was flesh and blood like any other man.

"No wonder she's scared," he mumbled as he pushed into the crafters' store and was enveloped in a rush of warm, dry air, feeling like an idiot for not sensing the reason for her withdrawal sooner.

But Domination wasn't only, or even primarily, about flesh and blood. Domination was about power exchange and trust as much as sex toys and spankings. He might not be able to throw Hannah over his shoulder and tie her up in a sex swing anytime soon, but he could still take her to the place of safety and abandon she had come to crave. He could still make it clear that he was in control and she could trust him with her pleasure and her pain.

But you can't promise not to die, leaving her vulnerable and alone.

Jackson frowned down at a row of antler bracelets and delicate white bone earrings carved into lace displayed in the case in front of him.

"Can I get something out for you?"

He glanced up to see an older woman with gently weathered brown skin and bright green eyes watching him from the other side of the display, her long graying hair pulled into a bun and her trim form encased in various shades of brown fleece. There was nothing remarkable about her—aside from the pretty shade of her eyes—but Jackson was struck by how relaxed and happy and *normal* she seemed.

This was the kind of life Hannah would have had if he hadn't taken her away from her aunt or taught her to crave sharp edges and pain with her pleasure. When she was happy, it was easy to defend the love they'd found, but watching her fret herself into losing five pounds in four days made him wonder if he was doing the right thing.

No matter how much he loved her, would his love be enough to keep her happy in a world designed for people like this? Normal people who didn't get off on games played in the shadows?

"Maybe these aren't quite your speed," the woman continued, seemingly unfazed by Jackson's lack of response. "That's all right. Bones and horns aren't for everyone."

"No." He shook his head. "I mean yes, you have some very

nice things. I'd like to see the earrings, please. The ones on the far left."

With a smile that crinkled the edges of her eyes, the woman unlocked the case and reached inside. "Excellent choice. These are my absolute favorites. It's amazing how Becky can make a little piece of animal bone look like a scrap of lace like that."

Jackson picked up one of the earrings, letting it dangle from his thick fingers, feeling clumsy and out of place. It had been so long since he'd bought a woman a gift, and even longer since he'd wanted her to like it as much as he wanted Hannah to like the things she unwrapped tomorrow morning.

He only wanted to please her, but somewhere between losing her in Tahiti and finding her in Florida with her hands creased and red from the fabric she'd used to kill a man, he seemed to have lost the knack for it.

"It's delicate but still strong," the woman mused, studying the earring from the other side of the case. "A beautiful contrast."

Delicate, but strong. Like Hannah.

"I'll take them," he said, setting the earring back beside its mate. "Do you gift wrap?"

"Not usually." The woman's grin widened. "But seeing as you're in a bit of a bind with that arm and it's the day before Christmas I can make an exception. Just let me go beg some paper from my friend across the way. Be back in two shakes of a lamb's tail."

Jackson nodded, moving off to one side of the case as two teenage girls pressed up against it, studying the bracelets.

It was true, bones and horns weren't for everyone. Neither was the lifestyle he and Hannah had chosen, but they could make it work, as long as he remembered to take care of every part of her—the strong and the delicate, the tender lover and the stubborn worrier who drove him crazy, the brave defender of the people she loved and the frightened woman who looked at him like he might vanish before her eyes leaving her alone.

But he was made of tougher stuff than that and as soon as he got Hannah home he was going to prove it.

With that in mind, he decided against the charm bracelet he'd been planning to buy her at the jewelry store, opting instead to look for something with a more significant meaning.

CHAPTER FIFTY-FOUR

Hannah

*H*annah barely had time to hang her hat on one of the many hooks inside the door and unzip her coat when Jackson slammed the door behind them and ordered—

"Clothes off, on your knees by the fireplace."

Startled by the abrupt return of his Dom voice, she spun over her shoulder, arousal and unease flooding through in equal measure, leaving her feeling like a light socket that had started to short circuit. "B-but you're still in pain, I don't think—"

"I didn't ask what you thought. I told you to take your clothes off and get on your knees." He tossed the bag he'd brought in from the car onto the floor and prowled toward her, a hungry look in his hooded eyes that made it clear he meant business.

Or pleasure, rather.

This was the side of Jackson that she usually associated with pleasure, the side that could make her knees weak with a look and her panties damp with a single command. But right now she didn't want to play games. She was too worried—about him, about the future, and about what Dominic was going to find out now that he'd tracked Harley and Jasper to a village in southern Thailand.

Just the thought of her secret calls to her new spy was enough to cool her desire.

"No. I don't want to, Jackson," she said, hanging her coat beside her hat.

Before she had time to say another word, he was across the wide foyer, his good hand fisting in her hair.

She gasped as his fingers tightened at the nape of her neck, her bones melting the way they always did when he touched her like this—like she was his to pleasure or punish as he saw fit. She hadn't realized how much she missed the thrill of danger mixed with seduction until he drew her tight to his chest and spoke in a dark whisper—

"You don't tell me no. No is not in your vocabulary when I want you naked and kneeling. Do you understand?"

Hannah bit her lip, torn between the lust spreading, hot and thick, through her mid-section and the fear that Jackson was going to hurt himself trying to prove something that didn't need to be proven. She was his. She belonged to him and they belonged together and there would be time for the game when he wasn't barely a week into healing from a gunshot wound.

"No is in my vocabulary when you're being an idiot," she said, arousal mixing with the anger in her tone. "I'll get on my knees, but you have to promise to sit down and take it easy."

"You don't give orders," he said, using the fist in her hair to half drag her across the room to the fireplace, proving he had more strength left in that big body of his than she'd assumed. "You don't tell me when to sit still or shut up or stop asking for what I need from you."

"Jackson stop, I—" Her words ended in a cry of pain as she tried to pull away and he answered her attempt by tightening his grip at the base of her neck.

"I'm hurt, but I'm not dying and I've still got more than

enough mental and physical strength left to top you, sunshine." His voice was so deep she could feel it vibrate the tips of her nerve endings, sending a fresh sizzle of desire tingling across her skin, making her nipples pucker. "Now take your clothes off and get on your knees. This is your last chance to have this end well for you."

Hannah glared up at him, her breath coming harsh and uneven. She was turned on, there was no doubt about it—and it was clear he was determined to have his way, even if he ended up ripping his stitches in the process—but instead of reaching for her sweater zipper, she shouted the first word that came to her mind.

"No!" Her volume was loud enough to echo through the room, but saying it once wasn't enough. Now that she'd started, she couldn't seem to stop. "No, no, no!"

"No?" Jackson repeated, soft and cold, his control stoking her anger.

"No!" she howled, barely resisting the urge to punch him in the stomach. "I said no, damn you, so let me go!"

"No isn't the word you use," he said, again in that completely calm, even tone that made her want to scream. "If you want this to stop you use your safe word. Anything else I'm going to assume is a challenge to up my game until you feel safe again."

"I'll never feel safe," she said, tears spilling down her cheeks, shocking her. She hadn't even realized she was about to cry.

"And why's that?" He pulled her closer, pinning her to the strong side of his body though she squirmed to get free. "Why can't you feel safe?"

"I don't know," she sobbed, overwhelmed by terror and rage she hadn't known she was feeling. "Let me go. I don't want to touch you right now."

"Why? Am I hurting you?"

"No," she snapped, then added with a sob, "Yes, now let me go."

"I'm never going to let you go," he said, vulnerability flickering behind his eyes. "You're mine. Your pleasure and pain are mine, your happiness and sadness are mine, your fear and hurt are mine." He leaned down, pressing his lips to her forehead before adding softly, "But I can't help you control any of those things unless you give me the reins, Hannah."

She sucked in a breath, fighting to keep her face from crumpling. "But I'm afraid," she said, trembling as the truth she'd been hiding from herself came clawing its way to the surface.

"What are you afraid of?" he asked, his voice gentle now though he didn't loosen his grip on her hair.

"You said you had respect for life, but not hers," Hannah said, a dam breaking inside of her. "You said you would never doom your child to having her for a mother. But what if you did, by accident? What are you going to do?"

Jackson froze before pulling back to look down into her face.

"What are you going to do?" Hannah choked out between sobs as Jackson's hand slid from her hair. "You can't take her son away. She loves him more than anything. I don't know what else to believe about Harley, but I believe that. Jasper is the only thing that matters to her, the only thing she's living for."

His lids closed, concealing his eyes, so she had no idea what he was thinking.

"I wanted to tell you right away," she babbled on, her nose beginning to run. "But I didn't have a chance to find out if Jasper was yours and I didn't want to upset you while you were trying to get better." She sucked in a breath. "But most of all I didn't want to think about you having a baby with my s-sister. I hated the thought so much I wasn't sure I was going to tell you, even when I knew the truth for sure."

She sniffed hard, ashamed of herself now that her secret was out. "But I should have been honest with you, even if I didn't want to be. I'm sorry."

Jackson's eyes opened, but he didn't look at her. He kept his gaze on the ground as he nodded toward the fireplace, "Sit down on the couch. I'm going to bring you something to drink."

Hannah gulped. "But I don't—"

"Sit down, Hannah," Jackson said, loud enough to make her jump before she backed away to sit down hard on the supple leather couch cushion.

She threaded her fingers together in her lap, heart racing as she watched Jackson move across the large open room to the kitchen. The average person wouldn't be able to tell that anything was wrong, but Hannah could read the tension in his movements as he fetched a glass from the cupboard and filled it with water from the refrigerator door.

He was upset, most likely angry, too, but her mind couldn't think past the relief coursing through her.

No matter how much she dreaded the conversation they were about to have, she was so grateful to sense the miserable distance between them beginning to fade away.

She accepted the glass Jackson offered and took a long drink as he crossed the room to the bookshelf and plucked a box of tissues from beside a set of leather-bound classics. By the time he returned—placing the tissues within her easy reach before sitting down on the wooden coffee table facing her—she'd stopped crying and was ready to accept whatever came next.

Even if he yelled at her or shut down and pushed her away as punishment, it would be better than the disconnect of the past week.

"Tell me everything," he said, the muscle leaping in his jaw the only outward sign of the stress he must be feeling. "Don't leave anything out, even if it seems like something small."

Hannah set her water on the side table near the lamp and took a bracing breath. "Harley and I were locked in a room at your father's house. She thought she was going to die, so she asked me to promise to take care of Jasper, her son, and love him like he was my own. I didn't find out much about him except that he's five and getting ready to go into kindergarten this coming year."

Jackson nodded, but his expression remained emotionless. "So the timeline is right for him to be mine. But I know she was sleeping with at least one other person that summer."

"Right," Hannah agreed, her stomach cramping. "Your friend. And there could have been others. Harley wasn't a big fan of monogamy back then." She tucked her thumbs inside her rolled fingers, resisting the urge to nibble the rough edge of her cuticle the way she did when she was nervous as a child. "I should have asked her who the father was, but I was too busy trying to figure out a way to get out before Adam or Ian came back."

"As you should have been," Jackson said. "Your safety is the most important thing."

Hannah dropped her gaze to the dark jewel tones of the carpet. "But if I'd asked, then I wouldn't have hired Dominic to spy for me or stolen your hair from your pillow while you slept."

Jackson sighed. "For a DNA test I assume?"

Hannah kept her eyes focused on the floor. "Dominic found Harley and Jasper yesterday. They're in Thailand. He's hoping to have samples of Jasper's hair soon and the test results not long after."

"And you've been worried that I would try to take the boy away from Harley. If it turns out he's mine."

"Not consciously," she said, shoulders hunching. "I didn't realize I was worried about that until it just...came out."

He grunted softly. "And I thought you were pushing me

away because you'd put so much trust in me and I'd betrayed it by going and getting myself shot."

Hannah glanced up sharply. "No, I... It has nothing to do with that, Jackson."

"Are you sure?" he asked, searching her face. "I imagine it would be scary to submit to someone and then have them prove they're not as strong as you thought they were."

"You were shot. That has nothing to do with strength or a lack of it," she said, wanting to reach out to him, but sensing he wasn't ready to be touched. "And I didn't mean to push you away. I just couldn't be the way we are together and keep a secret from you at the same time."

"No, you can't," he said. "I can't either. Trust is important in any relationship, but for us it's going to be critical. This is only going to work if we're honest with each other. Even when it hurts."

She nodded, pressing her lips together and fighting the tears trying to rise in her eyes. "I know. And I'm sorry."

"It's all right. I'm not in a place to judge," he said, running his good hand through his hair, which looked even silkier and shinier away from the island humidity. "I've been keeping something from you, too. Something your aunt told me when she learned you'd been taken."

Hannah sat motionless as Jackson briefly outlined Sybil's suspicions, absorbing the news that her father might have hired Ian to kill his brothers with less shock than she would have expected. But then, she'd sensed he'd done something horrible, something so dark and terrible that he would never be able to find the other side of it.

"I didn't want you to have to live with that," Jackson continued. "I didn't want you to wonder if there was some part of you—no matter how small—that was like him."

Hannah blinked, shocked by the ping of recognition deep inside of her. "I probably wouldn't have thought of that, at least not at first. But you're right. I will wonder. I guess a part of me already has been."

She bit her lip as she shook her head slowly back and forth. "I've changed so much in the past few months, but it hasn't really felt like change. It's felt like the real me, the person I kept hidden for so long, finally stepped out into the light and sometimes..." Hannah hesitated, but then forced herself to push on, knowing if anyone would understand her fears it would be Jackson. "Sometimes that person scares me."

He reached out, taking her hand. Energy hummed from his body to hers, filling her with the certainty that she wasn't alone.

"She shouldn't scare you," he said. "I love her. Even when she makes mistakes."

Hannah's mouth trembled. "But I killed a man. And I didn't...I *don't* feel bad about it. I really don't."

"*We* killed a man," he corrected. "And you shouldn't feel bad about it. It had to be done. There's a reason my mother hasn't reported him missing or called the authorities, Hannah. My father was a monster who had nothing left to offer the world but more violence and suffering." He squeezed her hand. "Regretting ending his life is a waste of energy you could be using to not keep secrets from me."

Her lips quirked at the edges before settling back into an uncertain line. "What are you going to do? About Jasper?"

"I don't know," he said with an openness that surprised her. "I'll wait until we know if the boy is mine and if he is... We'll decide what to do then."

"We?" she asked, brows lifting. "So you're not angry with me?"

"No," he said, before adding in a drier tone, "I'd prefer nothing like this happens again, but I'm just glad to get to the bottom of it. I've hated the distance the past few days. You've felt...out of reach, and I didn't like it."

"Me either." Hannah slid to her knees in front of him,

bringing her palms to rest lightly on his thighs. "If you still want me naked and kneeling, I'm ready."

He cupped her cheek. "To be honest, I'd rather make love than play. It seems like that's the side of us that needs attention right now." He grimaced lightly. "And though I hate to admit that you're right, after dragging you around my chest hurts like hell."

"Well, you were right, too." She turned her head, pressing a kiss to his palm. "I needed you to push me. If I hadn't needed it, I would have said my safe word." She curled her fingers into the thick muscles of his thighs, skin prickling as his fingertips traced a trail down her throat. "But that scares me sometimes, too. The way you seem to know me better than I know myself."

"I don't. I've just had more experience with power exchange."

"It's not just that." She dropped her head back, staring up into his beautiful face as he clasped the zipper holding her sweater closed and dragged it slowly down. "When my head feels clear, I love the game. I crave it and don't feel like I've gotten close enough to you if we go without it for too long," she said, voice breathy from a combination of longing and the prickle of fear inspired by being so vulnerable, even with someone she knew she could trust with her most breakable parts.

"But when you bring out things in me that I didn't even know were there," she continued, "it can start to feel like I'm out of control in a bad way. Does that make sense?"

"It does." He pushed her sweater off one shoulder and then the other.

Hannah caught her sleeves with opposite fingers, tugging the cozy knit down until it fell to the floor, leaving her in nothing but her camisole. Immediately, her nipples puckered, the combination of the cool air in the cabin and Jackson's fingertip slipping beneath one strap enough to make her nerve endings spark violently to life.

"But that just means we've reached territory we haven't explored before," Jackson continued, finger teasing up and down the length of her strap without easing it off her shoulder. "It's unfamiliar, but it doesn't have to be scary."

"But what if we reach ugly territory?" she asked softly. "Or territory you just don't care for?"

"I care for everything about you." His hand stilled as he held her gaze. "I care for the little girl you were, the woman you are, and the person you're going to become. When I said forever, I meant it. I don't make those kinds of promises lightly."

His warm fingers slipped down the front of her shirt, capturing her nipple and rolling it gently, but his eyes remained glued to hers, heightening the intimacy of the electric touch. "Tonight I'm going to prove that by making love to you until you understand that there is nothing I want more in the world than to be close to you. And tomorrow, I'll prove it by showing you that I can handle anything and everything you need to give me. How does that sound?"

"It sounds perfect." Hannah swallowed, fighting back another wave of tears. But they were grateful tears this time, the tears of a woman who was loved exactly the way she needed to be loved—sweet and gentle, hard and ruthless, coaxing and demanding, and everything in between.

"Now take off the rest of your clothes," he said, leaning in to kiss her forehead, his breath warm on her skin. "It feels like forever since I've seen you."

Knees already weaker, Hannah stood, studying Jackson's face as she unbuttoned her jeans and pushed them down to the floor. Her socks came next, then her camisole, and finally her panties. She hooked her thumbs at the sides of the lacy fabric, drawing them slowly down her hips and thighs until she reached the place where a gentle shimmy of her legs sent them slipping down her calves to fall at her feet.

The entire time, Jackson watched her, his eyes filling with a mixture of hunger and tenderness that made her feel like the most beautiful woman in the world. By the time she finished her brief striptease, she was wet and aching, so eager to be joined with him that she hoped he wouldn't delay their gratification for too long.

There were times when she craved teasing and a slow spiral out of control. But there were times when she simply needed to be as close as she could get to the man she loved, this dangerous man whose arms had become the only place where she felt safe.

Once, not long ago, she had been afraid of what Jackson would do next. Now, the only thing she feared was that, for some reason, she might not be around to see it.

Or that someone would take him away from her before she had time to love him in all the ways—and for all the years—she wanted to love him.

CHAPTER FIFTY-FIVE

Jackson

*J*ackson's breath caught and his fingers flexed restlessly at his sides, torn between reaching for Hannah and taking another moment to drink in how beautiful she looked.

"Maybe you were right about the other, too." Her tongue slipped out to dampen her lips as he did his best to memorize the way her skin glowed in the cool winter light filling the room. "Looking at a man like you, the last thing I used to think about was death. But now, I do. I think about death, and how quickly it can take away everything that matters."

"I think about that, too." Jackson stood, encircling her waist with his good arm, ignoring the dull pain throbbing through his bum shoulder as he hugged her close. "I thought about it the entire flight across the ocean to Florida, hating myself for failing to keep you safe and worrying that I'd waited too long to tell you the way I feel."

He leaned down, inhaling the smoke and winter smells lingering in her hair, an ache filling his chest that had nothing to do with his gunshot wound. But it was a sweet discomfort, the increasingly familiar pain of his heart stretching wider, making room to love her more.

"I promised myself if I got a second chance, I wouldn't hold anything back," he continued, hugging her closer, wishing he could draw her so close that nothing—not even death—could ever pull them apart. "I can't say with any certainty what happens after this life, but if energy can neither be created nor destroyed, neither can love like this."

She tipped her head back, tears filling her eyes even as she smiled that wide, nothing-to-hide smile he'd missed so much. "I would never have imagined the first law of thermodynamics could be so romantic."

"It isn't romantic; it's the truth," he said, hand slipping down to mold to the bare curve of her bottom. "Some part of me has always loved you. And some part of me, the best part, always will."

Hannah blinked fast, her throat working as she reached up to take his face in her hands. "What did I do to deserve you?"

His lips curved in a wry smile. "Nothing. Or everything, depending on which me we're talking about."

"There's only one you," she said with a confidence that made him believe he would continue to put the darkest hours of his life behind him. "And I love him and I need to take his clothes off as soon as possible."

His smiled widened. "Immediately works for me."

Hannah reached for the strap on his sling as he thumbed open the close of his jeans. A few moments later, she was back in his arms, her skin cool against the burning length of his cock as they backed toward the couch. She arched her hips as they moved, rubbing against his erection, making him groan as his lips found hers and his tongue pushed inside.

He needed to be inside her so desperately his balls felt bruised and tender, but he needed to kiss her everywhere first. He needed to claim her mouth, taste the honey and musk of the skin beneath her breasts, plunge his tongue into the slickness between her legs until he could feel her pussy pulsing around him, flooding his mouth with evidence of her desire.

He needed to make love to the backs of her knees and the small of her back and the place at the base of her neck that made her melt when he trapped it between his teeth and bit down.

"Sit," Hannah murmured against his lips as the back of his knees hit the couch. "Let me do the work so you don't have to put weight on your arm."

"This isn't work. This is all I've been able to think about lying next to you every night," Jackson said, but he allowed his weight to settle back onto the cool leather cushions, the thought of watching Hannah ride him too tempting to resist.

His cock jerked as she straddled him and his tip began to leak, but when she reached down to guide him inside her, he gripped her wrist and pushed her hand away.

"Not yet," he said, cupping her breasts in his hands. "I need to kiss you here first."

"Be careful," she said, breath catching as his thumbs brushed across her tight nipples. "The doctor said you shouldn't use that arm except when you're working on the physical therapy exercises."

"This is physical therapy." He drew his tongue across her nipple, moaning as the singular taste of her skin filled his mouth.

"Seriously, Jackson, I don't—" Her words became a gasp as he sucked her deeper, trapping her taut flesh between his teeth before flicking his tongue back and forth until she squirmed on his lap.

"Oh, God. God, Jackson." She threaded her fingers into his hair, holding on tight as he tortured her sensitive skin. "I've missed you. So much."

He transferred his attention to her other breast, shifting his leg until it was wedged between her thighs. Her hips undulated as she rubbed against him, riding his leg until her slickness coated his skin and his balls began to pulse with a heartbeat of their own.

Her breath grew faster and more erratic, her arms trembling as her fingernails dug into the skin at the back of his neck, sending a hot knife of pain through his pleasure, giving him the strength to draw out the anticipation for a little longer.

"Now your mouth," he said, continuing to tease her slick nipples with his fingers as he tilted his head back. "Give me your mouth."

Hannah leaned in, her lips parted as if she knew he meant to do something much more thorough than simply kiss her. And he did. He was going to show her who her mouth belonged to.

Her lips, her teeth, her tongue—they were all his. Every inch of her was his and he meant to make sure she knew it.

He drove his tongue into her warm, wet heat, fucking her mouth with the thick muscle, plunging in deep and hard until she had no choice but to relax her throat and open for him. She groaned, the sound vibrating their lips as he stroked deeper, his tongue dancing with hers as his grip pulsed on her nipples, pinching her skin between his fingers a little harder each time, until she was bucking into his leg.

Finally, she ripped her mouth from his with a gasp. "I'm going to come, Jackson. I can't stop it, I can't."

"Wait," he ordered, gritting his jaw as he reached down, squeezing her hip tight with one hand while he positioned his cock with the other. "Wait until I'm inside you."

"Yes, please." She bit her lip, whimpering as he guided his engorged head back and forth through her slick, swollen folds, unable to resist a few more seconds of sweet torture. "Please, Jackson. Please!"

"Not yet, wait for me," he said, circling her clit with his leaking tip though his balls were suffering and he wanted to be inside her more than he'd ever wanted anything.

But he wanted them both even closer to losing control, so close that the razor's edge of their desire would cut away everything that stood between them. "Wait, Hannah. Wait for me."

She made a sound that was half growl and half plea for mercy but held still, waiting for him to give her permission to move.

"Look at me," he said, needing to look into her eyes as she tumbled over. "Now, sweetness. Ride me now."

With a sob of relief, Hannah spread her thighs and dropped her hips, taking him deep, deep, deeper, until he was clutched in her heat, feeling her inner muscles squeeze tight around him.

But she didn't come. She bit her lip and held his gaze as she bent her knees and hooked her feet around the inside of his knees, giving her more control over the length and duration of her thrusts as she began to slide up and down him, fucking him with a slow, languid rhythm that scattered the coals threatening to burst into flames within him.

Jackson brought his hands to her sides, letting them skim the surface of her silken skin as she moved, so lost in her eyes he couldn't think what else to do with them. They'd made love like this before—close and connected, with her gaze locked on his, telling him so much more than words ever could—but this time it was even more intimate, more intense. He was naked with her in a way that had nothing to do with their physical bodies and everything to do with trust and love and the indestructible energy they created together, something so pure and right Jackson wouldn't have believed it existed before her.

Before Hannah, his love, his light, his everything.

"Everything," she echoed as if he'd said the words out loud.

But he supposed he had. There were ways to speak without saying a word. Her touch, her kiss, the shine in her eyes as she began to move faster, carrying them both closer to the precipice, told him as much as her words. They said he was loved and seen and exactly what she needed, no matter what the rest of the world might have to say about it.

"Closer," he said, bringing his hand to the small of her back. "I want to feel your skin against me."

She leaned forward, breasts rubbing against his chest as her hips pumped harder, faster. He shifted closer to the edge of the cushion, giving himself more freedom to move, to thrust up into her as her rhythm grew frantic and her breath came in shallow gasps that puffed against his lips.

"Are you going to come for me?" he asked, loving the sob that hitched her chest as she nodded. "Then come, baby. Come on my cock, let me feel you."

The skin around her eyes tightened as her pussy locked around him, but they didn't close. She kept her eyes open, staring into his as they came together, riding the sharp edge of their pleasure until it became a gentler wave, carrying them home even as it eroded more of the shoreline that separated them.

Someday soon, there would be no separation at all, nothing to keep him from the kind of union he hadn't known he craved until Hannah had proven to him that love was more powerful than anything that stood in its way.

"I love you," she murmured long minutes later, her lips kissing his throat as she spoke.

Even in the middle of claiming her pleasure, she had been careful to collapse on his uninjured side, but Jackson wasn't sure it mattered. He was suddenly feeling better than he had since the day he was shot, the bliss of union and release making him wonder if they needed to wait until tomorrow to attend to their other needs.

"And I'm so hungry I feel like I could eat all of the groceries we left out in the trunk," she said, her stomach confirming her claim with a long, irritable growl that made Jackson smile.

"Then why don't you go grab them," he said, patting her ass. "And I'll make you something decadent for lunch."

"You?" She lifted her head, shooting him an incredulous grin. "You're going to cook for me?"

"I'm an excellent cook," he said with a sniff that she apparently found funny.

She giggled, forcing his softening length from inside her, sending a ripple of regret skimming through him and making him even more determined to have her again before the day was over. He hadn't had his fill of her yet, not nearly, but he could wait long enough to prove that he had skill sets beyond those he'd proven in the bedroom.

"Get the bags, woman." He delivered a more serious swat to her backside, loving that it only made her smile wider. "I'm going to make you a lunch that will make your mouth come."

Hannah's eyes darkened. "Is that right?" Her tongue swept out, teasing across her lips. "Is that even possible?"

"Haven't you learned not to doubt me, yet," Jackson said, his blood beginning to simmer all over again. "I don't make promises I can't keep."

She sobered, a tender expression softening her face. "No, you don't. It's one of the many things I love about you." She kissed his cheek before slipping off his lap. "Let me get a cloth from the bathroom to clean up and I'll get dressed and get the bags."

"You don't have to get dressed," he said, admiring the sway of her hips as she crossed the room to the hall leading to the downstairs bathroom. "There's no one close enough to see you run outside."

"I'm not going out in twenty-degree weather naked, Jackson," she called out. "I enjoy a little pain, not torture."

He smiled. "But you'd look sexy wearing nothing but those furry boots you bought today."

Her laughter echoed down the hall as she came back into the room carrying a damp rag in one hand, a dry one in the other. "We can live out that fantasy later. Indoors."

Oh yes, they would. They would live out that fantasy and more.

Now that they'd reconnected and put the strangeness between them aside, it was time to make sure their other needs were met. There would be time to wonder what the hell he was going to do if he had a son he'd never met later. There would be time to sort out where he and Hannah went from here and what to do with his life now that he'd left his criminal past behind him.

But the rest of the day was his and Hannah's, and he intended to make sure it was a Christmas Eve neither of them would ever forget.

CHAPTER FIFTY-SIX

Hannah

*J*ackson couldn't chop vegetables one-handed, but he was excellent at telling her how to slice them to his satisfaction—big surprise. She teased him about being a control freak in the kitchen as well as the bedroom, but he only smiled and said—

"I want the carrots thinner, sunshine. I know you can get them thinner than that."

—and returned to whipping up an exotic blend of spices and cornmeal that he said was going to transform his version of chicken and dumplings into something taste-bud-orgasmic.

Hannah kept sneaking glances his way as they worked, surprised by how sexy she found it to see him moving confidently about the kitchen, setting water to boil and the oven to preheat. But she shouldn't be, she supposed. Everything about him was sexy, from the way he fisted his hand in her hair and pushed her out of her comfort zone to the way he held her gaze as she rode him, the look in his eyes making it clear there was nothing in the world that mattered to him as much as her happiness.

Whatever came next, they would face it together and they would come out whole on the other side. She believed that now. She'd made a stupid mistake, but instead of lashing out or getting angry, he'd simply forgiven her. As much as anything he'd said or done in the past that easy forgiveness made her certain she'd found the only person she wanted to share her life with.

It also made her wish he could see himself through her eyes. He shouldn't worry about what he might have inherited from his father. Jackson was one of the best people she'd ever met, a fact he proved as he cooked her an amazing lunch, helped clean up one-handed, and tucked her in for a nap though she could tell he was interested in more entertaining bedroom activities.

But she was exhausted from the stress of the past week and the adventures of the morning and determined to keep him from putting any more weight on his wounded side until tomorrow morning.

Besides, it was the perfect afternoon for a nap.

Outside the floor to ceiling picture windows of their loft bedroom, a gentle snow had begun to fall, coating the mountains with another layer of white, blurring the edges of the world until it felt like everything outside of their warm cocoon of covers was distant and small. Everything that mattered was right here, lying beside her with his fingers running lightly up and down her back as she snuggled close to his chest and fell into the deepest, most peaceful sleep she'd enjoyed in days.

*S*he slept hard, soaking in much-needed rest, and woke slowly, drifting back into her body with the nagging feeling that something wasn't quite right. Her skin was still warm from the flannel sheets and her head cradled by her pillow, but when she opened her eyes, the world remained dark.

She blinked, her lashes brushing against whatever it was that covered her eyes. She moved to pull the fabric away, but when she tried to shift her arms, she realized what else had changed since she'd fallen asleep. Her wrists were bound together and tied above her head and the bra and panties she'd worn to bed were gone.

She was naked, blindfolded, and tied to the headboard.

She was also immediately, mind-numbingly aroused.

Her lips parted to call out to Jackson and let him know she was awake, but before she could speak, a large hand covered her mouth and a rough voice whispered in her ear.

"Relax, sunshine, it's just me."

They were the first words he'd ever spoken to her, all those years ago when he'd made love to the wrong sister and proven there was nothing more right than the way they fit together. And now, they were going to relive that first time, knowing exactly who they were making love to.

Hannah moaned against his hand, wanting to tell him how perfect this was, but he kept his hand firmly over her lips.

"Remember when I told you I'd do all the dirty things you wanted me to do, as long as you would say you were mine?"

She nodded slowly, all of her available senses on high alert, not wanting to miss a moment of what he had planned.

"Well, now you're mine," he said. "Are you ready to play?"

"Yes," she whispered, lips moving against the rough skin of his palm.

"Good," he said, in his deep, delicious Dom voice. "But from here on out, don't speak unless you need to say your safe word."

She nodded again and his hand vanished, the mattress dipping as it gave up his weight. She wet her lips and rubbed them together, finding it harder to stay quiet than she usually did. The fact that she couldn't see what he was doing made her crave other forms of communication, but she forced herself to remain silent, listening to him move around the room.

She heard a rough scraping sound followed by a sizzle and

a whiff of sulfur that made her think he'd lit the candle on the bedside table. A moment later she heard his footsteps at the bottom of the bed, but then nothing. She held as still as she could, straining for some sign of what he was up to, her nerves growing progressively agitated as more time passed and nothing happened.

He didn't touch her, he didn't talk to her, he didn't give any sign that he was even still in the room, let alone in the midst of an erotic encounter.

Seconds became minutes and minutes seemed to drag on for hours as she lay tied to the bed, the sheets growing damp beneath her as she began to sweat. The air in the room was cool, but not knowing what the hell was going on was driving her crazy, ratcheting up her body temperature until she felt like she'd just come in from an afternoon on the slopes.

Finally, when her arm started to itch in a place she couldn't scratch, the soft sheets began to feel rough and gritty against her sensitized skin, and frustration had tied her throat into knots, she let her breath huff sharply through her lips.

She had no idea what Jackson thought he was doing, but she didn't like this game, not one bit. "Jackson, where are you?" she asked, her irritation clear in her tone.

In less than a second, he answered her.

Hannah cried out as his hand curved around her hip, flipping her roughly onto her stomach. She barely had time to lift her face from the pillow when his hand came down hard on her ass. She cried out, back arching as he delivered another stinging swat to her other cheek, alternating back and forth until her flesh began to burn.

Hands balling into fists, she fought to keep still and not to cry out—in pain or arousal—sensing her punishment for breaking her silence would be worse if she did. The spanking continued for twenty strokes and then thirty as Hannah's teeth dug into her lip. Her bottom flesh flamed so hot she was sure her ass must be bright red, and her pussy grew slick and swollen, jealous of so much attention being paid to another part of her body.

By the time Jackson finished, she was breathless from a heady combination of pain, arousal, and uncertainty about what he was going to do next. They'd never played a game like this before and the newness of it was nearly as nerve-racking as it was arousing. Nearly...

Fortunately, this time she didn't have long to wait.

"Trust means believing that I'm always there for you," he said in a soft, controlled voice. "Even when you can't see me. Even when your head tells you that my focus is elsewhere."

His fingertips traced the valley of her spine, collecting the drops of moisture that had gathered there as he spanked her. "But I am always thinking of you, always focused on you. There is nothing that matters to me as much as you and your trust and obedience when I'm proving that you're mine. Nod if you understand."

Hannah nodded, her head buzzing drunkenly as he gently urged her over to lie on her back. She was already high on the scene and they'd barely gotten started. She had a feeling Jackson didn't mean this encounter to be a mild one, and that she should do her best to hold onto her sanity as long as possible, but she didn't want to stay sane.

She wanted to get lost in him, in the things he did to her. She wanted to fall and fall and know that he would always be there to catch her.

"I'm going to tie floss to your nipples," Jackson said, his finger circling one tip and then the other, making her breath come faster as pleasure shivered from her breasts down to the hot, needy place between her legs. "I'm going to tie it tight enough to hurt, but not for your skin to go numb. If the pain is too much, use your safe word. If not, keep silent. Now arch your back."

Hannah obeyed, arching into his fingers as he plucked and teased her nipples into tight points and then wrapped each one in a little knot of torture. But it was delicious torture, the kind that made her nerve endings sizzle and her sex even wetter.

She held still for as long as she could but finally couldn't resist the urge to shift her thighs, restlessly seeking to ease the tension fisting between her legs.

"It looks like you're ready for more," Jackson said, a hint of amusement in his tone. "Spread your legs as wide as you can, sunshine. We're going to see how you like pain in a more intimate place."

Hannah slowly drew her legs apart, pulse leaping in her throat as she wondered what he was going to do next. Would he tie floss around her down there? And if so, how exactly would that work?

She was nibbling on her bottom lip, torn between eagerness and trepidation, when Jackson ran a finger down the center of her, making her entire body jerk in response.

"You're so wet," he said, his voice husky. "So responsive. I love seeing how much you want me."

His finger moved to one side of her entrance, pinching one of her outer lips lightly between his fingers before something harder pinched more firmly just below it. "I'll start with one clothespin on each side and give you a minute to adjust before I add more."

Pressing her lips together to suppress a whimper, Hannah held still as he applied a pin to her other side.

Dreamily, she swam through waves of hot and cold, exploring the pain and pleasure drifting through her as, after a moment, Jackson applied the next set of clothespins. He waited a long, sizzling moment before bringing a finger to her clit and tapping gently.

"This is not to make you come," he said, slowly, torturously tapping, hard enough to make her aware of how desperately she wanted release, but not enough pressure to take the edge off. "This is to remind you that even when I'm causing you pain, your pleasure is always utmost in my mind. I know you don't like one without the other, but there are times when you need this more than you think you do. You need to be reminded why you gave me your trust in the first place."

A second finger—or maybe a thumb, she couldn't be sure —found the tight puckered muscle of her ass and began to exert a similar pleasure.

"And I need your submission just as much. Nothing makes me feel safer or more loved than to know you trust me enough to give yourself to me. Completely." His thumb tested her hole, offering just enough pressure to make her aware of how much she wanted him there, too.

She wanted him in her ass and her pussy. She wanted him so far down her throat she couldn't breathe. She wanted him to fill her up, everywhere, in every way, because he was so exactly what she needed.

He was everything she wanted before she knew she wanted it. He was the mystery she would spend the rest of her life unraveling and never solve because he wasn't that kind of man. He wasn't a man you pinned down and sorted out; he was a wide, endless wilderness she could explore forever. He was the person she would keep falling deeper and deeper in love with until the last day she shared with this man—her lover, her master, her friend.

"I love it when you obey me without question," he said, words thick with desire. "But I love it when you make me work for it, too. Because every time you push me, I'm going to push right back."

He emphasized the words by slipping his thumb into her ass, drawing a soundless gasp of relief from her throat. It wasn't his cock or even close to everything she wanted, but it was a small mercy, a little more of him, the one thing she needed above all else.

"And every time we push," he continued, beginning to fuck her ass with slow, shallow strokes, driving her arousal even higher, "I see parts of you I've never seen before. And the more I see, the more I love you."

Hannah spread her legs wider, relishing in how right it felt to be pushed to the edge of what her body and soul could take. Yes, she wanted pleasure, but she wanted this, too. She wanted deeper and closer. She wanted to be seen and loved in ways she hadn't known were possible until she'd become Jackson's.

"But I see more of myself, too," he said, gently withdrawing his hand from between her legs. "While I was watching you sleep, I kept thinking about the ways people try to become the best versions of themselves."

The mattress dipped and she felt his heat beside her. "Some people use religion." He pressed a kiss to the side of her breast, bringing her attention back to the stinging pleasure of her bound nipple. "Some use a shrink or art or exercise or self-help books."

He flicked his tongue across her aching tip, summoning a sigh of bliss and surrender from her lips. "We use each other. And for everything I learn about being a better, stronger man, I'm rewarded by getting a little closer to you."

She swallowed, overwhelmed with sensation and emotion and not sure how much longer she could resist the urge to speak.

"So never doubt that you can trust me, sunshine," he said, urging her onto her side with a firm hand. "I won't hurt you, I won't let you down, and I won't leave, no matter how deep we go or what we find there." He curled his body behind hers, his cock teasing at her entrance, making her want to sob with relief. "I couldn't escape from you any more than I could escape from my own skin, and I wouldn't want to."

The erotic torment had driven her to the edge, but it was the love in his voice as he proved that he understood her better than anyone in the world that made her break.

She pulled in a breath, not sure what she was going to say,

only that she had to say something, when he whispered against her neck—

"Tell me if this makes the pain too intense."

—and pushed inside her, his thick cock spearing through where she was so swollen and wet.

She cried out, a desperate, guttural sound that came from a primal place inside of her only Jackson had ever reached. His thrust stretched the sensitive skin where the clothespins gripped her, intensifying the sting until it hurt, but the hurt was soon eclipsed by the bliss of Jackson sliding home, filling her completely.

Her head fell back with a groan. "Yes, sir."

"Yes, it's too much?" he asked, breath hot on her neck.

"No, sir," she panted. "Not too much. I like it. I love it. I love you."

"I love you, too." He kissed her shoulder, a tender kiss that became something darker when he parted his teeth and bit down, summoning another groan from her throat and a rush of heat between her legs.

"Yes, yes," she chanted, arching her back, easing the way for his next thrust to shove a little deeper. "Don't stop, sir. Don't ever stop."

With a growl, Jackson wrapped his arm more tightly around her waist, holding her tight as he began to fuck her harder, faster, driving them both toward that bright, clear place at the end of the game where they would burn together.

Hannah's fingers clawed at the air above her head and her arm muscles pulled whip tight, desperate to touch, to hold, to reach back and dig her fingernails into the thick muscles of Jackson's ass as he rode her, but she was bound too tight to escape.

And damn if the frustration didn't drive her need even higher.

By the time Jackson's palm slid down her belly to her clit, she was already a whisper away. All it took was the barest pressure of his fingertips on her sensitized skin and his sharp command to, "Come for me," and she was gone.

Gone. Lost. Found. Above it all but more a part of Jackson than she had ever been before.

Even as pleasure turned her body inside out, drowning her in bliss and magic, she was still with Jackson, so in tune with his every movement, his every breath, that she knew the exact moment he joined her in the fall. His cock swelled thicker, hotter inside of her and he came in long, wrenching bursts that made him cry out in what sounded like pain.

But it wasn't pain that made him squeeze her tight, holding on for dear life as they rode the waves of pleasure together. It wasn't pain that made him mumble sweet, wonderful things she could barely understand in her ear as they writhed together, drawing out the release until it felt like they would be like this forever, tangled and twisted and lost together in the best way.

And it wasn't pain that made him kiss her cheek tenderly as he removed the pins, the binding on her nipples, and the soft fabric tying her hands before reaching for the back of her blindfold and slipping the knot free.

Hannah blinked as she rubbed feeling back into her hands, waiting for the fuzziness to fade from the edges of her vision before she turned to look over her shoulder to find Jackson propped up on his good arm watching her. "Hi," she said, feeling shy, the way she sometimes did when they went some-where new together.

"Hi," he said, lips curving in a soft smile.

Hannah was returning the grin when she saw the blood staining the bandage covering Jackson's bullet wound and concern swept in to banish the rosy post-scene haze. "Jackson, you're bleeding."

"I don't care. It was worth it," he said, still smiling as he caught her arm, holding her on the bed beside him when she would have jumped up to grab the first aid supplies. "Stay. It won't hurt to put off a new bandage for ten minutes."

Hannah sighed as she relaxed back onto the sheets, knowing yelling at him wouldn't do any good now. And at least it wasn't a lot of blood.

Besides, she didn't want to leap out of bed just yet. She needed a few minutes to stare up into his eyes while her head and heart absorbed all the things she'd learned. "You're really good at that," she finally said.

"At what?" His smile went cocky around the edges.

Hannah laughed. "All that. All that *that* that you did just then."

"I'm glad," he said, grin fading though his eyes still sparkled. "I meant it. You make me better. This makes me better."

"I know. Me too." She turned, curling closer to his chest, inhaling the sweat and sex smell of him, knowing it would always be one of her favorite scents in the world. "I don't think we'll ever reach the end of that road, do you?"

"No." He rested his hand on her ass, giving her an affectionate pat. "But it sure will be fun trying."

She giggled again, so sated and pleasured and content that she was certain she wanted for nothing. And then Jackson said—

"Will you marry me, sunshine?"

—and she realized that there is always room for a little more happiness.

She propped up on one arm, meeting his soft gaze, awed that this was the same man she'd met two months ago. He was still strong, stubborn, and determined to have his way, but now he was also thoughtful and caring and loved her with a bravery that was humbling.

"Should I wait and ask against tomorrow morning?" His eyes searched hers, the spark of uncertainty in their depths as sweet as it was unnecessary. "I had something romantic planned involving mimosas, but I just...I didn't want to wait."

"Me either," she whispered, leaning in to kiss him with her next words. "Yes, Jackson Hawke, I will marry you."

"Thank you," he said, the relief in his voice making her smile against his lips.

"I'm already yours. Might as well make it official."

He hummed appreciatively into her mouth and kissed her gently, but thoroughly.

And as they made love again—slower and sweeter this time, coming together with the unpracticed ease of two people who were made to fit just right—Hannah silently gave thanks for the man in her arms. He was precious, irreplaceable, and no longer anything close to a monster.

He was all man now.

And all hers.

EPILOGUE

Jackson

Two Months Later

They were married in Samoa and decided to stay. Tropical islands without extradition treaties weren't easy to come by and the fact that Samoa was relatively close to Tahiti and Hannah's aunt was all it took to seal the deal. They settled into a cottage by the beach, spent their honeymoon making love until they lost track of where one of them ended and the other began, and started shopping for investment property.

After years of running an apparently cursed bed and breakfast, Hannah was reluctant to get back in the lodging business and Jackson had no interest in opening a restaurant or tourist shop. His finances were in excellent shape, but he preferred to operate businesses that were easier to keep in the black.

Near the end of January, Hannah had found a job working for a charity that helped native women start small businesses that lifted their families out of poverty. While Jackson was proud of her and the good work she was doing, he missed their long days on the beach and became increasingly aware that he had gone soft during his recovery.

He stepped up his workouts and eventually fell in with three men who ran the same route he did every morning. Over post-run coffee at a local café, he learned that they owned a gym near the town center and worked part time providing security for visiting dignitaries. Once they heard about Jackson's service in the marines, they were eager to hire him on to the team.

Needing something to occupy his hours while Hannah was gone, he agreed, with the stipulation that he had to be home no later than six Monday through Thursday and he never worked Friday through Sunday, Hannah's days off.

And so it was that Jackson found himself wearing a gun holster and an ear piece, standing outside the Chinese embassy in Apia, waiting for the ambassador he was shadowing to conclude his business for the day when a man in a straw hat and a white guayabera shirt walked out of the covered market across the street and up the steps into the shade beside him.

Normally, Jackson would have immediately been on alert, but there was something familiar about the man, something that put him at ease, even when the stranger stepped a little too close and kept his gaze tipped down, concealing his face.

"I heard you were out of the smuggling business," the man said in a light, easy voice. "But I didn't expect to see you in law enforcement."

"I'm not," Jackson said in an equally mild tone, even as he calculated how long it would take him to get his gun free. This man knew about his past and had come all the way to Samoa to find him. That didn't bode well, no matter how non-threatening he appeared. "I work part time as a personal protection specialist."

The man grunted in amusement. "A bodyguard. I wouldn't think there would be much need for that kind of thing in a place like this."

"People find things to be afraid of," Jackson replied, easing back a step, trying to get a look beneath the brim of the man's hat. "Even in paradise."

"I suppose so." The man tucked his chin closer to his chest. "And you've always been good at putting people's fears to rest."

"Who are you?" Jackson asked bluntly. His client could be out any minute and he needed to find out if this man was a threat to his or Hannah's safety before that happened. "What do you want?"

The man laughed. "I'm a ghost. But a friendly one. I don't mean you or your wife any harm. I saw her on her way to work this morning, by the way. She's the kind of person who has a smile for everyone isn't she?"

"I'm not going to discuss my wife with you," Jackson said, trying to keep the anger building inside of him from his voice. "And you still haven't answered my question."

"No, I suppose I haven't." The man sighed. "This seemed easier from half a world away. I didn't think it would still feel so raw, but it does. Even knowing she's not Harley, it was hard to watch her walk down the street."

Jackson reached out, gripping the stranger's arm, but the moment the man lifted his face he wasn't a stranger any longer. Jackson pulled his hand away with a shake of his head, certain he was seeing things.

But then, if Harley could come back from the dead, why not his best friend?

"Clay." Jackson shook his head again, still expecting the man's features to rearrange themselves into someone else's face. "I thought you were dead."

"I am. As far as anyone who used to know me is concerned." Clay's mouth twisted into a hard smile. "I can't tell you who I am now. I shouldn't be here at all, but I owe you things I don't owe anyone else. First and foremost among them, an apology."

"You don't owe me anything."

"I do," Clay insisted. "Because I believed her. I believed that you beat her and frightened her and all the other lies she told. I wanted it to be okay to fall in love with my best friend's girlfriend so I let myself believe."

He turned, staring out at the street, where sweating men on bicycles vied for space with tiny, rust-tinged cars. "And when I woke up in a hospital eight months after the crash, I kept on believing for years after I should have realized the truth. There's no excuse for what I did and I'm not here asking for forgiveness."

Jackson started to insist that he was too happy with the way his life had worked out to regret anything that had brought him to where he was now, but Clay turned to him and said—

"I'm just here to let you know that the boy is mine and I intend to take care of him."

"Harley's son?" he asked, pushing on when Clay nodded. "How do you know? I had a man working on a DNA test, but Harley and the boy disappeared again before he could get a hair sample."

"I have resources at my disposal not even you can imagine," Clay said, a hint of his old humor in his tone. "I know the boy is mine and I know you've been removed from the CIA's watch list."

Jackson's brows lifted. "Is that so?"

"It is. Though I wouldn't plan on a move back to the States anytime soon. Better to give everyone a cooling off period."

"I have no plans to move," he said, his thoughts racing. "My wife and I enjoy island living."

Was Clay CIA or simply higher up some criminal food chain than Jackson had ever climbed? He didn't know and he wasn't sure he wanted to. He trusted Clay's intelligence and he trusted that his old friend wanted nothing from him but to make amends. That was all he needed to know. Anything else would only put him and Hannah in danger.

But he couldn't resist asking for one small favor, for Hannah's sake.

"You won't hurt her," Jackson said softly. "I know she's a monster, but she's also my wife's sister."

Clay looked surprised, but only for a moment before he regained control of his features. "No, I won't hurt her. I haven't changed that much. But I'm going to make sure my son is taken care of."

"Hannah says Harley loves the boy," Jackson said though he couldn't believe he was putting in a good word for the bitch who had ruined his life.

But then, it wasn't ruined. Not anymore. He was the happiest he'd ever been. Hannah was worth the years of rage and all the injustice. She was worth every second of hell Harley had put him through and more.

"You *must* be happy," Clay said with a sharp laugh. "The Jackson I knew wasn't the kind to forgive or forget."

Jackson shrugged. "I had to make a choice between punishing the woman I hated and pleasing the woman I love. It wasn't a hard call to make."

Clay cast an appraising look his way before nodding slowly. "Well, I'm glad for you. You deserve the sweet life on the beach with a pretty girl."

"You know better than most that we don't get what we deserve," Jackson said, casting a glance over his shoulder at the door to the embassy before turning back to his friend. "But don't shut out the good in the world because of a few terrible people. There are good ones out there, too."

"Angels to make up for the devils?" Clay asked wryly.

"Something like that," Jackson said though he couldn't help thinking that Hannah was much more interesting—and far sexier—than any angel. "I'm just saying I learned the hard way how much revenge can steal from a life. I wouldn't want that for you."

Clay's blue eyes softened and for a moment Jackson saw

the kid he'd met in basic, the all-American boy who could make everyone laugh, even at the end of a day spent drilling until their muscles had turned to jelly. But then the shadows moved in behind his friend's eyes again, proving Clay was a long way from making his way out of the darkness.

"Thank you," he said though Jackson could tell his words had fallen on deaf ears. "I appreciate the advice and wish you the best. And please tell your wife thank you for me."

"For what?"

Clay smiled. "For getting you back on the straight and narrow before I had to put you in prison."

CIA then, Jackson thought, wondering why that didn't make him feel better about the road his friend was on.

Clay stepped away, lifting a hand. "Goodbye, Jackson, and good luck."

"Be careful," Jackson said, raising his voice slightly to be heard as Clay continued to walk away. "There's always something left to lose, man."

Clay waved in acknowledgment of Jackson's words, but he didn't turn around. A few minutes later he had disappeared in the crowd of shoppers swarming the outdoor market across the street. Jackson had a feeling he wouldn't see the man again.

*L*ater that night, as he and Hannah sat down to dinner on their lanai overlooking the ocean, he told her the news, downplaying his concerns about what Clay would do to her sister.

But she was no fool.

"Well, if Harley had given me any way to get in touch, I'd warn her trouble was coming but…" Hannah lifted her arms helplessly at her sides before plucking her napkin from the table and laying it in her lap. "I'll just have to send extra good vibes her and Jasper's way and hope for the best. There's nothing else I can do."

"Your good vibes are pretty powerful," Jackson said, admiring the way the setting sun caught the red highlights in her hair. "You're beautiful tonight."

"I am not," she said, smiling even as she rolled her eyes. "I was out in the heat sweating in a coconut field all day. My hair is a wreck."

"Your hair is fine and I like you sweaty."

She hummed knowingly beneath her breath as she speared a tomato from her plate. "I know you do, but don't even think about trying anything until I've showered."

"Is that a hard limit?"

"Jackson," she warned, narrowing her eyes.

"What if I wanted to sniff your sweaty panties while you shower?"

"Cheese biscuits," she retorted, plucking another tomato from her plate and tossing it at him across the table.

Jackson dodged easily, suppressing a laugh.

"No." She pointed a finger at his chest. "I'm not giving you my dirty panties."

"That's all right. I can get them out of the laundry basket later."

"Ew, Jackson," she said, wrinkling her nose. "You don't seriously have a stinky panty fetish do you?"

"Would you still love me if I did?"

"Of course," she said, without a moment's hesitation, making his heart feel a little lighter even though he was only teasing. "But it would take some getting used to. I'm not accustomed to sharing that part of my life with anyone but the washing machine."

He reached across the table, taking her hand and lifting it to his mouth. "I'm kidding." He kissed the tips of her fingers one by one, loving the way she flushed in response. "I have no designs on your panties, just the woman who wears them."

She curled her fingers, giving his palm a squeeze. "Harley's going to be okay, right?"

"I think so," Jackson said, knowing he had no choice but to be honest with her. They didn't do lies or secrets, not even to spare each other pain. "I asked Clay not to hurt her and he said he wouldn't, but I haven't seen the man in years. I don't know whether he's still the kind to tell the truth."

Hannah cocked her head. "You did? Really? You asked him not to hurt her?"

"I knew you would want me to."

She sighed. "You are my favorite husband I've ever had."

"I'm the only husband you've ever had," he said, rising from his chair. "And the only one you're going to have. Come get in the water with me."

"What about dinner?" she asked, but she was already standing beside him, letting him lead her down the steps toward the beach.

"Dinner will keep. The sunset won't and I want to fuck you in the waves with the sun in your hair."

And so he did and it was even better than the last time he'd made love to his wife because every day with Hannah was better than the last, every moment more priceless than the one before.

She was all the proof he needed to believe that life was beautiful, nearly as beautiful as the woman in his arms.

Ready for more dark, sexy romance?
Get addicted to Harley and Clay's story
in Filthy Wicked Love
Available Now.

Keep reading for a sneak peek!

Sign up for Lili's newsletter and
never miss a sale or
new release: http://bit.ly/1zXpwL6

TELL LILI YOUR FAVORITE PART!

I love reading your thoughts about the books and your review matters. Reviews help readers find new-to-them authors to enjoy. So if you could take a moment to leave a review letting me know your favorite part of the story—nothing fancy required, even a sentence or two would be wonderful—I would be deeply grateful.

ABOUT THE AUTHOR

Lili Valente has slept under the stars in Greece, eaten dinner at midnight with French men who couldn't be trusted to keep their mouths on their food, and walked alone through Munich's red light district after dark and lived to tell the tale.

These days you can find her writing in a tent beside the sea, drinking coconut water and thinking delightfully dirty thoughts.

Find Lili on the web…
www.lilivalente.com

ALSO BY LILI VALENTE

Standalone romances:

THE BABY MAKER

THE TROUBLEMAKER

Sexy, flirty, dirty romantic comedies!

MAGNIFICENT BASTARD

a USA Today Bestselling romantic comedy

SPECTACULAR RASCAL

INCREDIBLE YOU

MEANT FOR YOU

Sexy romantic comedies featuring hot hockey players!

HOT AS PUCK

SEXY MOTHERPUCKER

PUCK-AHOLIC

PUCK ME BABY

The Master Me Series, red HOT erotic Standalone novellas!

SNOWBOUND WITH THE BILLIONAIRE

SNOWED IN WITH THE BOSS

MASQUERADE WITH THE MASTER

Bought by the Billionaire Series—HOT novellas, must be read
in order.

DARK DOMINATION

DEEP DOMINATION

DESPERATE DOMINATION

DIVINE DOMINATION

Kidnapped by the Billionaire Series—HOT novellas, must be read in order.

FILTHY WICKED LOVE

CRAZY BEAUTIFUL LOVE

ONE MORE SHAMELESS NIGHT

Under His Command Series—HOT novellas, must be read in order.

CONTROLLING HER PLEASURE

COMMANDING HER TRUST

CLAIMING HER HEART

To the Bone Series—Sexy Romantic Suspense, must be read in order.

A LOVE SO DANGEROUS

A LOVE SO DEADLY

A LOVE SO DEEP

Fight for You Series—Emotional New Adult Romantic Suspense. Read in order.

RUN WITH ME

FIGHT FOR YOU

Bedding The Bad Boy Series—must be read in order.

THE BAD BOY'S TEMPTATION

THE BAD BOY'S SEDUCTION

THE BAD BOY'S REDEMPTION

The Lonesome Point Series—Sexy Cowboys written with Jessie Evans.

LEATHER AND LACE

SNEAK PEEK

Please enjoy this sneak peek of
FILTHY WICKED LOVE available now.

Warning: This is a dark enemies-to-lovers romance that contains violence, a damaged alpha male, and dirty twisted hate banging. Read at your own risk.

The first time CIA Agent Clay Hart fell for Harley Mason, she nearly killed him. But she won't get another chance at his heart or his life. He's going to take the son she's hidden from him for years, send her to jail where she belongs, and never look back.

Harley isn't the sick twisted person she used to be, but sins have a long half-life and rage an even longer reach. Now the only man she's ever loved is back from the dead and determined to take away her reason for living. But she won't give up her son without one hell of a dirty, twisted, sexy fight.

She won't give up.

He won't give in.

And neither of them is prepared for the sparks that fly between them or the shared enemy determined to destroy them both.

EXCERPT

Just a few more weeks.

Just a few more weeks, one last job, and she and Jasper would finally be safe.

Harley studied her reflection in the small mirror above the outdoor sink, trying to see if she was buying her own encouraging load of bullshit. But her blue eyes were cool and calm. Her eyes kept their secrets, refusing to say if they believed in happily ever after.

Happily ever after. Riiiight.

I'm sure that's right around the corner, along with Santa Claus and Prince Charming riding a unicorn.

She turned to face the beach with a sigh the sea breeze swept away. Happily ever after was definitely a long shot. At this point, she would settle for being able to stop looking over her shoulder and take for granted that she would live to see her thirtieth birthday. Ian Hawke—her father's enemy and the man who had nearly killed Harley and her twin sister, Hannah, last December—was dead, but her own enemies were still very much among the living.

Marlowe Reynolds considered her a friend, or at least a trusted associate, but if he realized she wanted out, she would see the terrifying side of the soft-spoken Brit. He was the most successful drug lord in Europe, and a man didn't run a multi-billion dollar cartel for over a decade without knowing how to keep his friends close, his enemies dead, and people who knew too much tucked firmly beneath his wing. Marlowe didn't let people walk away; he made the malcontent disappear. In order to make her escape, Harley was going to have to be very smart, very careful, and very lucky.

Smart and careful she could control, but luck didn't take directions.

Therefore, precautions had to be taken.

Harley's gaze drifted to the sheltered section of the private beach, where Jasper was busy digging a hole so deep only the top of his tousled blond hair showed above the sand. Before she and Dominic had started running sprints along the shoreline, she'd asked Jasper what he was digging for, but he'd refused to say, only giving her a mysterious grin and a vague "you'll see."

With his dark blond hair, murky blue eyes several shades darker than her own, and golden skin, Jasper looked like his father, but he kept his secrets close to his chest like his mother.

Sometimes Harley worried that he was too much like her, and that his insatiable curiosity would lead him into the same labyrinth she'd wandered most of her life, a place where the walls of perception were always shifting and each ugly new revelation only forced you deeper into the maze. But most of the time she believed in nurture triumphing over nature. She wasn't raising Jasper the way she had been raised. He was being taught that kindness was a strength, not a signal to attack at will, and as he grew she would continue to help him channel his curiosity into more productive pursuits than the ones she'd been steered toward.

Engineering, maybe. Jasper loved building things, even though he claimed he was going to be a "destruction worker" when he grew up.

"Is that smile for me?" Dominic asked, his dark eyes flashing as he walked up the trail from the beach.

Harley tilted her head to one side, letting her grin stretch wider. "It could be. If you say the torture is over for the day."

"Not yet, beautiful." Dominic's hand lingered on her waist. He nodded toward the makeshift weight room he'd set up on the covered patio. "Come on, let's do legs and abs and then we'll call it a day."

Her sister Hannah's former bodyguard had spent the past three months whipping Harley into the best physical shape of her life, insisting she needed to keep her body as sharp as her mind. In addition to serving as her personal trainer, he was also concealing her whereabouts from her sister's psychotic new husband, Jackson, a man Harley suspected wanted to kill her. Not that Jackson didn't have every reason to want her dead after what she'd done to him, but she had a son to raise. She had to stay alive and Dom was helping make that happen.

In exchange, Harley spent several hours a day sweating in the brutal Thai sun and her nights pretending she didn't realize that her lover would rather be sleeping with her sister.

"Let me get Jasper into the bath," she said, catching Dom's hand and giving it a light squeeze. "I'll meet you there."

"All right." He stretched his arms overhead, his white tee shirt riding up high enough to reveal the taut planes of his stomach. "I already put his boogie board away. All he needs to do is grab his sand toys."

"Thanks," she murmured, letting her eyes skim up and down Dom's frame. He was a beautiful man—long and lean, with muscles on top of muscles, caramel skin, amber-flecked eyes, and a classically handsome face. It had certainly been no hardship to spend a few months on a beach with him, but it wouldn't hurt to say goodbye. She had enjoyed their time together, but she wasn't looking for long-term attachments.

She only had space in her heart for Jasper. Her son was her first—and only—priority. There wasn't room in her crazy life for anything else.

"But don't be too long," Dom continued, backing away. "We should leave by four. Traffic's been bad getting in and out of town since the mudslide."

Harley nodded and started across the sand to help Jasper gather up his toys. He loved bath time and would play until his skin was pruned all over if she let him. Today she would set his timer for an hour. That should give her plenty of time to finish her workout, grab a quick shower, and finish packing Jasper's bag for the trip. Maybe his last trip.

Please let it be the last.

She didn't know how much longer she could keep sending her son away not knowing when or if she would ever see him again.

"Tub time," she said, forcing a smile as she squatted down at the edge of Jasper's sand pit. "Have you found the buried treasure yet?"

"I'm not finding it, I'm leaving it." Jasper scrambled out and began tossing his extensive collection of sand toys, favorite red shovel, and alligator beach towel down inside the hole. "I've already drawn a map to leave in my room. That way the next kid who lives here can go on a hunt for my treasure and then we'll be friends."

Harley's throat tightened. "So I guess you saw your suitcase in the laundry room."

"You can't take sand toys on the airplane," Jasper said, not meeting her eyes as he shoved a mound of sand toward the edge of the pit, sending it sliding down on top of his treasures. "A little help here, lady?"

"I'm not a lady, I'm your mother," she said, finishing her

part of their inside joke even though her heart wasn't in it. But neither was Jasper's, and he wasn't moping. He was burying treasures for a friend he would never meet.

She helped him fill in the hole, not bothering to tell him that the tide would probably wash away his treasures long before any other child came to find them. She'd chosen this island off the coast of Thailand because it was remote, sparsely populated, and far outside the stomping grounds of the typical tourist. The rental house they'd leased had stood empty for a year before they had come to stay and would probably stay empty for months after she had packed up their things.

After the sand was smooth again, she and Jasper stomped over the top a few times, tamping it down until a darker, damper spot than the surrounding sand was the only sign that the beach had been disturbed.

With one last stomp, Jasper took her hand. "Are you coming this time, Mama?"

"No," Harley said, leading the way back toward the bungalow. "Dominic is going to be your travel buddy. I have to take care of a few things and close up the house. Then I'll come meet you. It shouldn't be more than two weeks, three at the most."

Jasper frowned. "What about Miss Louisa? Am I still supposed to call her if something goes wrong?"

"Yes. Call Miss Louisa first and if she's not available call Mr. Tim and he'll know what to do." Harley hated that her six-year-old was so intimately acquainted with potential danger, but their plans and backup plans had kept Jasper safe when she was taken captive last December. If some of his innocence had to die in order to keep him alive, it was a price she was willing to pay. "But you know Dom is smart and careful. You shouldn't have any problems and you'll be having so much fun exploring a new city you won't even have a chance to miss me."

Jasper dropped her hand to turn on the waterspout near

the door and leaned down to rinse his arms and legs. "I would rather stay at the beach with you. I like the beach better than the city. Even Paris."

"Me, too," she said, ruffling his sandy hair. "Maybe someday soon we'll have a forever house on the beach."

Or you will, when I'm dead and you go to live with Hannah on her island.

Harley pushed the thought away and helped Jasper get the sand out from between his toes. She wasn't going to die and leave Jasper to be raised by someone else. Hannah would love him like her own, Harley was sure of it, but Hannah's husband, Jackson, was another matter.

Harley had done terrible, unforgivable things to Jackson back when she was a young woman with more lust for vengeance than sense. Framing a man for rape had been one of her uglier moments, but whether Jackson's hatred for her was justified or not, she didn't want her son raised by a man who might make Jasper pay for her sins.

Jasper had never known anything but a mother who loved him more than life and that's how things were going to stay. He was never going to know what it felt like to be shut out of a parental figure's heart.

"Can I bring my bath toys on the plane?" Jasper asked as they let themselves into the house and headed for the bathroom.

"We can buy more bath toys at our new place." Harley started the water running, making sure it was a little on the hot side since Jasper would be playing for a while, and turned to help him undress. "But I have a special surprise for you. I'll give it to you at the airport."

Jasper's head popped free of his blue rash guard, his eyes dancing. "Is it for my collection?"

Harley shrugged mysteriously. "You'll have to wait and see." She leaned in, cupping his chubby cheeks and pressing a kiss to his sun-warmed forehead. "Remember to turn the water off before it gets too full, okay? And scrub your hair good. You don't want to carry sand with you onto the plane."

"I don't care." Jasper shoved his trunks down, sending the sand in his swimsuit spilling out all over the tile. "I like sand."

"Obviously," Harley said dryly, watching him climb into the tub, her heart breaking a little bit.

He was so beautiful, so sweet, and so much like his father there was no way she would ever be able to forget the man she'd lost too soon, before she'd realized that punishing the people who'd wronged her would never fill the empty place in her soul.

But that was all right. She didn't want to forget Clay and she never wanted to take her son—or the way he'd changed her—for granted. Jasper had saved her life, pure and simple. He was her everything and she would do whatever it took to keep him safe.

Even if it meant one last dance with the devil in the pale moonlight.

Marlowe was a bad man, but Harley was no angel, and sometimes one thing must die for another to be born from the ashes.

With one last look at Jasper—doing her best to memorize the blissed-out expression on his face as he dumped his bath toys out of their bucket into the water—she closed the bathroom door and went to set the first stage of her plan into motion.

Get addicted to Harley and Clay's story
in Filthy Wicked Love
Available Now.

Made in the USA
Coppell, TX
07 March 2020

16609267R00246